EVERYMAN'S LIBRARY
EDITED BY ERNEST RHYS

FICTION

GOGOL'S DEAD SOULS
TRANSLATED BY D. J. HOGARTH
INTRODUCTION BY JOHN COURNOS

A TALE WHICH HOLDETH CHILDREN FROM PLAY & OLD MEN FROM THE CHIMNEY CORNER

SIR PHILIP SIDNEY

DEAD·SOULS BY·NIKOLAI VASIL'EVICH GOGOL

LONDON & TORONTO
PUBLISHED BY J·M·DENT
& SONS Ltd & IN NEW YORK
BY E·P·DUTTON & CO

First Issue of this Edition . 1915
Reprinted 1917

INTRODUCTION

Dead Souls, first published in 1842, is the great prose classic of Russia. That amazing institution, " the Russian novel," not only began its career with this unfinished masterpiece by Nikolai Vasil'evich Gogol, but practically all the Russian masterpieces that have come since have grown out of it, like the limbs of a single tree. Dostoieffsky goes so far as to bestow this tribute upon an earlier work by the same author, a short story entitled *The Cloak ;* this idea has been wittily expressed by another compatriot, who says: " We have all issued out of Gogol's Cloak."

Dead Souls, which bears the word " Poem " upon the title page of the original, has been generally compared to *Don Quixote* and to the *Pickwick Papers*, while E. M. Vogüe places its author somewhere between Cervantes and Le Sage. However considerable the influences of Cervantes and Dickens may have been—the first in the matter of structure, the other in background, humour, and detail of characterisation—the predominating and distinguishing quality of the work is undeniably something foreign to both and quite peculiar to itself; something which, for want of a better term, might be called the quality of the Russian soul. The English reader familiar with the works of Dostoieffsky, Turgenev, and Tolstoi, need hardly be told what this implies; it might be defined in the words of the French critic just named as " a tendency to pity." One might indeed go further and say that it implies a certain tolerance of one's characters even though they be, in the conventional sense, knaves, products, as the case might be, of conditions or circumstance, which after all is the thing to be criticised and not the man. But pity and tolerance are rare in satire, even in clash with it, producing in the result a deep sense of tragic humour. It is this that makes of *Dead Souls* a unique work, peculiarly Gogolian, peculiarly Russian, and distinct from its author's Spanish and English masters.

Still more profound are the contradictions to be seen in the author's personal character; and unfortunately they prevented him from completing his work. The trouble is that he made his art out of life, and when in his final years he carried his struggle, as Tolstoi did later, back into life, he repented of all he had written, and in the frenzy of a wakeful night burned all his manuscripts, including the second part of *Dead Souls*, only fragments of which were saved. There was yet a third part to be written. Indeed, the second part had been written and burned twice. Accounts differ as to why he had burned it finally. Religious remorse, fury at adverse criticism, and despair at not reaching ideal perfection are among the reasons given. Again it is said that he had destroyed the manuscript with others altogether inadvertently.

The poet Pushkin, who said of Gogol that " behind his laughter you feel the unseen tears," was his chief friend and inspirer. It was he who suggested the plot of *Dead Souls* as well as the plot of the earlier work *The Revisor*, which is almost the only comedy in Russian. The importance of both is their introduction of the social element in Russian literature, as Prince Kropotkin points out. Both hold up the mirror to Russian officialdom and the effects it has produced on the national character. The plot of *Dead Souls* is simple enough, and is said to have been suggested by an actual episode.

It was the day of serfdom in Russia, and a man's standing was often judged by the numbers of " souls " he possessed. There was a periodical census of serfs, say once every ten or twenty years. This being the case, an owner had to pay a tax on every " soul " registered at the last census, though some of the serfs might have died in the meantime. Nevertheless, the system had its material advantages, inasmuch as an owner might borrow money from a bank on the " dead souls " no less than on the living ones. The plan of Chichikov, Gogol's hero-villain, was therefore to make a journey through Russia and buy up the " dead souls," at reduced rates of course, saving their owners the government tax, and acquiring for himself a list of fictitious serfs, which he meant to mortgage to a bank for a considerable sum. With this money he would buy an estate and some real live serfs, and make the beginning of a fortune.

Obviously, this plot, which is really no plot at all but merely a ruse to enable Chichikov to go across Russia in a *troika*, with Selifan the coachman as a sort of Russian Sancho Panza, gives Gogol a magnificent opportunity to reveal his genius as a painter of Russian panorama, peopled with characteristic native types commonplace enough but drawn in comic relief. "The comic," explained the author yet at the beginning of his career, "is hidden everywhere, only living in the midst of it we are not conscious of it; but if the artist brings it into his art, on the stage say, we shall roll about with laughter and only wonder we did not notice it before." But the comic in *Dead Souls* is merely external. Let us see how Pushkin, who loved to laugh, regarded the work. As Gogol read it aloud to him from the manuscript the poet grew more and more gloomy and at last cried out: "God! What a sad country Russia is!" And later he said of it: "Gogol invents nothing; it is the simple truth, the terrible truth."

The work on one hand was received as nothing less than an exposure of all Russia—what would foreigners think of it? The liberal elements, however, the critic Belinsky among them, welcomed it as a revelation, as an omen of a freer future. Gogol, who had meant to do a service to Russia and not to heap ridicule upon her, took the criticisms of the Slavophiles to heart; and he palliated his critics by promising to bring about in the succeeding parts of his novel the redemption of Chichikov and the other "knaves and block-heads." But the "Westerner" Belinsky and others of the liberal camp were mistrustful. It was about this time (1847) that Gogol published his *Correspondence with Friends*, and aroused a literary controversy that is alive to this day. Tolstoi is to be found among his apologists.

Opinions as to the actual significance of Gogol's masterpiece differ. Some consider the author a realist who has drawn with meticulous detail a picture of Russia; others, Merejkovsky among them, see in him a great symbolist; the very title *Dead Souls* is taken to describe the living of Russia as well as its dead. Chichikov himself is now generally regarded as a universal character. We find an American professor, William Lyon Phelps,[1] of Yale, holding the opinion that "no one can travel far in America without meeting scores of Chichikovs; indeed, he is an accurate portrait of the American promoter, of the successful commercial traveller whose success depends entirely not on the real value and usefulness of his stock-in-trade, but on his knowledge of human nature and of the persuasive power of his tongue." This is also the opinion held by Prince Kropotkin,[2] who says: "Chichikov may buy

[1] *Essays on Russian Novelists.* Macmillan.
[2] *Ideals and Realities in Russian Literature.* Duckworth and Co.

dead souls, or railway shares, or he may collect funds for some charitable institution, or look for a position in a bank, but he is an immortal international type; we meet him everywhere; he is of all lands and of all times; he but takes different forms to suit the requirements of nationality and time."

Again, the work bears an interesting relation to Gogol himself. A romantic, writing of realities, he was appalled at the commonplaceness of life, at finding no outlet for his love of colour derived from his Cossack ancestry. He realised that he had drawn a host of "heroes," "one more commonplace than another, that there was not a single palliating circumstance, that there was not a single place where the reader might find pause to rest and to console himself, and that when he had finished the book it was as though he had walked out of an oppressive cellar into the open air." He felt perhaps inward need to redeem Chichikov; in Merejkovsky's opinion he really wanted to save his own soul, but had succeeded only in losing it. His last years were spent morbidly; he suffered torments and ran from place to place like one hunted; but really always running from himself. Rome was his favourite refuge, and he returned to it again and again. In 1848, he made a pilgrimage to the Holy Land, but he could find no peace for his soul. Something of this mood had reflected itself even much earlier in the *Memoirs of a Madman* : " Oh, little mother, save your poor son! Look how they are tormenting him. . . . There's no place for him on earth! He's being driven! . . . Oh, little mother, take pity on thy poor child."

All the contradictions of Gogol's character are not to be disposed of in a brief essay. Such a strange combination of the tragic and the comic was truly seldom seen in one man. He, for one, realised that "it is dangerous to jest with laughter." " Everything that I laughed at became sad." " And terrible," adds Merejkovsky. But earlier his humour was lighter, less tinged with the tragic; in those days Pushkin never failed to be amused by what Gogol had brought to read to him. Even *Revizor* (1835), with its tragic undercurrent, was a trifle compared to *Dead Souls*, so that one is not astonished to hear that not only did the Tsar, Nicholas I., give permission to have it acted, in spite of its being a criticism of official rottenness, but laughed uproariously, and led the applause. Moreover, he gave Gogol a grant of money, and asked that its source should not be revealed to the author lest " he might feel obliged to write from the official point of view."

Gogol was born at Sorotchinetz, Little Russia, in March 1809. He left college at nineteen and went to St. Petersburg, where he secured a position as copying clerk in a government department. He did not keep his position long, yet long enough to store away in his mind a number of bureaucratic types which proved useful later. He quite suddenly started for America with money given to him by his mother for another purpose, but when he got as far as Lübeck he turned back. He then wanted to become an actor, but his voice proved not strong enough. Later he wrote a poem which was unkindly received. As the copies remained unsold, he gathered them all up at the various shops and burned them in his room.

His next effort, *Evenings at the Farm of Dikanka* (1831), was more successful. It was a series of gay and colourful pictures of Ukraine, the land he knew and loved, and if he is occasionally a little over romantic here and there, he also achieves some beautifully lyrical passages. Then came another even finer series called *Mirgorod*, which won the admiration of Pushkin. Next he planned a " History of Little Russia " and a " History of the Middle Ages," this last work to be in eight or nine volumes. The result of all this study was a beautiful and short Homeric epic in prose, called *Taras Bulba*. His appointment to a professorship in history was a ridiculous episode in his life. After a brilliant first lecture, in which he had evidently said all he had to say, he settled to a life of boredom for himself and his pupils. When he resigned he said joyously: " I am once more a free Cossack." Between 1834 and 1835 he produced a new series of stories, including his famous *Cloak*, which may be regarded as the legitimate beginning of the Russian novel.

Gogol knew little about women, who played an equally minor rôle in his life and in his books. This may be partly because his personal appearance was not prepossessing. He is described by a contemporary as " a little man with legs too short for his body. He walked crookedly; he was clumsy, ill-dressed, and rather ridiculous-looking, with his long lock of hair flapping on his forehead, and his large prominent nose."

From 1835 Gogol spent almost his entire time abroad; some strange unrest—possibly his Cossack blood—possessed him like a demon, and he never stopped anywhere very long. After his pilgrimage in 1848 to Jerusalem, he returned to

Moscow, his entire possessions in a little bag; these consisted
of pamphlets, critiques, and newspaper articles mostly inimical
to himself. He wandered about with these from house to
house. Everything he had of value he gave away to the poor.
He ceased work entirely. According to all accounts he spent
his last days in praying and fasting. Visions came to him.
His death, which came in 1852, was extremely fantastic. His
last words, uttered in loud frenzy, were: "A ladder! Quick,
a ladder!" This call for a ladder—"a spiritual ladder," in
the words of Merejkovsky—had been made on an earlier occasion by a certain Russian saint, who used almost the same
language. "I shall laugh my bitter laugh"[1] was the inscription placed on Gogol's grave.

JOHN COURNOS.

[1] This is generally referred to in the Russian criticisms of Gogol
as a quotation from Jeremiah. It appears upon investigation,
however, that it actually occurs only in the Slavonic version from
the Greek, and not in the Russian translation made direct from
the Hebrew.

Evenings on the Farm near the Dikanka, 1829-31; Mirgorod, 1831-33;
Taras Bulba, 1834; Arabesques (includes tales, The Portrait and A Mad-
man's Diary), 1831-35; The Cloak, 1835; The Revizor (The Inspector-
General), 1836; Dead Souls, 1842; Correspondence with Friends, 1847.
     ENGLISH TRANSLATIONS: Cossack Tales (The Night of Christmas Eve,
Tarass Boolba), trans. by G. Tolstoy, 1860; St. John's Eve and Other
Stories, trans. by Isabel F. Hapgood, New York, Crowell, 1886; Taras
Bulba: Also St. John's Eve and Other Stories, London, Vizetelly, 1887;
Taras Bulba, trans. by B. C. Baskerville, London, Scott, 1907; The In-
spector: a Comedy, Calcutta, 1890; The Inspector-General, trans. by A. A.
Sykes, London, Scott, 1892; Revizor, trans. for the Yale Dramatic Asso-
ciation by Max S. Mandell, New Haven, Conn., 1908; Home Life in
Russia (adaptation of Dead Souls), London, Hurst, 1854; Tchitchikoff's
Journeys; or Dead Souls, trans. by Isabel F. Hapgood, New York,
Crowell, 1886; Dead Souls, London, Vizetelly, 1887; Dead Souls, London,
Maxwell, 1887; Meditations on the Divine Liturgy, trans. by L. Alexeieff,
London, A. R. Mowbray and Co., 1913.
     LIVES, etc.: (Russian) Kotlyarevsky (N. A.), 1903; Shenrok (V. I.),
Materials for a Biography, 1892; (French) Leger (L.), Nicholas Gogol, 1914.

AUTHOR'S PREFACE

TO THE FIRST PORTION OF THIS WORK

SECOND EDITION PUBLISHED IN 1846

From the Author to the Reader

READER, whosoever or wheresoever you be, and whatsoever be your station—whether that of a member of the higher ranks of society or that of a member of the plainer walks of life—I beg of you, if God shall have given you any skill in letters, and my book shall fall into your hands, to extend to me your assistance.

For in the book which lies before you, and which, probably, you have read in its first edition, there is portrayed a man who is a type taken from our Russian Empire. This man travels about the Russian land, and meets with folk of every condition —from the nobly-born to the humble toiler. Him I have taken as a type to show forth the vices and the failings, rather than the merits and the virtues, of the commonplace Russian individual; and the characters which revolve around him have also been selected for the purpose of demonstrating our national weaknesses and shortcomings. As for men and women of the better sort, I propose to portray them in subsequent volumes. Probably much of what I have described is improbable and does not happen as things customarily happen in Russia; and the reason for that is that for me to learn all that I have wished to do has been impossible, in that human life is not sufficiently long to become acquainted with even a hundredth part of what takes place within the borders of the Russian Empire. Also, carelessness, inexperience, and lack of time have led to my perpetrating numerous errors and inaccuracies of detail; with the result that in every line of the book there is something which calls for correction. For these reasons I beg of you, my reader, to act also as my corrector. Do not despise the task, for, however superior be your education, and however lofty your station, and however insignificant, in your eyes, my book, and however

A

trifling the apparent labour of correcting and commenting upon that book, I implore you to do as I have said. And you too, O reader of lowly education and simple status, I beseech you not to look upon yourself as too ignorant to be able in some fashion, however small, to help me. Every man who has lived in the world and mixed with his fellow men will have remarked something which has remained hidden from the eyes of others; and therefore I beg of you not to deprive me of your comments, seeing that it cannot be that, should you read my book with attention, you will have *nothing* to say at some point therein.

For example, how excellent it would be if some reader who is sufficiently rich in experience and the knowledge of life to be acquainted with the sort of characters which I have described herein would annotate in detail the book, without missing a single page, and undertake to read it precisely as though, laying pen and paper before him, he were first to peruse a few pages of the work, and then to recall his own life, and the lives of folk with whom he has come in contact, and everything which he has seen with his own eyes or has heard of from others, and to proceed to annotate, in so far as may tally with his own experience or otherwise, what is set forth in the book, and to jot down the whole exactly as it stands pictured to his memory, and, lastly to send me the jottings as they may issue from his pen, and to continue so doing until he has covered the entire work! Yes, he would indeed do me a vital service! Of style or beauty of expression he would need to take no account, for the value of a book lies in its truth and its actuality rather than in its wording. No would he need to consider my feelings if at any point he should feel minded to blame or to upbraid me, or to demonstrate th harm rather than the good which has been done through an lack of thought or verisimilitude of which I have been guilty In short, for anything and for everything in the way of criticisn I should be thankful.

Also, it would be an excellent thing if some reader in the highe walks of life, some person who stands remote, both by life an by education, from the circle of folk which I have pictured i my book, but who knows the life of the circle in which he himse revolves, would undertake to read my work in similiar fashio and methodically to recall to his mind any members of superic social classes whom he has met, and carefully to observe wheth there exists any resemblance between one such class and anothe and whether, at times, there may not be repeated in a high sphere what is done in a lower, and likewise to note any add tional fact in the same connection which may occur to him (that is to say, any fact pertaining to the higher ranks of society which would seem to confirm or to disprove his conclusions), and, lastly, to record that fact as it may have occurred within his own experience, while giving full details of persons (of individual manners, tendencies, and customs) and also of inanimate surroundings (of dress, furniture, fittings of houses, and so forth). For I need knowledge of the classes in question, which are the flower of our people. In fact, this very reason the reason that I do not yet know Russian life in all its aspects, and in the degree to which it is necessary for me to know it in order to become a successful author—is what has, until now, prevented me from publishing any subsequent volumes of this story.

Again, it would be an excellent thing if some one who is endowed with the faculty of imagining and vividly picturing to himself the various situations wherein a character may be placed, and of mentally following up a character's career in one field and another—by this I mean some one who possesses the power of entering into and developing the ideas of the author whose work he may be reading—would scan each character herein portrayed, and tell me how each character ought to have acted at a given juncture, and what, to judge from the beginnings of each character, ought to have become of that character later, and what new circumstances might be devised in connection therewith, and what new details might advantageously be added to those already described. Honestly can I say that to consider these points against the time when a new edition of my book may be published in a different and a better form would give me the greatest possible pleasure.

One thing in particular would I ask of any reader who may be willing to give me the benefit of his advice. That is to say, I would beg of him to suppose, while recording his remarks, that it is for the benefit of a man in no way his equal in education, or similar to him in tastes and ideas, or capable of apprehending criticisms without full explanation appended, that he is doing so. Rather would I ask such a reader to suppose that before him there stands a man of incomparably inferior enlightenment and schooling—a rude country bumpkin whose life, thoroughout, has been passed in retirement—a bumpkin to whom it is necessary to explain each circumstance in detail, while never forgetting to be as simple of speech as though he were a child, and at every step there were a danger of employing terms beyond his understanding. Should these precautions be kept constantly in view by any reader undertaking to annotate my book, that reader's remarks will exceed in weight and interest even his own expectations, and will bring me very real advantage.

Thus, provided that my earnest request be heeded by my readers, and that among them there be found a few kind spirits to do as I desire, the following is the manner in which I would request them to transmit their notes for my consideration. Inscribing the package with my name, let them then enclose that package in a second one addressed either to the Rector of the University of St. Petersburg or to Professor Shevirev of the University of Moscow, according as the one or the other of those two cities may be the nearer to the sender.

Lastly, while thanking all journalists and *litterateurs* for their previously published criticisms of my book—criticisms which, in spite of a spice of that intemperance and prejudice which is common to all humanity, have proved of the greatest use both to my head and to my heart—I beg of such writers again to favour me with their reviews. For in all sincerity I can assure them that whatsoever they may be pleased to say for my improvement and my instruction will be received by me with naught but gratitude.

DEAD SOULS

PART I

I

To the door of an inn in the provincial town of N. there drew
up a smart *britchka*—a light spring-carriage of the sort affected
by bachelors, retired lieutenant-colonels, staff-captains, landowners possessed of about a hundred souls, and, in short, all
persons who rank as gentlemen of the intermediate category.
In the *britchka* was seated such a gentleman—a man who, though
not handsome, was not ill-favoured, not over-fat, and not over-
thin. Also, though not over-elderly, he was not over-young.
His arrival produced no stir in the town, and was accompanied
by no particular incident, beyond that a couple of peasants who
happened to be standing at the door of a dramshop exchanged
a few comments with reference to the equipage rather than to the
individual who was seated in it. " Look at that carriage," one
of them said to the other. " Think you it will be going as far
as Moscow? " " I think it will," replied his companion. " But
not as far as Kazan, eh? " " No, not as far as Kazan." With
that the conversation ended. Presently, as the *britchka* was
approaching the inn, it was met by a young man in a pair of
very short, very tight breeches of white dimity, a quasi-fashion-
able frockcoat, and a dickey fastened with a pistol-shaped
bronze tie-pin. The young man turned his head as he passed the
britchka and eyed it attentively; after which he clapped his
hand to his cap (which was in danger of being removed by the
wind) and resumed his way. On the vehicle reaching the inn
door, its occupant found standing there to welcome him the
polevoi, or waiter, of the establishment—an individual of such
nimble and brisk movement that even to distinguish the character of his face was impossible. Running out with a napkin in one
hand and his lanky form clad in a tailcoat, reaching almost to
the nape of his neck, he tossed back his locks, and escorted the
gentleman upstairs, along a wooden gallery, and so to the bed-

chamber which God had prepared for the gentleman's reception. The said bedchamber was quite of ordinary appearance, since the inn belonged to the species to be found in all provincial towns—the species wherein, for two roubles a day, travellers may obtain a room swarming with black-beetles, and communicating by a doorway with the apartment adjoining. True, the doorway may be blocked up with a wardrobe; yet behind it, in all probability, there will be standing a silent, motionless neighbour whose ears are burning to learn every possible detail concerning the latest arrival. The inn's exterior corresponded with its interior. Long, and consisting only of two storeys, the building had its lower half destitute of stucco; with the result that the dark-red bricks, originally more or less dingy, had grown yet dingier under the influence of atmospheric changes. As for the upper half of the building, it was, of course, painted the usual tint of unfading yellow. Within, on the ground floor, there stood a number of benches heaped with horse-collars, rope, and sheepskins; while the window-seat accommodated a *sbitentshik*,[1] cheek by jowl with a *samovar*[2]—the latter so closely resembling the former in appearance that, but for the fact of the *samovar* possessing a pitch-black lip, the *samovar* and the *sbitentshik* might have been two of a pair.

During the traveller's inspection of his room his luggage was brought into the apartment. First came a portmanteau of white leather whose raggedness indicated that the receptacle had made several previous journeys. The bearers of the same were the gentleman's coachman, Selifan (a little man in a large overcoat), and the gentleman's valet, Petrushka—the latter a fellow of about thirty, clad in a worn, over-ample jacket which formerly had graced his master's shoulders, and possessed of a nose and a pair of lips whose coarseness communicated to his face rather a sullen expression. Behind the portmanteau came a small dispatch-box of redwood, lined with birch bark, a boot-case, and (wrapped in blue paper) a roast fowl; all of which having been deposited, the coachman departed to look after his horses, and the valet to establish himself in the little dark anteroom or kennel where already he had stored a cloak, a bagful of livery, and his own peculiar smell. Pressing the narrow bedstead back against the wall, he covered it with the tiny remnant of mattress —a remnant as thin and flat (perhaps also as greasy) as a pan-cake—which he had managed to beg of the landlord of the establishment.

[1] An urn for brewing honey tea. [2] An urn for brewing ordinary tea.

While the attendants had been thus setting things straight the gentleman had repaired to the common parlour. The appearance of common parlours of the kind is known to every one who travels. Always they have varnished walls which, grown black in their upper portions with tobacco smoke, are, in their lower, grown shiny with the friction of customers' backs — more especially with that of the backs of such local tradesmen as, on market-days, make it their regular practice to resort to the local hostelry for a glass of tea. Also, parlours of this kind invariably contain smutty ceilings, an equally smutty chandelier, a number of pendant shades which jump and rattle whenever the waiter scurries across the shabby oilcloth with a trayful of glasses (the glasses looking like a flock of birds roosting by the seashore), and a selection of oil paintings. In short, there are certain objects which one sees in every inn. In the present case the only outstanding feature of the room was the fact that in one of the paintings a nymph was portrayed as possessing breasts of a size such as the reader can never in his life have beheld. A similar caricaturing of nature is to be noted in the historical pictures (of unknown origin, period, and creation) which reach us— sometimes through the instrumentality of Russian magnates who profess to be connoisseurs of art—from Italy; owing to the said magnates having made such purchases solely on the advice of the couriers who have escorted them.

To resume, however—our traveller removed his cap, and divested his neck of a parti-coloured woollen scarf of the kind which a wife makes for her husband with her own hands, while accompanying the gift with interminable injunctions as to how best such a garment ought to be folded. True, bachelors also wear similar gauds, but, in their case, God alone knows who may have manufactured the articles! For my part, I cannot endure them. Having unfolded the scarf, the gentleman ordered dinner, and whilst the various dishes were being got ready— cabbage soup, a pie several weeks old, a dish of marrow and peas, a dish of sausages and cabbage, a roast fowl, some salted cucumber, and the sweet tart which stands perpetually ready for use in such establishments; whilst, I say, these things were either being warmed up or brought in cold, the gentleman induced the waiter to retail certain fragments of tittle-tattle concerning the late landlord of the hostelry, the amount of income which the hostelry produced, and the character of its present proprietor. To the last-mentioned inquiry the waiter returned the answer invariably given in such cases—namely,

"My master is a terribly hard man, sir." Curious that in enlightened Russia so many people cannot even take a meal at an inn without chattering to the attendant and making free with him! Nevertheless not *all* the questions which the gentleman asked were aimless ones, for he inquired who was Governor of the town, who President of the Local Council, and who Public Prosecutor. In short, he omitted no single official of note, while asking also (though with an air of detachment) the most exact particulars concerning the landowners of the neighbourhood. Which of them, he inquired, possessed serfs, and how many of them? How far from the town did those landowners reside? What was the character of each landowner, and was he in the habit of paying frequent visits to the town? The gentleman also made searching inquiries concerning the hygienic condition of the countryside. Was there, he asked, much sickness about— whether sporadic fever, fatal forms of ague, smallpox, or what not? Yet, though his solicitude concerning these matters showed more than ordinary curiosity, his bearing retained its gravity unimpaired, and from time to time he blew his nose with portentous fervour. Indeed, the manner in which he accomplished this latter feat was marvellous in the extreme, for, though that member emitted sounds equal to those of a trumpet in intensity, he could yet, with his accompanying air of guileless dignity, evoke the waiter's undivided respect—so much so that, whenever the sounds of the nose reached that menial's ears, he would shake back his locks, straighten himself into a posture of marked solicitude, and inquire afresh, with head slightly inclined, whether the gentleman happened to require anything further. After dinner the guest consumed a cup of coffee, and then, seating himself upon the sofa, with, behind him, one of those wool-covered cushions which, in Russian taverns, resemble nothing so much as a cobblestone or a brick, fell to snoring; whereafter, returning with a start to consciousness, he ordered himself to be conducted to his room, flung himself at full length upon the bed, and once more slept soundly for a couple of hours. Aroused, eventually, by the waiter, he, at the latter's request, inscribed a fragment of paper with his name, his surname, and his rank (for communication, in accordance with the law, to the police): and on that paper the waiter, leaning forward from the corridor, read, syllable by syllable: "Paul Ivanovitch Chichikov, Collegiate Councillor — Landowner — Travelling on Private Affairs." The waiter had just time to accomplish this feat before Paul Ivanovitch Chichikov set forth to inspect the town. Ap-

parently the place succeeded in satisfying him, and, to tell the
truth, it was at least up to the usual standard of our provincial
capitals. Where the staring yellow of stone edifices did not
greet his eye he found himself confronted with the more modest
grey of wooden ones; which, consisting, for the most part, of
one or two storeys (added to the range of attics which provincial
architects love so well), looked almost lost amid the expanses of
street and intervening medleys of broken or half-finished parti-
tion-walls. At other points evidence of more life and movement
was to be seen, and here the houses stood crowded together and
displayed dilapidated, rain-blurred signboards whereon boots or
cakes or pairs of blue breeches inscribed " Arshavski, Tailor,"
and so forth, were depicted. Over a shop containing hats and
caps was written " Vassili Thedorov, Foreigner"; while, at
another spot, a signboard portrayed a billiard table and two
players—the latter clad in frockcoats of the kind usually affected
by actors whose part it is to enter the stage during the closing
act of a piece, even though, with arms sharply crooked and legs
slightly bent, the said billiard players were taking the most
careful aim, but succeeding only in making abortive strokes in
the air. Each emporium of the sort had written over it: " This
is the best establishment of its kind in the town." Also, *al fresco*
in the streets there stood tables heaped with nuts, soap, and
gingerbread (the latter but little distinguishable from the soap),
and at an eating-house there was displayed the sign of a plump
fish transfixed with a gaff. But the sign most frequently to be
discerned was the insignia of the State, the double-headed
eagle (now replaced, in this connection, with the laconic inscription " Dramshop "). As for the paving of the town, it was
uniformly bad.

The gentleman peered also into the municipal gardens, which
contained only a few sorry trees that were poorly selected,
requiring to be propped with oil-painted, triangular green
supports, and able to boast of a height no greater than that of
an ordinary walking-stick. Yet recently the local paper had
said (*apropos* of a gala) that, " Thanks to the efforts of our Civil
Governor, the town has become enriched with a pleasaunce full
of umbrageous, spaciously-branching trees. Even on the most
sultry day they afford agreeable shade, and indeed gratifying
was it to see the hearts of our citizens panting with an impulse
of gratitude as their eyes shed tears in recognition of all that
their Governor has done for them! "

Next, after inquiring of a gendarme as to the best ways and

means of finding the local council, the local law-courts, and the local Governor, should he (Chichikov) have need of them, the gentleman went on to inspect the river which ran through the town. *En route* he tore off a notice affixed to a post, in order that he might the more conveniently read it after his return to the inn. Also, he bestowed upon a lady of pleasant exterior who, escorted by a footman laden with a bundle, happened to be passing along a wooden sidewalk a prolonged stare. Lastly, he threw around him a comprehensive glance (as though to fix in his mind the general topography of the place) and betook himself home. There, gently aided by the waiter, he ascended the stairs to his bedroom, drank a glass of tea, and, seating himself at the table, called for a candle; which having been brought him, he produced from his pocket the notice, held it close to the flame, and conned its tenour—slightly contracting his right eye as he did so. Yet there was little in the notice to call for remark. All that it said was that shortly one of Kotzebue's [1] plays would be given, and that one of the parts in the play was to be taken by a certain Monsieur Poplevin, and another by a certain Mademoiselle Ziablova, while the remaining parts were to be filled by a number of less important personages. Nevertheless the gentleman perused the notice with careful attention, and even jotted down the prices to be asked for seats for the performance. Also, he remarked that the bill had been printed at the press of the Provincial Government. Next, he turned over the paper, in order to see if anything further was to be read on the reverse side; but, finding nothing there, he refolded the document, placed it in the box which served him as a receptacle for odds and ends, and brought the day to a close with a portion of cold veal, a bottle of pickles, and a sound sleep.

The following day he devoted to paying calls upon the various municipal officials—a first, and a very respectful, visit being paid to the Governor. This personage turned out to resemble Chichikov himself in that he was neither fat nor thin. Also, he wore the riband of the order of Saint Anna around his neck, and was reported to have been recommended also for the star. For the rest, he was large and good-natured, and had a habit of amusing himself with occasional spells of knitting. Next, Chichikov repaired to the Vice-Governor's, and thence to the house of the Public Prosecutor, to that of the President of the Local Council, to that of the Chief of Police, to that of the Commis-

---

[1] A German dramatist (1761–1819) who also filled sundry posts in the service of the Russian Government.

sioner of Taxes, and to that of the local Director of State Factories. True, the task of remembering every big-wig in this world of ours is not a very easy one; but at least our visitor displayed the greatest activity in his work of paying calls, seeing that he went so far as to pay his respects also to the Inspector of the Municipal Department of Medicine and to the City Architect. Thereafter he sat thoughtfully in his *britchka*—plunged in meditation on the subject of whom else it might be well to visit. However, not a single magnate had been neglected, and in conversation with his hosts he had contrived to flatter each separate one. For instance to the Governor he had hinted that a stranger, on arriving in his, the Governor's province, would conceive that he had reached Paradise, so velvety were the roads.. "Governors who appoint capable subordinates," had said Chichikov, "are deserving of the most ample meed of praise." Again, to the Chief of Police our hero had passed a most gratifying remark on the subject of the local gendarmery; while in his conversation with the Vice-Governor and the President of the Local Council (neither of whom had, as yet, risen above the rank of State Councillor) he had twice been guilty of the *gaucherie* of addressing his interlocutors with the title of "Your Excellency"—a blunder which had not failed to delight them. In the result the Governor had invited him to a reception the same evening, and certain other officials had followed suit by inviting him, one of them to dinner, a second to a tea-party, and so forth, and so forth.

Of himself, however, the traveller had spoken little; or, if he had spoken at any length, he had done so in a general sort of way and with marked modesty. Indeed, at moments of the kind his discourse had assumed something of a literary vein, in that invariably he had stated that, being a worm of no account in the world, he was deserving of no consideration at the hands of his fellows; that in his time he had undergone many strange experiences; that subsequently he had suffered much in the cause of Truth; that he had many enemies seeking his life; and that, being desirous of rest, he was now engaged in searching for a spot wherein to dwell—wherefore, having stumbled upon the town in which he now found himself, he had considered it his bounden duty to evince his respect for the chief authorities of the place. This, and no more, was all that, for the moment, the town succeeded in learning about the new arrival. Naturally he lost no time in presenting himself at the Governor's evening party. First, however, his preparations for that function occupied a space of over two hours, and necessitated an attention to his toilet of a kind not commonly seen. That is to say, after a brief post-prandial nap he called for soap and water, and spent a considerable period in the task of scrubbing his cheeks (which, for the purpose, he supported from within with his tongue) and then of drying his full, round face, from the ears downwards, with a towel which he took from the waiter's shoulder. Twice he snorted into the waiter's countenance as he did this, and then he posted himself in front of the mirror, donned a false shirt-front, plucked out a couple of hairs which were protruding from his nose, and appeared vested in a frockcoat of bilberry-coloured check. Thereafter driving through broad streets sparsely lighted with lanterns, he arrived at the Governor's residence to find it illuminated as for a ball. Barouches with gleaming lamps, a couple of gendarmes posted before the doors, a babel of pos-tillions' cries—nothing of a kind likely to be impressive was wanting; and, on reaching the *salon*, the visitor actually found himself obliged to close his eyes for a moment, so strong was the mingled sheen of lamps, candles, and feminine apparel. Every-thing seemed suffused with light, and everywhere, flitting and flashing, were to be seen black coats—even as on a hot summer's day flies revolve around a sugar loaf while the old housekeeper is cutting it into cubes before the open window, and the children of the house crowd around her to watch the movements of her rugged hands as those members ply the smoking pestle; and airy squadrons of flies, borne on the breeze, enter boldly, as though free of the house, and, taking advantage of the fact that the glare of the sunshine is troubling the old lady's sight, disperse themselves over broken and unbroken fragments alike, even though the lethargy induced by the opulence of summer and the rich shower of dainties to be encountered at every step has induced them to enter less for the purpose of eating than for that of showing themselves in public, of parading up and down the sugar loaf, of rubbing both their hindquarters and their fore against one another, of cleaning their bodies under the wings, of extending their forelegs over their heads and grooming themselves, and of flying out of the window again to return with other predatory squadrons. Indeed, so dazed was Chichikov that scarcely did he realise that the Governor was taking him by the arm and presenting him to his (the Governor's) lady. Yet the newly-arrived guest kept his head sufficiently to con-trive to murmur some such compliment as might fittingly come from a middle-aged individual of a rank neither excessively high now excessively low. Next, when couples had been formed for dancing and the remainder of the company found itself pressed back against the walls, Chichikov folded his arms, and carefully scrutinised the dancers. Some of the ladies were dressed well and in the fashion, while the remainder were clad in such garments as God usually bestows upon a provincial town. Also here, as elsewhere, the men belonged to two separate and distinct categories; one of which comprised slender individuals who, flitting around the ladies, were scarcely to be distinguished from denizens of the metropolis, so carefully, so artistically, groomed were their whiskers, so presentable their oval, clean-shaven faces, so easy the manner of their dancing attendance upon their womenfolk, so glib their French conversation as they quizzed their female companions. As for the other category, it comprised individuals who, stout, or of the same build as Chichikov (that is to say, neither very portly nor very lean), backed and sidled away from the ladies, and kept peering hither and thither to see whether the Governor's footmen had set out green tables for whist. Their features were full and plump, some of them had beards, and in no case was their hair curled or waved or arranged in what the French call " the devil-may-care " style. On the contrary, their heads were either close-cropped or brushed very smooth, and their faces were round and firm. This category represented the more respectable officials of the town. In passing, I may say that in business matters fat men always prove superior to their leaner brethren; which is probably the reason why the latter are mostly to be found in the Political Police, or acting as mere ciphers whose existence is a purely hopeless, airy, trivial one. Again, stout individuals never take a back seat, but always a front one, and, wheresoever it be, they sit firmly, and with confidence, and decline to budge even though the seat crack and bend with their weight. For comeliness of exterior they care not a rap, and therefore a dress coat sits less easily on their figures than is the case with figures of leaner individuals. Yet invariably fat men amass the greater wealth. In three years' time a thin man will have not a single serf whom he has left unpledged; whereas—well, pray look at a fat man's fortunes, and what will you see? First of all a suburban villa, and then a larger suburban villa, and then a villa close to a town, and, lastly, a country estate which comprises every amenity! That is to say, having served both God and the State, the stout individual has won universal respect, and will end by retiring from business, reordering his mode of life, and becoming a Russian landowner—in other words, a fine gentleman who dispenses hospitality, lives in comfort and luxury, and is destined to leave his property to heirs who are purposing to squander the same on foreign travel.

That the foregoing represents pretty much the gist of Chichikov's reflections as he stood watching the company I will not attempt to deny. And of those reflections the upshot was that he decided to join himself to the stouter section of the guests, among whom he had already recognised several familiar faces —namely, those of the Public Prosecutor (a man with beetling brows over eyes which seemed to be saying with a wink, " Come into the next room, my friend, for I have something to say to you "—though, in the main, their owner was a man of grave and taciturn habit), of the Postmaster (an insignificant-looking individual, yet a would-be wit and a philosopher), and of the President of the Local Council (a man of much amiability and good sense). These three personages greeted Chichikov as an old acquaintance, and to their salutations he responded with a sidelong, yet a sufficiently civil, bow. Also, he became acquainted with an extremely unctuous and approachable landowner named Manilov, and with a landowner of more uncouth exterior named Sobakevitch—the latter of whom began the acquaintance by treading heavily upon Chichikov's toes, and then begging his pardon. Next, Chichikov received an offer of a " cut in " at whist, and accepted the same with his usual courteous inclination of the head. Seating themselves at a green table, the party did not rise therefrom until supper time; and during that period all conversation between the players became hushed, as is the custom when men have given themselves up to a really serious pursuit. Even the Postmaster—a talkative man by nature—had no sooner taken the cards into his hands than he assumed an expression of profound thought, pursed his lips, and retained this attitude unchanged throughout the game. Only when playing a court card was it his custom to strike the table with his fist, and to exclaim (if the card happened to be a queen), " Now, old *popadia !* " [1] and (if the card happened to be a king), " Now, peasant of Tambov! " To which ejaculations invariably the President of the Local Council retorted, " Ah, I have him by the ears, I have him by the ears! " And from the neighbourhood of the table other strong ejaculations relative to the play would arise, interposed with one or another of those nicknames which participants in a game are apt to apply to members of the various suits. I need hardly add that, the game over, the players fell to

[1] Priest's wife.

quarrelling, and that in the dispute our friend joined, though so artfully as to let every one see that, in spite of the fact that he was wrangling, he was doing so only in the most amicable fashion possible. Never did he say outright, "You played the wrong card at such and such a point." No, he always employed some such phrase as, "You permitted yourself to make a slip, and thus afforded me the honour of covering your deuce." Indeed, the better to keep in accord with his antagonists, he kept offering them his silver enamelled snuff box (at the bottom of which lay a couple of violets, placed there for the sake of their scent). In particular did the newcomer pay attention to landowners Manilov and Sobakevitch; so much so that his haste to arrive on good terms with them led to his leaving the President and the Postmaster rather in the shade. At the same time, certain questions which he put to those two landowners evinced not only curiosity, but also a certain amount of sound intelligence; for he began by asking how many peasant souls each of them possessed, and how their affairs happened at present to be situated, and then proceeded to enlighten himself also as to their standing and their families. Indeed, it was not long before he had succeeded in fairly enchanting his new friends. In particular did Manilov—a man still in his prime, and possessed of a pair of eyes which, sweet as sugar, blinked whenever he laughed—find himself unable to make enough of his enchanter. Clasping Chichikov long and fervently by the hand, he besought him to do him, Manilov, the honour of visiting his country house (which he declared to lie at a distance of not more than fifteen versts from the boundaries of the town); and in return Chichikov averred (with an exceedingly affable bow and a most sincere handshake) that he was prepared not only to fulfil his friend's behest, but also to look upon the fulfilling of it as a sacred duty. In the same way Sobakevitch said to him laconically: "And do you pay *me* a visit," and then proceeded to shuffle a pair of boots of such dimensions that to find a pair to correspond with them would have been indeed difficult—more especially at the present day, when the race of epic heroes is beginning to die out in Russia.

Next day Chichikov dined and spent the evening at the house of the Chief of Police—a residence where, three hours after dinner, every one sat down to whist, and remained so seated until two o'clock in the morning. On this occasion Chichikov made the acquaintance of, among others, a landowner named Nozdrev—a dissipated little fellow of thirty who had no sooner

exchanged three or four words with his new acquaintance
than he began to address him in the second person singular.
Yet although he did the same to the Chief of Police and the
Public Prosecutor, the company had no sooner seated themselves
at the card-table than both the one and the other of those
functionaries started to keep a careful eye upon Nozdrev's
tricks, and to watch practically every card which he played.
The following evening Chichikov spent with the President of the
Local Council, who received his guests—even though the latter
included two ladies—in a greasy dressing-gown. Upon that
followed an evening at the Vice-Governor's, a large dinner party
at the house of the Commissioner of Taxes, a smaller dinner-
party at the house of the Public Prosecutor (a very wealthy
man), and a subsequent reception given by the Mayor. In short,
not an hour of the day did Chichikov find himself forced to spend
at home, and his return to the inn became necessary only for
purposes of sleeping. Somehow or other he had landed on his
feet, and everywhere he figured as an experienced man of the
world. No matter what the conversation chanced to be about,
he always contrived to maintain his part in the same. Did the
discourse turn upon horse-breeding, upon horse-breeding he
happened to be peculiarly well qualified to speak. Did the
company fall to discussing well-bred dogs, at once he had
remarks of the most pertinent kind possible to offer. Did the
company touch upon a prosecution which had recently been
carried out by the Excise Department, instantly he showed that
he too was not wholly unacquainted with legal affairs. Did an
opinion chance to be expressed concerning billiards, on that
subject too he was at least able to avoid committing a blunder.
Did a reference occur to virtue, concerning virtue he hastened
to deliver himself in a way which brought tears to every eye.
Did the subject in hand happen to be the distilling of brandy
—well, that was a matter concerning which he had the soundest
of knowledge. Did any one happen to mention Customs officials
and inspectors, from that moment he expatiated as though he too
had been both a minor functionary and a major. Yet a remarkable fact was the circumstance that he always contrived to temper
his omniscience with a certain readiness to give way, a certain
ability so to keep a rein upon himself that never did his utterances become too loud or too soft, or transcend what was
perfectly befitting. In a word, he was always a gentleman of
excellent manners, and every official in the place felt pleased
when he saw him enter the door. Thus the Governor gave it as his

opinion that Chichikov was a man of excellent intentions; the Public Prosecutor, that he was a good man of business; the Chief of Gendarmery, that he was a man of education; the President of the Local Council, that he was a man of breeding and refinement; and the wife of the Chief of Gendarmery, that his politeness of behaviour was equalled only by his affability of bearing. Nay, even Sobakevitch—who as a rule never spoke well of *any one*—said to his lanky wife when, on returning late from the town, he undressed and betook himself to bed by her side: "My dear, this evening, after dining with the Chief of Police, I went on to the Governor's, and met there, among others, a certain Paul Ivanovitch Chichikov, who is a Collegiate Councillor and a very pleasant fellow." To this his spouse replied "Hm!" and then dealt him a hearty kick in the ribs.

Such were the flattering opinions earned by the newcomer to the town; and these opinions he retained until the time when a certain speciality of his, a certain scheme of his (the reader will learn presently what it was), plunged the majority of the townsfolk into a sea of perplexity.

II

FOR more than two weeks the visitor lived amid a round of evening parties and dinners; wherefore he spent (as the saying goes) a very pleasant time. Finally he decided to extend his visits beyond the urban boundaries by going and calling upon landowners Manilov and Sobakevitch, seeing that he had promised on his honour to do so. Yet what really incited him to this may have been a more essential cause, a matter of greater gravity, a purpose which stood nearer to his heart, than the motive which I have just given; and of that purpose the reader will learn if only he will have the patience to read this prefatory narrative (which, lengthy though it be, may yet develop and expand in proportion as we approach the *dénouement* with which the present work is destined to be crowned).

One evening, therefore, Selifan the coachman received orders to have the horses harnessed in good time next morning; while Petrushka received orders to remain behind, for the purpose of looking after the portmanteau and the room. In passing, the reader may care to become more fully acquainted with the two serving-men of whom I have spoken. Naturally, they were not persons of much note, but merely what folk call characters of secondary, or even of tertiary, importance. Yet, despite the fact that the springs and the thread of this romance will not *depend* upon them, but only touch upon them, and occasionally include them, the author has a passion for circumstantiality, and, like the average Russian, such a desire for accuracy as even a German could not rival. To what the reader already knows concerning the personages in hand it is therefore necessary to add that Petrushka usually wore a cast-off brown jacket of a size too large for him, as also that he had (according to the custom of individuals of his calling) a pair of thick lips and a very prominent nose. In temperament he was taciturn rather than loquacious, and he cherished a yearning for self-education. That is to say, he loved to read books, even though their contents came alike to him whether they were books of heroic adventure or mere grammars or liturgical compendia. As I say, he perused every book with an equal amount of attention, and, had he been offered a work on chemistry, would have accepted that also. Not the words which he read, but the mere solace derived from the act of reading, was what especially pleased his mind; even though at any moment there might launch itself from the page some devil-sent word whereof he could make neither head nor tail. For the most part, his task of reading was performed in a recumbent position in the anteroom; which circumstance ended by causing his mattress to become as ragged and as thin as a wafer. In addition to his love of poring over books, he could boast of two habits which constituted two other essential features of his character—namely, a habit of retiring to rest in his clothes (that is to say, in the brown jacket above-mentioned) and a habit of everywhere bearing with him his own peculiar atmosphere, his own peculiar smell—a smell which filled any lodging with such subtlety that he needed but to make up his bed anywhere, even in a room hitherto untenanted, and to drag thither his greatcoat and other impedimenta, for that room at once to assume an air of having been lived in during the past ten years. Nevertheless, though a fastidious, and even an irritable, man, Chichikov would merely frown when his nose caught this smell amid the freshness of the morning, and exclaim with a toss of his head: " The devil only knows what is up with you! Surely you sweat a good deal, do you not? The best thing you can do is to go and take a bath." To this Petrushka would make no reply, but, approaching, brush in hand, the spot where his master's coat would be pendent, or starting to arrange one and another article in order, would strive to seem wholly immersed in his work. Yet of what was he thinking as he remained thus silent? Perhaps he was saying to himself: "My master is a good fellow, but for him to keep on saying the same thing forty times over is a little wearisome." Only God knows and sees all things; wherefore for a mere human being to know what is in the mind of a servant while his master is scolding him is wholly impossible. However, no more need be said about Petrushka. On the other hand, Coachman Selifan——

But here let me remark that I do not like engaging the reader's attention in connection with persons of a lower class than himself; for experience has taught me that we do not willingly familiarise ourselves with the lower orders—that it is the custom of the average Russian to yearn exclusively for information concerning persons on the higher rungs of the social ladder. In fact, even a bowing acquaintance with a prince or a lord counts, in his eyes, for more than do the most intimate of relations with ordinary folk. For the same reason the author of this story feels apprehensive on his hero's account, seeing that he has made that hero a mere Collegiate Councillor—a mere person with whom Aulic Councillors might consort, but upon whom persons of the grade of full General[1] would probably bestow one of those glances proper to a man who is cringing at their august feet. Worse still, such persons of the grade of General are likely to treat Chichikov with studied negligence — and to an author studied negligence spells death.

However, in spite of the distressfulness of the foregoing possibilities, it is time that I returned to my hero. After issuing, overnight, the necessary orders, he awoke early, washed himself, rubbed himself from head to foot with a wet sponge (a performance executed only on Sundays—and the day in question happened to be a Sunday), shaved his face with such care that his cheeks issued of absolutely satin-like smoothness and polish, donned first his bilberry-coloured, spotted frockcoat, and then his bearskin overcoat, descended the staircase (attended, throughout, by the waiter) and entered his *britchka*. With a loud rattle the vehicle left the inn-yard, and issued into the street. A passing priest doffed his cap, and a few urchins in grimy shirts shouted, "Gentleman, please give a poor orphan a trifle!" Presently the driver noticed that a sturdy young rascal was on the point of climbing on to the splashboard; wherefore he

[1] In this case the term General refers to a civil grade equivalent to the military rank of the same title.

cracked his whip and the *britchka* leapt forward with increased speed over the cobblestones. At last, with a feeling of relief, the travellers caught sight of macadam ahead, which promised an end both to the cobblestones and to sundry other annoyances. And, sure enough, after his head had been bumped a few more times against the boot of the conveyance, Chichikov found himself bowling over softer ground. On the town receding into the distance, the sides of the road began to be varied with the usual hillocks, fir trees, clumps of young pine, trees with old, scarred trunks, bushes of wild juniper, and so forth. Presently there came into view also strings of country villas which, with their carved supports and grey roofs (the latter looking like pendent, embroidered tablecloths), resembled, rather, bundles of old faggots. Likewise the customary peasants, dressed in sheepskin jackets, could be seen yawning on benches before their huts, while their womenfolk, fat of feature and swathed of bosom, gazed out of upper windows, and the windows below displayed, here a peering calf, and there the unsightly jaws of a pig. In short, the view was one of the familiar type. After passing the fifteenth verst-stone Chichikov suddenly recollected that, according to Manilov, fifteen versts was the exact distance between his country house and the town; but the sixteenth verst stone flew by, and the said country house was still nowhere to be seen. In fact, but for the circumstance that the travellers happened to encounter a couple of peasants, they would have come their errand in vain. To a query as to whether the country house known as Zamanilovka was anywhere in the neighbourhood the peasants replied by doffing their caps; after which one of them who seemed to boast of a little more intelligence than his companion, and who wore a wedge-shaped beard, made answer:

" Perhaps you mean Manilovka—not Zamanilovka? "

" Yes, yes—Manilovka."

" Manilovka, eh? Well, you must continue for another verst, and then you will see it straight before you, on the right."

" On the right? " re-echoed the coachman.

" Yes, on the right," affirmed the peasant. " You are on the proper road for Manilovka, but Zamanilovka—well, there is no such place. The house you mean is called Manilovka because Manilovka is its name; but no house at all is called Zamanilovka. The house you mean stands there, on that hill, and is a stone house in which a gentleman lives, and its name is Manilovka; but Zamanilovka does not stand hereabouts, nor ever has stood."

So the travellers proceeded in search of Manilovka, and, after driving an additional two versts, arrived at a spot whence there branched off a by-road. Yet two, three, or four versts of the by-road had been covered before they saw the least sign of a two-storied stone mansion. Then it was that Chichikov suddenly recollected that, when a friend has invited one to visit his country house, and has said that the distance thereto is fifteen versts, the distance is sure to turn out to be at least thirty.

Not many people would have admired the situation of Manilov's abode, for it stood on an isolated rise and was open to every wind that blew. On the slope of the rise lay closely-mown turf, while, disposed here and there, after the English fashion, were flower-beds containing clumps of lilac and yellow acacia. Also, there were a few insignificant groups of slender-leaved, pointed-tipped birch trees, with, under two of the latter, an arbour having a shabby green cupola, some blue-painted wooden supports, and the inscription " This is the Temple of Solitary Thought." Lower down the slope lay a green-coated pond— green-coated ponds constitute a frequent spectacle in the gardens of Russian landowners; and, lastly, from the foot of the declivity there stretched a line of mouldy, log-built huts which, for some obscure reason or another, our hero set himself to count. Up to two hundred or more did he count, but nowhere could he perceive a single leaf of vegetation or a single stick of timber. The only thing to greet the eye was the logs of which the huts were constructed. Nevertheless the scene was to a certain extent enlivened by the spectacle of two peasant women who, with clothes picturesquely tucked up, were wading knee-deep in the pond and dragging behind them, with wooden handles, a ragged fishing-net, in the meshes of which two crawfish and a roach with glistening scales were entangled. The women appeared to have cause of dispute between themselves—to be rating one another about something. In the background, and to one side of the house, showed a faint, dusky blur of pinewood, and even the weather was in keeping with the surroundings, since the day was neither clear nor dull, but of the grey tint which may be noted in uniforms of garrison soldiers which have seen long service. To complete the picture, a cock, the recognised harbinger of atmospheric mutations, was present; and, in spite of the fact that a certain connection with affairs of gallantry had led to his having had his head pecked bare by other cocks, he flapped a pair of wings—appendages as bare as two pieces of bast—and crowed loudly.

As Chichikov approached the courtyard of the mansion he caught sight of his host (clad in a green frock coat) standing on the verandah and pressing one hand to his eyes to shield them from the sun and so get a better view of the approaching carriage. In proportion as the *britchka* drew nearer and nearer to the verandah, the host's eyes assumed a more and more delighted expression, and his smile a broader and broader sweep.

" Paul Ivanovitch! " he exclaimed when at length Chichikov leapt from the vehicle. " Never should I have believed that you would have remembered us! "

The two friends exchanged hearty embraces, and Manilov then conducted his guest to the drawing-room. During the brief time that they are traversing the hall, the anteroom, and the dining-room, let me try to say something concerning the master of the house. But such an undertaking bristles with difficulties —it promises to be a far less easy task than the depicting of some outstanding personality of a type which calls but for a wholesale dashing of colours upon the canvas—the colours of a pair of dark, burning eyes, a pair of dark, beetling brows, a forehead seamed with wrinkles, a black, or a fiery-red, cloak thrown backwards over the shoulder, and so forth, and so forth. Yes, so numerous are Russian serf owners that, though careful scrutiny reveals to one's sight a quantity of *outré* peculiarities, they are, as a class, exceedingly difficult to portray, and one needs to strain one's faculties to the utmost before it becomes possible to pick out their variously subtle, their almost invisible, features. In short, one needs, before doing this, to carry out a prolonged probing with the aid of an insight sharpened in the acute school of research.

Only God can say what Manilov's real character was. A class of men exists whom the proverb has described as " men unto themselves, neither this nor that—neither Bogdan of the city nor Selifan of the village." And to that class we had better assign also Manilov. Outwardly he was presentable enough, for his features were not wanting in amiability, but that amiability was a quality into which there entered too much of the sugary element, so that his every gesture, his every attitude, seemed to connote an excess of eagerness to curry favour and cultivate a closer acquaintance. On first speaking to the man, his ingratiating smile, his flaxen hair, and his blue eyes would lead one to say, " What a pleasant, good-tempered fellow he seems! " yet during the next moment or two one would feel inclined to say nothing at all, and, during the third moment, only to say, " The devil alone knows what he is! " And should, thereafter, one not hasten to depart, one would inevitably become overpowered with the deadly sense of *ennui* which comes of the intuition that nothing in the least interesting is to be looked for, but only a series of wearisome utterances of the kind which are apt to fall from the lips of a man whose hobby has once been touched upon. For every man *has* his hobby. One man's may be sporting dogs; another man's may be that of believing himself to be a lover of music, and able to sound the art to its inmost depths; another's may be that of posing as a connoisseur of *récherché* cookery; another's may be that of aspiring to play rôles of a kind higher than nature has assigned him; another's (though this is a more limited ambition) may be that of getting drunk, and of dreaming that he is edifying both his friends, his acquaintances, and people with whom he has no connection at all by walking arm-in-arm with an Imperial aide-de-camp; another's may be that of possessing a hand able to chip corners off aces and deuces of diamonds; another's may be that of yearning to set things straight—in other words, to approximate his personality to that of a stationmaster or a director of posts. In short, almost every man has his hobby or his leaning; yet Manilov had none such, for at home he spoke little, and spent the greater part of his time in meditation—though God only knows what that meditation comprised! Nor can it be said that he took much interest in the management of his estate, for he never rode into the country, and the estate practically managed itself. Whenever the bailiff said to him, " It might be well to have such-and-such a thing done," he would reply, " Yes, that is not a bad idea," and then go on smoking his pipe—a habit which he had acquired during his service in the army, where he had been looked upon as an officer of modesty, delicacy, and refinement. " Yes, it is *not* a bad idea," he would repeat. Again, whenever a peasant approached him and, rubbing the back of his neck, said, " *Barin*, may I have leave to go and work for myself, in order that I may earn my *obrok* [1]? " he would snap out, with pipe in mouth as usual, " Yes, go! " and never trouble his head as to whether the peasant's real object might not be to go and get drunk. True, at intervals he would say, while gazing from the verandah to the courtyard, and from the courtyard to the pond, that it would be indeed splendid if a carriage drive could suddenly materialise, and the

[1] An annual tax upon peasants, payment of which secured to the payer the right of removal.

pond as suddenly become spanned with a stone bridge, and little shops as suddenly arise whence pedlars could dispense the petty merchandise of the kind which peasantry most need. And at such moments his eyes would grow winning, and his features assume an expression of intense satisfaction. Yet never did these projects pass beyond the stage of debate. Likewise there lay in his study a book with the fourteenth page permanently turned down. It was a book which he had been reading for the past two years! In general, something seemed to be wanting in the establishment. For instance, although the drawing-room was filled with beautiful furniture, and upholstered in some fine silken material which clearly had cost no inconsiderable sum, two of the chairs lacked any covering but bast, and for some years past the master had been accustomed to warn his guests with the words, " Do not sit upon those chairs; they are not yet ready for use." Another room contained no furniture at all, although, a few days after the marriage, it had been said: " My dear, to-morrow let us set about procuring at least some *temporary* furniture for this room." Also, every evening would see placed upon the drawing-room table a fine bronze candelabrum, a statuette representative of the Three Graces, a tray inlaid with mother-of-pearl, and a rickety, lop-sided copper *invalide*. Yet of the fact that all four articles were thickly coated with grease neither the master of the house nor the mistress nor the servants seemed to entertain the least suspicion. At the same time, Manilov and his wife were quite satisfied with one another. More than eight years had elapsed since their marriage, yet one of them was for ever offering his or her partner a piece of apple or a bonbon or a nut, while murmuring some tender something which voiced a whole-hearted affection. "Open your mouth, dearest "—thus ran the formula—" and let me pop into it this titbit." You may be sure that on such occasions the " dearest mouth " parted its lips most graciously! For their mutual birthdays the pair always contrived some " surprise present " in the shape of a glass receptacle for tooth-powder, or what not; and as they sat together on the sofa he would suddenly, and for some unknown reason, lay aside his pipe, and she her work (if at the moment she happened to be holding it in her hands) and husband and wife would imprint upon one another's cheeks such a prolonged and languishing kiss that during its continuance you could have smoked a small cigar. In short, they were what is known as " a very happy couple." Yet it may be remarked that a household requires other pursuits to be engaged in than lengthy embracings and the preparing of cunning " surprises." Yes, many a function calls for fulfilment. For instance, why should it be thought foolish or low to superintend the kitchen? Why should care not be taken that the storeroom never lacks supplies? Why should a housekeeper be allowed to thieve? Why should slovenly and drunken servants exist? Why should a domestic staff be suffered to indulge in bouts of unconscionable debauchery during its leisure time? Yet none of these things were thought worthy of consideration by Manilov's wife, for she had been gently brought up, and gentle nurture, as we all know, is to be acquired only in boarding schools, and boarding schools, as we know, hold the three principal subjects which constitute the basis of human virtue to be the French language (a thing indispensable to the happiness of married life), piano-playing (a thing wherewith to beguile a husband's leisure moments), and that particular department of housewifery which is comprised in the knitting of purses and other " surprises." Nevertheless changes and improvements have begun to take place, since things now are governed more by the personal inclinations and idiosyncracies of the keepers of such establishments. For instance, in some seminaries the regimen places piano-playing first, and the French language next, and then the above department of housewifery; while in other seminaries the knitting of " surprises " heads the list, and then the French language, and then the playing of pianos —so diverse are the systems in force! None the less, I may remark that Madame Manilov——

But let me confess that I always shrink from saying too much about ladies. Moreover, it is time that we returned to our heroes, who, during the past few minutes, have been standing in front of the drawing-room door, and engaged in urging one another to enter first.

" Pray be so good as not to inconvenience yourself on my account," said Chichikov. " *I* will follow *you*."

" No, Paul Ivanovitch—no! You are my guest." And Manilov pointed towards the doorway.

" Make no difficulty about it, I pray," urged Chichikov. " I beg of you to make no difficulty about it, but to pass into the room."

" Pardon me, I will not. Never could I allow so distinguished and so welcome a guest as yourself to take second place."

" Why call me ' distinguished,' my dear sir? I beg of you to proceed."

" Nay; be *you* pleased to do so."

" And why? "

" For the reason which I have stated." And Manilov smiled his very pleasantest smile.

Finally the pair entered simultaneously and sideways; with the result that they jostled one another not a little in the process.

" Allow me to present to you my wife," continued Manilov. " My dear—Paul Ivanovitch."

Upon that Chichikov caught sight of a lady whom hitherto he had overlooked, but who, with Manilov, was now bowing to him in the doorway. Not wholly of unpleasing exterior, she was dressed in a well-fitting, high-necked morning dress of pale-coloured silk; and as the visitor entered the room her small white hands threw something upon the table and clutched her embroidered skirt before rising from the sofa where she had been seated. Not without a sense of pleasure did Chichikov take her hand as, lisping a little, she declared that she and her husband were greatly gratified by his coming, and that, of late, not a day had passed without her husband recalling him to mind.

" Yes," affirmed Manilov; " and every day *she* has said to *me :* ' Why does not your friend put in an appearance? ' ' Wait a little dearest,' I have always replied. ' 'Twill not be long now before he comes.' And you *have* come, you *have* honoured us with a visit, you *have* bestowed upon us a treat—a treat destined to convert this day into a gala day, a true birthday of the heart."

The intimation that matters had reached the point of the occasion being destined to constitute a " true birthday of the heart" caused Chichikov to become a little confused; wherefore he made modest reply that, as a matter of fact, he was neither of distinguished origin nor distinguished rank.

" Ah, you *are* so," interrupted Manilov with his fixed and engaging smile. " You are all that, and more."

" How like you our town? " queried Madame. " Have you spent an agreeable time in it? "

" Very," replied Chichikov. " The town is an exceedingly nice one, and I have greatly enjoyed its hospitable society."

" And what think you of our Governor? "

" Yes; *is* he not a most engaging and dignified personage? " added Manilov.

" He is all that," assented Chichikov. " Indeed, he is a man worthy of the greatest respect. And how thoroughly he performs his duty according to his lights! Would that we had more like him!"

"And the tactfulness with which he greets every one!" added Manilov, smiling, and half-closing his eyes, like a cat which is being tickled behind the ears.

"Quite so," assented Chichikov. "He is a man of the most eminent civility and approachableness. And what an artist! Never should I have thought he could have worked the marvellous household samplers which he has done! Some specimens of his needlework which he showed me could not well have been surpassed by any lady in the land!"

"And the Vice-Governor, too—he is a nice man, is he not?" inquired Manilov with renewed blinkings of the eyes.

"Who? The Vice-Governor? Yes, a most worthy fellow!" replied Chichikov.

"And what of the Chief of Police? Is it not a fact that he too is in the highest degree agreeable?"

"Very agreeable indeed. And what a clever, well-read individual! With him and the Public Prosecutor and the President of the Local Council I played whist until the cocks uttered their last morning crow. He is a most excellent fellow."

"And what of his wife?" queried Madame Manilov. "Is she not a most gracious personality?"

"One of the best among my limited acquaintance," agreed Chichikov.

Nor were the President of the Local Council and the Postmaster overlooked; until the company had run through the whole list of urban officials. And in every case those officials appeared to be persons of the highest possible merit.

"Do you devote your time entirely to your estate?" asked Chichikov, in his turn.

"Well, most of it," replied Manilov; "though also we pay occasional visits to the town, in order that we may mingle with a little well-bred society. One grows a trifle rusty if one lives for ever in retirement."

"Quite so," agreed Chichikov.

"Yes, quite so," capped Manilov. "At the same time, it would be a different matter if the neighbourhood were a *good* one—if, for example, one had a friend with whom one could discuss manners and polite deportment, or engage in some branch of science, and so stimulate one's wits. For that sort of thing gives one's intellect an airing. It, it——" At a loss for further words, he ended by remarking that his feelings were apt to carry him away; after which he continued with a gesture: "What I mean is that, were that sort of thing possible, I, for one, should find the country and an isolated life possessed of great attractions. But, as matters stand, such a thing is *not* possible. All that I can manage to do is, occasionally, to read a little of *A Son of the Fatherland*."

With these sentiments Chichikov expressed entire agreement: adding that nothing could be more delightful than to lead a solitary life in which there should be comprised only the sweet contemplation of nature and the intermittent perusal of a book.

"Nay, but even *that* were worth nothing had not one a friend with whom to share one's life," remarked Manilov.

"True, true," agreed Chichikov. "Without a friend, what are all the treasures in the world? 'Possess not money,' a wise man has said, ' but rather good friends to whom to turn in case of need.' "

"Yes, Paul Ivanovitch," said Manilov with a glance not merely sweet, but positively luscious—a glance akin to the mixture which even clever physicians have to render palatable before they can induce a hesitant patient to take it. "Consequently you may imagine what happiness—what *perfect* happiness, so to speak—the present occasion has brought me, seeing that I am permitted to converse with you and to enjoy your conversation."

"But *what* of my conversation?" replied Chichikov. "I am an insignificant individual, and, beyond that, nothing."

"Oh, Paul Ivanovitch!" cried the other. "Permit me to be frank, and to say that I would give half my property to possess even a *portion* of the talents which you possess."

"On the contrary, I should consider it the highest honour in the world if——"

The lengths to which this mutual outpouring of soul would have proceeded had not a servant entered to announce luncheon must remain a mystery.

"I humbly invite you to join us at table," said Manilov. "Also, you will pardon us for the fact that we cannot provide a banquet such as is to be obtained in our metropolitan cities? We partake of simple fare, according to the Russian custom— we confine ourselves to *shtchi*,[1] but we do so with a single heart. Come, I humbly beg of you."

After another contest for the honour of yielding precedence,

[1] Cabbage soup.

Chichikov succeeded in making his way (in zigzag fashion) to the dining-room, where they found awaiting them a couple of youngsters. These were Manilov's sons, and boys of the age which admits of their presence at table, but necessitates the continued use of high chairs. Beside them was their tutor, who bowed politely and smiled; after which the hostess took her seat before her soup plate, and the guest of honour found himself ensconsed between her and the master of the house, while the servant tied up the boys' necks in bibs.

"What charming children!" said Chichikov as he gazed at the pair. "And how old are they?"

"The eldest is eight," replied Manilov, "and the younger one attained the age of six yesterday."

"Themistocleus," went on the father, turning to his first-born, who was engaged in striving to free his chin from the bib with which the footman had encircled it. On hearing this distinctly Greek name (to which, for some unknown reason, Manilov always appended the termination "eus"), Chichikov raised his eyebrows a little, but hastened, the next moment, to restore his face to a more befitting expression.

"Themistocleus," repeated the father, "tell me which is the finest city in France."

Upon this the tutor concentrated his attention upon Themistocleus, and appeared to be trying hard to catch his eye. Only when Themistocleus had muttered "Paris" did the preceptor grow calmer, and nod his head.

"And which is the finest city in Russia?" continued Manilov.

Again the tutor's attitude became wholly one of concentration.

"St. Petersburg," replied Themistocleus.

"And what other city?"

"Moscow," responded the boy.

"Clever little dear!" burst out Chichikov, turning with an air of surprise to the father. "Indeed, I feel bound to say that the child evinces the greatest possible potentialities."

"You do not know him fully," replied the delighted Manilov. "The amount of sharpness which he possesses is extraordinary. Our younger one, Alkid, is not so quick; whereas his brother—well, no matter what he may happen upon (whether upon a cow-bag or upon a water-beetle or upon anything else), his little eyes begin jumping out of his head, and he runs to catch the thing, and to inspect it. For *him* I am reserving a diplomatic post. Themistocleus," added the father, again turning to his son, "do you wish to become an ambassador?"

" Yes, I do," replied Themistocleus, chewing a piece of bread, and wagging his head from side to side.

At this moment the lacquey who had been standing behind the future ambassador wiped the latter's nose; and well it was that he did so, since otherwise an inelegant and superfluous drop would have been added to the soup. After that the conversation turned upon the joys of a quiet life—though occasionally it was interrupted by remarks from the hostess on the subject of acting and actors. Meanwhile the tutor kept his eyes fixed upon the speakers' faces; and whenever he noticed that they were on the point of laughing he at once opened his mouth, and laughed with enthusiasm. Probably he was a man of grateful heart who wished to repay his employers for the good treatment which he had received. Once, however, his features assumed a look of grimness as, fixing his eyes upon his *vis-à-vis*, the boys, he tapped sternly upon the table. This happened at a juncture when Themistocleus had bitten Alkid on the ear, and the said Alkid, with frowning eyes and open mouth, was preparing himself to sob in piteous fashion; until, recognising that for such a proceeding he might possibly be deprived of his plate, he hastened to restore his mouth to its original expression, and fell tearfully to gnawing a mutton bone—the grease from which had soon covered his cheeks.

Every now and again the hostess would turn to Chichikov with the words, " You are eating nothing—you have indeed taken little; " but invariably her guest replied: " Thank you, I have had more than enough. A pleasant conversation is worth all the dishes in the world."

At length the company rose from table. Manilov was in high spirits, and, laying his hand upon his guest's shoulder, was on the point of conducting him to the drawing-room, when suddenly Chichikov intimated to him, with a meaning look, that he wished to speak to him on a very important matter.

" That being so," said Manilov, " allow me to invite you into my study." And he led the way to a small room which faced the blue of the forest. " This is my sanctum," he added.

" What a pleasant apartment! " remarked Chichikov as he eyed it carefully. And, indeed, the room did not lack a certain attractiveness. The walls were painted a sort of blueish-grey colour, and the furniture consisted of four chairs, a settee, and a table—the latter of which bore a few sheets of writing-paper and the book of which I have before had occasion to speak. But the most prominent feature of the room was tobacco, which appeared in many different guises—in packets, in a tobacco jar, and in a loose heap strewn about the table. Likewise, both window sills were studded with little heaps of ash, arranged, not without artifice, in rows of more or less tidiness. Clearly smoking afforded the master of the house a frequent means of passing the time.

" Permit me to offer you a seat on this settee," said Manilov. " Here you will be quieter than you would be in the drawing-room."

" But I should prefer to sit upon this chair."

" I cannot allow that," objected the smiling Manilov. " The settee is specially reserved for my guests. Whether you choose or no, upon it you *must* sit."

Accordingly Chichikov obeyed.

" And also let me hand you a pipe."

" No, I never smoke," answered Chichikov civilly, and with an assumed air of regret.

" And why? " inquired Manilov—equally civilly, but with a regret that was wholly genuine.

" Because I fear that I have never quite formed the habit, owing to my having heard that a pipe exercises a desiccating effect upon the system."

" Then allow me to tell you that that is mere prejudice. Nay, I would even go so far as to say that to smoke a pipe is a healthier practice than to take snuff. Among its members our regiment numbered a lieutenant—a most excellent, well-educated fellow—who was simply *incapable* of removing his pipe from his mouth, whether at table or (pardon me) in other places. He is now forty, yet no man could enjoy better health than he has always done."

Chichikov replied that such cases were common, since nature comprised many things which even the finest intellect could not compass.

" But allow me to put to you a question," he went on in a tone in which there was a strange—or, at all events, *rather* a strange—note. For some unknown reason, also, he glanced over his shoulder. For some equally unknown reason, Manilov glanced over *his*.

" How long is it," inquired the guest, " since you last rendered a census return? "

" Oh, a long, long time. In fact, I cannot remember when it was."

" And since then have many of your serfs died? "

" I do not know. To ascertain that I should need to ask my bailiff. Footman, go and call the bailiff. I think he will be at home to-day.

Before long the bailiff made his appearance. He was a man of under forty, clean-shaven, clad in a smock, and evidently used to a quiet life, seeing that his face was of that puffy fullness, and the skin encircling his slit-like eyes was of that sallow tint, which shows that the owner of those features is well acquainted with a feather bed. In a trice it could be seen that he had played his part in life as all such bailiffs do—that, originally a young serf of elementary education, he had married some Agashka of a housekeeper or a mistress's favourite, and then himself become housekeeper, and, subsequently, bailiff; after which he had proceeded according to the rules of his tribe—that is to say, he had consorted with and stood in with the more well-to-do serfs on the estate, and added the poorer ones to the list of forced payers of *obrok*, while himself leaving his bed at nine o'clock in the morning, and, when the *samovar* had been brought, drinking his tea at leisure.

" Look here, my good man," said Manilov. " How many of our serfs have died since the last census revision? "

" How many of them have died? Why, a great many." The bailiff hiccoughed, and slapped his mouth lightly after doing so.

" Yes, I imagined that to be the case," corroborated Manilov. " In fact, a *very* great many serfs have died." He turned to Chichikov and repeated the words.

" How many, for instance? " asked Chichikov.

" Yes; how many? " re-echoed Manilov.

" *How* many? " re-echoed the bailiff. " Well, no one knows the exact number, for no one has kept any account."

" Quite so," remarked Manilov. " I supposed the death-rate to have been high, but was ignorant of its precise extent."

" Then would you be so good as to have it computed for me? " said Chichikov. " And also to have a detailed list of the deaths made out? "

" Yes, I will—a detailed list," agreed Manilov.

" Very well."

The bailiff departed.

" For what purpose do you want it? " inquired Manilov when the bailiff had gone.

The question seemed to embarrass the guest, for in Chichikov's face there dawned a sort of tense expression, and it reddened as though its owner were striving to express something not easy to put into words. True enough, Manilov was now destined to hear such strange and unexpected things as never before had greeted human ears.

" You ask me," said Chichikov, " for what purpose I want the list. Well, my purpose in wanting it is this—that I desire to purchase a few peasants." And he broke off with a gulp.

" But may I ask *how* you desire to purchase those peasants? " asked Manilov. " With land, or merely as souls for transferment —that is to say, by themselves, and without any land? "

" I want the peasants themselves only," replied Chichikov. " And I want dead ones at that."

" What?—— Excuse me, but I am a trifle deaf. Really, your words sound most strange! "

" All that I am proposing to do," replied Chichikov, " is to purchase the dead peasants who, at the last census, were returned by you as alive."

Manilov dropped his pipe upon the floor, and sat gaping. Yes, the two friends who had just been discussing the joys of *camaraderie* sat staring at one another like the portraits which, of old, used to hang on opposite sides of a mirror. At length Manilov picked up his pipe, and, while doing so, glanced covertly at Chichikov to see whether there was any trace of a smile to be detected on his lips—whether, in short, he was joking. But nothing of the sort could be discerned. On the contrary, Chichikov's face looked even graver than usual. Next, Manilov wondered whether, for some unknown reason, his guest had lost his wits; wherefore he spent some time in gazing at him with anxious intentness. But the guest's eyes seemed clear—they contained no spark of the wild, restless fire which is apt to wander in the eyes of madmen. All was as it should be. Consequently, in spite of Manilov's cogitations, he could think of nothing better to do than to sit letting a stream of tobacco smoke escape from his mouth.

" So," continued Chichikov, " what I desire to know is whether you are willing to hand over to me—to resign—these actually non-living, but legally living, peasants; or whether you have any better proposal to make? "

Manilov felt too confused and confounded to do aught but continue staring at his interlocutor.

" I think that you are disturbing yourself unnecessarily," was Chichikov's next remark.

" I? Oh no! Not at all! " stammered Manilov. " Only— pardon me—I do not quite comprehend you. You see, never has it fallen to my lot to acquire the brilliant polish which is, so to speak, manifest in your every movement. Nor have I ever been able to attain the art of expressing myself well. Consequently, although there is a possibility that in the—er—utterances which have just fallen from your lips there may lie something else concealed, it may equally be that—er—you have been pleased so to express yourself for the sake of the beauty of the terms wherein that expression found shape?"

"Oh, no," asserted Chichikov. "I mean what I say and no more. My reference to such of your peasant souls as are dead was intended to be taken literally."

Manilov still felt at a loss—though also he was conscious that he *must* do something, he *must* propound some question. But what question? The devil alone knew! In the end he merely expelled some more tobacco smoke—this time from his nostrils as well as from his mouth.

"So," went on Chichikov, "if no obstacle stands in the way, we might as well proceed to the completion of the purchase."

"What? Of the purchase of the dead souls?"

"Of the 'dead' souls? Oh dear no! Let us write them down as *living* ones, seeing that that is how they figure in the census returns. Never do I permit myself to step outside the civil law, great though has been the harm which that rule has wrought me in my career. In my eyes an obligation is a sacred thing. In the presence of the law I am dumb."

These last words reassured Manilov not a little: yet still the meaning of the affair remained to him a mystery. By way of answer, he fell to sucking at his pipe with such vehemence that at length the pipe began to gurgle like a bassoon. It was as though he had been seeking of it inspiration in the present unheard-of juncture. But the pipe only gurgled, *et præterea nihil*.

"Perhaps you feel doubtful about the proposal?" said Chichikov.

"Not at all," replied Manilov. "But you will, I know, excuse me if I say (and I say it out of no spirit of prejudice, nor yet as criticising yourself in any way)—you will, I know, excuse me if I say that possibly this—er—this, er, *scheme* of yours, this—er—*transaction* of yours, may fail altogether to accord with the Civil Statutes and Provisions of the Realm?"

And Manilov, with a slight gesture of the head, looked meaningly into Chichikov's face, while displaying in his every feature including his closely-compressed lips, such an expression o:

profundity as never before was seen on any human countenance
—unless on that of some particularly sapient Minister of State
who is debating some particularly abstruse problem.

Nevertheless Chichikov rejoined that the kind of scheme or
transaction which he had adumbrated in no way clashed with
the Civil Statutes and Provisions of Russia; to which he added
that the Treasury would even *benefit* by the enterprise, seeing
it would draw therefrom the usual legal percentage.

" What, then, do you propose? " asked Manilov.

" I propose only what is above-board, and nothing else."

" Then, that being so, it is another matter, and I have nothing
to urge against it," said Manilov, apparently reassured to the full.

" Very well," remarked Chichikov. " Then we need only to
agree as to the price."

" As to the price? " began Manilov, and then stopped. Presently he went on: " Surely you cannot suppose me capable of
taking money for souls which, in one sense at least, have completed their existence? Seeing that this fantastic whim of yours
(if I may so call it?) has seized upon you to the extent that it has,
I, on my side, shall be ready to surrender to you those souls
unconditionally, and to charge myself with the whole expenses
of the sale."

I should be greatly to blame if I were to omit that, as soon
as Manilov had pronounced these words, the face of his guest
became replete with satisfaction. Indeed, grave and prudent
a man though Chichikov was, he had much ado to refrain from
executing a leap that would have done credit to a goat (an
animal which, as we all know, finds itself moved to such exertions
only during moments of the most ecstatic joy). Nevertheless
the guest did at least execute such a convulsive shuffle that the
material with which the cushions of the chair were covered
came apart, and Manilov gazed at him with some misgiving.
Finally Chichikov's gratitude led him to plunge into a stream
of acknowledgement of a vehemence which caused his host to
grow confused, to blush, to shake his head in deprecation, and
to end by declaring that the concession was nothing, and that,
his one desire being to manifest the dictates of his heart and the
psychic magnetism which his friend exercised, he, in short,
looked upon the dead souls as so much worthless rubbish.

" Not at all," replied Chichikov, pressing his hand; after
which he heaved a profound sigh. Indeed, he seemed in the
right mood for outpourings of the heart, for he continued—not
without a ring of emotion in his tone: " If you but knew the

service which you have rendered to an apparently insignificant individual who is devoid both of family and kindred! For what have I not suffered in my time—I, a drifting barque amid the tempestuous billows of life? What harryings, what persecutions, have I not known? Of what grief have I not tasted? And why? Simply because ever I have kept the truth in view, because ever I have preserved inviolate an unsullied conscience, because ever I have stretched out a helping hand to the defenceless widow and the hapless orphan!" After which outpouring Chichikov pulled out his handkerchief, and wiped away a brimming tear.

Manilov's heart was moved to the core. Again and again did the two friends press one another's hands in silence as they gazed into one another's tear-filled eyes. Indeed, Manilov *could* not let go our hero's hand, but clasped it with such warmth that the hero in question began to feel himself at a loss how best to wrench it free: until, quietly withdrawing it, he observed that to have the purchase completed as speedily as possible would not be a bad thing; wherefore he himself would at once return to the town to arrange matters. Taking up his hat, therefore, he rose to make his adieus.

"What? Are you departing already?" said Manilov, suddenly recovering himself, and experiencing a sense of misgiving. At that moment his wife sailed into the room.

"Is Paul Ivanovitch leaving us so soon, dearest Lizanka?" she said with an air of regret.

"Yes. Surely it must be that we have wearied him?" her spouse replied.

"By no means," asserted Chichikov, pressing his hand to his heart. "In this breast, madam, will abide for ever the pleasant memory of the time which I have spent with you. Believe me, I could conceive of no greater blessing than to reside, if not under the same roof as yourselves, at all events in your immediate neighbourhood."

"Indeed?" exclaimed Manilov, greatly pleased with the idea. "How splendid it would be if you *did* come to reside under our roof, so that we could recline under an elm tree together, and talk philosophy, and delve to the very root of things!"

"Yes, it *would* be a paradisaical existence!" agreed Chichikov with a sigh. Nevertheless he shook hands with Madame. "Farewell, *sudarina*," he said. "And farewell to *you*, my esteemed host. Do not forget what I have requested you to do."

"Rest assured that I will not," responded Manilov. "Only for a couple of days will you and I be parted from one another."

With that the party moved into the drawing-room.

" Farewell, dearest children," Chichikov went on as he caught sight of Alkid and Themistocleus, who were playing with a wooden hussar which lacked both a nose and one arm. " Farewell, dearest pets. Pardon me for having brought you no presents, but, to tell the truth, I was not, until my visit, aware of your existence. However, now that I shall be coming again, I will not fail to bring you gifts. Themistocleus, to you I will bring a sword. You would like that, would you not? "

" I should," replied Themistocleus.

" And to you, Alkid, I will bring a drum. That would suit you, would it not? " And he bowed in Alkid's direction.

" Zeth—a dwum," lisped the boy, hanging his head.

" Good! Then a drum it shall be—*such* a beautiful drum! What a tur-r-r-ru-ing and a tra-ta-ta-ta-ing you will be able to kick up! Farewell, my darling." And, kissing the boy's head, he turned to Manilov and Madame with the slight smile which one assumes before assuring parents of the guileless merits of their offspring.

" But you had better stay, Paul Ivanovitch," said the father as the trio stepped out on to the verandah. " See how the clouds are gathering! "

" They are only small ones," replied Chichikov.

" And you know your way to Sobakevitch's? "

" No, I do not, and should be glad if you would direct me."

" If you like I will tell your coachman." And in very civil fashion Manilov did so, even going so far as to address the man in the second person plural. On hearing that he was to pass two turnings, and then to take the third, Selifan remarked, " We shall get there all right, sir," and Chichikov departed amid a prolonged salvo of salutations and wavings of handkerchiefs on the part of his host and hostess, who raised themselves on tiptoe in their enthusiasm.

For a long while Manilov stood following the departing *britchka* with his eyes. In fact, he continued to smoke his pipe and gaze after the vehicle even when it had become lost to view. Then he re-entered the drawing-room, seated himself upon a chair, and surrendered his mind to the thought that he had shown his guest most excellent entertainment. Next, his mind passed imperceptibly to other matters, until at last it lost itself God only knows where. He thought of the amenities of a life, of friendship, and of how nice it would be to live with a comrade on, say, the bank of some river, and to span the river with a bridge of his own, and to build an enormous mansion with a façade lofty enough even to afford a view to Moscow. On that façade he and his wife and friend would drink afternoon tea in the open air, and discuss interesting subjects; after which, in a fine carriage, they would drive to some reunion or other, where with their pleasant manners they would so charm the company that the Imperial Government, on learning of their merits, would raise the pair to the grade of General or God knows what —that is to say, to heights whereof even Manilov himself could form no idea. Then suddenly Chichikov's extraordinary request interrupted the dreamer's reflections, and he found his brain powerless to digest it, seeing that, turn and turn the matter about as he might, he could not properly explain its bearing. Smoking his pipe, he sat where he was until supper time.

III

MEANWHILE, Chichikov, seated in his *britchka* and bowling along the turnpike, was feeling greatly pleased with himself. From the preceding chapter the reader will have gathered the principal subject of his bent and inclinations: wherefore it is no matter for wonder that his body and his soul had ended by becoming wholly immersed therein. To all appearances the thoughts, the calculations, and the projects which were now reflected in his face partook of a pleasant nature, since momentarily they kept leaving behind them a satisfied smile. Indeed, so engrossed was he that he never noticed that his coachman, elated with the hospitality of Manilov's domestics, was making remarks of a didactic nature to the off horse of the *troika*,[1] a skewbald. This skewbald was a knowing animal, and made only a show of pulling; whereas its comrades, the middle horse (a bay, and known as the Assessor, owing to his having been acquired from a gentleman of that rank) and the near horse (a roan), would do their work gallantly, and even evince in their eyes the pleasure which they derived from their exertions.

" Ah, you rascal, you rascal! *I'll* get the better of you! " ejaculated Selifan as he sat up and gave the lazy one a cut with his whip. " *You* know your business all right, you German pantaloon! The bay is a good fellow, and does his duty, and I will give him a bit over his feed, for he is a horse to be respected;

[1] Three horses harnessed abreast.

and the Assessor too is a good horse. But what are *you* shaking your ears for? You are a fool, so just mind when you're spoken to. 'Tis good advice I'm giving you, you blockhead. Ah! You *can* travel when you like." And he gave the animal another cut, and then shouted to the trio, " Gee up, my beauties! " and drew his whip gently across the backs of the skewbald's comrades —not as a punishment, but as a sign of his approval. That done, he addressed himself to the skewbald again.

" Do you think," he cried, " that I don't see what you are doing? You can behave quite decently when you like, and make a man respect you."

With that he fell to recalling certain reminiscences.

" They *were* nice folk, those folk at the gentleman's yonder," he mused. " I *do* love a chat with a man when he is a good sort. With a man of that kind I am always hail-fellow-well-met, and glad to drink a glass of tea with him, or to eat a biscuit. One *can't* help respecting a decent fellow. For instance, this gentleman of mine—why, every one looks up to him, for he has been in the Government's service, and is a Collegiate Councillor."

Thus soliloquising, he passed to more remote abstractions; until, had Chichikov been listening, he would have learnt a number of interesting details concerning himself. However, his thoughts were wholly occupied with his own subject, so much so that not until a loud clap of thunder awoke him from his reverie did he glance around him. The sky was completely covered with clouds, and the dusty turnpike beginning to be sprinkled with drops of rain. At length a second and a nearer and a louder peal resounded, and the rain descended as from a bucket. Falling slantwise, it beat upon one side of the basket-work of the tilt until the splashings began to spurt into his face, and he found himself forced to draw the curtains (fitted with circular openings through which to obtain a glimpse of the way-side view), and to shout to Selifan to quicken his pace. Upon that the coachman, interrupted in the middle of his harangue, bethought him that no time was to be lost; wherefore, extracting from under the box-seat a piece of old blanket, he covered over his sleeves, resumed the reins, and cheered on his threefold team (which, it may be said, had so completely succumbed to the influence of the pleasant lassitude induced by Selifan's discourse that it had taken to scarcely placing one leg before the other). Unfortunately, Selifan could not clearly remember whether two turnings had been passed or three. Indeed, on collecting his faculties, and dimly recalling the lie of the road, he became filled with a shrewd suspicion that *a very large number* of turnings had been passed. But since, at moments which call for a hasty decision, a Russian is quick to discover what may conceivably be the best course to take, our coachman put away from him all ulterior reasoning, and, turning to the right at the next cross-road, shouted, "Hi, my beauties!" and set off at a gallop. Never for a moment did he stop to think whither the road might lead him!

It was long before the clouds had discharged their burden, and, meanwhile, the dust on the road became kneaded into mire, and the horses' task of pulling the *britchka* heavier and heavier. Also, Chichikov had taken alarm at his continued failure to catch sight of Sobakevitch's country house. According to his calculations, it ought to have been reached long ago. He gazed about him on every side, but the darkness was too dense for the eye to pierce.

"Selifan!" he exclaimed, leaning forward in the *britchka*.

"What is it, *barin?*" replied the coachman.

"Can you see the country house anywhere?"

"No, *barin.*" After which, with a flourish of his whip, the man broke into a sort of endless, drawling song. In that song everything had a place. By "everything" I mean both the various encouraging and stimulating cries with which Russian folk urge on their horses, and a random, unpremeditated selection of adjectives.

Meanwhile Chichikov began to notice that the *britchka* was swaying violently, and dealing him occasional bumps. Consequently he suspected that it had left the road and was being dragged over a ploughed field. Upon Selifan's mind there appeared to have dawned a similar inkling, for he had ceased to hold forth.

"You rascal, what road are you following?" inquired Chichikov.

"I don't know," retorted the coachman. "What can a man do at a time of night when the darkness won't let him even see his whip?" And as Selifan spoke the vehicle tilted to an angle which left Chichikov no choice but to hang on with hands and teeth. At length he realised the fact that Selifan was drunk.

"Stop, stop, or you will upset us!" he shouted to the fellow.

"No, no, *barin,*" replied Selifan. "*How* could I upset you? To upset people is wrong. I know that very well, and should never dream of such conduct."

Here he started to turn the vehicle round a little—and kept

on doing so until the *britchka* capsized on to its side, and Chichikov landed in the mud on his hands and knees. Fortunately Selifan succeeded in stopping the horses, although they would have stopped of themselves, seeing that they were utterly worn out. This unforeseen catastrophe evidently astonished their driver. Slipping from the box, he stood resting his hands against the side of the *britchka,* while Chichikov tumbled and floundered about in the mud, in a vain endeavour to wriggle clear of the stuff.

" Ah, you! " said Selifan meditatively to the *britchka.* " To think of upsetting us like this! "

" You are as drunk as a lord! " exclaimed Chichikov.

" No, no, *barin.* Drunk, indeed? Why, I know my manners too well. A word or two with a friend—that is all that I have taken. Any one may talk with a decent man when he meets him. There is nothing wrong in that. Also, we had a snack together. There is nothing wrong in a snack—especially a snack with a decent man."

" What did I say to you when last you got drunk? " asked Chichikov. " Have you forgotten what I said then? "

" No, no, *barin. How* should I forget it? I know what is what, and know that it is not right to get drunk. All that I have been having is a word or two with a decent man, for the reason that——"

"Well, if I lay the whip about you, you'll know then how to talk to a decent fellow, I'll warrant! "

" As you please, *barin,*" replied the complacent Selifan. " Should you whip me, you will whip me, and I shall have nothing to complain of. Why should you not whip me if I deserve it? 'Tis for you to do as you like. Whippings are necessary sometimes, for a peasant often plays the fool, and discipline ought to be maintained. If I have deserved it, beat me. Why should you not? "

This reasoning seemed, at the moment, irrefutable, and Chichikov said nothing more. Fortunately fate had decided to take pity on the pair, for from afar their ears caught the barking of a dog. Plucking up courage, Chichikov gave orders for the *britchka* to be righted, and the horses to be urged forward; and since a Russian driver has at least this merit, that, owing to a keen sense of smell being able to take the place of eyesight, he can, if necessary, drive at random and yet reach a destination of some sort, Selifan succeeded, though powerless to discern a single object, in directing his steeds to a country house near by, and that with such a certainty of instinct that it was not until the shafts had collided with a garden wall, and thereby made it clear that to proceed another pace was impossible, that he stopped. All that Chichikov could discern through the thick veil of pouring rain was something which resembled a verandah. So he dispatched Selifan to search for the entrance gates, and that process would have lasted indefinitely had it not been shortened by the circumstance that, in Russia, the place of a Swiss footman is frequently taken by watchdogs; of which animals a number now proclaimed the travellers' presence so loudly that Chichikov found himself forced to stop his ears. Next, a light gleamed in one of the windows, and filtered in a thin stream to the garden wall—thus revealing the whereabouts of the entrance gates; whereupon Selifan fell to knocking at the gates until the bolts of the house door were withdrawn and there issued therefrom a figure clad in a rough cloak.

"Who is that knocking? What have you come for?" shouted the hoarse voice of an elderly woman.

"We are travellers, good mother," said Chichikov. "Pray allow us to spend the night here."

"Out upon you for a pair of gadabouts!" retorted the old woman. "A fine time of night to be arriving! We don't keep an hotel, mind you. This is a lady's residence."

"But what are we to do, mother? We have lost our way, and cannot spend the night out of doors in such weather."

"No, we cannot. The night is dark and cold," added Selifan.

"Hold your tongue, you fool!" exclaimed Chichikov.

"Who *are* you, then?" inquired the old woman.

"A *dvorianin*,[1] good mother."

Somehow the word *dvorianin* seemed to give the old woman food for thought.

"Wait a moment," she said, "and I will tell the mistress."

Two minutes later she returned with a lantern in her hand, the gates were opened, and a light glimmered in a second window. Entering the courtyard, the *britchka* halted before a moderate-sized mansion. The darkness did not permit of very accurate observation being made, but, apparently, the windows only of one-half of the building were illuminated, while a quagmire in front of the door reflected the beams from the same. Meanwhile the rain continued to beat sonorously down upon the wooden roof, and could be heard trickling into a water

[1] A member of the gentry class.

butt; nor for a single moment did the dogs cease to bark with all the strength of their lungs. One of them, throwing up its head, kept venting a howl of such energy and duration that the animal seemed to be howling for a handsome wager; while another, cutting in between the yelpings of the first animal, kept restlessly reiterating, like a postman's bell, the notes of a very young puppy. Finally, an old hound which appeared to be gifted with a peculiarly robust temperament kept supplying the part of *contrabasso*, so that his growls resembled the rumbling of a bass singer when a chorus is in full cry, and the tenors are rising on tiptoe in their efforts to compass a particularly high note, and the whole body of choristers are wagging their heads before approaching a climax, and the *contrabasso* alone is tucking his bearded chin into his collar, and sinking almost to a squatting posture on the floor, in order to produce a note which shall cause the windows to shiver and their panes to crack. Naturally, from a canine chorus of such executants it might reasonably be inferred that the establishment was one of the utmost respectability. To that, however, our damp, cold hero gave not a thought, for all his mind was fixed upon bed. Indeed, the *britchka* had hardly come to a standstill before he leapt out upon the doorstep, missed his footing, and came within an ace of falling. To meet him there issued a female younger than the first, but very closely resembling her; and on his being conducted to the parlour, a couple of glances showed him that the room was hung with old striped curtains, and ornamented with pictures of birds and small, antique mirrors —the latter set in dark frames which were carved to resemble scrolls of foliage. Behind each mirror was stuck either a letter or an old pack of cards or a stocking, while on the wall hung a clock with a flowered dial. More, however, Chichikov could not discern, for his eyelids were as heavy as though smeared with treacle. Presently the lady of the house herself entered—an elderly woman in a sort of nightcap (hastily put on) and a flannel neck wrap. She belonged to that class of lady landowners who are for ever lamenting failures of the harvest and their losses thereby; to the class who, drooping their heads despondently, are all the while stuffing money into striped purses, which they keep hoarded in the drawers of cupboards. Into one purse they will stuff rouble pieces, into another half roubles, and into a third *tchetvertachki*,[1] although from their mien you would suppose that the cupboard contained only linen

[1] Pieces equal in value to twenty-five kopecks (a quarter of a rouble).

and nightshirts and skeins of wool and the piece of shabby material which is destined—should the old gown become scorched during the baking of holiday cakes and other dainties, or should it fall to pieces of itself—to become converted into a new dress. But the gown never does get burnt or wear out, for the reason that the lady is too careful; wherefore the piece of shabby material reposes in its unmade-up condition until the priest advises that it be given to the niece of some widowed sister, together with a quantity of other such rubbish.

Chichikov apologised for having disturbed the household with his unexpected arrival.

"Not at all, not at all," replied the lady. "But in what dreadful weather God has brought you hither! What wind and what rain! You could not help losing your way. Pray excuse us for being unable to make better preparations for you at this time of night."

Suddenly there broke in upon the hostess' words the sound of a strange hissing, a sound so loud that the guest started in alarm, and the more so seeing that it increased until the room seemed filled with adders. On glancing upwards, however, he recovered his composure, for he perceived the sound to be emanating from the clock, which appeared to be in a mind to strike. To the hissing sound there succeeded a wheezing one, until, putting forth its best efforts, the thing struck two with as much clatter as though some one had been hitting an iron pot with a cudgel. That done, the pendulum returned to its right-left, right-left oscillation.

Chichikov thanked his hostess kindly, and said that he needed nothing, and she must not put herself about: only for rest was he longing—though also he should like to know whither he had arrived, and whether the distance to the country house of land-owner Sobakevitch was anything very great. To this the lady replied that she had never so much as heard the name, since no gentleman of the name resided in the locality.

"But at least you are acquainted with landowner Manilov?" continued Chichikov.

"No. Who is he?"

"Another landed proprietor, madam."

"Well, neither have I heard of him. No such landowner lives hereabouts."

"Then who *are* your local landowners?"

"Bobrov, Svinin, Kanapatiev, Khapakin, Trepakin, and Plieshakov."

" Are they rich men? "

" No, none of them.   One of them may own twenty souls, and another thirty, but of gentry who own a hundred there are none."

Chichikov reflected that he had indeed fallen into an aristocratic wilderness!

" At all events, is the town far away? " he inquired.

" About sixty versts.   How sorry I am that I have nothing for you to eat!   Should you care to drink some tea? "

" I thank you, good mother, but I require nothing beyond a bed."

" Well, after such a journey you must indeed be needing rest, so you shall lie upon this sofa.   Fetinia, bring a quilt and some pillows and sheets.   What weather God has sent us!   And what dreadful thunder!   Ever since sunset I have had a candle burning before the *ikon* in my bedroom.   My God!   Why, your back and sides are as muddy as a wild boar's!   However have you managed to get into such a state? "

" That I am nothing worse than muddy is indeed fortunate, since, but for the Almighty, I should have had my ribs broken."

" Dear, dear!   To think of all that you must have been through.   Had I not better wipe your back? "

" I thank you, I thank you, but you need not trouble.   Merely be so good as to tell your maid to dry my clothes."

" Do you hear that, Fetinia? " said the hostess, turning to a woman who was engaged in dragging in a feather bed and deluging the room with feathers.   " Take this coat and this vest, and, after drying them before the fire—just as we used to do for your late master—give them a good rub, and fold them up neatly."

" Very well, mistress," said Fetinia, spreading some sheets over the bed, and arranging the pillows.

" Now your bed is ready for you," said the hostess to Chichikov.   " Good-night, dear sir.   I wish you good-night.   Is there anything else that you require?   Perhaps you would like to have your heels tickled before retiring to rest?   Never could my late husband get to sleep without that having been done."

But the guest declined the proffered heel-tickling, and, on his hostess taking her departure, hastened to divest himself of his clothing, both upper and under, and to hand the garments to Fetinia.   She wished him good-night, and removed the wet trappings; after which he found himself alone.   Not without satisfaction did he eye his bed, which reached almost to the

ceiling. Clearly Fetinia was a past mistress in the art of beating up such a couch, and, as the result, he had no sooner mounted
it with the aid of a chair than it sank well-nigh to the floor, and
the feathers, squeezed out of their proper confines, flew hither
and thither into every corner of the apartment. Nevertheless
he extinguished the candle, covered himself over with the chintz
quilt, snuggled down beneath it, and instantly fell asleep. Next
day it was late in the morning before he awoke. Through the
window the sun was shining into his eyes, and the flies which,
overnight, had been roosting quietly on the walls and ceiling
now turned their attention to the visitor. One settled on his
lip, another on his ear, a third hovered as though intending to
lodge in his very eye, and a fourth had the temerity to alight
just under his nostrils. In his drowsy condition he inhaled the
latter insect, sneezed violently, and so returned to consciousness.
He glanced around the room, and perceived that not all the
pictures were representative of birds, since among them hung
also a portrait of Kutuzov[1] and an oil painting of an old man
in a uniform with red facings such as were worn in the days of
the Emperor Paul.[2] At this moment the clock uttered its usual
hissing sound, and struck ten, while a woman's face peered in
at the door, but at once withdrew, for the reason that, with the
object of sleeping as well as possible, Chichikov had removed
every stitch of his clothing. Somehow the face seemed to him
familiar, and he set himself to recall whose it could be. At
length he recollected that it was the face of his hostess. His
clothes he found lying, clean and dry, beside him; so he dressed
and approached the mirror, meanwhile sneezing again with such
vehemence that a cock which happened at the moment to be
near the window (which was situated at no great distance from
the ground) chuckled a short, sharp phrase. Probably it
meant, in the bird's alien tongue, " Good morning to you! "
Chichikov retorted by calling the bird a fool, and then himself
approached the window to look at the view. It appeared to
comprise a poulterer's premises. At all events, the narrow yard
in front of the window was full of poultry and other domestic
creatures—of game fowls and barn door fowls, with, among
them, a cock which strutted with measured gait, and kept
shaking its comb, and tilting its head as though it were trying
to listen to something. Also, a sow and her family were helping

---

[1] A Russian general who, in 1812, stoutly opposed Napoleon at the
battle of Borodino.
[2] The late eighteenth century.

to grace the scene. First, she rooted among a heap of litter; then, in passing, she ate up a young pullet; lastly, she proceeded carelessly to munch some pieces of melon rind. To this small yard or poultry-run a length of planking served as a fence, while beyond it lay a kitchen garden containing cabbages, onions, potatoes, beetroots, and other household vegetables. Also, the garden contained a few stray fruit trees that were covered with netting to protect them from the magpies and sparrows; flocks of which were even then wheeling and darting from one spot to another. For the same reason a number of scarecrows with outstretched arms stood reared on long poles, with, surmounting one of the figures, a cast-off cap of the hostess's. Beyond the garden again there stood a number of peasants' huts. Though scattered, instead of being ranged in regular rows, these appeared to Chichikov's eye to comprise well-to-do inhabitants, since all rotten planks in their roofing had been replaced with new ones, and none of their doors were askew, and such of their tiltsheds as faced him evinced evidence of the presence of a spare waggon —in some cases almost a new one.

" This lady owns by no means a poor village," said Chichikov to himself; wherefore he decided then and there to have a talk with his hostess, and to cultivate her closer acquaintance. Accordingly he peeped through the chink of the door whence her head had recently protruded, and, on seeing her seated at a tea table, entered and greeted her with a cheerful, kindly smile.

" Good morning, dear sir," she responded as she rose. " How have you slept? " She was dressed in better style than she had been on the previous evening. That is to say, she was now wearing a gown of some dark colour, and lacked her nightcap, and had swathed her neck in something stiff.

" I have slept exceedingly well," replied Chichikov, seating himself upon a chair. " And how are *you*, good madam? "

" But poorly, my dear sir."

" And why so? "

" Because I cannot sleep. A pain has taken me in my middle, and my legs, from the ankles upwards, are aching as though they were broken."

" That will pass, that will pass, good mother. You must pay no attention to it."

" God grant that it *may* pass. However, I have been rubbing myself with lard and turpentine. What sort of tea will you take? In this jar I have some of the scented kind."

"Excellent, good mother! Then I will take that."

Probably the reader will have noticed that, for all his expressions of solicitude, Chichikov's tone towards his hostess partook of a freer, a more unceremonious, nature than that which he had adopted towards Madame Manilov. And here I should like to assert that, howsoever much, in certain respects, we Russians may be surpassed by foreigners, at least we surpass them in adroitness of manner. In fact the various shades and subtleties of our social intercourse defy enumeration. A Frenchman or a German would be incapable of envisaging and understanding all its peculiaries and differences, for his tone in speaking to a millionaire differs but little from that which he employs towards a small tobacconist—and that in spite of the circumstance that he is accustomed to cringe in spirit before the former. With us, however, things are different. In Russian society there exist clever folk who can speak in one manner to a landowner possessed of two hundred peasant souls, and in another to a landowner possessed of three hundred, and in another to a landowner possessed of five hundred. In short, up to the number of a million souls the Russian will have ready for each landowner a suitable mode of address. For example, suppose that somewhere there exists a government office, and that in that office there exists a director. I would beg of you to contemplate him as he sits among his myrmidons. Sheer nervousness will prevent you from uttering a word in his presence, so great are the pride and the superiority depicted on his countenance. Also, were you to sketch him, you would be sketching a veritable Prometheus, for his glance is as that of an eagle, and he walks with measured, stately stride. Yet no sooner will the eagle have left the room to seek the study of his superior officer than he will go scurrying along (papers held close to his nose) like any partridge. But in society, and at the evening party (should the rest of those present be of lesser rank than himself) the Prometheus will once more become Prometheus, and the man who stands a step below him will treat him in a way never dreamt of by Ovid, seeing that each fly is of lesser account than its superior fly, and becomes, in the presence of the latter, even as a grain of sand. "Surely that is not Ivan Petrovitch?" you will say of such and such a man as you regard him. "Ivan Petrovitch is tall, whereas this man is small and spare.. Ivan Petrovitch has a loud, deep voice, and never smiles, whereas this man (whoever he may be) is twittering like a sparrow, and smiling all the time." Yet approach and take a good look at the fellow and you will see that it *is* Ivan Petrovitch. "Alack, alack!" will be the only remark that you can make.

Let us return to our characters in real life. We have seen that, on this occasion, Chichikov decided to dispense with ceremony; wherefore, taking up the teapot, he went on as follows:

"You have a nice little village here, madam. How many souls does it contain?"

"A little less than eighty, dear sir. But the times are hard, and I have lost a great deal through last year's harvest having proved a failure."

"But your peasants look fine, strong fellows. May I enquire your name? Through arriving so late at night I have quite lost my wits."

"Korobotchka, the widow of a Collegiate Secretary."

"I humbly thank you. And your Christian name and patronymic?"

"Nastasia Petrovna."

"Nastasia Petrovna! Those are excellent names. I have a maternal aunt named like yourself."

"And *your* name?" queried the lady. "May I take it that you are a Government Assessor?"

"No, madam," replied Chichikov with a smile. "I am not an Assessor, but a traveller on private business."

"Then you must be a buyer of produce? How I regret that I have sold my honey so cheaply to other buyers! Otherwise *you* might have bought it, dear sir."

"I never buy honey."

"Then *what* do you buy, pray? Hemp? I have a little of that by me, but not more than half a *pood* [1] or so."

"No, madam. It is in other wares that I deal. Tell me, have you, of late years, lost many of your peasants by death?"

"Yes; no fewer than eighteen," responded the old lady with a sigh. "Such a fine lot, too—all good workers! True, others have since grown up, but of what use are *they*? Mere striplings. When the Assessor last called upon me I could have wept; for, though those workmen of mine are dead, I have to keep on paying for them as though they were still alive! And only last week my blacksmith got burnt to death! Such a clever hand at his trade he was!"

"What? A fire occurred at your place?"

"No, no, God preserve us all! It was not so bad as that. You

[1] Forty Russian pounds.

must understand that the blacksmith *set himself* on fire—he got set on fire in his bowels through overdrinking. Yes, all of a sudden there burst from him a blue flame, and he smouldered and smouldered until he had turned as black as a piece of charcoal! Yet what a clever blacksmith he was! And now I have no horses to drive out with, for there is no one to shoe them."

"In everything the will of God, madam," said Chichikov with a sigh. "Against the divine wisdom it is not for us to rebel. Pray hand them over to me, Nastasia Petrovna."

"Hand over whom?"

"The dead peasants."

"But how could I do that?"

"Quite simply. Sell them to me, and I will give you some money in exchange."

"But how am I to sell them to you? I scarcely understand what you mean. Am I to dig them up again from the ground?"

Chichikov perceived that the old lady was altogether at sea, and that he must explain the matter; wherefore in a few words he informed her that the transfer or purchase of the souls in question would take place merely on paper—that the said souls would be listed as still alive.

"And what good would they be to you?" asked his hostess, staring at him with her eyes distended.

"That is *my* affair."

"But they are *dead* souls."

"Who said they were not? The mere fact of their being dead entails upon you a loss as dead as the souls, for you have to continue paying the tax upon them, whereas *my* plan is to relieve you both of the tax and of the resultant trouble. *Now* do you understand? And I will not only do as I say, but also hand you over fifteen roubles per soul. Is that clear enough?"

"Yes—but I do not know," said his hostess diffidently. "You see, never before have I sold dead souls."

"Quite so. It would be a surprising thing if you had. But surely you do not think that these dead souls are in the least worth keeping?"

"Oh no, indeed! Why should they be worth keeping? I am sure they are not so. The only thing which troubles me is the fact that they are *dead*."

"She seems a truly obstinate old woman!" was Chichikov's inward comment. "Look here, madam," he added aloud. "You reason well, but you are simply ruining yourself by continuing to pay the tax upon dead souls as though they were still alive."

"Oh, good sir, do not speak of it!" the lady exclaimed. "Three weeks ago I took a hundred and fifty roubles to the Assessor, and buttered him up, and——"

"Then you see how it is, do you not? Remember that, according to my plan, you will never again have to butter up the Assessor, seeing that it will be I who will be paying for those peasants—*I*, not *you*, for I shall have taken over the dues upon them, and have transferred them to myself as so many *bona fide* serfs. Do you understand *at last* ? "

However, the old lady still communed with herself. She could see that the transaction would be to her advantage, yet it was one of such a novel and unprecedented nature that she was beginning to fear lest this purchaser of souls intended to cheat her. Certainly he had come from God only knew where, and at the dead of night, too!

"Let us shake hands over it," advised Chichikov.

"But, sir, I have never in my life sold dead folk—only living ones. Three years ago I transferred two wenches to Protopopov for a hundred roubles apiece, and he thanked me kindly, for they turned out splendid workers—able to make napkins or anything else."

"Yes, but with the living we have nothing to do, damn it! I am asking you only about *dead* folk."

"Yes, yes, of course. But at first sight I felt afraid lest I should be incurring a loss—lest you should be wishing to outwit me, good sir. You see, the dead souls are worth rather more than you have offered for them."

"See here, madam. (What a woman it is!) *How* could they be worth more? Think for yourself. They are so much loss to you—so much loss, do you understand? Take any worthless, rubbishy article you like—a piece of old rag, for example. That rag will yet fetch its price, for it can be bought for paper-making. But these dead souls are good for *nothing at all*. Can you name anything that they *are* good for? "

"True, true—they *are* good for nothing. But what troubles me is the fact that they are dead."

"What a blockhead of a creature!" said Chichikov to himself, for he was beginning to lose patience. "Bless her heart, I may as well be going. She has thrown me into a perfect sweat, the cursed old shrew! "

He took a handkerchief from his pocket, and wiped the

perspiration from his brow. Yet he need not have flown into such a passion. More than one respected statesman reveals himself, when confronted with a business matter, to be just such another as Madame Korobotchka, in that, once he has got an idea into his head, there is no getting it out of him—you may ply him and ply him with daylight-clear arguments, yet they will rebound from his brain as an india-rubber ball rebounds from a flagstone. Nevertheless, wiping away the perspiration, Chichikov resolved to try whether he could not bring her back to the road by another path.

" Madam," he said, " either you are declining to understand what I say or you are talking for the mere sake of talking. If I hand you over some money—fifteen roubles for each soul, do you understand?—it is *money*, not something which can be picked up haphazard in the street. For instance, tell me how much you sold your honey for? "

" For twelve roubles per *pood*."

" Ah! Then by those words, madam, you have laid a trifling sin upon your soul; for you did *not* sell the honey for twelve roubles."

" By the Lord God I did! "

" Well, well! Never mind. Honey is only honey. Now, you had collected that stuff, it may be, for a year, and with infinite care and labour. You had fussed after it, you had trotted to and fro, you had duly frozen out the bees, and you had fed them in the cellar throughout the winter. But these dead souls of which I speak are quite another matter, for in this case you have put forth no exertions—it was merely God's will that they should leave the world, and thus decrease the *personnel* of your establishment. In the former case you received (so you allege) twelve roubles per *pood* for your labour; but in this case you will receive money for having done nothing at all. Nor will you receive twelve roubles per item, but *fifteen*—and roubles not in silver, but roubles in good paper currency."

That these powerful inducements would certainly cause the old woman to yield Chichikov had not a doubt.

" True," his hostess replied. " But how strangely business comes to me as a widow! Perhaps I had better wait a little longer, seeing that other buyers might come along, and I might be able to compare prices."

" For shame, madam! For shame! Think what you are saying. Who else, I would ask, would care to buy those souls? What use could they be to any one ? "

" If that is so, they might come in useful to *me*," mused the old woman aloud; after which she sat staring at Chichikov with her mouth open and a face of nervous expectancy as to his possible rejoinder.

" Dead folk useful in a household!" he exclaimed. " Why, what could you do with them? Set them up on poles to frighten away the sparrows from your garden? "

" The Lord save us, but what things you say! " she ejaculated, crossing herself.

" Well, *what* could you do with them? By this time they are so much bones and earth. That is all there is left of them. Their transfer to myself would be *on paper* only. Come, come! At least give me an answer."

Again the old woman communed with herself.

" What are you thinking of, Nastasia Petrovna? " inquired Chichikov.

" I am thinking that I scarcely know what to do. Perhaps I had better sell you some hemp? "

" What do I want with hemp? Pardon me, but just when I have made to you a different proposal altogether you begin fussing about hemp! Hemp is hemp, and though I may want some when I *next* visit you, I should like to know what you have to say to the suggestion under discussion."

" Well, I think it a very queer bargain. Never have I heard of such a thing."

Upon this Chichikov lost all patience, upset his chair, and bid her go to the devil; of which personage even the mere mention terrified her extremely.

" Do not speak of him, I beg of you! " she cried, turning pale. " May God, rather, bless him! Last night was the third night that he has appeared to me in a dream. You see, after saying my prayers, I bethought me of telling my fortune by the cards; and God must have sent him to me as a punishment. He looked so horrible, and had horns longer than a bull's! "

" I wonder you don't see *scores* of devils in your dreams! Merely out of Christian charity he had come to you to say, ' I perceive a poor widow to be going to rack and ruin, and likely soon to stand in danger of want.' Well, go to rack and ruin— yes, you and all your village together! "

" The insults! " exclaimed the old woman, glancing at her visitor in terror.

" I should think so! " continued Chichikov. " Indeed, I cannot find words to describe you. To say no more about it, you are like a dog in a manger. You don't want to eat the hay yourself, yet you won't let any one else touch it. All that I am seeking to do is to purchase certain domestic products of yours, for the reason that I have certain Government contracts to fulfil." This last he added in passing, and without any ulterior motive, save that it came to him as a happy thought. Nevertheless the mention of Government contracts exercised a powerful influence upon Nastasia Petrovna, and she hastened to say in a tone that was almost supplicatory:

" Why should you be so angry with me? Had I known that you were going to lose your temper in this way, I should never have discussed the matter."

" No wonder that I lose my temper! An egg too many is no great matter, yet it may prove exceedingly annoying."

" Well, well, I will let you have the souls for fifteen roubles each. Also, with regard to those contracts, do not forget me if at any time you should find yourself in need of rye-meal or buckwheat or groats or dead meat."

" No, I shall *never* forget you, madam!" he said, wiping his forehead, whence three separate streams of perspiration were trickling down his face. Then he asked her whether in the town she had any acquaintance or agent whom she could empower to complete the transference of the serfs, and to carry out whatsoever else might be necessary.

" Certainly," replied Madame Korobotchka. " The son of our arch-priest, Father Cyril, himself is a lawyer."

Upon that Chichikov begged her to accord the gentleman in question a power of attorney, while, to save extra trouble, he himself would then and there compose the requisite letter.

" It would be a fine thing if he were to buy up all my meal and stock for the Government," thought Madame to herself. " I must encourage him a little. There has been some dough standing ready since last night, so I will go and tell Fetinia to fry a few pancakes. Also, it might be well to try him with an egg pie. We make them nicely here, and they do not take long in the making."

So she departed to translate her thoughts into action, as well as to supplement the pie with other products of the domestic cuisine; while, for his part, Chichikov returned to the drawing-room where he had spent the night, in order to procure from his dispatch-box the necessary writing-paper. The room had now been set in order, the sumptuous feather bed removed, and a table set before the sofa. Depositing his dispatch-box upon the table, he heaved a gentle sigh on becoming aware that he was so soaked with perspiration that he might almost have been dipped in a river. Everything, from his shirt to his socks, was dripping. " May she starve to death, the cursed old harridan! " he ejaculated after a moment's rest. Then he opened his dispatch-box. In passing, I may say that I feel certain that at least *some* of my readers will be curious to know the contents and the internal arrangements of that receptacle. Why should I not gratify their curiosity? To begin with, the centre of the box contained a soap-dish, with, disposed around it, six or seven compartments for razors. Next came square partitions for a sand-box [1] and an inkstand, as well as (scooped out in their midst) a hollow for pens, sealing-wax, and anything else that required more room. Lastly there were all sorts of little divisions, both with and without lids, for articles of a smaller nature, such as visiting cards, memorial cards, theatre tickets, and things which Chichikov had laid by as souvenirs. This portion of the box could be taken out, and below it were both a space for manuscripts and a secret money-box—the latter made to draw out from the side of the receptacle.

Chichikov set to work to clean a pen, and then to write. Presently his hostess entered the room.

" What a beautiful box you have got, my dear sir! " she exclaimed as she took a seat beside him. " Probably you bought it in Moscow? "

" Yes—in Moscow," replied Chichikov without interrupting his writing.

" I thought so. One *can* get good things there. Three years ago my sister brought me a few pairs of warm shoes for my sons, and they were such excellent articles! To this day my boys wear them. And what nice stamped paper you have! " (she had peered into the dispatch-box, where, sure enough, there lay a further store of the paper in question). " Would you mind letting me have a sheet of it? I am without any at all, although I shall soon have to be presenting a plea to the land court, and possess not a morsel of paper to write it on."

Upon this Chichikov explained that the paper was not the sort proper for the purpose—that it was meant for serf-indenturing, and not for the framing of pleas. Nevertheless, to quiet her, he gave her a sheet stamped to the value of a rouble. Next, he handed her the letter to sign, and requested, in return, a list of

[1] To serve as blotting-paper. (N.B.—This work was written more than seventy years ago.)

her peasants. Unfortunately, such a list had never been compiled, let alone any copies of it, and the only way in which she
knew the peasants' names was by heart. However, he told her
to dictate them. Some of the names greatly astonished our hero,
as, still more, did the surnames. Indeed, frequently, on hearing
the latter, he had to pause before writing them down. Especially did he halt before a certain "Peter Saveliev Nëuvazhai
Korito." "What a string of titles!" involuntarily he ejaculated. To the Christian name of another serf was appended
"Korovi Kirpitch," and to that of a third "Koleso Ivan."
However, at length the list was compiled, and he caught a deep
breath; which latter proceeding caused him to catch also the
attractive odour of something fried in fat.

"I beseech you to have a morsel," murmured his hostess.
Chichikov looked up, and saw that the table was spread with
mushrooms, pies, and other viands.

"Try this freshly-made pie and an egg," continued Madame.
Chichikov did so, and having eaten more than half of what
she offered him, praised the pie highly. Indeed, it was a tooth-
some dish, and, after his difficulties and exertions with his
hostess, it tasted even better than it might otherwise have
done.

"And also a few pancakes?" suggested Madame.
For answer Chichikov folded three together, and, having
dipped them in melted butter, consigned the lot to his mouth,
and then wiped his mouth with a napkin. Twice more was the
process repeated, and then he requested his hostess to order the
britchka to be got ready. In dispatching Fetinia with the necessary instructions, she ordered her to return with a second batch
of hot pancakes.

"Your pancakes are indeed splendid," said Chichikov,
applying himself to the second consignment of fried dainties
when they had arrived.

"Yes, we make them well here," replied Madame. "Yet how
unfortunate it is that the harvest should have proved so poor
as to have prevented me from earning anything on my—— But
why should you be in such a hurry to depart, good sir?" She
broke off on seeing Chichikov reach for his cap. "The *britchka*
is not yet ready."

"Then it is being got so, madam, it is being got so, and I shall
need a moment or two to pack my things."

"As you please, dear sir; but do not forget me in connection
with those Government contracts."

" No, I have said that *never* shall I forget you," replied Chichikov as he hurried into the hall.

"And would you like to buy some lard?" continued his hostess, pursuing him.

" Lard? Oh, certainly. Why not? Only, only—I will do so *another* time."

" I shall have some ready at about Christmas."

" Quite so, madam. *Then* I will buy anything and everything —the lard included."

" And perhaps you will be wanting also some feathers? I shall be having some for sale about St. Philip's Day."

" Very well, very well, madam."

" There you see! " she remarked as they stepped on to the verandah. " The *britchka* is *not* yet ready."

" But it soon will be, it soon will be. Only direct me to the main road."

" How am I to do that? " said Madame. " 'Twould puzzle a wise man to do so, for in these parts there are so many turnings. However, I will send a girl to guide you. You could find room for her on the box-seat, could you not? "

" Yes, of course."

" Then I will send her. She knows the way thoroughly. Only do not carry her off for good. Already some traders have deprived me of one of my girls."

Chichikov reassured his hostess on the point, and Madame plucked up courage enough to scan, first of all, the housekeeper, who happened to be issuing from the storehouse with a bowl of honey, and, next, a young peasant who happened to be standing at the gates; and, while thus engaged, she became wholly absorbed in her domestic pursuits. But why pay her so much attention? The Widow Korobotchka, Madame Manilov, domestic life, non-domestic life—away with them all! How strangely are things compounded! In a trice may joy turn to sorrow, should one halt long enough over it: in a trice only God can say what ideas may strike one. You may fall even to thinking: " After all, did Madame Korobotchka stand so very low in the scale of human perfection? Was there really such a very great gulf between her and Madame Manilov—between her and the Madame Manilov whom we have seen entrenched behind the walls of a genteel mansion in which there were a fine staircase of wrought metal and a number of rich carpets; the Madame Manilov who spent most of her time in yawning behind half-read books, and in hoping for a visit from some socially distinguished person in order that she might display her wit and carefully rehearsed thoughts—thoughts which had been *de rigeur* in town for a week past, yet which referred, not to what was going on in her household or on her estate—both of which properties were at odds and ends, owing to her ignorance of the art of managing them—but to the coming political revolution in France and the direction in which fashionable Catholicism was supposed to be moving? But away with such things! Why need we speak of them? Yet how comes it that suddenly into the midst of our careless, frivolous, unthinking moments there may enter another, and a very different, tendency?—that the smile may not have left a human face before its owner will have radically changed his or her nature (though not his or her environment) with the result that the face will suddenly become lit with a radiance never before seen there? . . .

"Here is the *britchka*, here is the *britchka!*" exclaimed Chichikov on perceiving that vehicle slowly advancing. "Ah, you blockhead!" he went on to Selifan. "Why have you been loitering about? I suppose last night's fumes have not yet left your brain?"

To this Selifan returned no reply.

"Good-bye, madam," added the speaker. "But where is the girl whom you promised me?"

"Here, Pelagea!" called the hostess to a wench of about eleven who was dressed in home-dyed garments and could boast of a pair of bare feet which, from a distance, might almost have been mistaken for boots, so encrusted were they with fresh mire. "Here, Pelagea! Come and show this gentleman the way."

Selifan helped the girl to ascend to the box-seat. Placing one foot upon the step by which the gentry mounted, she covered the said step with mud, and then, ascending higher, attained the desired position beside the coachman. Chichikov followed in her wake (causing the *britchka* to heel over with his weight as he did so), and then settled himself back into his place with an "All right! Good-bye, madam!" as the horses moved away at a trot.

Selifan looked gloomy as he drove, but also very attentive to his business. This was invariably his custom when he had committed the fault of getting drunk. Also, the horses looked unusually well-groomed. In particular, the collar on one of them had been neatly mended, although hitherto its state of dilapidation had been such as perennially to allow the stuffing to protrude through the leather. The silence preserved was well-nigh complete. Merely flourishing his whip, Selifan spoke to the team no word of instruction, although the skewbald was as ready as usual to listen to conversation of a didactic nature, seeing that at such times the reins hung loosely in the hands of the loquacious driver, and the whip wandered merely as a matter of form over the backs of the *troika*. This time, however, there could be heard issuing from Selifan's sullen lips only the uniformly unpleasant exclamation, " Now then, you brutes! Get on with you, get on with you! " The bay and the Assessor too felt put out at not hearing themselves called " my pets " or " good lads "; while, in addition, the skewbald came in for some nasty cuts across his sleek and ample quarters. " What has put master out like this? " thought the animal as it shook its head. " Heaven knows where he does not keep beating me —across the back, and even where I am tenderer still. Yes, he keeps catching the whip in my ears, and lashing me under the belly."

" To the right, eh? " snapped Selifan to the girl beside him as he pointed to a rain-soaked road which trended away through fresh green fields.

" No, no," she replied. " I will show you the road when the time comes."

" Which way, then? " he asked again when they had proceeded a little further.

" This way." And she pointed to the road just mentioned.

" Get along with you! " retorted the coachman. " That *does* go to the right. You don't know your right hand from your left."

The weather was fine, but the ground so excessively sodden that the wheels of the *britchka* collected mire until they had become caked as with a layer of felt, a circumstance which greatly increased the weight of the vehicle, and prevented it from clearing the neighbouring parishes before the afternoon was arrived. Also, without the girl's help the finding of the way would have been impossible, since roads wriggled away in every direction, like crabs released from a net, and, but for the assist-ance mentioned, Selifan would have found himself left to his own devices. Presently she pointed to a building ahead, with the words, " *There* is the main road."

" And what is the building? " asked Selifan.

" A tavern," she said.

" Then we can get along by ourselves," he observed. " Do you get down, and be off home."

With that he stopped, and helped her to alight—muttering as he did so: " Ah, you blackfooted creature! "

Chichikov added a copper groat, and she departed well pleased with her ride in the gentleman's carriage.

IV

On reaching the tavern, Chichikov called a halt. His reasons for this were twofold—namely, that he wanted to rest the horses, and that he himself desired some refreshment. In this connection the author feels bound to confess that the appetite and the capacity of such men are greatly to be envied. Of those well-to-do folk of St. Petersburg and Moscow who spend their time in considering what they shall eat on the morrow, and in composing a dinner for the day following, and who never sit down to a meal without first of all injecting a pill and then swallowing oysters and crabs and a quantity of other monsters, while eternally departing for Karlsbad or the Caucasus, the author has but a small opinion. Yes, *they* are not the persons to inspire envy. Rather, it is the folk of the middle classes—folk who at one posthouse call for bacon, and at another for a sucking pig, and at a third for a steak of sturgeon or a baked pudding with onions, and who can sit down to table at any hour, as though they had never had a meal in their lives, and can devour fish of all sorts, and guzzle and chew it with a view to provoking further appetite—these, I say, are the folk who enjoy heaven's most favoured gift. To attain such a celestial condition the great folk of whom I have spoken would sacrifice half their serfs and half their mortgaged and non-mortgaged property, with the foreign and domestic improvements thereon, if thereby they could compass such a stomach as is possessed by the folk of the middle class. But, unfortunately, neither money nor real estate, whether improved or non-improved, can purchase such a stomach.

The little wooden tavern, with its narrow, but hospitable, curtain suspended from a pair of rough-hewn doorposts like old church candlesticks, seemed to invite Chichikov to enter. True, the establishment was only a Russian hut of the ordinary type, but it was a hut of larger dimensions than usual, and had around its windows and gables carved and patterned cornices of bright-coloured wood which threw into relief the darker hue of the walls, and consorted well with the flowered pitchers painted on the shutters.

Ascending the narrow wooden staircase to the upper floor, and arriving upon a broad landing, Chichikov found himself confronted with a creaking door and a stout old woman in a striped print gown. "This way, if you please," she said. Within the apartment designated Chichikov encountered the old friends which one invariably finds in such roadside hostelries—to wit, a hoary *samovar*, four smooth, bescratched walls of white pine, a three-cornered press with cups and teapots, egg-cups of gilded china standing in front of *ikons* suspended by blue and red ribands, a cat lately delivered of a family, a mirror which gives one four eyes instead of two and a pancake for a face, and, beside the *ikons*, some bunches of herbs and carnations of such faded dustiness that, should one attempt to smell them, one is bound to burst out sneezing.

"Have you a sucking-pig?" Chichikov inquired of the landlady as she stood expectantly before him.

"Yes."

"And some horse-radish and sour cream?"

"Yes."

"Then serve them."

The landlady departed for the purpose, and returned with a plate, a napkin (the latter starched to the consistency of dried bark), a knife with a bone handle beginning to turn yellow, a two-pronged fork as thin as a wafer, and a salt-cellar incapable of being made to stand upright.

Following the accepted custom, our hero entered into conversation with the woman, and inquired whether she herself or a landlord kept the tavern; how much income the tavern brought in; whether her sons lived with her; whether the eldest was a bachelor or married; whom the eldest had taken to wife; whether the dowry had been large; whether the father-in-law had been satisfied; and whether the said father-in-law had not complained of receiving too small a present at the wedding. In short, Chichikov, touched on every conceivable point. Likewise (of course) he displayed some curiosity as to the landowners of the neighbourhood. Their names, he ascertained, were Blochin, Potchitaev, Milnoi, Cheprakov, and Sobakevitch.

"Then you are acquainted with Sobakevitch?" he said; whereupon the old woman informed him that she knew not only Sobakevitch, but also Manilov, and that the latter was the more delicate eater of the two, since, whereas Manilov always ordered a roast fowl and some veal and mutton, and then tasted merely a morsel of each, Sobakevitch would order one dish only, but consume the whole of it, and then demand more at the same price.

Whilst Chichikov was thus conversing and partaking of the sucking pig until only a fragment of it seemed likely to remain, the sound of an approaching vehicle made itself heard. Peering through the window, he saw draw up to the tavern door a light *britchka* drawn by three fine horses. From it there descended two men—one flaxen-haired and tall, and the other dark-haired and of slighter build. While the flaxen-haired man was clad in a dark-blue coat, the other one was wrapped in a coat of striped pattern. Behind the *britchka* stood a second, but an empty, turn-out, drawn by four long-coated steeds in ragged collars and rope harness. The flaxen-haired man lost no time in ascending the staircase, while his darker friend remained below to fumble at something in the *britchka*, talking, as he did so, to the driver of the vehicle which stood hitched behind. Somehow the dark-haired man's voice struck Chichikov as familiar; and as he was taking another look at him the flaxen-haired gentleman entered the room. The newcomer was a man of lofty stature, with a small red moustache and a lean, hard-bitten face whose redness made it evident that its acquaintance, if not with the smoke of gunpowder, at all events with that of tobacco, was intimate and extensive. Nevertheless he greeted Chichikov civilly, and the latter returned his bow. Indeed, the pair would have entered into conversation, and have made one another's acquaintance (since a beginning was made with their simultaneously expressing satisfaction at the circumstance that the previous night's rain had laid the dust on the roads, and thereby made driving cool and pleasant) when the gentleman's darker-favoured friend also entered the room, and, throwing his cap upon the table, pushed back a mass of dishevelled black locks from his brow. The latest arrival was a man of medium height, but well put together, and possessed of a pair of full red cheeks, a set of teeth as white as snow, and coal-black whiskers. Indeed, so fresh was his complexion that it seemed to have been compounded of blood and milk, while health danced in his every feature.

" Ha, ha, ha! " he cried with a gesture of astonishment at the sight of Chichikov. " What chance brings *you* here? "

Upon that Chichikov recognised Nozdrev—the man whom he had met at dinner at the Public Prosecutor's, and who, within a minute or two of the introduction, had become so intimate with his fellow-guest as to address him in the second person singular, in spite of the fact that Chichikov had given him no opening for doing so.

"Where have you been to-day?" Nozdrev inquired, and, without waiting for an answer, went on: "For myself, I am just from the fair, and completely cleaned out. Believe me, never in my life have I been so cleaned out. Actually, I have had to do the journey back with stage horses! Look out of the window, and see them for yourself." And he turned Chichikov's head so sharply in the desired direction that he came very near to bumping it against the window-frame. "Did you ever see such a bag of tricks? The cursed things have only just managed to get here. In fact, on the way I had to transfer myself to this fellow's *britchka*." He indicated his companion with his finger. "By the way, don't you know one another? He is Mizhuev, my brother-in-law. He and I were talking of you only this morning. ' Just you see,' said I to him, ' if we do not fall in with Chichikov before we have done.' Heavens, how completely cleaned out I am! Not only have I lost four good horses, but also my watch and chain." Chichikov perceived that in very truth his interlocutor was minus the articles named, as well as that one of Nozdrev's whiskers was less bushy in appearance than the other one. "Had I had another twenty roubles in my pocket," went on Nozdrev, "I should have won back all that I have lost, as well as have pouched a further thirty thousand. Yes, I give you my word of honour on that."

"But you were saying the same thing when last I met you," put in the flaxen-haired man. "Yet, even though I lent you fifty roubles, you lost them all."

"But I should not have lost them *this* time. Don't try to make me out a fool. I should *not* have lost them, I tell you. Had I only played the right card, I should have broken the bank."

"But you did *not* break the bank," remarked the flaxen-haired man.

"No. That was because I did not play my cards right. But what about your precious major's play? Is *that* good? "

"Good or not, at least he beat you."

"Splendid of him! Nevertheless I will get my own back. Let him play me at doubles, and we shall soon see what sort of a player he is! Friend Chichikov, at first we had a glorious time, for the fair was a tremendous success. Indeed, the tradesmen said that never had there been such a gathering. I myself managed to sell everything from my estate at a good price. In fact, we had a magnificent time. I can't help thinking of it, devil take me! But what a pity *you* were not there! Three versts from the town there is quartered a regiment of dragoons, and you would scarcely believe what a lot of officers it has. Forty at least there are, and they do a fine lot of knocking about the town and drinking. In particular, Staff-Captain Potsieluev is a *splendid* fellow! You should just see his moustache! Why, he calls good claret 'trash'! 'Bring me some of the usual trash,' is his way of ordering it. And Lieutenant Kuvshinnikov, too! He is as delightful as the other man. In fact, I may say that every one of the lot is a rake. I spent my whole time with them, and you can imagine that Ponomarev, the wine merchant, did a fine trade indeed! All the same, he is a rascal, you know, and ought not to be dealt with, for he puts all sorts of rubbish into his liquor—Indian wood and burnt cork and elderberry juice, the villain! Nevertheless, get him to produce a bottle from what he calls his 'special cellar,' and you will fancy yourself in the seventh heaven of delight. And what quantities of champagne we drank! Compared with it, provincial stuff is *kvass*.[1] Try to imagine not merely Clicquot, but a sort of a blend of Clicquot and Matradura—Clicquot of double strength. Also Ponomarev produced a bottle of French stuff which he calls 'Bonbon.' Had it a bouquet, ask you? Why, it had the bouquet of a rose garden, of anything else you like. What times we had, to be sure! Just after we had left Ponomarev's place, some prince or another arrived in the town, and sent out for some champagne; but not a bottle was there left, for the officers had drunk every one! Why, I myself got through seventeen bottles at a sitting."

"Come, come! You *can't* have got through seventeen," remarked the flaxen-haired man.

"But I did, I give you my word of honour," retorted Nozdrev.

"Imagine what you like, but you didn't drink even *ten* bottles at a sitting."

"Will you bet that I did not?"

"No; for what would be the use of betting about it?"

"Then at least wager the gun which you have bought."

"No, I am not going to do anything of the kind."

"Just as an experiment?"

"No."

---

[1] A liquor distilled from fermented bread crusts or sour fruit.

"It is as well for you that you don't, since, otherwise, you would have found yourself minus both gun and cap. However, friend Chichikov, it is a pity you were not there. Had you been there, I feel sure you would have found yourself unable to part with Lieutenant Kuvshinnikov. You and he would have hit it off splendidly. You know, he is quite a different sort from the Public Prosecutor and our other provincial skinflints—fellows who shiver in their shoes before they will spend a single kopeck. *He* will play faro, or anything else, and at any time. Why did you not come with us, instead of wasting your time on cattle breeding or something of the sort? But never mind. Embrace me. I like you immensely. Mizhuev, see how curiously things have turned out. Chichikov has nothing to do with me, or I with him, yet here is he come from God knows where, and landed in the very spot where I happen to be living! I may tell you that, no matter how many carriages I possessed, I should gamble the lot away. Recently I went in for a turn at billiards, and lost two jars of pomade, a china teapot, and a guitar. Then I staked some more things, and, like a fool, lost them all, and six roubles in addition. What a dog is that Kuvshinnikov! He and I attended nearly every ball in the place. In particular, there was a woman—*décolletée*, and such a swell! I merely thought to myself, 'The devil take her!' but Kuvshinnikov is such a wag that he sat down beside her, and began paying her strings of compliments in French. However, I did not neglect the damsels altogether—though *he* calls that sort of thing 'going in for strawberries.' By the way, I have a splendid piece of fish and some caviare with me. 'Tis all I *have* brought back! In fact it is a lucky chance that I happened to buy the stuff before my money was gone. Where are you for?"

"I am about to call on a friend."

"On what friend? Let him go to the devil, and come to my place instead."

"I cannot, I cannot. I have business to do."

"Oh, business again! I thought so!"

"But I *have* business to do—and pressing business at that."

"I wager that you're lying. If not, tell me whom you're going to call upon."

"Upon Sobakevitch."

Instantly Nozdrev burst into the laugh compassable only by a healthy man in whose head every tooth still remains as white as sugar. By this I mean the laugh of quivering cheeks, the laugh which causes a neighbour who is sleeping behind double doors three rooms away to leap from his bed and exclaim with distended eyes, " Hullo! Something *has* upset him! "

" What is there to laugh at? " asked Chichikov, a trifle nettled; but Nozdrev laughed more unrestrainedly than ever, ejaculating: " Oh, spare us all! The thing is so amusing that I shall die of it! "

" I say that there is nothing to laugh at," repeated Chichikov. " It is in fulfilment of a promise that I am on my way to Sobakevitch's."

" Then you will scarcely be glad to be alive when you've got there, for he is the veriest miser in the countryside. Oh, *I* know you. However, if you think to find there either faro or a bottle of ' Bonbon ' you are mistaken. Look here, my good friend. Let Sobakevitch go to the devil, and come to *my* place, where at least I shall have a piece of sturgeon to offer you for dinner. Ponomarev said to me on parting: ' This piece is just the thing for you. Even if you were to search the whole market, you would never find a better one.' But of course he is a terrible rogue. I said to him outright: ' You and the Collector of Taxes are the two greatest skinflints in the town.' But he only stroked his beard and smiled. Every day I used to breakfast with Kuvshinnikov in his restaurant. Well, what I was nearly forgetting is this: that, though I am aware that you can't forgo your engagement, I am not going to give you up—no, not for ten thousand roubles of money. I tell you that in advance."

Here he broke off to run to the window and shout to his servant (who was holding a knife in one hand and a crust of bread and a piece of sturgeon in the other—he had contrived to filch the latter while fumbling in the *britchka* for something else):

" Hi, Porphyri! Bring here that puppy, you rascal! What a puppy it is! Unfortunately that thief of a landlord has given it nothing to eat, even though I have promised him the roan filly which, as you may remember, I swopped from Khvostirev." As a matter of fact, Chichikov had never in his life seen either Khvostirev or the roan filly.

" *Barin,* do you wish for anything to eat? " inquired the landlady as she entered.

" No, nothing at all. Ah, friend Chichikov, what times we had! Yes, give me a glass of *vodka,* old woman. What sort do you keep? "

" Aniseed."

" Then bring me a glass of it," repeated Nozdrev.

" And one for me as well," added the flaxen-haired man.

" At the theatre," went on Nozdrev, " there was an actress who sang like a canary. Kuvshinnikov, who happened to be sitting with me, said: ' My boy, you had better go and gather that strawberry.' As for the booths at the fair, they numbered, I should say, fifty." At this point he broke off to take the glass of *vodka* from the landlady, who bowed low in acknowledgment of his doing so. At the same moment Porphyri—a fellow dressed like his master (that is to say, in a greasy, wadded overcoat)—entered with the puppy.

" Put the brute down here," commanded Nozdrev, " and then fasten it up."

Porphyri deposited the animal upon the floor; whereupon it proceeded to act after the manner of dogs.

" *There's* a puppy for you! " cried Nozdrev, catching hold of it by the back, and lifting it up. The puppy uttered a piteous yelp.

" I can see that you haven't done what I told you to do," he continued to Porphyri after an inspection of the animal's belly. " You have quite forgotten to brush him."

" I *did* brush him," protested Porphyri.

" Then where do these fleas come from? "

" I cannot think. Probably they have leapt into his coat out of the *britchka*."

" You liar! As a matter of fact, you have forgotten to brush him. Nevertheless, look at those ears, Chichikov. Just feel them."

" Why should I? Without doing that, I can see that he is well-bred."

" Nevertheless, catch hold of his ears and feel them."

To humour the fellow Chichikov did as he had requested, remarking: " Yes, he seems likely to turn out well."

" And feel the coldness of his nose! Just take it in your hand."

Not wishing to offend his interlocutor, Chichikov felt the puppy's nose, saying: " Some day he will have an excellent scent."

" Yes, will he not? 'Tis the right sort of muzzle for that. I must say I have long been wanting such a puppy. Porphyri, take him away again."

Porphyri lifted up the puppy, and bore it downstairs.

" Look here, Chichikov," resumed Nozdrev. " You *must* come to my place. It lies only five versts away, and we can go there like the wind, and you can visit Sobakevitch afterwards."

" Shall I, or shall I not, go to Nozdrev's? " reflected Chichikov. " Is he likely to prove any more useful than the rest? Well, at least he is as promising, even though he has lost so much at play. But he has a head on his shoulders, and therefore I must go carefully if I am to tackle him concerning my scheme."

With that he added aloud: "Very well, I *will* come with you, but do not let us be long, for my time is very precious."

"That's right, that's right!" cried Nozdrev. "Splendid, splendid! Let me embrace you!" And he fell upon Chichikov's neck. "All three of us will go."

"No, no," put in the flaxen-haired man. "You must excuse me, for I must be off home."

"Rubbish, rubbish! I am *not* going to excuse you."

"But my wife will be furious with me. You and Monsieur Chichikov must change into the other *britchka*."

"Come, come! The thing is not to be thought of."

The flaxen-haired man was one of those people in whose character, at first sight, there seems to lurk a certain grain of stubbornness—so much so that, almost before one has begun to speak, they are ready to dispute one's words, and to disagree with anything that may be opposed to their peculiar form of opinion. For instance, they will decline to have folly called wisdom, or any tune danced to but their own. Always, however, will there become manifest in their character a soft spot, and in the end they will accept what hitherto they have denied, and call what is foolish sensible, and even dance—yes, better than any one else will do—to a tune set by some one else. In short, they generally begin well, but always end badly.

"Rubbish!" said Nozdrev in answer to a further objection on his brother-in-law's part. And, sure enough, no sooner had Nozdrev clapped his cap upon his head than the flaxen-haired man started to follow him and his companion.

"But the gentleman has not paid for the *vodka*?" put in the old woman.

"All right, all right, good mother. Look here, brother-in-law. Pay her, will you, for I have not a kopeck left."

"How much?" inquired the brother-in-law.

"What, sir? Eighty kopecks, if you please," replied the old woman.

"A lie! Give her half a rouble. That will be quite enough."

"No, it will *not, barin*," protested the old woman. However, she took the money gratefully, and even ran to the door to open it for the gentlemen. As a matter of fact, she had lost nothing by the transaction, since she had demanded fully a quarter more than the *vodka* was worth.

The travellers then took their seats, and since Chichikov's *britchka* kept alongside the *britchka* wherein Nozdrev and his brother-in-law were seated, it was possible for all three men to converse together as they proceeded. Behind them came Nozdrev's smaller buggy, with its team of lean stage horses and Porphyri and the puppy. But inasmuch as the conversation which the travellers maintained was not of a kind likely to interest the reader, I might do worse than say something concerning Nozdrev himself, seeing that he is destined to play no small rôle in our story.

Nozdrev's face will be familiar to the reader, seeing that every one must have encountered many such. Fellows of the kind are known as " gay young sparks," and, even in their boy-hood and school days, earn a reputation for being *bons camarades* (though with it all they come in for some hard knocks) for the reason that their faces evince an element of frankness, directness, and enterprise which enables them soon to make friends, and, almost before you have had time to look round, to start address-ing you in the second person singular. Yet, while cementing such friendships for all eternity, almost always they begin quarrel-ling the same evening, since, throughout, they are a loquacious, dissipated, high-spirited, over-showy tribe. Indeed, at thirty-five Nozdrev was just what he had been at eighteen and twenty —he was just such a lover of fast living. Nor had his marriage in any way changed him, and the less so since his wife had soon departed to another world, and left behind her two children, whom he did not want, and who were therefore placed in the charge of a good-looking nursemaid. Never at any time could he remain at home for more than a single day, for his keen scent could range over scores and scores of versts, and detect any fair which promised balls and crowds. Consequently in a trice he would be there—quarrelling, and creating disturbances over the gaming-table (like all men of his type, he had a perfect passion for cards) yet playing neither a faultless nor an over-clean game, since he was both a blunderer and able to indulge in a large number of illicit cuts and other devices. The result was that the game often ended in another kind of sport altogether. That is to say, either he received a good kicking, or he had his thick and very handsome whiskers pulled; with the result that on certain occasions he returned home with one of those appendages looking decidedly ragged. Yet his plump, healthy-looking cheeks were so robustly constituted, and contained such an abundance of recreative vigour, that a new whisker soon sprouted in place of the old one, and even surpassed its predecessor. Again (and the following is a phenomenon peculiar to Russia) a very short time would have elapsed before once more he would be consorting with the very cronies who had recently cuffed him—and consorting with them as though nothing whatsoever had happened—no reference to the subject being made by him, and they too holding their tongues.

In short, Nozdrev was, at it were, a man of incident. Never was he present at any gathering without some sort of a *fracas* occurring thereat. Either he would require to be expelled the room by gendarmes, or his friends would have to kick him out into the street. At all events, should neither of those occurrences take place, at least he did something of a nature which would not otherwise have been witnessed. That is to say, should he not play the fool in a buffet to such an extent as to make every one smile, you may be sure that he was engaged in lying to a degree which at times abashed even himself. Moreover, the man lied without reason. For instance, he would begin telling a story to the effect that he possessed a blue-coated or a red-coated horse; until, in the end, his listeners would be forced to leave him with the remark, " You are giving us some fine stuff, old fellow! " Also, men like Nozdrev have a passion for insulting their neighbours without the least excuse afforded. (For that matter, even a man of good standing and of respectable exterior—a man with a star on his breast—may unexpectedly press your hand one day, and begin talking to you on subjects of a nature to give food for serious thought. Yet just as unexpectedly may that man start abusing you to your face—and do so in a manner worthy of a collegiate registrar rather than of a man who wears a star on his breast and aspires to converse on subjects which merit reflection. All that one can do in such a case is to stand shrugging one's shoulders in amazement.) Well, Nozdrev had just such a weakness. The more he became friendly with a man, the sooner would he insult him, and be ready to spread calumnies as to his reputation. Yet all the while he would consider himself the insulted one's friend, and, should he meet him again, would greet him in the most amicable style possible, and say, " You rascal, why have you given up coming to see me." Thus, taken all round, Nozdrev was a person of many aspects and numerous potentialities. In one and the same breath would he propose to go with you whithersoever you might choose (even to the very ends of the world should you so require) or to enter upon any sort of an enterprise with you, or to exchange any commodity for any other commodity which you might care to name. Guns, horses, dogs, all were subjects for barter—though not for profit so far as *you* were concerned. Such traits are mostly the outcome of a boisterous temperament, as is additionally exemplified by the fact that if at a fair he chanced to fall in with a simpleton and to fleece him, he would then proceed to buy a quantity of the very first articles which came to hand—horse-collars, cigar-lighters, dresses for his nursemaid, foals, raisins, silver ewers, lengths of holland, wheatmeal, tobacco, revolvers, dried herrings, pictures, whetstones, crockery, boots, and so forth, until every atom of his money was exhausted. Yet seldom were these articles conveyed home, since, as a rule, the same day saw them lost to some more skilful gambler, in addition to his pipe, his tobacco-pouch, his mouthpiece, his four-horsed turn-out, and his coach-man: with the result that, stripped to his very shirt, he would be forced to beg the loan of a vehicle from a friend.

Such was Nozdrev. Some may say that characters of his type have become extinct, that the Nozdrevs no longer exist. Alas! such as say this will be wrong; for many a day must pass before the Nozdrevs will have disappeared from our ken. Everywhere they are to be seen in our midst—the only difference between the new and the old being a difference of garments. Persons of superficial observation are apt to consider that a man clad in a different coat is quite a different person from what he used to be.

To continue. The three vehicles bowled up to the steps of Nozdrev's house, and their occupants alighted. But no prepara-tions whatsoever had been made for the guests' reception, for on some wooden trestles in the centre of the dining-room a couple of peasants were engaged in whitewashing the ceiling and drawling out an endless song as they splashed their stuff about the floor. Hastily bidding peasants and trestles be gone, Nozdrev departed to another room with further instructions. Indeed, so audible was the sound of his voice as he ordered dinner that Chichikov—who was beginning to feel hungry once more—was enabled to gather that it would be at least five o'clock before a meal of any kind would be available. On his return, Nozdrev invited his companions to inspect his establish-ment—even though as early as two o'clock he had to announce that nothing more was to be seen.

The tour began with a view of the stables, where the party saw two mares (the one a grey, and the other a roan) and a colt; which latter animal, though far from showy, Nozdrev declared to have cost him ten thousand roubles.

"You *never* paid ten thousand roubles for the brute!" exclaimed the brother-in-law. "He isn't worth even a thousand."

"By God, I *did* pay ten thousand!" asserted Nozdrev.

"You can swear that as much as you like," retorted the other.

"Will you bet that I did not?" asked Nozdrev, but the brother-in-law declined the offer.

Next, Nozdrev showed his guests some empty stalls where a number of equally fine animals (so he alleged) had lately stood. Also there was on view the goat which an old belief still considers to be an indispensable adjunct to such places, even though its apparent use is to pace up and down beneath the noses of the horses as though the place belonged to it. Thereafter the host took his guests to look at a young wolf which he had got tied to a chain. "He is fed on nothing but raw meat," he explained, "for I want him to grow up as fierce as possible." Then the party inspected a pond in which there were "fish of such a size that it would take two men all their time to lift one of them out."

This piece of information was received with renewed incredulity on the part of the brother-in-law.

"Now, Chichikov," went on Nozdrev, "let me show you a truly magnificent brace of dogs. The hardness of their muscles will surprise you, and they have jowls as sharp as needles."

So saying, he led the way to a small, but neatly-built, shed surrounded on every side with a fenced-in run. Entering this run, the visitors beheld a number of dogs of all sorts and sizes and colours. In their midst Nozdrev looked like a father lording it over his family circle. Erecting their tails—their "stems," as dog fanciers call those members—the animals came bounding to greet the party, and fully a score of them laid their paws upon Chichikov's shoulders. Indeed, one dog was moved with such friendliness that, standing on its hind legs, it licked him on the lips, and so forced him to spit. That done, the visitors duly inspected the couple already mentioned, and expressed astonishment at their muscles. True enough, they were fine animals. Next, the party looked at a Crimean bitch which, though blind and fast nearing her end, had, two years ago, been a truly magnificent dog. At all events, so said Nozdrev. Next came another bitch —also blind; then an inspection of the water-mill, which lacked the spindle-socket wherein the upper stone ought have been revolving—"fluttering," to use the Russian peasant's quaint expression. "But never mind," said Nozdrev. "Let us proceed to the blacksmith's shop." So to the blacksmith's shop the party proceeded, and when the said shop had been viewed, Nozdrev said as he pointed to a field:

" In this field I have seen such numbers of hares as to render the ground quite invisible. Indeed, on one occasion I, with my own hands, caught a hare by the hind legs."

" You never caught a hare by the hind legs with your hands! " remarked the brother-in-law.

" But I *did* " reiterated Nozdrev. " However, let me show you the boundary where my lands come to an end."

So saying, he started to conduct his guests across a field which consisted mostly of moleheaps, and in which the party had to pick their way between strips of ploughed land and of harrowed. Soon Chichikov began to feel weary, for the *terrain* was so low-lying that in many spots water could be heard squelching underfoot, and though for a while the visitors watched their feet, and stepped carefully, they soon perceived that such a course availed them nothing, and took to following their noses, without either selecting or avoiding the spots where the mire happened to be deeper or the reverse. At length, when a considerable distance had been covered, they caught sight of a boundary-post and a narrow ditch.

" That is the boundary," said Nozdrev. " Everything that you see on this side of the post is mine, as well as the forest on the other side of it, and what lies beyond the forest."

" *When* did that forest become yours? " asked the brother-in-law. " It cannot be long since you purchased it, for it never *used* to be yours."

" Yes, it isn't long since I purchased it," said Nozdrev.

" How long? "

" How long? Why, I purchased it three days ago, and gave a pretty sum for it, as the devil knows! "

" Indeed? Why, three days ago you were at the fair? "

" Wiseacre! Cannot one be at a fair and buy land at the same time? Yes, I *was* at the fair, and my steward bought the land in my absence."

" Oh, your *steward* bought it." The brother-in-law seemed doubtful, and shook his head.

The guests returned by the same route as that by which they had come; whereafter, on reaching the house, Nozdrev conducted them to his study, which contained not a trace of the things usually to be found in such apartments—such things as books and papers. On the contrary, the only articles to be seen were a sword and a brace of guns—the one " of them worth three hundred roubles," and the other " about eight hundred." The brother-in-law inspected the articles in question, and then shook his head as before. Next, the visitors were shown some " real Turkish " daggers, of which one bore the inadvertent inscription, " Saveli Sibiriakov,[1] Master Cutler." Then came a barrel-organ, on which Nozdrev started to play some tune or another. For a while the sounds were not wholly unpleasing, but suddenly something seemed to go wrong, for a mazurka started, to be followed by " Marlborough has gone to the war," and to this, again, there succeeded an antiquated waltz. Also, long after Nozdrev had ceased to turn the handle, one particularly shrill-pitched pipe which had, throughout, refused to harmonise with the rest kept up a protracted whistling on its own account. Then followed an exhibition of tobacco pipes—pipes of clay, of wood, of meerschaum, pipes smoked and non-smoked; pipes wrapped in chamois leather and not so wrapped; an amber-mounted hookah (a stake won at cards) and a tobacco pouch (worked, it was alleged, by some countess who had fallen in love with Nozdrev at a posthouse, and whose handiwork Nozdrev averred to constitute the "sublimity of superfluity"—a term which, in the Nozdrevian vocabulary, purported to signify the acme of perfection).

Finally, after some *hors-d'œuvres* of sturgeon's back, they sat down to table—the time being then nearly five o'clock. But the meal did not constitute by any means the best of which Chichikov had ever partaken, seeing that some of the dishes were overcooked, and others were scarcely cooked at all. Evidently their compounder had trusted chiefly to inspiration—she had laid hold of the first thing which had happened to come to hand. For instance, had pepper represented the nearest article within reach, she had added pepper wholesale. Had a cabbage chanced to be so encountered, she had pressed it also into the service. And the same with milk, bacon, and peas. In short, her rule seemed to have been " Make a hot dish of some sort, and some sort of a taste will result." For the rest, Nozdrev drew heavily upon the wine. Even before the soup had been served, he had poured out for each guest a bumper of port and another of " *haut* " sauterne. (Never in provincial towns is ordinary, vulgar sauterne even procurable). Next, he called for a bottle of madeira—" as fine a tipple as ever a field-marshal drank "; but the madeira only burnt the mouth, since the dealers, familiar with the taste of our landed gentry (who love

[1] That is to say, a distinctively Russian name.

" good " madeira) invariably doctor the stuff with copious
dashes of rum and Imperial *vodka*, in the hope that Russian
stomachs will thus be enabled to carry off the lot. After this
bottle Nozdrev called for another and " a very special " brand
—a brand which he declared to consist of a blend of burgundy
and champagne, and of which he poured generous measures
into the glasses of Chichikov and the brother-in-law as they
sat to right and left of him. But since Chichikov noticed that,
after doing so, he added only a scanty modicum of the mixture
to his own tumbler, our hero determined to be cautious, and
therefore took advantage of a moment when Nozdrev had
again plunged into conversation and was yet a third time
engaged in refilling his brother-in-law's glass, to contrive to
upset his (Chichikov's) glass over his plate. In time there came
also to table a tart of mountain-ashberries—berries which the
host declared to equal, in taste, ripe plums, but which, curiously
enough, smacked more of corn brandy. Next, the company
consumed a sort of pasty of which the precise name has escaped
me, but which the host rendered differently even on the second
occasion of its being mentioned. The meal over, and the whole
tale of wines tried, the guests still retained their seats—a circumstance which embarrassed Chichikov, seeing that he had no
mind to propound his pet scheme in the presence of Nozdrev's
brother-in-law, who was a complete stranger to him. No, that
subject called for amicable and *private* conversation. Nevertheless, the brother-in-law appeared to bode little danger, seeing
that he had taken on board a full cargo, and was now engaged
in doing nothing of a more menacing nature than picking his
nose. At length he himself noticed that he was not altogether in
a responsible condition; wherefore he rose and began to make
excuses for departing homewards, though in a tone so drowsy
and lethargic that, to quote the Russian proverb, he might
almost have been " pulling a collar on to a horse by the clasps."

" No, no ! " cried Nozdrev. " I am *not* going to let you go."

" But I *must* go," replied the brother-in-law. " Don't try to
hinder me. You are annoying me greatly."

" Rubbish! We are going to play a game of banker."

" No, no. You must play it without me, my friend. My wife
is expecting me at home, and I must go and tell her all about
the fair. Yes, I *must* go if I am to please her. Do not try to
detain me."

" Your wife be——! But have you *really* an important piece
of business with her ? "

"No, no, my friend. The real reason is that she is a good and trustful woman, and that she does a great deal for me. The tears spring to my eyes as I think of it. Do not detain me. As an honourable man I say that I must go. Of that I do assure you in all sincerity."

"Oh, let him go," put in Chichikov under his breath. "What use will he be here?"

"Very well," said Nozdrev, "though, damn it, I do not like fellows who lose their heads." Then he added to his brother-in-law: "All right, Thetuk.[1] Off you go to your wife and your woman's talk, and may the devil go with you!"

"Do not insult me with the term Thetuk," retorted the brother-in-law. "To her I owe my life, and she is a dear, good woman, and has shown me much affection. At the very thought of it I could weep. You see, she will be asking me what I have seen at the fair, and tell her about it I must, for she is such a dear, good woman."

"Then off you go to her with your pack of lies. Here is your cap."

"No, good friend, you are not to speak of her like that. By so doing you offend me greatly—— I say that she is a dear, good woman."

"Then run along home to her."

"Yes, I am just going. Excuse me for having been unable to stay. Gladly would I have stayed, but really I cannot."

The brother-in-law repeated his excuses again and again without noticing that he had entered the *britchka*, that it had passed through the gates, and that he was now in the open country. Permissibly we may suppose that his wife succeeded in gleaning from him few details of the fair.

"What a fool!" said Nozdrev as, standing by the window, he watched the departing vehicle. "Yet his off-horse is not such a bad one. For a long time past I have been wanting to get hold of it. A man like that is simply impossible. Yes, he is a Thetuk, a regular Thetuk."

With that they repaired to the parlour, where, on Porphyri bringing candles, Chichikov perceived that his host had produced a pack of cards.

"I tell you what," said Nozdrev, pressing the sides of the pack together, and then slightly bending them, so that the pack

---

[1] A jeering appellation which owes its origin to the fact that certain Russians cherish a prejudice against the initial character of the word— namely, the Greek θ or *th*.

cracked and a card flew out. " How would it be if, to pass the time, I were to make a bank of three hundred? "

Chichikov pretended not to have heard him, but remarked with an air of having just recollected a forgotten point:

" By the way, I had omitted to say that I have a request to make of you."

" What request? "

" First give me your word that you will grant it."

" What is the request, I say? "

" Then you give me your word, do you? "

" Certainly."

" Your word of honour? "

" My word of honour."

" This, then, is my request. I presume that you have a large number of dead serfs whose names have not yet been removed from the revision list? "

" I have. But why do you ask? "

" Because I want you to make them over to me."

" Of what use would they be to you? "

" Never mind. I have a purpose in wanting them."

" What purpose? "

" A purpose which is strictly my own affair. In short, I need them."

" You seem to have hatched a very fine scheme. Out with it, now! What is in the wind? "

" How could I have hatched such a scheme as you say? One could not very well hatch a scheme out of such a trifle as this."

" Then for what purpose do you want the serfs? "

" Oh, the curiosity of the man! He wants to poke his fingers into and smell over every detail! "

" Why do you decline to say what is in your mind? At all events, until you *do* say I shall not move in the matter."

" But how would it benefit you to know what my plans are? A whim has seized me. That is all. Nor are you playing fair. You have given me your word of honour, yet now you are trying to back out of it."

" No matter what you desire me to do, I decline to do it until you have told me your purpose."

" What am I to say to the fellow? " thought Chichikov. He reflected for a moment, and then explained that he wanted the dead souls in order to acquire a better standing in society, since at present he possessed little landed property, and only a handful of serfs.

"You are lying," said Nozdrev without even letting him finish. "Yes, you are lying my good friend."

Chichikov himself perceived that his device had been a clumsy one, and his pretext weak. "I must tell him straight out," he said to himself as he pulled his wits together.

"Should I tell you the truth," he added aloud, "I must beg of you not to repeat it. The truth is that I am thinking of getting married. But, unfortunately, my betrothed's father and mother are very ambitious people, and do not want me to marry her, since they desire the bridegroom to own not less than three hundred souls, whereas I own but a hundred and fifty, and that number is not sufficient."

"Again you are lying," said Nozdrev.

"Then look here; I have been lying only to this extent." And Chichikov marked off upon his little finger a minute portion.

"Nevertheless I will bet my head that you have been lying throughout."

"Come, come! That is not very civil of you. Why should I have been lying?"

"Because I know you, and know that you are a regular skinflint. I say that in all friendship. If I possessed any power over you I should hang you to the nearest tree."

This remark hurt Chichikov, for at any time he disliked expressions gross or offensive to decency, and never allowed any one—no, not even persons of the highest rank—to behave towards him with an undue measure of familiarity. Consequently his sense of umbrage on the present occasion was unbounded.

"By God, I *would* hang you!" repeated Nozdrev. "I say this frankly, and not for the purpose of offending you, but simply to communicate to you my friendly opinion."

"To everything there are limits," retorted Chichikov stifly. "If you want to indulge in speeches of that sort you had better return to the barracks."

However, after a pause he added:

"If you do not care to give me the serfs, why not *sell* them?"

"*Sell* them? *I* know you, you rascal! You wouldn't give me very much for them, *would* you?"

"A nice fellow! Look here. What are they to you? So many diamonds, eh?"

"I thought so! *I* know you!"

"Pardon me, but I could wish that you were a member of the Jewish persuasion. You would give them to me fast enough then."

" On the contrary, to show you that I am not a usurer, I will decline to ask of you a single kopeck for the serfs. All that you need do is to buy that colt of mine, and then I will throw in the serfs in addition."

" But what should *I* want with your colt? " said Chichikov, genuinely astonished at the proposal.

" What should *you* want with him? Why, I have bought him for ten thousand roubles, and am ready to let you have him for four."

" I ask you again: of what use could the colt possibly be to me? I am not the keeper of a breeding establishment."

" Ah! I see that you fail to understand me. Let me suggest that you pay down at once three thousand roubles of the purchase money, and leave the other thousand until later."

" But I do not mean to buy the colt, damn him! "

" Then buy the roan mare."

" No, nor the roan mare."

" Then you shall have both the mare and the grey horse which you have seen in my stables for two thousand roubles."

" I require no horses at all."

" But you would be able to sell them again. You would be able to get thrice their purchase price at the very first fair that was held."

" Then sell them at that fair yourself, seeing that you are so certain of making a triple profit."

" Oh, I should make it fast enough, only I want *you* to benefit by the transaction."

Chichikov duly thanked his interlocutor, but continued to decline either the grey horse or the roan mare.

" Then buy a few dogs," said Nozdrev. " I can sell you a couple with hides a-quiver, ears will pricked, coats like quills, ribs barrel-shaped, and paws so tucked up as scarcely to graze the ground when they run."

" Of what use would those dogs be to me? I am not a sportsman."

" But I *want* you to have the dogs. Listen. If you won't have the dogs, then buy my barrel-organ. 'Tis a splendid instrument. As a man of honour I tell you that, when new, it cost me fifteen hundred roubles. Well, you shall have it for nine hundred."

" Come, come! What should I want with a barrel-organ? I am not a German, to go hauling it about the roads and begging for coppers."

" But this is quite a different kind of organ from the one which

Germans take about with them. You see, it is a *real* organ. Look at it for yourself. It is made of the best wood. I will take you to have another view of it."

And seizing Chichikov by the hand, Nozdrev drew him towards the other room, where, in spite of the fact that Chichikov, with his feet planted firmly on the floor, assured his host, again and again, that he knew exactly what the organ was like, he was forced once more to hear how Marlborough went to the war.

" Then, since you don't care to give me any money for it," persisted Nozdrev, " listen to the following proposal. I will give you the barrel-organ and all the dead souls which I possess, and in return you shall give me your *britchka*, and another three hundred roubles into the bargain."

" Listen to the man! In that case, what should I have left to drive in? "

" Oh, I would stand you another *britchka*. Come to the coach-house, and I will show you the one I mean. It only needs re-painting to look a perfectly splendid *britchka*."

" The ramping, incorrigible devil! " thought Chichikov to himself as at all hazards he resolved to escape from *britchkas*, organs, and every species of dog, however marvellously barrel-ribbed and tucked up of paw.

" And in exchange, you shall have the *britchka*, the barrel-organ, and the dead souls," repeated Nozdrev.

" I must decline the offer," said Chichikov.

" And why? "

" Because I don't *want* the things—I am full up already."

" I can see that you don't know how things should be done between good friends and comrades. Plainly you are a man of two faces."

" What do you mean, you fool? Think for yourself. Why should I acquire articles which I don't want? "

" Say no more about it, if you please. I have quite taken your measure. But see here. Should you care to play a game of banker? I am ready to stake both the dead souls and the barrel-organ at cards."

" No; to leave an issue to cards means to submit oneself to the unknown," said Chichikov, covertly glancing at the pack which Nozdrev had got in his hands. Somehow the way in which his companion had cut that pack seemed to him suspicious.

" Why ' to the unknown '? " asked Nozdrev. " There is no such thing as ' the unknown.' Should luck be on your side, you may win the devil knows what a haul. Oh, luck, luck!" he went on, beginning to deal, in the hope of raising a quarrel. "Here is the cursed nine upon which, the other night, I lost everything. All along I knew that I should lose my money. Said I to myself: 'The devil take you, you false, accursed card!'"

Just as Nozdrev uttered the words Porphyri entered with a fresh bottle of liquor; but Chichikov declined either to play or to drink.

"Why do you refuse to play?" asked Nozdrev.

"Because I feel indisposed to do so. Moreover, I must confess that I am no great hand at cards."

"*Why* are you no great hand at them?"

Chichikov shrugged his shoulders. "Because I am not," he replied.

"You are no great hand at *anything*, I think."

"What does that matter? God has made me so."

"The truth is you are a Thetuk, and nothing else. Once upon a time I believed you to be a good fellow, but now I see that you don't understand civility. One cannot speak to you as one would to an intimate, for there is no frankness or sincerity about you. You are a regular Sobakevitch—just such another as he."

"For what reason are you abusing me? Am I in any way at fault for declining to play cards? Sell me those souls if you are the man to hesitate over such rubbish."

"The foul fiend take you! I was about to have given them to you for nothing, but now you shan't have them at all—not if you offer me three kingdoms in exchange. Henceforth I will have nothing to do with you, you cobbler, you dirty blacksmith! Porphyri, go and tell the ostler to give the gentleman's horses no oats, but only hay."

This development Chichikov had scarcely expected.

"And do you," added Nozdrev to his guest, "get out of my sight."

Yet in spite of this, host and guest took supper together— even though on this occasion the table was adorned with no wines of fictitious nomenclature, but only with a bottle which reared its solitary head beside a jug of what is usually known as *vin ordinaire*. When supper was over Nozdrev said to Chichikov as he conducted him to a side room where a bed had been made up:

"This is where you are to sleep. I cannot very well wish you good-night."

Left to himself on Nozdrev's departure, Chichikov felt in a

most unenviable frame of mind. Full of inward vexation, he blamed himself bitterly for having come to see this man and so wasted valuable time; but even more did he blame himself for having told him of his scheme—for having acted as carelessly as a child or a madman. Of a surety the scheme was not one which ought to have been confided to a man like Nozdrev, for he was a worthless fellow who might lie about it, and append additions to it, and spread such stories as would give rise to God knows what scandals. "This is indeed bad!" Chichikov said to himself. "I have been an absolute fool." Consequently he spent an uneasy night—his uneasiness being increased by the fact that a number of small, but vigorous, insects so feasted upon him that he could do nothing but scratch the spots and exclaim, "The devil take you and Nozdrev alike!" Only when morning was approaching did he fall asleep. On rising, he made it his first business (after donning dressing-gown and slippers) to cross the courtyard to the stable, for the purpose of ordering Selifan to harness the *britchka*. Just as he was returning from his errand he encountered Nozdrev, clad in a dressing-gown, and holding a pipe between his teeth.

Host and guest greeted one another in friendly fashion, and Nozdrev inquired how Chichikov had slept.

"Fairly well," replied Chichikov, but with a touch of dryness in his tone.

"The same with myself," said Nozdrev. "The truth is that such a lot of nasty brutes kept crawling over me that even to speak of it gives me the shudders. Likewise, as the effect of last night's doings, a whole squadron of soldiers seemed to be camping on my chest, and giving me a flogging. Ugh! And whom also do you think I saw in a dream? You would never guess. Why, it was Staff-Captain Potsieluev and Lieutenant Kuvshinnikov!"

"Yes," thought Chichikov to himself, "and I wish that they too would give you a public thrashing!"

"I felt so ill!" went on Nozdrev. "And just after I had fallen asleep something *did* come and sting me. Probably it was a party of hag fleas. Now, dress yourself, and I will be with you presently. First of all I must give that scoundrel of a bailiff a wigging."

Chichikov departed to his room to wash and dress; which process completed, he entered the dining-room to find the table laid with tea-things and a bottle of rum. Clearly no broom had yet touched the place, for there remained traces of the previous night's dinner and supper in the shape of crumbs strewn over the floor and tobacco ash on the tablecloth. The host himself, when he entered, was still clad in a dressing-gown exposing a hairy chest; and as he sat holding his pipe in his hand, and drinking tea from a cup, he would have made a model for the sort of painter who prefers to portray gentlemen of the less curled and scented order.

"What think you?" he asked of Chichikov after a short silence. "Are you willing *now* to play me for those souls?"

"I have told you that I never play cards. If the souls are for sale, I will buy them."

"I decline to sell them. Such would not be the course proper between friends. But a game of banker would be quite another matter. Let us deal the cards."

"I have told you that I decline to play."

"And you will not agree to an exchange?"

"No."

"Then look here. Suppose we play a game of chess. If you win, the souls shall be yours. There are a lot which I should like to see crossed off the revision list. Hi, Porphyri! Bring me the chessboard."

"You are wasting your time. I will play neither chess nor cards."

"But chess is different from playing with a bank. In chess there can be neither luck nor cheating, for everything depends upon skill. In fact, I warn you that I cannot possibly play with you unless you allow me a move or two in advance."

"The same with me," thought Chichikov. "Shall I, or shall I not, play this fellow? I used not to be a bad chess-player, and it is a sport in which he would find it more difficult to be up to his tricks."

"Very well," he added aloud. "I *will* play you at chess."

"And stake the souls for a hundred roubles?" asked Nozdrev.

"No. Why for a hundred? Would it not be sufficient to stake them for fifty?"

"No. What would be the use of fifty? Nevertheless, for the hundred roubles I will throw in a moderately old puppy, or else a gold seal and watch-chain."

"Very well," assented Chichikov.

"Then how many moves are you going to allow me?"

"Is *that* to be part of the bargain? Why, none, of course."

"At least allow me two."

"No, none. I myself am only a poor player."

" *I* know you and your poor play," said Nozdrev, moving a chessman.

" In fact, it is a long time since last I had a chessman in my hand," replied Chichikov, also moving a piece.

" Ah! *I* know you and your poor play," repeated Nozdrev, moving a second chessman.

" I say again that it is a long time since last I had a chessman in my hand." And Chichikov, in his turn, moved.

" Ah! *I* know you and your poor play," repeated Nozdrev, for the third time as he made a third move. At the same moment the cuff of one of his sleeves happened to dislodge another chessman from its position.

" Again, I say," said Chichikov, " that 'tis a long time since last——But hi! look here! Put that piece back in its place! "

" What piece? "

" This one." And almost as Chichikov spoke he saw a third chessman coming into view between the queens. God only knows whence that chessman had materialised.

" No, no! " shouted Chichikov as he rose from the table. " It is impossible to play with a man like you. People don't move three pieces at once."

" How ' three pieces'? All that I have done is to make a mistake—to move one of my pieces by accident. If you like, I will forfeit it to you."

" And whence has the third piece come? "

" What third piece? "

" The one now standing between the queens? "

" 'Tis one of your own pieces. Surely you are forgetting? "

" No, no, my friend. I have counted every move, and can remember each one. That piece has only just become added to the board. Put it back in its place, I say."

" Its place? Which *is* its place? " But Nozdrev had reddened a good deal. " I perceive you to be a strategist at the game."

" No, no, good friend. *You* are the strategist—though an unsuccessful one, as it happens."

" Then of what are you supposing me capable? Of cheating you? "

" I am not supposing you capable of anything. All that I say is that I will not play with you any more."

" But you can't refuse to," said Nozdrev, growing heated. " You see, the game has begun."

" Nevertheless I have a right not to continue it, seeing that you are not playing as an honest man should do."

" You are lying—you cannot truthfully say that."

" 'Tis you who are lying."

" But I have *not* cheated. Consequently you cannot refuse to play, but must continue the game to a finish."

" You cannot force me to play," retorted Chichikov coldly as, turning to the chessboard, he swept the pieces into confusion.

Nozdrev approached Chichikov in a manner so threatening that the other fell back a couple of paces.

" I *will* force you to play," said Nozdrev. " It is no use your making a mess of the chessboard, for I can remember every move. We will replace the chessmen exactly as they were."

" No, no, my friend. The game is over, and I play you no more."

" You say that you will not? "

" Yes. Surely you can see for yourself that such a thing is impossible? "

" That cock won't fight. Say at once that you refuse to play with me." And Nozdrev approached a step nearer.

" Very well; I *do* say that," replied Chichikov, and at the same moment raised his hands towards his face, for the dispute was growing heated. Nor was the act of caution altogether unwarranted, for Nozdrev also raised his fist, and it may be that one of our hero's plump, pleasant-looking cheeks would have sustained an indelible insult had not he (Chichikov) parried the blow and, seizing Nozdrev by his whirling arms, held them fast.

" Porphyri! Pavlushka! " shouted Nozdrev as madly he strove to free himself.

On hearing the words, Chichikov, both because he wished to avoid rendering the servants witnesses of the unedifying scene and because he felt that it would be of no avail to hold Nozdrev any longer, let go of the latter's arms; but at the same moment Porphyri and Pavlushka entered the room—a pair of stout rascals with whom it would be unwise to meddle.

" Do you, or do you not, intend to finish the game? " said Nozdrev. " Give me a direct answer."

" No; it will not be possible to finish the game," replied Chichikov, glancing out of the window. He could see his *britchka* standing ready for him, and Selifan evidently awaiting orders to draw up to the entrance steps. But from the room there was no escape, since in the doorway was posted the couple of well-built serving-men.

" Then it is as I say? You refuse to finish the game? " repeated Nozdrev, his face as red as fire.

" I would have finished it had you played like a man of honour. But, as it is, I cannot."

" You cannot, eh, you villain? You find that you cannot as soon as you find that you are not winning? Thrash him, you fellows!" And as he spoke Nozdrev grasped the cherrywood shank of his pipe. Chichikov turned as white as a sheet. He tried to say something, but his quivering lips emitted no sound. " Thrash him!" again shouted Nozdrev as he rushed forward in a state of heat and perspiration more proper to a warrior who is attacking an impregnable fortress. " Thrash him!" again he shouted in a voice like that of some half-demented lieutenant whose desperate bravery has acquired such a reputation that orders have had to be issued that his hands shall be held lest he attempt deeds of over-presumptuous daring. Seized with the military spirit, however, the lieutenant's head begins to whirl, and before his eye there flits the image of Suvorov.[1] He advances to the great encounter, and impulsively cries, " Forward, my sons!"—cries it without reflecting that he may be spoiling the plan of the general attack, that millions of rifles may be protruding their muzzles through the embrasures of the impregnable, towering walls of the fortress, that his own impotent assault may be destined to be dissipated like dust before the wind, and that already there may have been launched on its whistling career the bullet which is to close for ever his vociferous throat. However, if Nozdrev resembled the headstrong, desperate lieutenant whom we have just pictured as advancing upon a fortress, at least the fortress itself in no way resembled the impregnable stronghold which I have described. As a matter of fact, the fortress became seized with a panic which drove its spirit into its boots. First of all, the chair with which Chichikov (the fortress in question) sought to defend himself was wrested from his grasp by the serfs, and then—blinking and half alive nor dead—he turned to parry the Circassian pipe-stem of his host. In fact, God only knows what would have happened had not the fates been pleased by a miracle to deliver Chichikov's elegant back and shoulders from the onslaught. Suddenly, and as unexpectedly as though the sound had come from the clouds, there made itself heard the tinkling notes of a collar-bell, and then the rumble of wheels approaching the entrance steps, and, lastly, the snorting and hard breathing of a team of horses as a

[1] The great Russian general who, after winning fame in the Seven Years' War, met with disaster when attempting to assist the Austrians against the French in 1799.

vehicle came to a standstill. Involuntarily all present glanced through the window, and saw a man clad in a semi-military greatcoat leap from a buggy. After making an inquiry or two in the hall, he entered the dining-room just at the juncture when Chichikov, almost swooning with terror, had found himself placed in about as awkward a situation as could well befall a mortal man.

" Kindly tell me which of you gentlemen is Monsieur Nozdrev? " said the unknown with a glance of perplexity both at the person named (who was still standing with pipe-shank upraised) and at Chichikov (who was just beginning to recover from his unpleasant predicament).

" Kindly tell *me* whom I have the honour of addressing? " retorted Nozdrev as he approached the official.

" I am the Superintendent of Rural Police."

" And what do you want? "

" I have come to fulfil a commission imposed upon me. That is to say, I have come to place you under arrest until your case shall have been decided."

" Rubbish! What case, pray? "

" The case in which you involved yourself when, in a drunken condition, and through the instrumentality of a walking-stick, you offered grave offence to the person of Landowner Maksimov."

" You lie! To your face I tell you that never in my life have I set eyes upon Landowner Maksimov."

" Good sir, allow me to represent to you that I am a Government officer. Speeches like that you may address to your servants, but not to me."

At this point Chichikov, without waiting for Nozdrev's reply, seized his cap, slipped behind the Superintendent's back, rushed out on to the verandah, sprang into his *britchka*, and ordered Selifan to drive like the wind.

V

CERTAINLY Chichikov was a thorough coward, for, although the *britchka* pursued its headlong course until Nozdrev's establishment had disappeared behind hillocks and hedgerows, our hero continued to glance nervously behind him, as though every moment expecting to see a stern chase begin. His breath came with difficulty, and when he tried his heart with his hands he could feel it fluttering like a quail caught in a net.

"What a sweat the fellow has thrown me into!" he thought to himself, while many a dire and forceful aspiration passed through his mind. Indeed, the expressions to which he gave vent were most inelegant in their nature. But what was to be done next? He was a Russian, and thoroughly aroused. The affair had been no joke. "But for the Superintendent," he reflected, "I might never again have looked upon God's daylight—I might have vanished like a bubble on a pool, and left neither trace nor posterity nor property nor an honourable name for my future offspring to inherit!" (it seemed that our hero was particularly anxious with regard to his possible issue).

"What a scurvy *barin!*" mused Selifan as he drove along. "Never have I seen such a *barin*. I should like to spit in his face. 'Tis better to allow a man nothing to eat than to refuse to feed a horse properly. A horse needs his oats—they are his proper fare. Even if you make a man procure his meals at his own expense, don't deny a horse his oats, for he ought always to have them."

An equally poor opinion of Nozdrev seemed to be cherished also by the steeds, for not only were the bay and the Assessor clearly out of spirits, but even the skewbald was wearing a dejected air. True, at home the skewbald got none but the poorer sort of oats to eat, and Selifan never filled his trough without having first called him a villain; but at least they *were* oats, and not hay—they were stuff which could be chewed with a certain amount of relish. Also, there was the fact that at intervals he could intrude his long nose into his companions' troughs (especially when Selifan happened to be absent from the stable) and ascertain what *their* provender was like. But at Nozdrev's there had been nothing but hay! That was not right. All three horses felt greatly discontented.

But presently the malcontents had their reflections cut short in a very rude and unexpected manner. That is to say, they were brought back to practicalities by coming into violent collision with a six-horsed vehicle, while upon their heads descended both a babel of cries from the ladies inside and a storm of curses and abuse from the coachman. "Ah, you damned fool!" he vociferated. "I shouted to you loud enough! Draw out, you old raven, and keep to the right! Are you drunk." Selifan himself felt conscious that he had been careless, but since a Russian does not care to admit a fault in the presence of strangers, he retorted with dignity: "Why have you run into *us?* Did you leave your eyes behind you at the last tavern that you stopped at?" With that he started to back the *britchka*, in the hope that it might get clear of the other's harness; but this would not do, for the pair were too hopelessly intertwined. Meanwhile the skewbald snuffed curiously at his new acquaintances as they stood planted on either side of him; while the ladies in the vehicle regarded the scene with an expression of terror. One of them was an old woman, and the other a damsel of about sixteen. A mass of golden hair fell daintily from a small head, and the oval of her comely face was as shapely as an egg, and white with the transparent whiteness seen when the hands of a housewife hold a new-laid egg to the light to let the sun's rays filter through its shell. The same tint marked the maiden's ears where they glowed in the sunshine, and, in short, what with the tears in her wide-open, arresting eyes, she presented so attractive a picture that our hero bestowed upon it more than a passing glance before he turned his attention to the hubbub which was being raised among the horses and the coachmen.

"Back out, you rook of Nizhni Novgorod!" the strangers' coachman shouted. Selifan tightened his reins, and the other driver did the same. The horses stepped back a little, and then came together again—this time getting a leg or two over the traces. In fact, so pleased did the skewbald seem with his new friends that he refused to stir from the *mêlée* into which an unforeseen chance had plunged him. Laying his muzzle lovingly upon the neck of one of his recently-acquired acquaintances, he seemed to be whispering something in that acquaintance's ear—and whispering pretty nonsense, too, to judge from the way in which that confidant kept shaking his ears.

At length peasants from a village which happened to be near the scene of the accident tackled the mess; and since a spectacle of that kind is to the Russian *muzhik* what a newspaper or a club-meeting is to the German, the vehicles soon became the centre of a crowd, and the village denuded even of its old women and children. The traces were disentangled, and a few slaps on the nose forced the skewbald to draw back a little; after which the teams were straightened out and separated. Nevertheless, either sheer obstinacy or vexation at being parted from their new friends caused the strange team absolutely to refuse to move a leg. Their driver laid the whip about them, but still they stood as though rooted to the spot. At length the participatory efforts of the peasants rose to an unprecedented degree of enthusiasm, and they shouted in an intermittent chorus the advice, "Do you, Andrusha, take the head of the trace horse on the right, while Uncle Mitai mounts the shaft horse. Get up, Uncle Mitai."

Upon that the lean, long, and red-bearded Uncle Mitai mounted
the shaft horse; in which position he looked like a village steeple
or the winder which is used to raise water from wells. The
coachman whipped up his steeds afresh, but nothing came of
it, and Uncle Mitai had proved useless. " Hold on, hold on! "
shouted the peasants again. " Do you, Uncle Mitai, mount the
trace horse, while Uncle Minai mounts the shaft horse." Whereupon Uncle Minai—a peasant with a pair of broad shoulders, a
beard as black as charcoal, and a belly like the huge *samovar* in
which *sbiten* is brewed for all attending a local market—hastened
to seat himself upon the shaft horse, which almost sank to the
ground beneath his weight. " *Now* they will go all right! " the
muzhiks exclaimed. " Lay it on hot, lay it on hot! Give that
sorrel horse the whip, and make him squirm like a *koramora*." [1]
Nevertheless the affair in no way progressed; wherefore, seeing
that flogging was of no use, Uncles Mitai and Minai *both* mounted
the sorrel, while Andrusha seated himself upon the trace horse.
Then the coachman himself lost patience, and sent the two
Uncles about their business—and not before it was time, seeing
that the horses were steaming in a way that made it clear that,
unless they were first winded, they would never reach the next
posthouse. So they were given a moment's rest. That done,
they moved off of their own accord!

Throughout, Chichikov had been gazing at the young unknown with great attention, and had even made one or two
attempts to enter into conversation with her: but without
success. Indeed, when the ladies departed, it was as in a dream
that he saw the girl's comely presence, the delicate features of
her face, and the slender outline of her form vanish from his
sight; it was as in a dream that once more he saw only the road,
the *britchka*, the three horses, Selifan, and the bare, empty fields.
Everywhere in life—yes, even in the plainest, the dingiest ranks
of society, as much as in those which are uniformly bright and
presentable—a man may happen upon some phenomenon which
is so entirely different from anything hitherto known to his
experience that it arouses in him feelings different from those
which have hitherto fallen to his lot. Everywhere through the
web of sorrow of which our lives are woven there may suddenly
break a clear, radiant thread of joy; even as suddenly along the
street of some poor, poverty-stricken village which, ordinarily,
sees nought but a farm waggon there may come bowling a
gorgeous coach with plated harness, picturesque horses, and a

[1] A kind of large gnat.

glitter of glass, so that the peasants stand gaping, and do not resume their caps until long after the strange equipage has become lost to sight. Thus the golden-haired maiden makes a sudden, unexpected appearance in our story, and as suddenly, as unexpectedly, disappears. Indeed, had it not been that the person concerned was Chichikov, and not some youth of twenty summers—a hussar or a student or, in general, a man standing on the threshold of life—what thoughts would not have sprung to birth, and stirred and spoken, within him; for what a length of time would he not have stood entranced as he stared into the distance and forgot alike his journey, the business still to be done, the possibility of incurring loss through lingering—himself, his vocation, the world, and everything else that the world contains!

But in the present case the hero was a man of middle-age, and of cautious and frigid temperament. True, he pondered over the incident, but in more deliberate fashion than a younger man would have done. That is to say, his reflections were not so irresponsible and unsteady. "She was a comely damsel," he said to himself as he opened his snuff-box and took a pinch. "But the important point is: Is she also a *nice damsel?* One thing she has in her favour—and that is that she appears only just to have left school, and not to have had time to become womanly in the worser sense. At present, therefore, she is like a child. Everything in her is simple, and she says just what she thinks, and laughs merely when she feels inclined. Such a damsel might be made into anything—or she might be turned into worthless rubbish. The latter, I surmise, for trudging after her she will have a fond mother and a bevy of aunts, and so forth—persons who, within a year, will have filled her with womanishness to the point where her own father wouldn't know her. And to that there will be added pride and affectation, and she will begin to observe established rules, and to rack her brains as to how, and how much, she ought to talk, and to whom, and where, and so forth. Every moment will see her growing timorous and confused lest she be saying too much. Finally, she will develop into a confirmed prevaricator, and end by marrying the devil knows whom!" Chichikov paused awhile. Then he went on: "Yet I should like to know who she is, and who her father is, and whether he is a rich landowner of good standing, or merely a respectable man who has acquired a fortune in the service of the Government. Should he allow her, on marriage, a dowry of, say, two hundred thousand roubles, she will be a very nice catch indeed. She might even, so to speak, make a man of good breeding happy."

Indeed, so attractively did the idea of the two hundred thousand roubles begin to dance before his imagination that he felt a twinge of self-reproach because, during the hubbub, he had not inquired of the postillion or the coachman who the travellers might be. But soon the sight of Sobakevitch's country house dissipated his thoughts, and forced him to return to his stock subject of reflection.

Sobakevitch's country house and estate were of very fair size, and on each side of the mansion were expanses of birch and pine forest in two shades of green. The wooden edifice itself had dark-grey walls and a red-gabled roof, for it was a mansion of the kind which Russia builds for her military settlers and for German colonists. A noticeable circumstance was the fact that the taste of the architect had differed from that of the proprietor —the former having manifestly been a pedant and desirous of symmetry, and the latter having wished only for comfort. Consequently he (the proprietor) had dispensed with all windows on one side of the mansion, and had caused to be inserted, in their place, only a small aperture which, doubtless, was intended to light an otherwise dark lumber-room. Likewise, the architect's best efforts had failed to cause the pediment to stand in the centre of the building, since the proprietor had had one of its four original columns removed. Evidently durability had been considered throughout, for the courtyard was enclosed by a strong and very high wooden fence, and both the stables, the coach-house, and the culinary premises were partially constructed of beams warranted to last for centuries. Nay, even the wooden huts of the peasantry were wonderful in the solidity of their construction, and not a clay wall or a carved pattern or other device was to be seen. Everything fitted exactly into its right place, and even the draw-well of the mansion was fashioned of the oakwood usually thought suitable only for mills or ships. In short, wherever Chichikov's eye turned he saw nothing that was not free from shoddy and well and skilfully arranged. As he approached the entrance steps he caught sight of two faces peering from a window. One of them was that of a woman in a mobcap with features as long and as narrow as a cucumber, and the other that of a man with features as broad and as short as the Moldavian pumpkins (known as *gorlianki*) whereof *balalaiki*—the species of light, two-stringed instrument which constitutes the pride and the joy of the gay young fellow of twenty as he sits winking and smiling at the white-necked, white-bosomed maidens who have gathered to listen to his low-pitched tinkling—are fashioned. This scrutiny made, both faces withdrew, and there came out on to the entrance steps a lacquey clad in a grey jacket and a stiff blue collar. This functionary conducted Chichikov into the hall, where he was met by the master of the house himself, who requested his guest to enter, and then led him into the inner part of the mansion.

A covert glance at Sobakevitch showed our hero that his host exactly resembled a moderate-sized bear. To complete the resemblance, Sobakevitch's long frockcoat and baggy trousers were of the precise colour of a bear's hide, while, when shuffling across the floor, he made a criss-cross motion of the legs, and had, in addition, a constant habit of treading upon his companion's toes. As for his face, it was of the warm, ardent tint of a *piatok*.[1] Persons of this kind—persons to whose designing nature has devoted not much thought, and in the fashioning of whose frames she has used no instruments so delicate as a file or a gimlet and so forth—are not uncommon. Such persons she merely roughhews. One cut with a hatchet, and there results a nose; another such cut with a hatchet, and there materialises a pair of lips; two thrusts with a drill, and there issues a pair of eyes. Lastly, scorning to plane down the roughness, she sends out that person into the world, saying: "Here is another live creature." Sobakevitch was just such a ragged, curiously put together figure—though the above model would seem to have been followed more in his upper portion than in his lower. One result was that he seldom turned his head to look at the person with whom he was speaking, but, rather, directed his eyes towards, say, the stove corner or the doorway. As host and guest crossed the dining-room Chichikov directed a second glance at his companion. "He is a bear, and nothing but a bear," he thought to himself. And, indeed, the strange comparison was inevitable. Incidentally, Sobakevitch's Christian name and patronymic were Michael Semenovitch. Of his habit of treading upon other people's toes Chichikov had become fully aware; wherefore he stepped cautiously, and, throughout, allowed his host to take the lead. As a matter of fact, Sobakevitch himself seemed conscious of his failing, for at intervals he would inquire: "I hope I have not hurt you?" and Chichikov, with a word of thanks, would reply that as yet he had sustained no injury.

[1] A copper coin worth five kopecks.

At length they reached the drawing-room, where Sobakevitch pointed to an armchair, and invited his guest to be seated. Chichikov gazed with interest at the walls and the pictures. In every such picture there were portrayed either young men or Greek generals of the type of Mavrogordato (clad in a red uniform and breeches), Kanaris, and others; and all these heroes were depicted with a solidity of thigh and a wealth of moustache which made the beholder simply shudder with awe. Among them there were placed also, according to some unknown system, and for some unknown reason, firstly, Bagration [1]—tall and thin, and with a cluster of small flags and cannon beneath him, and the whole set in the narrowest of frames—and, secondly, the Greek heroine, Bobelina, whose legs looked larger than do the whole bodies of the drawing-room dandies of the present day. Apparently the master of the house was himself a man of health and strength, and therefore liked to have his apartments adorned with none but folk of equal vigour and robustness. Lastly, in the window, and suspended cheek by jowl with Bobelina, there hung a cage whence at intervals there peered forth a white-spotted blackbird. Like everything else in the apartment, it bore a strong resemblance to Sobakevitch. When host and guest had been conversing for two minutes or so the door opened, and there entered the hostess—a tall lady in a cap adorned with ribands of domestic colouring and manufacture. She entered deliberately, and held her head as erect as a palm.

" This is my wife, Theodulia Ivanovna," said Sobakevitch.

Chichikov approached and took her hand. The fact that she raised it nearly to the level of his lips apprised him of the circumstance that it had just been rinsed in cucumber oil.

" My dear, allow me to introduce Paul Ivanovitch Chichikov," added Sobakevitch. " He has the honour of being acquainted both with our Governor and with our Postmaster."

Upon this Theodulia Ivanovna requested her guest to be seated, and accompanied the invitation with the kind of bow usually employed only by actresses who are playing the rôle of queens. Next, she took a seat upon the sofa, drew around her her merino gown, and sat thereafter without moving an eyelid or an eyebrow. As for Chichikov, he glanced upwards, and once more caught sight of Kanaris with his fat thighs and interminable moustache, and of Bobelina and the blackbird. For fully five minutes all present preserved a complete silence — the only

[1] A Russian general who fought against Napoleon, and was mortally wounded at Borodino.

sound audible being that of the blackbird's beak against the wooden floor of the cage as the creature fished for grains of corn. Meanwhile Chichikov again surveyed the room, and saw that everything in it was massive and clumsy in the highest degree; as also that everything was curiously in keeping with the master of the house. For example, in one corner of the apartment there stood a hazelwood bureau with a bulging body on four grotesque legs—the perfect image of a bear. Also, the tables and the chairs were of the same ponderous, unrestful order, and every single article in the room appeared to be saying either, " I, too, am a Sobakevitch," or " I am exactly like Sobakevitch."

" I heard speak of you one day when I was visiting the President of the Council," said Chichikov, on perceiving that no one else had a mind to begin a conversation. " That was on Thursday last. We had a very pleasant evening."

" Yes, on that occasion I was not there," replied Sobakevitch.

" What a nice man he is ! "

" Who is ? " inquired Sobakevitch, gazing into the corner by the stove.

" The President of the Local Council."

" Did he seem so to you? True, he is a mason, but he is also the greatest fool that the world ever saw."

Chichikov started a little at this mordant criticism, but soon pulled himself together again, and continued:

" Of course, every man has his weakness. Yet the President seems to be an excellent fellow."

" And do you think the same of the Governor? "

" Yes. Why not? "

" Because there exists no greater rogue than he."

" What? The Governor a rogue? " ejaculated Chichikov, at a loss to understand how the official in question could come to be numbered with thieves. " Let me say that I should never have guessed it. Permit me also to remark that his conduct would scarcely seem to bear out your opinion—he seems so gentle a man." And in proof of this Chichikov cited the purses which the Governor knitted, and also expatiated on the mildness of his features.

" He has the face of a robber," said Sobakevitch. " Were you to give him a knife, and to turn him loose on a turnpike, he would cut your throat for about two kopecks. And the same with the Vice-Governor. The pair are just Gog and Magog."

" Evidently he is not on good terms with them," thought Chichikov to himself. " I had better pass to the Chief of Police, with whom he *does* seem to be friendly." Accordingly he added aloud: "For my own part, I should give the preference to the Head of the Gendarmery. What a frank, outspoken nature he has! And what an element of simplicity does his expression contain!"

"He is mean to the core," remarked Sobakevitch coldly. "He will sell you and cheat you, and then dine at your table. Yes, I know them all, and every one of them is a swindler, and the town a nest of rascals engaged in robbing one another. Not a man of the lot is there but would sell Christ. Yet stay: *one* decent fellow there is—the Public Prosecutor; though even *he*, if the truth be told, is little better than a pig."

After these eulogia Chichikov saw that it would be useless to continue running through the list of officials—more especially since suddenly he had remembered that Sobakevitch was not at any time given to commending his fellow man.

"Let us go to luncheon, my dear," put in Theodulia Ivanovna to her spouse.

"Yes; pray come to table," said Sobakevitch to his guest; whereupon they consumed the customary glass of *vodka* (accompanied by sundry snacks of salted cucumber and other dainties) with which Russians, both in town and country, preface a meal. Then they filed into the dining-room in the wake of the hostess, who sailed on ahead like a goose swimming across a pond. The small dining-table was found to be laid for four persons—the fourth place being occupied by a lady or a young girl (it would have been difficult to say which exactly) who might have been either a relative, the housekeeper, or a casual visitor. Certain persons in the word exist, not as personalities in themselves, but as spots or specks on the personalities of others. Always they are to be seen sitting in the same place, and holding their heads at exactly the same angle, so that one comes within an ace of mistaking them for furniture, and thinks to oneself that never since the day of their birth can they have spoken a single word.

"My dear," said Sobakevitch, "the cabbage soup is excellent." With that he finished his portion, and helped himself to a generous measure of *niania* [1]—the dish which follows *shtchi* and consists of a sheep's stomach stuffed with black porridge, brains, and other things. "What *niania* this is!" he added to Chichikov. "Never would you get such stuff in a town, where one is given the devil knows what."

"Nevertheless the Governor keeps a fair table," said Chichikov.

[1] Literally, "nursemaid."

" Yes; but do you know what all the stuff is *made of*? " retorted Sobakevitch. " If you *did* know you would never touch it."

" Of course I am not in a position to say how it is prepared, but at least the pork cutlets and the boiled fish seemed excellent."

" Ah, it might have been thought so; yet I know the way in which such things are bought in the market-place. They are bought by some rascal of a cook whom a Frenchman has taught how to skin a tomcat and then serve it up as hare."

" Ugh! What horrible things you say! " put in Madame.

" Well, my dear, that is how things are done, and it is no fault of mine that it is so. Moreover, everything that is left over —everything that *we* (pardon me for mentioning it) cast into the slop-pail—is used by such folk for making soup."

" Always at table you begin talking like this! " objected his helpmeet.

" And why not? " said Sobakevitch. " I tell you straight that I would not eat such nastiness, even had I made it myself. Sugar a frog as much as you like, but never shall it pass *my* lips. Nor would I swallow an oyster, for I know only too well what an oyster may resemble. But have some mutton, friend Chichikov. It is shoulder of mutton, and very different stuff from the mutton which they cook in noble kitchens—mutton which has been kicking about the market-place four days or more. All that sort of cookery has been invented by French and German doctors, and I should like to hang them for having done so. They go and prescribe diets and a hunger cure as though what suits their flaccid German systems will agree with a Russian stomach! Such devices are no good at all." Sobakevitch shook his head wrathfully. " Fellows like those are for ever talking of civilisa- tion. As if *that* sort of thing was civilisation! Phew! " (Perhaps the speaker's concluding exclamation would have been even stronger had he not been seated at table.) " For myself, I will have none of it. When I eat pork at a meal, give me the *whole* pig; when mutton, the *whole* sheep; when goose, the *whole* of the bird. Two dishes are better than a thousand, provided that one can eat of them as much as one wants."

And he proceeded to put precept into practice by taking half the shoulder of mutton on to his plate, and then devouring it down to the last morsel of gristle and bone.

" My word! " reflected Chichikov. " The fellow has a pretty good holding capacity! "

" None of it for me," repeated Sobakevitch as he wiped his

hands on his napkin. " I don't intend to be like a fellow named Plushkin, who owns eight hundred souls, yet dines worse than does my shepherd."

" Who is Plushkin ? " asked Chichikov.

" A miser," replied Sobakevitch. " Such a miser as never you could imagine. Even convicts in a prison live better than he does. And he starves his servants as well."

" Really ? " ejaculated Chichikov, greatly interested. " Should you, then, say that he has lost many peasants by death ? "

" Certainly. They keep dying like flies."

" Then how far from here does he reside ? "

" About five versts."

" Only five versts ? " exclaimed Chichikov, feeling his heart beating joyously. " Ought one, when leaving your gates, to turn to the right or to the left ? "

" I should be sorry to tell you the way to the house of such a cur," said Sobakevitch. " A man had far better go to hell than to Plushkin's."

" Quite so," responded Chichikov. " My only reason for asking you is that it interests me to become acquainted with any and every sort of locality."

To the shoulder of mutton there succeeded, in turn, cutlets (each one larger than a plate), a turkey of about the size of a calf, eggs, rice, pastry, and every conceivable thing which could possibly be put into a stomach. There the meal ended. When he rose from table Chichikov felt as though a *pood's* weight were inside him. In the drawing-room the company found dessert awaiting them in the shape of pears, plums, and apples; but since neither host nor guest could tackle these particular dainties the hostess removed them to another room. Taking advantage of her absence, Chichikov turned to Sobakevitch (who, prone in an armchair, seemed, after his ponderous meal, to be capable of doing little beyond belching and grunting— each such grunt or belch necessitating a subsequent signing of the cross over the mouth), and intimated to him a desire to have a little private conversation concerning a certain matter. At this moment the hostess returned.

" Here is more dessert," she said. " Pray have a few radishes stewed in honey."

" Later, later," replied Sobakevitch. " Do you go to your room, and Paul Ivanovitch and I will take off our coats and have a nap."

Upon this the good lady expressed her readiness to send for

feather beds and cushions, but her husband expressed a preference for slumbering in an armchair, and she therefore departed. When she had gone Sobakevitch inclined his head in an attitude of willingness to listen to Chichikov's business. Our hero began in a sort of detached manner—touching lightly upon the subject of the Russian Empire, and expatiating upon the immensity of the same, and saying that even the Empire of Ancient Rome had been of considerably smaller dimensions. Meanwhile Sobakevitch sat with his head drooping.

From that Chichikov went on to remark that, according to the statutes of the said Russian Empire (which yielded to none in glory—so much so that foreigners marvelled at it), peasants on the census lists who had ended their earthly careers were nevertheless, on the rendering of new lists, returned equally with the living, to the end that the courts might be relieved of a multitude of trifling, useless emendations which might complicate the already sufficiently complex mechanism of the State. Nevertheless, said Chichikov, the general equity of this measure did not obviate a certain amount of annoyance to landowners, since it forced them to pay upon a non-living article the tax due upon a living. Hence (our hero concluded) he (Chichikov) was prepared, owing to the personal respect which he felt for Sobakevitch, to relieve him, in part, of the irksome obligation referred to (in passing, it may be said that Chichikov referred to his principal point only guardedly, for he called the souls which he was seeking not " dead," but " non-existent ").

Meanwhile Sobakevitch listened with bent head; though something like a trace of expression dawned in his face as he did so. Ordinarily his body lacked a soul—or, if he did possess a soul, he seemed to keep it elsewhere than where it ought to have been; so that, buried beneath mountains (as it were) or enclosed within a massive shell, its movements produced no sort of agitation on the surface.

" Well? " said Chichikov—though not without a certain tremor of diffidence as to the possible response.

" You are after dead souls? " were Sobakevitch's perfectly simple words. He spoke without the least surprise in his tone, and much as though the conversation had been turning on grain.

" Yes," replied Chichikov, and then, as before, softened down the expression " dead souls."

" They are to be found," said Sobakevitch. " Why should they not be? "

" Then of course you will be glad to get rid of any that you may chance to have? "

" Yes, I shall have no objection to *selling* them." At this point the speaker raised his head a little, for it had struck him that surely the would-be buyer must have some advantage in view.

" The devil! " thought Chichikov to himself. " Here is he selling the goods before I have even had time to utter a word! "

" And what about the price? " he added aloud. " Of course, the articles are not of a kind very easy to appraise."

" I should be sorry to ask too much," said Sobakevitch. " How would a hundred roubles per head suit you? "

" What? A hundred roubles per head? " Chichikov stared open-mouthed at his host—doubting whether he had heard aright, or whether his host's slow-moving tongue might not have inadvertently substituted one word for another.

" Yes. Is that too much for you? " said Sobakevitch. Then he added: " What is your own price? "

" My own price? I think that we cannot properly have understood one another—that you must have forgotten of what the goods consist. With my hand on my heart do I submit that eight *grivni* per soul would be a handsome, a *very* handsome, offer."

" What? Eight *grivni*? "

" In my opinion, a higher offer would be impossible."

" But I am not a seller of boots."

" No; yet you, for your part, will agree that these souls are not live human beings? "

" I suppose you hope to find fools ready to sell you souls on the census list for a couple of groats apiece? "

" Pardon me, but why do you use the term ' on the census list '? The souls themselves have long since passed away, and have left behind them only their names. Not to trouble you with any further discussion of the subject, I can offer you a rouble and a half per head, but no more."

" You should be ashamed even to mention such a sum! Since you deal in articles of this kind, quote me a genuine price."

" I cannot, Michael Semenovitch. Believe me, I cannot. What a man cannot do, that he cannot do." The speaker ended by advancing another half-rouble per head.

" But why hang back with your money? " said Sobakevitch. " Of a truth I am not asking much of you. Any other rascal than myself would have cheated you by selling you old rubbish instead of good, genuine souls, whereas I should be ready to give you of my best, even were you buying only nut-kernels. For instance, look at wheelwright Michiev. Never was there such a one to build spring carts! And his handiwork was not like your Moscow handiwork—good only for an hour. No, he did it all himself, even down to the varnishing."

Chichikov opened his mouth to remark that, nevertheless, the said Michiev had long since departed this world; but Sobakevitch's eloquence had got too thoroughly into its stride to admit of any interruption.

"And look, too, at Probka Stepan, the carpenter," his host went on. "I will wager my head that nowhere else would you find such a workman. What a strong fellow he was! He had served in the Guards, and the Lord only knows what they had given for him, seeing that he was over three *arshins* in height."

Again Chichikov tried to remark that Probka was dead, but Sobakevitch's tongue was borne on the torrent of its own verbiage, and the only thing to be done was to listen.

"And Milushkin, the bricklayer! He could build a stove in any house you liked! And Maksim Teliatnikov, the bootmaker! Anything that he drove his awl into became a pair of boots—and boots for which you would be thankful, although he *was* a bit foul of the mouth. And Eremi Sorokoplechin, too! He was the best of the lot, and used to work at his trade in Moscow, where he paid a tax of five hundred roubles. Well, *there's* an assortment of serfs for you!—a very different assortment from what Plushkin would sell you!"

"But permit me," at length put in Chichikov, astounded at this flood of eloquence to which there appeared to be no end. "Permit me, I say, to inquire why you enumerate the talents of the deceased, seeing that they are all of them dead, and that therefore there can be no sense in doing so. 'A dead body is only good to prop a fence with,' says the proverb."

"Of course they are dead," replied Sobakevitch, but rather as though the idea had only just occurred to him, and was giving him food for thought. "But tell me, now: what is the use of listing them as still alive? And what is the use of them themselves? They are flies, not human beings."

"Well," said Chichikov, "they exist, though only in idea."

"But no—*not* only in idea. I tell you that nowhere else would you find such a fellow for working heavy tools as was Michiev. He had the strength of a horse in his shoulders." And, with the words, Sobakevitch turned, as though for corroboration, to the portrait of Bagration, as is frequently done by one of the parties in a dispute when he purports to appeal to an extraneous individual who is not only unknown to him, but wholly unconnected with the subject in hand; with the result that the individual is left in doubt whether to make a reply, or whether to betake himself elsewhere.

"Nevertheless I *cannot* give you more than two roubles per head," said Chichikov.

"Well, as I don't want you to swear that I have asked too much of you and won't meet you halfway, suppose, for friendship's sake, that you pay me seventy-five roubles in *assignats* ?"

"Good heavens!" thought Chichikov to himself. "Does the man take me for a fool?" Then he added aloud: "The situation seems to me a strange one, for it is as though we were performing a stage comedy. No other explanation would meet the case. Yet you appear to be a man of sense, and possessed of some education. The matter is a very simple one. The question is: what is a dead soul worth, and is it of any use to any one?"

"It is of use to *you*, or you would not be buying such articles."

Chichikov bit his lip, and stood at a loss for a retort. He tried to say something about "family and domestic circumstances," but Sobakevitch cut him short with:

"I don't want to know your private affairs, for I never poke my nose into such things. You need the souls, and I am ready to sell them. Should you not buy them, I think you will repent it."

"Two roubles is my price," repeated Chichikov.

"Come, come! As you have named that sum, I can understand your not liking to go back upon it; but quote me a *bona fide* figure."

"The devil fly away with him!" mused Chichikov. "However, I will add another half-rouble." And he did so.

"Indeed?" said Sobakevitch. "Well, my last word upon it is—fifty roubles in *assignats*. That will mean a sheer loss to me, for nowhere else in the world could you buy better souls than mine."

"The old skinflint!" muttered Chichikov. Then he added aloud, with irritation in his tone: "See here. This is a serious matter. Any one but you would be thankful to get rid of the souls. Only a fool would stick to them, and continue to pay the tax."

"Yes, but remember (and I say it wholly in a friendly way) that transactions of this kind are not generally allowed, and that any one would say that a man who engages in them must have some rather doubtful advantage in view."

"Have it your own way," said Chichikov with assumed indifference. "As a matter of fact, I am not purchasing for profit, as you suppose, but to humour a certain whim of mine. Two and a half roubles is the most that I can offer."

"Bless your heart!" retorted the host. "At least give me thirty roubles in *assignats*, and take the lot."

"No, for I see that you are unwilling to sell. I must say good-day to you."

"Hold on, hold on!" exclaimed Sobakevitch, retaining his guest's hand, and at the same moment treading heavily upon his toes—so heavily, indeed, that Chichikov gasped and danced with the pain.

"I *beg* your pardon!" said Sobakevitch hastily. "Evidently I have hurt you. Pray sit down again."

"No," retorted Chichikov. "I am merely wasting my time, and must be off."

"Oh, sit down just for a moment. I have something more agreeable to say." And, drawing closer to his guest, Sobakevitch whispered in his ear, as though communicating to him a secret: "How about twenty-five roubles?"

"No, no, no!" exclaimed Chichikov. "I won't give you even a *quarter* of that. I won't advance another kopeck."

For a while Sobakevitch remained silent, and Chichikov did the same. This lasted for a couple of minutes, and, meanwhile, the aquiline-nozed Bagration gazed from the wall as though much interested in the bargaining.

"What is your outside price?" at length said Sobakevitch.

"Two and a half roubles."

"Then you seem to rate a human soul at about the same value as a boiled turnip. At least give me *three* roubles."

"No, I cannot."

"Pardon me, but you are an impossible man to deal with. However, even though it will mean a dead loss to me, and you have not shown a very nice spirit about it, I cannot well refuse to please a friend. I suppose a purchase deed had better be made out in order to have everything in order?"

"Of course."

"Then for that purpose let us repair to the town."

The affair ended in their deciding to do this on the morrow, and to arrange for the signing of a deed of purchase. Next, Chichikov requested a list of the peasants; to which Sobakevitch readily agreed. Indeed, he went to his writing-desk then and there, and started to indite a list which gave not only the peasants' names, but also their late qualifications.

Meanwhile Chichikov, having nothing else to do, stood looking at the spacious form of his host; and as he gazed at his back as broad as that of a cart horse, and at the legs as massive as the iron standards which adorn a street, he could not help inwardly ejaculating:

"Truly God has endowed you with much! Though not adjusted with nicety, at least you are strongly built. I wonder whether you were born a bear or whether you have come to it through your rustic life, with its tilling of crops and its trading with peasants? Yet no; I believe that, even if you had received a fashionable education, and had mixed with society, and had lived in St. Petersburg, you would still have been just the *kulak*[1] that you are. The only difference is that circumstances, as they stand, permit of your polishing off a stuffed shoulder of mutton at a meal; whereas in St. Petersburg you would have been unable to do so. Also, as circumstances stand, you have under you a number of peasants, whom you treat well for the reason that they are your property; whereas, otherwise, you would have had under you *tchinovniks :*[2] whom you would have bullied because they were *not* your property. Also, you would have robbed the Treasury, since a *kulak* always remains a money-grubber.

"The list is ready," said Sobakevitch, turning round.

"Indeed? Then please let me look at it." Chichikov ran his eye over the document, and could not but marvel at its neatness and accuracy. Not only were there set forth in it the trade, the age, and the pedigree of every serf, but on the margin of the sheet were jotted remarks concerning each serf's conduct and sobriety. Truly it was a pleasure to look at it.

"And do you mind handing me the earnest money?" said Sobakevitch.

"Yes, I do. Why need that be done? You can receive the money in a lump sum as soon as we visit the town."

"But it is always the custom, you know," asserted Sobakevitch.

"Then I cannot follow it, for I have no money with me. However, here are ten roubles."

"Ten roubles, indeed? You might as well hand me fifty while you are about it."

[1] Village factor or usurer.   [2] Subordinate government officials.

Once more Chichikov started to deny that he had any money upon him, but Sobakevitch insisted so strongly that this was not so that at length the guest pulled out another fifteen roubles, and added them to the ten already produced.

" Kindly give me a receipt for the money," he added.

" A receipt? Why should I give you a receipt? "

" Because it is better so, in order to guard against mistakes."

" Very well; but first hand me over the money."

" The money? I have it here. Do you write out the receipt, and then the money shall be yours."

" Pardon me, but how am I to write out the receipt before I have seen the cash? "

Chichikov placed the notes in Sobakevitch's hand; whereupon the host moved nearer to the table, and added to the list of serfs a note that he had received for the peasants, therewith sold, the sum of twenty-five roubles, as earnest money. This done, he counted the notes once more.

" This is a very *old* note," he remarked, holding one up to the light. " Also, it is a trifle torn. However, in a friendly transaction one must not be too particular."

" What a *kulak !* " thought Chichikov to himself. " And what a brute beast! "

" Then you do not want any *women* souls? " queried Sobakevitch.

" I thank you, no."

" I could let you have some cheap—say, as between friends, at a rouble a head? "

" No, I should have no use for them."

" Then, that being so, there is no more to be said. There is no accounting for tastes. ' One man loves the priest, and another the priest's wife,' says the proverb."

Chichikov rose to take his leave. " Once more I would request of you," he said, " that the bargain be left as it is."

" Of course, of course. What is done between friends holds good because of their mutual friendship. Good-bye, and thank you for your visit. In advance I would beg that, whenever you should have an hour or two to spare, you will come and lunch with us again. Perhaps we might be able to do one another further service? "

" Not if I know it! " reflected Chichikov as he mounted his *britchka*. " Not I, seeing that I have had two and a half roubles per soul squeezed out of me by a brute of a *kulak !* "

Altogether he felt dissatisfied with Sobakevitch's behaviour.

In spite of the man being a friend of the Governor and the Chief of Police, he had acted like an outsider in taking money for what was worthless rubbish. As the *britchka* left the court-yard Chichikov glanced back and saw Sobakevitch still standing on the verandah—apparently for the purpose of watching to see which way the guest's carriage would turn.

"The old villain, to be still standing there!" muttered Chichikov through his teeth; after which he ordered Selifan to proceed so that the vehicle's progress should be invisible from the mansion—the truth being that he had a mind next to visit Plushkin (whose serfs, to quote Sobakevitch, had a habit of dying like flies), but not to let his late host learn of his intention. Accordingly, on reaching the further end of the village, he hailed the first peasant whom he saw—a man who was in the act of hoisting a ponderous beam on to his shoulder before setting off with it, ant-like, to his hut.

"Hi!" shouted Chichikov. "How can I reach landowner Plushkin's place without first going past the mansion here?"

The peasant seemed nonplussed by the question.

"Don't you know?" queried Chichikov.

"No, *barin*," replied the peasant.

"What? You don't know skinflint Plushkin who feeds his people so badly?"

"Of course I do!" exclaimed the fellow, and added thereto an uncomplimentary expression of a species not ordinarily employed in polite society. We may guess that it was a pretty apt expression, since long after the man had become lost to view Chichikov was still laughing in his *britchka*. And, indeed, the language of the Russian populace is always forcible in its phraseology.

VI

CHICHIKOV'S amusement at the peasant's outburst prevented him from noticing that he had reached the centre of a large and populous village; but, presently, a violent jolt aroused him to the fact that he was driving over wooden pavements of a kind compared with which the cobblestones of the town had been as nothing. Like the keys of a piano, the planks kept rising and falling, and unguarded passage over them entailed either a bump on the back of the neck or a bruise on the forehead or a bite on the tip of one's tongue. At the same time Chichikov noticed a look of decay about the buildings of the village. The beams of the huts had grown dark with age, many of their roofs were riddled with holes, others had but a tile of the roof remaining, and yet others were reduced to the rib-like framework of the same. It would seem as though the inhabitants themselves had removed the laths and traverses, on the very natural plea that the huts were no protection against the rain, and therefore, since the latter entered in bucketfuls, there was no particular object to be gained by sitting in such huts when all the time there was the tavern and the highroad and other places to resort to.

Suddenly a woman appeared from an outbuilding—apparently the housekeeper of the mansion, but so roughly and dirtily dressed as almost to seem indistinguishable from a man. Chichikov inquired for the master of the place.

" He is not at home," she replied, almost before her interrogator had had time to finish. Then she added: " What do you want with him? "

" I have some business to do," said Chichikov.

" Then pray walk into the house," the woman advised. Then she turned upon him a back that was smeared with flour and had a long slit in the lower portion of its covering. Entering a large, dark hall which reeked like a tomb, he passed into an equally dark parlour that was lighted only by such rays as contrived to filter through a crack under the door. When Chichikov opened the door in question, the spectacle of the untidiness within struck him almost with amazement. It would seem that the floor was never washed, and that the room was used as a receptacle for every conceivable kind of furniture. On a table stood a ragged chair, with, beside it, a clock minus a pendulum and covered all over with cobwebs. Against a wall leant a cupboard, full of old silver, glassware, and china. On a writing table, inlaid with mother-of-pearl which, in places, had broken away and left behind it a number of yellow grooves (stuffed with putty), lay a pile of finely written manuscript, an overturned marble press (turning green), an ancient book in a leather cover with red edges, a lemon dried and shrunken to the dimensions of a hazelnut, the broken arm of a chair, a tumbler containing the dregs of some liquid and three flies (the whole covered over with a sheet of notepaper), a pile of rags, two ink-encrusted pens, and a yellow tookpick with which the master of the house had picked his teeth (apparently) at least before the coming of the French to Moscow. As for the walls, they were hung with a medley of pictures. Among the latter was a long engraving of a battle scene, wherein soldiers in three-cornered hats were brandishing huge drums and slender lances. It lacked a glass, and was set in a frame ornamented with bronze fretwork and bronze corner rings. Beside it hung a huge, grimy oil painting representative of some flowers and fruit, half a water melon, a boar's head, and the pendent form of a dead wild duck. Attached to the ceiling there was a chandelier in a holland covering — the covering so dusty as closely to resemble a huge cocoon enclosing a caterpillar. Lastly, in one corner of the room lay a pile of articles which had evidently been adjudged unworthy of a place on the table. Yet what the pile consisted of it would have been difficult to say, seeing that the dust on the same was so thick that any hand which touched it would have at once resembled a glove. Prominently protruding from the pile was the shaft of a wooden spade and the antiquated sole of a shoe. Never would one have supposed that a living creature had tenanted the room, were it not that the presence of such a creature was betrayed by the spectacle of an old nightcap resting on the table.

Whilst Chichikov was gazing at this extraordinary mess, a side door opened and there entered the housekeeper who had met him near the outbuildings. But now Chichikov perceived this person to be a man rather than a woman, since a female housekeeper would have had no beard to shave, whereas the chin of the newcomer, with the lower portion of his cheeks, strongly resembled the curry-comb which is used for grooming horses. Chichikov assumed a questioning air, and waited to hear what the housekeeper might have to say. The housekeeper did the same. At length, surprised at the misunderstanding, Chichikov decided to ask the first question.

" Is the master at home ? " he inquired.

" Yes," replied the person addressed.

" Then where is he ? " continued Chichikov.

" Are you blind, my good sir ? " retorted the other. " *I* am the master."

Involuntarily our hero started and stared. During his travels it had befallen him to meet various types of men—some of them, it may be, types which you and I have never encountered; but even to Chichikov this particular species was new. In the old man's face there was nothing very special—it was much like the wizened face of many another dotard, save that the chin so greatly projected that whenever he spoke he was forced to wipe it with a handkerchief to avoid dribbling, and that his small eyes were not yet grown dull, but twinkled under their overhanging brows like the eyes of mice when, with attentive ears and sensitive whiskers, they snuff the air and peer forth from their holes to see whether a cat or a boy may not be in the vicinity. No, the most noticeable feature about the man was his clothes. In no way could it have been guessed of what his coat was made, for both its sleeves and its skirts were so ragged and filthy as to defy description, while instead of two posterior tails, there dangled four of those appendages, with, projecting from them, a torn newspaper. Also, around his neck there was wrapped something which might have been a stocking, a garter, or a stomacher, but was certainly not a tie. In short, had Chichikov chanced to encounter him at a church door, he would have bestowed upon him a copper or two (for, to do our hero justice, he had a sympathetic heart and never refrained from presenting a beggar with alms), but in the present case there was standing before him, not a mendicant, but a landowner—and a landowner possessed of fully a thousand serfs, the superior of all his neighbours in wealth of flour and grain, and the owner of storehouses, and so forth, that were crammed with homespun cloth and linen, tanned and undressed sheepskins, dried fish, and every conceivable species of produce. Nevertheless, such a phenomenon is rare in Russia, where the tendency is rather to prodigality than to parsimony.

For several minutes Plushkin stood mute, while Chichikov remained so dazed with the appearance of his host and everything else in the room, that he, too, could not begin a conversation, but stood wondering how best to find words in which to explain the object of his visit. For a while he thought of expressing himself to the effect that, having heard so much of his host's benevolence and other rare qualities of spirit, he had considered it his duty to come and pay a tribute of respect; but presently even *he* came to the conclusion that this would be overdoing the thing, and, after another glance round the room, decided that the phrase "benevolence and other rare qualities of spirit" might to advantage give place to "economy and genius for method." Accordingly, the speech mentally composed, he said aloud that, having heard of Plushkin's talents for thrifty and systematic management, he had considered himself bound to make the acquaintance of his host, and to present him with his personal compliments (I need hardly say that

Chichikov could easily have alleged a better reason, had any better one happened, at the moment, to have come into his head).

With toothless gums Plushkin murmured something in reply, but nothing is known as to its precise terms beyond that it included a statement that the devil was at liberty to fly away with Chichikov's compliments. However, the laws of Russian hospitality do not permit even of a miser infringing their rules; wherefore Plushkin added to the foregoing a more civil invitation to be seated.

"It is long since I last received a visitor," he went on. "Also, I feel bound to say that I can see little good in their coming. Once introduce the abominable custom of folk paying calls, and forthwith there will ensue such ruin to the management of estates that landowners will be forced to feed their horses on hay. Not for a long, long time have I eaten a meal away from home—although my own kitchen is a poor one, and has its chimney in such a state that, were it to become overheated, it would instantly catch fire."

"What a brute!" though Chichikov. "I am lucky to have got through so much pasty and stuffed shoulder of mutton at Sobakevitch's!"

"Also," went on Plushkin, "I am ashamed to say that hardly a wisp of fodder does the place contain. But how can I get fodder? My lands are small, and the peasantry lazy fellows who hate work and think of nothing but the tavern. In the end, therefore, I shall be forced to go and spend my old age in roaming about the world."

"But I have been told that you possess over a thousand serfs?" said Chichikov.

"Who told you that? No matter who it was, you would have been justified in giving him the lie. He must have been a jester who wanted to make a fool of you. A thousand souls, indeed! Why, just reckon the taxes on them, and see what there would be left! For these three years that accursed fever has been killing off my serfs wholesale."

"Wholesale, you say?" echoed Chichikov, greatly interested.

"Yes, wholesale," replied the old man.

"Then might I ask you the exact number?"

"Fully eighty."

"Surely not?"

"But it is so."

"Then might I also ask whether it is from the date of the last census revision that you are reckoning these souls?"

"Yes, damn it! And since that date I have been bled for taxes upon a hundred and twenty souls in all."

"Indeed? Upon a hundred and twenty souls in all!" And Chichikov's surprise and elation were such that, this said, he remained sitting open-mouthed.

"Yes, good sir," replied Plushkin. "I am too old to tell you lies, for I have passed my seventieth year."

Somehow he seemed to have taken offence at Chichikov's almost joyous exclamation; wherefore the guest hastened to heave a profound sigh, and to observe that he sympathised to the full with his host's misfortunes.

"But sympathy does not put anything into one's pocket," retorted Plushkin. "For instance, I have a kinsman who is constantly plaguing me. He is a captain in the army, damn him, and all day he does nothing but call me 'dear uncle,' and kiss my hand, and express sympathy until I am forced to stop my ears. You see, he has squandered all his money upon his brother-officers, as well as made a fool of himself with an actress; so now he spends his time in telling me that he has a sympathetic heart!"

Chichikov hastened to explain that *his* sympathy had nothing in common with the captain's, since he dealt, not in empty words alone, but in actual deeds; in proof of which he was ready then and there (for the purpose of cutting the matter short, and of dispensing with circumlocution) to transfer to himself the obligation of paying the taxes due upon such serfs of Plushkin's as had, in the unfortunate manner just described, departed this world. The proposal seemed to astonish Plushkin, for he sat staring open-eyed. At length he inquired:

"My dear sir, have you seen military service?"

"No," replied the other warily, "but I have been a member of the *Civil* Service."

"Oh! Of the *Civil* Service?" And Plushkin sat moving his lips as though he were chewing something. "Well, what of your proposal?" he added presently. "Are you prepared to lose by it?"

"Yes, certainly, if thereby I can please you."

"My dear sir! My good benefactor!" In his delight Plushkin lost sight of the fact that his nose was caked with snuff of the consistency of thick coffee, and that his coat had parted in front and was disclosing some very unseemly underclothing. "What comfort you have brought to an old man! Yes, as God is my witness!"

For the moment he could say no more. Yet barely a minute

had elapsed before this instantaneously aroused emotion had, as instantaneously, disappeared from his wooden features. Once more they assumed a careworn expression, and he even wiped his face with his handkerchief, then rolled it into a ball, and rubbed it to and fro against his upper lip.

" If it will not annoy you again to state the proposal," he went on, " what you undertake to do is to pay the annual tax upon these souls, and to remit the money either to me or to the Treasury? "

" Yes, that is how it shall be done. We will draw up a deed of purchase as though the souls were still alive and you had sold them to myself."

" Quite so—a deed of purchase," echoed Plushkin, once more relapsing into thought and the chewing motion of the lips. " But a deed of such a kind will entail certain expenses, and lawyers are so devoid of conscience! In fact, so extortionate is their avarice that they will charge one half a rouble, and then a sack of flour, and then a whole waggon-load of meal. I wonder that no one has yet called attention to the system."

Upon that Chichikov intimated that, out of respect for his host, he himself would bear the cost of the transfer of souls. This led Plushkin to conclude that his guest must be the kind of unconscionable fool who, while pretending to have been a member of the Civil Service, has in reality served in the army and run after actresses; wherefore the old man no longer disguised his delight, but called down blessings alike upon Chichikov's head and upon those of his children (he had never even inquired whether Chichikov possessed a family). Next, he shuffled to the window, and, tapping one of its panes, shouted the name of " Proshka." Immediately some one ran quickly into the hall, and, after much stamping of feet, burst into the room. This was Proshka—a thirteen-year-old youngster who was shod with boots of such dimensions as almost to engulf his legs as he walked. The reason why he entered thus shod was that Plushkin kept only one pair of boots for the whole of his domestic staff. This universal pair was stationed in the hall of the mansion, so that any servant who was summoned to the house might don the said boots after wading barefooted through the mud of the courtyard, and enter the parlour dry-shod— subsequently leaving the boots where he had found them, and departing in his former barefooted condition. Indeed, had any one, on a slushy winter's morning, glanced from a window into the said courtyard, he would have seen Plushkin's servitors performing saltatory feats worthy of the most vigorous of stage-dancers.

"Look at that boy's face!" said Plushkin to Chichikov as he pointed to Proshka. "It is stupid enough, yet, lay anything aside, and in a trice he will have stolen it. Well, my lad, what do you want?"

He paused a moment or two, but Proshka made no reply.

"Come, come!" went on the old man. "Set out the *samovar*, and then give Mavra the key of the store-room—here it is—and tell her to get out some loaf sugar for tea. Here! Wait another moment, fool! Is the devil in your legs that they itch so to be off? Listen to what more I have to tell you. Tell Mavra that the sugar on the outside of the loaf has gone bad, so that she must scrape it off with a knife, and *not* throw away the scrapings, but give them to the poultry. Also, see that you yourself don't go into the storeroom, or I will give you a birching that you won't care for. Your appetite is good enough already, but a better one won't hurt you. Don't even *try* to go into the storeroom, for I shall be watching you from this window."

"You see," the old man added to Chichikov, "one can never trust these fellows." Presently, when Proshka and the boots had departed, he fell to gazing at his guest with an equally distrustful air, since certain features in Chichikov's benevolence now struck him as a little open to question, and he had begun to think to himself: "After all, the devil only knows who he is—whether a braggart, like most of these spendthrifts, or a fellow who is lying merely in order to get some tea out of me." Finally, his circumspection, combined with a desire to test his guest, led him to remark that it might be well to complete the transaction *immediately*, since he had not overmuch confidence in humanity, seeing that a man might be alive to-day and dead to-morrow.

To this Chichikov assented readily enough—merely adding that he should like first of all to be furnished with a list of the dead souls. This reassured Plushkin as to his guest's intention of doing business, so he got out his keys, approached a cupboard, and, having pulled back the door, rummaged among the cups and glasses with which it was filled. At length he said:

"I cannot find it now, but I used to possess a splendid bottle of liquor. Probably the servants have drunk it all, for they are such thieves. Oh no: perhaps this is it!"

Looking up, Chichikov saw that Plushkin had extracted a decanter coated with dust.

" My late wife made the stuff," went on the old man, " but that rascal of a housekeeper went and threw away a lot of it, and never even replaced the stopper. Consequently bugs and other nasty creatures got into the decanter, but I cleaned it out, and now beg to offer you a glassful."

The idea of a drink from such a receptacle was too much for Chichikov, so he excused himself on the ground that he had just had luncheon.

" You have just had luncheon? " re-echoed Plushkin. " Now, *that* shows how invariably one can tell a man of good society, wheresoever one may be. A man of that kind never eats anything —he always says that he has had enough. Very different that from the ways of a rogue, whom one can never satisfy, however much one may give him. For instance, that captain of mine is constantly begging me to let him have a meal—though he is about as much my nephew as I am his grandfather. As it happens, there is never a bite of anything in the house, so he has to go away empty. But about the list of those good-for-nothing souls—I happen to possess such a list, since I have drawn one up in readiness for the next revision."

With that Plushkin donned his spectacles, and once more started to rummage in the cupboard, and to smother his guest with dust as he untied successive packages of papers—so much so that his victim burst out sneezing. Finally he extracted a much-scribbled document in which the names of the deceased peasants lay as close-packed as a cloud of midges, for there were a hundred and twenty of them in all. Chichikov grinned with joy at the sight of the multitude. Stuffing the list into his pocket, he remarked that, to complete the transaction, it would be necessary to return to the town.

" To the town? " repeated Plushkin. " But why? Moreover, how could I leave the house, seeing that every one of my servants is either a thief or a rogue? Day by day they pilfer things, until soon I shall have not a single coat to hang on my back."

" Then you possess acquaintances in the town? "

" Acquaintances? No. Every acquaintance whom I ever possessed has either left me or is dead. But stop a moment. I *do* know the President of the Council. Even in my old age he has once or twice come to visit me, for he and I used to be schoolfellows, and to go climbing walls together. Yes, him I do know. Shall I write him a letter? "

" By all means."

"Yes, him I know well, for we were friends together at school."

Over Plushkin's wooden features there had gleamed a ray of warmth—a ray which expressed, if not feeling, at all events feeling's pale reflection. Just such a phenomenon may be witnessed when, for a brief moment, a drowning man makes a last re-appearance on the surface of a river, and there rises from the crowd lining the banks a cry of hope that even yet the exhausted hands may clutch the rope which has been thrown him—may clutch it before the surface of the unstable element shall have resumed for ever its calm, dread vacuity. But the hope is short-lived, and the hands disappear. Even so did Plushkin's face, after its momentary manifestation of feeling, become meaner and more insensible than ever.

"There used to be a sheet of clean writing paper lying on the table," he went on. "But where it is now I cannot think. That comes of my servants being such rascals."

With that he fell to looking also under the table, as well as to hurrying about with cries of "Mavra, Mavra!" At length the call was answered by a woman with a plateful of the sugar of which mention has been made; whereupon there ensued the following conversation.

"What have you done with my piece of writing paper, you pilferer?"

"I swear I have seen no paper except the bit with which you covered the glass."

"Your very face tells me that you have made off with it."

"Why should I make off with it? 'Twould be of no use to me, for I can neither read nor write."

"You lie! You have taken it away for the sexton to scribble upon."

"Well, if the sexton wanted paper he could get some for himself. Neither he nor I have set eyes upon your piece."

"Ah! Wait a bit, for on the Judgment Day you will be roasted by devils on iron spits. Just see if you are not!"

"But why should I be roasted when I have never even *touched* the paper? You might accuse me of any other fault than theft."

"Nay, devils shall roast you, sure enough. They will say to you, 'Bad woman, we are doing this because you robbed your master,' and then stoke up the fire still hotter."

"Nevertheless *I* shall continue to say, 'You are roasting me for nothing, for I never stole anything at all.' Why, *there* it is, lying on the table! You have been accusing me for no reason whatever!"

And, sure enough, the sheet of paper was lying before Plushkin's very eyes. For a moment or two he chewed silently. Then he went on:

"Well, and what are you making such a noise about? If one says a single word to you, you answer back with ten. Go and fetch me a candle to seal a letter with. And mind you bring a *tallow* candle, for it will not cost so much as the other sort. And bring me a match too."

Mavra departed, and Plushkin, seating himself, and taking up a pen, sat turning the sheet of paper over and over, as though in doubt whether to tear from it yet another morsel. At length he came to the conclusion that it was impossible to do so, and therefore, dipping the pen into the mixture of mouldy fluid and dead flies which the ink bottle contained, started to indite the letter in characters as bold as the notes of a music score, while momentarily checking the speed of his hand, lest it should meander too much over the paper, and crawling from line to line as though he regretted that there was so little vacant space left on the sheet.

"And do you happen to know any one to whom a few runaway serfs would be of use?" he asked as subsequently he folded the letter.

"What? You have some runaways as well?" exclaimed Chichikov, again greatly interested.

"Certainly I have. My son-in-law has laid the necessary information against them, but says that their tracks have grown cold. However, he is only a military man—that is to say, good at clinking a pair of spurs, but of no use for laying a plea before a court."

"And how many runaways have you?"

"About seventy."

"Surely not?"

"Alas, yes. Never does a year pass without a certain number of them making off. Yet so gluttonous and idle are my serfs that they are simply bursting with food, whereas I scarcely get enough to eat. I will take any price for them that you may care to offer. Tell your friends about it, and, should they find even a score of the runaways, it will repay them handsomely, seeing that a living serf on the census list is at present worth five hundred roubles."

"Perhaps so, but I am not going to let any one but myself

have a finger in this," thought Chichikov to himself; after which he explained to Plushkin that a friend of the kind mentioned would be impossible to discover, since the legal expenses of the enterprise would lead to the said friend having to cut the very tail from his coat before he would get clear of the lawyers.

" Nevertheless," added Chichikov, " seeing that you are so hard pressed for money, and that I am so interested in the matter, I feel moved to advance you—well, to advance you such a trifle as would scarcely be worth mentioning."

" But how much is it? " asked Plushkin eagerly, and with his hands trembling like quicksilver.

" Twenty-five kopecks per soul."

" What? In ready money? "

" Yes—in money down."

" Nevertheless, consider my poverty, dear friend, and make it *forty* kopecks per soul."

" Venerable sir, would that I could pay you not merely forty kopecks, but five hundred roubles. I should be only too delighted if that were possible, since I perceive that you, an aged and respected gentleman, are suffering for your own goodness of heart."

" By God, that is true, that is true." Plushkin hung his head, and wagged it feebly from side to side. " Yes, all that I have done I have done purely out of kindness."

" See how instantaneously I have divined your nature! By now it will have become clear to you why it is impossible for me to pay you five hundred roubles per runaway soul: for by now you will have gathered the fact that I am not sufficiently rich. Nevertheless, I am ready to add another five kopecks, and so to make it that each runaway serf shall cost me, in all, thirty kopecks."

" As you please, dear sir. Yet stretch another point, and throw in another two kopecks."

" Pardon me, but I cannot. How many runaway serfs did you say that you possess? Seventy? "

" No; seventy-eight."

" Seventy-eight souls at thirty kopecks each will amount to— to——" only for a moment did our hero halt, since he was strong in his arithmetic, " —will amount to twenty-four roubles, ninety-six kopecks." [1]

---

[1] Nevertheless Chichikov would appear to have erred, since most people would make the sum amount to twenty-three roubles, forty kopecks. If so, Chichikov cheated himself of one rouble, fifty-six kopecks.

With that he requested Plushkin to make out the receipt, and then handed him the money. Plushkin took it in both hands, bore it to a bureau with as much caution as though he were carrying a liquid which might at any moment splash him in the face, and, arrived at the bureau, and glancing round once more, carefully packed the cash in one of his money bags, where, doubtless, it was destined to lie buried until, to the intense joy of his daughters and his son-in-law (and, perhaps, of the captain who claimed kinship with him), he should himself receive burial at the hands of Fathers Carp and Polycarp, the two priests attached to his village. Lastly, the money concealed, Plushkin re-seated himself in the armchair, and seemed at a loss for further material for conversation.

"Are you thinking of starting?" at length he inquired, on seeing Chichikov make a trifling movement, though the movement was only to extract from his pocket a handkerchief. Nevertheless the question reminded Chichikov that there was no further excuse for lingering.

"Yes, I must be going," he said as he took his hat.

"Then what about the tea?"

"Thank you, I will have some on my next visit."

"What? Even though I have just ordered the *samovar* to be got ready? Well, well! I myself do not greatly care for tea, for I think it an expensive beverage. Moreover, the price of sugar has risen terribly."

"Proshka!" he then shouted. "The *samovar* will not be needed. Return the sugar to Mavra, and tell her to put it back again. But no. Bring the sugar here, and *I* will put it back."

"Good-bye, dear sir," finally he added to Chichikov. "May the Lord bless you! Hand that letter to the President of the Council, and let him read it. Yes, he is an old friend of mine. We knew one another as schoolfellows."

With that this strange phenomenon, this withered old man, escorted his guest to the gates of the courtyard, and, after the guest had departed, ordered the gates to be closed, made the round of the outbuildings for the purpose of ascertaining whether the numerous watchmen were at their posts, peered into the kitchen (where, under the pretence of seeing whether his servants were being properly fed, he made a light meal of cabbage soup and gruel), rated the said servants soundly for their thievishness and general bad behaviour, and then returned to his room. Meditating in solitude, he fell to thinking how best he could contrive to recompense his guest for the latter's measureless benevolence. " I will present him," he thought to himself, " with a watch. It is a good silver article—not one of those cheap metal affairs; and though it has suffered some damage, he can easily get that put right. A young man always needs to give a watch to his betrothed."

" No," he added after further thought. " I will leave him the watch in my will, as a keepsake."

Meanwhile our hero was bowling along in high spirit. Such an unexpected acquisition both of dead souls and of runaway serfs had come as a windfall. Even before reaching Plushkin's village he had had a presentiment that he would do successful business there, but not business of such pre-eminent profitableness as had actually resulted. As he proceeded he whistled, hummed with hand placed trumpetwise to his mouth, and ended by bursting into a burst of melody so striking that Selifan, after listening for a while, nodded his head and exclaimed, " My word, but the master *can* sing ! "

By the time they had reached the town darkness had fallen, and changed the character of the scene. The *britchka* bounded over the cobblestones, and at length turned into the hostelry's courtyard, where the travellers were met by Petrushka. With one hand holding back the tails of his coat (which he never liked to see fly apart), the valet assisted his master to alight. The waiter ran out with candle in hand and napkin on shoulder. Whether or not Petrushka was glad to see the *barin* return it is impossible to say, but at all events he exchanged a wink with Selifan, and his ordinarily morose exterior seemed momentarily to brighten.

" Then you have been travelling far, sir ? " said the waiter, as he lit the way upstairs.

" Yes," said Chichikov. " What has happened here in the meanwhile ? "

" Nothing, sir," replied the waiter, bowing, " except that last night there arrived a military lieutenant. He has got room number sixteen."

" A lieutenant ? "

" Yes. He came from Riazan, driving three grey horses."

On entering his room, Chichikov clapped his hand to his nose, and asked his valet why he had never had the windows opened.

" But I did have them opened," replied Petrushka. Nevertheless this was a lie, as Chichikov well knew, though he was too tired to contest the point. After ordering and consuming a light supper of sucking pig, he undressed, plunged beneath the bedclothes, and sank into the profound slumber which comes only to such fortunate folk as are troubled neither with mosquitoes nor fleas nor excessive activity of brain.

VII

WHEN Chichikov awoke he stretched himself and realised that he had slept well. For a moment or two he lay on his back, and then suddenly clapped his hands at the recollection that he was now owner of nearly four hundred souls. At once he leapt out of bed without so much as glancing at his face in the mirror, though, as a rule, he had much solicitude for his features, and especially for his chin, of which he would make the most when in company with friends, and more particularly should any one happen to enter while he was engaged in the process of shaving. " Look how round my chin is! " was his usual formula. On the present occasion, however, he looked neither at chin nor at any other feature, but at once donned his flower-embroidered slippers of morocco leather (the kind of slippers in·which, thanks to the Russian love for a dressing-gowned existence, the town of Torzhok does such a huge trade), and, clad only in a meagre shirt, so far forgot his elderliness and dignity as to cut a couple of capers after the fashion of a Scottish highlander—alighting neatly, each time, on the flat of his heels. Only when he had done that did he proceed to business. Planting himself before his dispatch-box, he rubbed his hands with a satisfaction worthy of an incorruptible rural magistrate when adjourning for luncheon; after which he extracted from the receptacle a bundle of papers. These he had decided not to deposit with a lawyer, for the reason that he would hasten matters, as well as save expense, by himself framing and fair-copying the necessary deeds of indenture; and since he was thoroughly acquainted with the necessary terminology, he proceeded to inscribe in large characters the date, and then in smaller ones, his name and rank. By two o'clock the whole was finished, and as he looked at the sheets of names representing bygone peasants who had ploughed, worked at handicrafts, cheated their masters, fetched, carried, and got drunk (though *some* of them may have behaved well), there came over him a strange, unaccountable sensation. To his eye each list of names seemed to possess a character of its own; and even individual peasants therein seemed to have taken on certain qualities peculiar to themselves. For instance, to the majority of Madame Korobotchka's serfs there were appended nicknames and other additions; Plushkin's list was distinguished by a conciseness of exposition which had led to certain of the items being represented merely by Christian name, patronymic, and a couple of dots; and Sobakevitch's list was remarkable for its amplitude and circumstantiality, in that not a single peasant had such of his peculiar characteristics omitted as that the deceased had been "excellent at joinery," or "sober and ready to pay attention to his work." Also, in Sobakevitch's list there was recorded who had been the father and the mother of each of the deceased, and how those parents had behaved themselves. Only against the name of a certain Thedotov was there inscribed: "Father unknown, Mother the maidservant Kapitolina, Morals and Honesty good." These details communicated to the document a certain air of freshness, they seemed to connote that the peasants in question had lived but yesterday. As Chichikov scanned the list he felt softened in spirit, and said with a sigh:

"My friends, what a concourse of you is here! How did you all pass your lives, my brethren? And how did you all come to depart hence?"

As he spoke his eyes halted at one name in particular—that of the same Peter Saveliev Nëuvazhai Korito who had once been the property of the widow Korobotchka. Once more he could not help exclaiming:

"What a series of titles! They occupy a whole line! Peter Saveliev, I wonder whether you were an artisan or a plain *muzhik*. Also, I wonder how you came to meet your end; whether in a tavern, or whether through going to sleep in the middle of the road, and being run over by a train of waggons. Again, I see the name, 'Probka Stepan, carpenter, very sober.' That must be the hero of whom the Guards would have been so glad to get hold. How well I can imagine him tramping the country with an axe in his belt and his boots on his shoulder, and living on a few groats'-worth of bread and dried fish per day, and taking home a couple of half-rouble pieces in his purse, and sewing the notes into his breeches, or stuffing them into his boots! In what manner came you by your end, Probka Stepan? Did you, for good wages, mount a scaffold around the cupola of the village church, and, climbing thence to the cross above, miss your footing on a beam, and fall headlong with none at hand but Uncle Michai—the good uncle who, scratching the back of his neck, and muttering, ' Ah, Vania, for once you have been too clever! ' straightway lashed himself to a rope, and took your place? ' Maksim Teliatnikov, shoemaker.' A shoemaker, indeed? ' As drunk as a shoemaker,' says the proverb. *I* know what you were like, my friend. If you wish, I will tell you your whole history. You were apprenticed to a German, who fed you and your fellows at a common table, thrashed you with a strap, kept you indoors whenever you had made a mistake, and spoke of you in uncomplimentary terms to his wife and friends. At length, when your apprenticeship was over, you said to yourself, ' I am going to set up on my own account, and not just to scrape together a kopeck here and a kopeck there, as the Germans do, but to grow rich quick.' Hence you took a shop at a high rent, bespoke a few orders, and set to work to buy up some rotten leather out of which you could make, on each pair of boots, a double profit. But those boots split within a fortnight, and brought down upon your head dire showers of maledictions; with the result that gradually your shop grew empty of customers, and you fell to roaming the streets and exclaiming, ' The world is a very poor place indeed! A Russian cannot make a living for German competition.' Well, well! ' Elizabeta Vorobei! ' But that is a *woman's* name! How comes *she* to be on the list? That villain Sobakevitch must have sneaked her in without my knowing it."

" ' Grigori Doiezhai-ne-Doiedesh,' " he went on. " What sort of a man were *you*, I wonder? Were you a carrier who, having set up a team of three horses and a tilt waggon, left your home, your native hovel, for ever, and departed to cart merchandise to market? Was it on the highway that you surrendered your soul to God, or did your friends first marry you to some fat, red-faced soldier's daughter; after which your harness and team of rough, but sturdy, horses caught a highwayman's fancy, and you, lying on your pallet, thought things over until, willy-nilly, you felt that you must get up and make for the tavern, thereafter blundering into an icehole? Ah, our peasant of Russia! Never do you welcome death when it comes! "

" And you, my friends? " continued Chichikov, turning to the sheet whereon were inscribed the names of Plushkin's absconded serfs. " Although you are still alive, what is the good of you? You are practically dead. Whither, I wonder, have your fugitive feet carried you? Did you fare hardly at Plushkin's, or was it that your natural inclinations led you to prefer roaming the wilds and plundering travellers? Are you, by this time, in gaol, or have you taken service with other masters for the tillage of their lands? ' Eremei Kariakin, Nikita Volokita and Anton Volokita (son of the foregoing).' To judge from your surnames, you would seem to have been born gadabouts.[1] ' Popov, household serf.' Probably you are an educated man, good Popov, and go in for polite thieving, as distinguished from the more vulgar cut-throat sort. In my mind's eye I seem to see a Captain of Rural Police challenging you for being without a passport; whereupon you stake your all upon a single throw. ' To whom do you belong? ' asks the Captain, probably adding to his question a forcible expletive. ' To such and such a landowner,' stoutly you reply. ' And what are you doing here? ' continues the Captain. ' I have just received permission to go and earn my *obrok*,' is your fluent explanation. ' Then where is your passport? ' ' At *Miestchanin*[2] Pimenov's.' ' Pimenov's? Then are you Pimenov himself? ' ' Yes, I am Pimenov himself.' ' He has given you his passport? ' ' No, he has not given me his passport.' ' Come, come! ' shouts the Captain with another forcible expletive. ' You are lying! ' ' No, I am not,' is your dogged reply. ' It is only that last night I could not return him his passport, because I came home late; so I handed it to Antip Prochorov, the bell-ringer, for him to take care of.' ' Bell-ringer, indeed! Then *he* gave you a passport? ' ' No; I did not receive a passport from him either.' ' What? '—and here the Captain shouts another expletive—' How dare you keep on lying? Where is *your own* passport? ' ' I had one all right,' you reply cunningly, ' but must have dropped it somewhere on the road as I came along.' ' And what about that soldier's coat? ' asks the Captain with an impolite addition. ' Whence did you get it? And what of the priest's cashbox and copper money? ' ' About them I know nothing,' you reply doggedly. ' Never at any time have I committed a theft.' ' Then how is it that the coat was found at your place? ' ' I do not know. Probably some one else put it there.' ' You rascal, you rascal! ' shouts the Captain, shaking his head, and closing in upon you. ' Put the leg-irons upon him, and off with him to prison! ' ' With pleasure,' you reply as, taking a snuff-box from your pocket, you offer a pinch to each of the two gendarmes who are manacling you, while also inquiring how long they have been discharged from the army, and in what wars they may have served. And in prison

---

[1] The names Kariakin and Volokita might, perhaps, be translated as " Gallant " and " Loafer."

[2] Tradesman or citizen.

you remain until your case comes on, when the justice orders you to be removed from Tsarev-Kokshaiska to such and such another prison, and a second justice orders you to be transferred thence to Vesiegonsk or somewhere else, and you go flitting from gaol to gaol, and saying each time, as you eye your new habitation, ' The last place was a good deal cleaner than this one is, and one could play *babki*[1] there, and stretch one's legs, and see a little society.' "

" ' Abakum Thirov,' " Chichikov went on after a pause. " What of *you*, brother? Where, and in what capacity, are *you* disporting yourself? Have you gone to the Volga country, and become bitten with the life of freedom, and joined the fishermen of the river? "

Here, breaking off, Chichikov relapsed into silent meditation. Of what was he thinking as he sat there? Was he thinking of the fortunes of Abakum Thirov, or was he meditating as meditates every Russian when his thoughts once turn to the joys of an emancipated existence?

" Ah, well! " he sighed, looking at his watch. " It has now gone twelve o'clock. Why have I so forgotten myself? There is still much to be done, yet I go shutting myself up and letting my thoughts wander! What a fool I am! "

So saying, he exchanged his Scottish costume (of a shirt and nothing else) for attire of a more European nature; after which he pulled tight the waistcoat over his ample stomach, sprinkled himself with eau-de-Cologne, tucked his papers under his arm, took his fur cap, and set out for the municipal offices, for the purpose of completing the transfer of souls. The fact that he hurried along was not due to a fear of being late (seeing that the President of the Local Council was an intimate acquaintance of his, as well as a functionary who could shorten or prolong an interview at will, even as Homer's Zeus was able to shorten or to prolong a night or a day, whenever it became necessary to put an end to the fighting of his favourite heroes, or to enable them to join battle), but rather to a feeling that he would like to have the affair concluded as quickly as possible, seeing that, throughout, it had been an anxious and difficult business. Also, he could not get rid of the idea that his souls were unsubstantial things, and that therefore, under the circumstances, his shoulders had better be relieved of their load with the least possible delay. Pulling on his cinnamon-coloured, bear-lined overcoat as he went, he had just stepped thoughtfully into the street

[1] The game of knucklebones.

when he collided with a gentleman dressed in a similar coat and an ear-lappeted fur cap. Upon that the gentleman uttered an exclamation. Behold, it was Manilov! At once the friends became folded in a strenuous embrace, and remained so locked for fully five minutes. Indeed, the kisses exchanged were so vigorous that both suffered from toothache for the greater portion of the day. Also, Manilov's delight was such that only his nose and lips remained visible—the eyes completely disappeared. Afterwards he spent about a quarter of an hour in holding Chichikov's hand and chafing it vigorously. Lastly, he, in the most pleasant and exquisite of terms possible, intimated to his friend that he had just been on his way to embrace Paul Ivanovitch; and upon this followed a compliment of the kind which would more fittingly have been addressed to a lady who was being asked to accord a partner the favour of a dance. Chichikov had opened his mouth to reply—though even *he* felt at a loss how to acknowledge what had just been said— when Manilov cut him short by producing from under his coat a roll of paper tied with red riband.

"What have you there?" asked Chichikov.

"The list of my souls."

"Ah!" And as Chichikov unrolled the document and ran his eye over it he could not but marvel at the elegant neatness with which it had been inscribed.

"It is a beautiful piece of writing," he said. "In fact, there will be no need to make a copy of it. Also, it has a border around its edge! Who worked that exquisite border?"

"Do not ask me," said Manilov.

"Did *you* do it?"

"No; my wife."

"Dear, dear!" Chichikov cried. "To think that I should have put her to so much trouble!"

"*Nothing* could be too much trouble where Paul Ivanovitch is concerned."

Chichikov bowed his acknowledgements. Next, on learning that he was on his way to the municipal offices for the purpose of completing the transfer, Manilov expressed his readiness to accompany him; wherefore the pair linked arm in arm and proceeded together. Whenever they encountered a slight rise in the ground—even the smallest unevenness or difference of level—Manilov supported Chichikov with such energy as almost to lift him off his feet, while accompanying the service with a smiling implication that not if *he* could help it should

Paul Ivanovitch slip or fall. Nevertheless this conduct appeared to embarrass Chichikov, either because he could not find any fitting words of gratitude or because he considered the proceeding tiresome; and it was with a sense of relief that he debouched upon the square where the municipal offices—a large, three-storied building of a chalky whiteness which probably symbolised the purity of the souls engaged within—were situated. No other building in the square could vie with them in size, seeing that the remaining edifices consisted only of a sentry-box, a shelter for two or three cabmen, and a long hoarding—the latter adorned with the usual bills, posters, and scrawls in chalk and charcoal. At intervals, from the windows of the second and third stories of the municipal offices, the incorruptible heads of certain of the attendant priests of Themis would peer quickly forth, and as quickly disappear again—probably for the reason that a superior official had just entered the room. Meanwhile the two friends ascended the staircase —nay, almost flew up it, since, longing to get rid of Manilov's ever-supporting arm, Chichikov hastened his steps, and Manilov kept darting forward to anticipate any possible failure on the part of his companion's legs. Consequently the pair were breathless when they reached the first corridor. In passing it may be remarked that neither corridors nor rooms evinced any of that cleanliness and purity which marked the exterior of the building, for such attributes were not troubled about within, and anything that was dirty remained so, and donned no meritricious, purely external, disguise. It was as though Themis received her visitors in *négligé* and a dressing-gown. The author would also give a description of the various offices through which our hero passed, were it not that he (the author) stands in awe of such legal haunts.

Approaching the first desk which he happened to encounter, Chichikov inquired of the two young officials who were seated at it whether they would kindly tell him where business relating to serf-indenture was transacted.

" Of what nature, precisely, *is* your business? " countered one of the youthful officials as he turned himself round.

" I desire to make an application."

" In connection with a purchase? "

" Yes. But, as I say, I should like first to know where I can find the desk devoted to such business. Is it here or elsewhere? "

" You must state what it is you have bought, and for how much. *Then* we shall be happy to give you the information."

Chichikov perceived that the officials' motive was merely one of curiosity, as often happens when young *tchinovniks* desire to cut a more important and imposing figure than is rightfully theirs.

" Look here, young sirs," he said. " I know for a fact that all serf business, no matter to what value, is transacted at one desk alone. Consequently I again request you to direct me to that desk. Of course, if you do not know your business I can easily ask some one else."

To this the *tchinovniks* made no reply beyond pointing towards a corner of the room where an elderly man appeared to be engaged in sorting some papers. Accordingly Chichikov and Manilov threaded their way in his direction through the desks; whereupon the elderly man became violently busy.

" Would you mind telling me," said Chichikov, bowing, " whether this is the desk for serf affairs? "

The elderly man raised his eyes, and said stiffly:

" This is *not* the desk for serf affairs."

" Where is it, then? "

" In the Serf Department."

" And where might the Serf Department be? "

" In charge of Ivan Antonovitch."

" And where is Ivan Antonovitch? "

The elderly man pointed to another corner of the room; whither Chichikov and Manilov next directed their steps. As they advanced, Ivan Antonovitch cast an eye backwards, and viewed them askance. Then, with renewed ardour, he resumed his work of writing.

" Would you mind telling me," said Chichikov, bowing, " whether this is the desk for serf affairs? "

It appeared as though Ivan Antonovitch had not heard, so completely did he bury himself in his papers and return no reply. Instantly it became plain that *he* at least was of an age of discretion, and not one of your jejune chatterboxes and harum-scarums; for, although his hair was still thick and black, he had long ago passed his fortieth year. His whole face tended towards the nose—it was what, in common parlance, is known as a " pitcher mug."

" Would you mind telling me," repeated Chichikov, " whether this is the desk for serf affairs? "

" It is that," said Ivan Antonovitch, again lowering his jug-shaped jowl, and resuming his writing.

" Then I should like to transact the following business. From various landowners in this canton I have purchased a number of peasants for transfer. Here is the purchase list, and it needs but to be registered."

" Have you also the vendors here? "

" Some of them, and from the rest I have obtained powers of attorney."

" And have you your statement of application? "

" Yes. I desire—indeed, it is necessary for me so to do—to hasten matters a little. Could the affair, therefore, be carried through to-day? "

" To-day? Oh, dear no! " said Ivan Antonovitch. " Before that can be done you must furnish me with further proofs that no impediments exist."

" Then, to expedite matters, let me say that Ivan Grigorievitch, the President of the Council, is a very intimate friend of mine."

" Possibly," said Ivan Antonovitch without enthusiasm. " But Ivan Grigorievitch alone will not do—it is customary to have others as well.'

" Yes, but the absence of others will not altogether invalidate the transaction. I too have been in the service, and know how things can be done."

" You had better go and see Ivan Grigorievitch," said Ivan Antonovitch more mildly. " Should he give you an order addressed to whom it may concern, we shall soon be able to settle the matter."

Upon that Chichikov pulled from his pocket a paper, and laid it before Ivan Antonovitch. At once the latter covered it with a book. Chichikov again attempted to show it to him, but, with a movement of his head, Ivan Antonovitch signified that that was unnecessary.

" A clerk," he added, " will now conduct you to Ivan Grigorievitch's room."

Upon that one of the toilers in the service of Themis—a zealot who had offered her such heartfelt sacrifice that his coat had burst at the elbows and lacked a lining—escorted our friends (even as Virgil once escorted Dante) to the apartment of the Presence. In this sanctum were some massive armchairs, a table laden with two or three fat books, and a large looking-glass. Lastly, in (apparently) sunlike isolation, there was seated at the table the President. On arriving at the door of the apartment, our modern Virgil seemed to become so overwhelmed with awe that, without daring even to intrude a foot, he turned back, and, in so doing, once more exhibited a back as shiny as a mat, and having adhering to it, in one spot, a chicken's feather. As soon as the two friends had entered the hall of the Presence they perceived that the President was *not* alone, but, on the contrary, had seated by his side Sobakevitch, whose form had hitherto been concealed by the intervening mirror. The new-comers' entry evoked sundry exclamations and the pushing back of a pair of Government chairs as the voluminous-sleeved Sobakevitch rose into view from behind the looking-glass. Chichikov the President received with an embrace, and for a while the hall of the Presence resounded with osculatory salutations as mutually the pair inquired after one another's health. It seemed that both had lately had a touch of that pain under the waistband which comes of a sedentary life. Also, it seemed that the President had just been conversing with Sobakevitch on the subject of the sales of souls, since now he proceeded to congratulate Chichikov on the same—a proceeding which rather embarrassed our hero, seeing that Manilov and Sobakevitch, two of the vendors, and persons with whom he had bargained in the strictest privacy, were now confronting one another direct. However, Chichikov duly thanked the President, and then, turning to Sobakevitch, inquired after *his* health.

" Thank God, I have nothing to complain of," replied Sobakevitch: which was true enough, seeing that a piece of iron would have caught cold and taken to sneezing sooner than would that uncouthly fashioned landowner.

" Ah, yes; you have always had good health, have you not? " put in the President. " Your late father was equally strong."

" Yes, he even went out bear hunting alone," replied Sobakevitch.

" I should think that you too could worst a bear if you were to try a tussle with him," rejoined the President.

" Oh no," said Sobakevitch. " My father was a stronger man than I am." Then with a sigh the speaker added: " But nowadays there are no such men as he. What is even a life like mine worth? "

" Then you do not have a comfortable time of it? " exclaimed the President.

" No; far from it," rejoined Sobakevitch, shaking his head. " Judge for yourself, Ivan Grigorievitch. I am fifty years old, yet never in my life have I been ill, except for an occasional carbuncle or boil. That is not a good sign. Sooner or later I shall have to pay for it." And he relapsed into melancholy.

E

" Just listen to the fellow!" was Chichikov's and the President's joint inward comment. " What on earth has *he* to complain of?"

" I have a letter for you, Ivan Grigorievitch," went on Chichikov aloud as he produced from his pocket Plushkin's epistle.

" From whom?" inquired the President. Having broken the seal, he exclaimed: " Why, it is from Plushkin! To think that *he* is still alive! What a strange world it is! He used to be such a nice fellow, and now——"

" And now he is a cur," concluded Sobakevitch, " as well as a miser who starves his serfs to death."

" Allow me a moment," said the President. Then he read the letter through. When he had finished he added: " Yes, I am quite ready to act as Plushkin's attorney. When do you wish the purchase deeds to be registered, Monsieur Chichikov, —now or later?"

" Now, if you please," replied Chichikov. " Indeed, I beg that, if possible, the affair may be concluded to-day, since to-morrow I wish to leave the town. I have brought with me both the forms of indenture and my statement of application."

" Very well. Nevertheless we cannot let you depart so soon. The indentures shall be completed to-day, but you must continue your sojourn in our midst. I will issue the necessary orders at once."

So saying, he opened the door into the general office, where the clerks looked like a swarm of bees around a honeycomb (if I may liken affairs of Government to such an article?).

" Is Ivan Antonovitch here?" asked the President.

" Yes," replied a voice from within.

" Then send him here."

Upon that the pitcher-faced Ivan Antonovitch made his appearance in the doorway, and bowed.

" Take these indentures, Ivan Antonovitch," said the President, " and see that they——"

" But first I would ask you to remember," put in Sobakevitch, " that witnesses ought to be in attendance—not less than two on behalf of either party. Let us, therefore, send for the Public Prosecutor, who has little to do, and has even that little done for him by his chief clerk, Zolotucha. The Inspector of the Medical Department is also a man of leisure, and likely to be at home—if he has not gone out to a card party. Others also there are—all men who cumber the ground for nothing."

" Quite so, quite so," agreed the President, and at once dispatched a clerk to fetch the persons named.

" Also," requested Chichikov, " I should be glad if you would send for the accredited representative of a certain lady landowner with whom I have done business. He is the son of a Father Cyril, and a clerk in your offices."

" Certainly we will call him here," replied the President. " Everything shall be done to meet your convenience, and I forbid you to present any of our officials with a gratuity. That is a special request on my part. No friend of mine ever pays a copper."

With that he gave Ivan Antonovitch the necessary instructions; and though they scarcely seemed to meet with that functionary's approval, upon the President the purchase deeds had evidently produced an excellent impression, more especially since the moment when he had perceived the sum-total to amount to nearly a hundred thousand roubles. For a moment or two he gazed into Chichikov's eyes with an expression of profound satisfaction. Then he said:

" Well done, Paul Ivanovitch! You have indeed made a nice haul!"

" That is so," replied Chichikov.

" Excellent business! Yes, excellent business!"

" I, too, conceive that I could not well have done better. The truth is that never until a man has driven home the piles of his life's structure upon a lasting bottom, instead of upon the wayward chimeras of youth, will his aims in life assume a definite end." And, that said, Chichikov went on to deliver himself of a very telling indictment of Liberalism and our modern young men. Yet in his words there seemed to lurk a certain lack of conviction. Somehow he seemed secretly to be saying to himself, " My good sir, you are talking the most absolute rubbish, and nothing but rubbish." Nor did he even throw a glance at Sobakevitch and Manilov. It was as though he were uncertain what he might not encounter in their expression. Yet he need not have been afraid. Never once did Sobakevitch's face move a muscle, and, as for Manilov, he was too much under the spell of Chichikov's eloquence to do aught beyond nod his approval at intervals, and strike the kind of attitude which is assumed by lovers of music when a lady singer has, in rivalry of an accompanying violin, produced a note whereof the shrillness would exceed even the capacity of a bird's throstle.

" But why not tell Ivan Grigorievitch precisely what you

have bought?" inquired Sobakevitch of Chichikov. "And why, Ivan Grigorievitch, do *you* not ask Monsieur Chichikov precisely what his purchases have consisted of? What a splendid lot of serfs, to be sure! I myself have sold him my wheelwright, Michiev."

"What? You have sold him Michiev?" exclaimed the President. "I know the man well. He is a splendid craftsman, and, on one occasion, made me a *drozhki*.[1] Only, only—well, lately didn't you tell me that he is dead?"

"That Michiev is dead?" re-echoed Sobakevitch, coming perilously near to laughing. "Oh dear no! That was his brother. Michiev himself is very much alive, and in even better health than he used to be. Any day he could knock you up a *britchka* such as you could not procure even in Moscow. However, he is now bound to work only for one master."

"Indeed a splendid craftsman!" repeated the President. "My only wonder is that you can have brought yourself to part with him."

"Then think you that Michiev is the *only* serf with whom I have parted? Nay, for I have parted also with Probka Stepan, my carpenter, with Milushkin, my bricklayer, and with Teliatnikov, my bootmaker. Yes, the whole lot have I sold."

And to the President's inquiry why he had so acted, seeing that the serfs named were all skilled workers and indispensable to a household, Sobakevitch replied that a mere whim had led him to do so, and thus the sale had owed its origin to a piece of folly. Then he hung his head as though already repenting of his rash act, and added:

"Though a man of grey hairs, I have not yet learned wisdom."

"But," inquired the President further, "how comes it about, Paul Ivanovitch, that you have purchased peasants apart from land? Is it for transferment elsewhere that you need them?"

"Yes."

"Very well, then. That is quite another matter. To what part of the country?"

"To the province of Kherson."

"Indeed? That region contains some splendid land," said the President; whereupon he proceeded to expatiate on the fertility of the Kherson pastures.

"And have you *much* land there?" he continued.

"Yes; quite sufficient to accommodate the serfs whom I have purchased."

[1] A sort of low, four-wheeled carriage.

" And is there a river on the estate or a lake? "

" Both."

After this reply Chichikov involuntarily threw a glance at Sobakevitch; and though that landowner's face was as motionless as ever, the other seemed to detect in it: " You liar! Don't tell *me* that you own both a river and a lake, as well as the land which you say you do."

Whilst the foregoing conversation had been in progress, various witnesses had been arriving on the scene. They consisted of the constantly blinking Public Prosecutor, the Inspector of the Medical Department, and others—all, to quote Sobakevitch, " men who cumbered the ground for nothing." With some of them, however, Chichikov was altogether unacquainted, since certain substitutes and supernumeraries had to be pressed into the service from among the ranks of the subordinate staff. There also arrived, in answer to the summons, not only the son of Father Cyril before mentioned, but also Father Cyril himself. Each such witness appended to his signature a full list of his dignities and qualifications: one man in printed characters, another in a flowing hand, a third in topsy-turvy characters of a kind never before seen in the Russian alphabet, and so forth. Meanwhile our friend Ivan Antonovitch comported himself with not a little address; and after the indentures had been signed, docketed, and registered, Chichikov found himself called upon to pay only the merest trifle in the way of Government percentage and fees for publishing the transaction in the Official Gazette. The reason of this was that the President had given orders that only half the usual charges were to be exacted from the present purchaser—the remaining half being somehow debited to the account of another applicant for serf registration.

" And now," said Ivan Grigorievitch when all was completed, " we need only to wet the bargain."

" For that too I am ready," replied Chichikov. " Do you but name the hour. If, in return for your most agreeable company, I were not to set a few champagne corks flying, I should be indeed in default."

" But we are not going to let you charge yourself with anything whatsoever. *We* must provide the champagne, for you are our guest, and it is for us—it is our duty, it is our bounden obligation—to entertain you. Look here, gentlemen. Let us adjourn to the house of the Chief of Police. He is the magician who needs but to wink when passing a fishmonger's or a wine merchant's. Not only shall we fare well at his place, but also we shall get a game of whist."

To this proposal no one had any objection to offer, for the mere mention of the fish shop aroused the witnesses' appetite. Consequently, the ceremony being over, there was a general reaching for hats and caps. As the party were passing through the general office, Ivan Antonovitch whispered in Chichikov's ear, with a courteous inclination of his jug-shaped physiognomy:

" You have given a hundred thousand roubles for the serfs, but have paid *me* only a trifle for my trouble."

" Yes," replied Chichikov in a similar whisper, " but what sort of serfs do you suppose them to be? They are a poor, useless lot, and not worth even half the purchase money."

This gave Ivan Antonovitch to understand that the visitor was a man of strong character—a man from whom nothing more was to be expected.

" Why have you gone and purchased souls from Plushkin? " whispered Sobakevitch in Chichikov's other ear.

" Why did *you* go and add the woman Vorobei to your list? " retorted Chichikov.

" Vorobei? Who is Vorobei? "

" The woman ' Elizabet ' Vorobei—' Elizabet,' not ' Eliza-beta? ' "

" I added no such name," replied Sobakevitch, and straight-way joined the other guests.

At length the party arrived at the residence of the Chief of Police. The latter proved indeed a man of spells, for no sooner had he learnt what was afoot than he summoned a brisk young constable, whispered in his ear, adding laconically, " You understand, do you not? " and brought it about that, during the time that the guests were cutting for partners at whist in an adjoining room, the dining-table became laden with sturgeon, caviare, salmon, herrings, cheese, smoked tongue, fresh roe, and a potted variety of the same—all procured from the local fish market, and reinforced with additions from the host's own kitchen. The fact was that the worthy Chief of Police filled the office of a sort of father and general benefactor to the town, and that he moved among the citizens as though they constituted part and parcel of his own family, and watched over their shops and markets as though those establishments were merely his own private larder. Indeed, it would be difficult to say—so thoroughly did he perform his duties in this respect—whether the post most fitted him, or he the post. Matters were also so arranged that though his income more than doubled that of his predecessors, he had never lost the affection of his fellow townsmen. In particular did the tradesmen love him, since he was never above standing godfather to their children or dining at their tables. True, he had differences of opinion with them, and serious differences at that; but always these were skilfully adjusted by his slapping the offended ones jovially on the shoulder, drinking a glass of tea with them, promising to call at their houses and play a game of chess, asking after their belongings, and, should he learn that a child of theirs was ill, prescribing the proper medicine. In short, he bore the reputation of being a very good fellow.

On perceiving the feast to be ready, the host proposed that his guests should finish their whist after luncheon; whereupon all proceeded to the room whence for some time past an agreeable odour had been tickling the nostrils of those present, and towards the door of which Sobakevitch in particular had been glancing since the moment when he had caught sight of a huge sturgeon reposing on the sideboard. After a glassful of warm, olive-coloured *vodka* apiece—*vodka* of the tint to be seen only in the species of Siberian stone whereof seals are cut—the company applied themselves to knife-and-fork work, and, in so doing, evinced their several characteristics and tastes. For instance, Sobakevitch, disdaining lesser trifles, tackled the large sturgeon, and, during the time that his fellow guests were eating minor comestibles, and drinking and talking, contrived to consume more than a quarter of the whole fish; so that, on the host remembering the creature, and, with fork in hand, leading the way in its direction and saying, "What, gentlemen, think you of this striking product of nature?" there ensued the discovery that of the said product of nature there remained little beyond the tail, while Sobakevitch, with an air as though at least *he* had not eaten it, was engaged in plunging his fork into a much more diminutive piece of fish which happened to be resting on an adjacent platter. After his divorce from the sturgeon, Sobakevitch ate and drank no more, but sat frowning and blinking in an armchair.

Apparently the host was not a man who believed in sparing the wine, for the toasts drunk were innumerable. The first toast (as the reader may guess) was quaffed to the health of the new landowner of Kherson; the second to the prosperity of his peasants and their safe transferment; and the third to the beauty of his future wife—a compliment which brought to our hero's lips a flickering smile. Lastly, he received from the company a pressing, as well as an unanimous, invitation to extend his stay in the town for at least another fortnight, and, in the meanwhile, to allow a wife to be found for him.

" Quite so," agreed the President. " Fight us tooth and nail though you may, we intend to have you married. You have happened upon us by chance, and you shall have no reason to repent of it. We are in earnest on this subject."

" But why should I fight you tooth and nail? " said Chichikov, smiling. " Marriage would not come amiss to me, were I but provided with a betrothed."

" Then a betrothed you shall have. Why not? We will do as you wish."

" Very well," assented Chichikov.

" Bravo, bravo!" the company shouted. " Long live Paul Ivanovitch! Hurrah! Hurrah!" And with that every one approached to clink glasses with him, and he readily accepted the compliment, and accepted it many times in succession. Indeed, as the hours passed on, the hilarity of the company increased yet further, and more than once the President (a man of great urbanity when thoroughly in his cups) embraced the chief guest of the day with the heartfelt words, " My dearest fellow! My own most precious of friends!" Nay, he even started to crack his fingers, to dance around Chichikov's chair, and to sing snatches of a popular song. To the champagne succeeded Hungarian wine, which had the effect of still further heartening and enlivening the company. By this time every one had forgotten about whist, and given himself up to shouting and disputing. Every conceivable subject was discussed, including politics and military affairs; and in this connection guests voiced jejune opinions for the expression of which they would, at any other time, have soundly spanked their offspring. Chichikov, like the rest, had never before felt so gay, and, imagining himself really and truly to be a landowner of Kherson, spoke of various improvements in agriculture, of the three-field system of tillage,[1] and of the beatific felicity of a union between two kindred souls. Also, he started to recite poetry to Sobakevitch, who blinked as he listened, for he greatly desired to go to sleep. At length the guest of the evening realised that matters had gone far enough, so begged to be given a lift home, and was accommodated with the Public Prosecutor's *drozhki*. Luckily the driver

---

[1] The system by which, in annual rotation, two-thirds of a given area are cultivated, and the remaining third is left fallow.

of the vehicle was a practised man at his work, for, while driving with one hand, he succeeded in leaning backwards and, with the other, holding Chichikov securely in his place. Arrived at the inn, our hero continued babbling awhile about a flaxen-haired damsel with rosy lips and a dimple in her right cheek, about villages of his in Kherson, and about the amount of his capital. Nay, he even issued seignorial instructions that Selifan should go and muster the peasants about to be transferred, and make a complete and detailed inventory of them. For a while Selifan listened in silence; then he left the room, and instructed Petrushka to help the *barin* to undress. As it happened, Chichikov's boots had no sooner been removed than he managed to perform the rest of his toilet without assistance, to roll on to the bed (which creaked terribly as he did so), and to sink into a sleep in every way worthy of a landowner of Kherson. Meanwhile Petrushka had taken his master's coat and trousers of bilberry-coloured check into the corridor; where, spreading them over a clothes' horse, he started to flick and to brush them, and to fill the whole corridor with dust. Just as he was about to replace them in his master's room he happened to glance over the railing of the gallery, and saw Selifan returning from the stable. Glances were exchanged, and in an instant the pair had arrived at an instinctive understanding—an understanding to the effect that the *barin* was sound asleep, and that therefore one might consider one's own pleasure a little. Accordingly Petrushka proceeded to restore the coat and trousers to their appointed places, and then descended the stairs; whereafter he and Selifan left the house together. Not a word passed between them as to the object of their expedition. On the contrary, they talked solely of extraneous subjects. Yet their walk did not take them far; it took them only to the other side of the street, and thence into an establishment which immediately confronted the inn. Entering a mean, dirty courtyard covered with glass, they passed thence to a cellar where a number of customers were seated around small wooden tables. What thereafter was done by Selifan and Petrushka God alone knows. At all events, within an hour's time they issued, arm in arm, and in profound silence, yet remaining markedly assiduous to one another, and ever ready to help one another around an awkward corner. Still linked together—never once releasing their mutual hold—they spent the next quarter of an hour in attempting to negotiate the stairs of the inn; but at length even that ascent had been mastered, and they proceeded further on their way. Halting before his mean little pallet, Petrushka stood awhile in thought. His difficulty was how best to assume a recumbent position. Eventually he lay down on his face, with his legs trailing over the floor; after which Selifan also stretched himself upon the pallet, with his head resting upon Petrushka's stomach, and his mind wholly oblivious of the fact that he ought not to have been sleeping there at all, but in the servants' quarters, or in the stable beside his horses. Scarcely a moment had passed before the pair were plunged in slumber and emitting the most raucous snores; to which their master (next door) responded with snores of a whistling and nasal order. Indeed, before long every one in the inn had followed their soothing example, and the hostelry lay plunged in complete restfulness. Only in the window of the room of the newly-arrived lieutenant from Riazan did a light remain burning. Evidently he was a devotee of boots, for he had purchased four pairs, and was now trying on a fifth. Several times he approached the bed with a view to taking off the boots and retiring to rest; but each time he failed, for the reason that the boots were so alluring in their make that he had no choice but to lift up first one foot, and then the other, for the purpose of scanning their elegant welts.

VIII

It was not long before Chichikov's purchases had become the talk of the town; and various were the opinions expressed as to whether or not it was expedient to procure peasants for trans-ferment. Indeed such was the interest taken by certain citizens in the matter that they advised the purchaser to provide himself and his convoy with an escort, in order to ensure their safe arrival at the appointed destination; but though Chichikov thanked the donors of this advice for the same, and declared that he should be very glad, in case of need, to avail himself of it, he declared also that there was no real necessity for an escort, seeing that the peasants whom he had purchased were exception-ally peace-loving folk, and that, being themselves consenting parties to the transferment, they would undoubtedly prove in every way tractable.

One particularly good result of this advertisement of his scheme was that he came to rank as neither more nor less than a millionaire. Consequently, much as the inhabitants had liked our hero in the first instance (as seen in Chapter I.), they now liked him more than ever. As a matter of fact, they were citizens of an exceptionally quiet, good-natured, easy-going disposition; and some of them were even well educated. For instance, the President of the Local Council could recite the whole of Zhukovski's *Ludmilla* by heart, and give such an impressive rendering of the passage " The pine forest was asleep and the valley at rest " (as well as of the exclamation " Phew ! ") that one felt, as he did so, that the pine forest and the valley really *were* as he described them. The effect was also further heightened by the manner in which, at such moments, he assumed the most portentous frown. For his part, the Post-master went in more for philosophy, and diligently perused such works as Young's *Night Thoughts*, and Eckhartshausen's *A Key to the Mysteries of Nature ;* of which latter work he would make copious extracts, though no one had the slightest notion what they referred to. For the rest, he was a witty, florid little individual, and much addicted to a practice of what he called " embellishing " whatsoever he had to say—a feat which he performed with the aid of such by-the-way phrases as " my dear sir," " my good So-and-So," " you know," " you understand," " you may imagine," " relatively speaking," " for instance," and " et cetera "; of which phrases he would add sackfuls to his speech. He could also " embellish " his words by the simple expedient of half-closing, half-winking one eye; which trick communicated to some of his satirical utterances quite a mordant effect. Nor were his colleagues a wit inferior to him in enlighten-ment. For instance, one of them made a regular practice of reading *Karamzin*, another of conning the *Moscow Gazette*, and a third of never looking at a book at all. Likewise, although they were the sort of men to whom, in their more intimate movements, their wives would very naturally address such nicknames as " Toby Jug," " Marmot," " Fatty," " Pot Belly," " Smutty," " Kiki," and " Buzz-Buzz," they were men also of good heart, and very ready to extend their hospitality and their friendship when once a guest had eaten of their bread and salt, or spent an evening in their company. Particularly, there-fore, did Chichikov earn these good folk's approval with his taking methods and qualities—so much so that the expression of that approval bid fair to make it difficult for him to quit the town, seeing that, wherever he went, the one phrase dinned into his ears was " Stay another week with us, Paul Ivanovitch."

In short, he had ceased to be a free agent. But incomparably more striking was the impression (a matter for unbounded surprise!) which he produced upon the ladies. Properly to explain this phenomenon I should need to say a great deal about the ladies themselves, and to describe in the most vivid of colours their social intercourse and spiritual qualities. Yet this would be a difficult thing for me to do, since, on the one hand, I should be hampered by my boundless respect for the womenfolk of all Civil Service officials, and, on the other hand—well, simply by the innate arduousness of the task. The ladies of N. were—— But no, I cannot do it; my heart has already failed me. Come, come! The ladies of N. were distinguished for—— But it is of no use; somehow my pen seems to refuse to move over the paper—it seems to be weighted as with a plummet of lead. Very well. That being so, I will merely say a word or two concerning the most prominent tints on the feminine palette of N.—merely a word or two concerning the outward appearance of its ladies, and a word or two concerning their more superficial characteristics. The ladies of N. were pre-eminently what is known as " presentable." Indeed, in that respect they might have served for a model to the ladies of many another town. That is to say, in whatever pertained to " tone," etiquette, the intricacies of decorum, and strict observance of the prevailing mode, they surpassed even the ladies of Moscow and St. Petersburg, seeing that they dressed with taste, drove about in carriages in the latest fashions, and never went out without the escort of a footman in a gold-laced livery. Again, they looked upon a visiting card—even upon a make-shift affair consisting of an ace of diamonds or a two of clubs—as a sacred thing; so sacred that on one occasion two closely related ladies who had also been closely attached friends were known to fall out with one another over the mere fact of an omission to return a social call! Yes, in spite of the best efforts of husbands and kinsfolk to reconcile the antagonists, it became clear that, though all else in the world might conceivably be possible, never could the hatchet be buried between ladies who had quarrelled over a neglected visit. Likewise strenuous scenes used to take place over questions of precedence—scenes of a kind which had the effect of inspiring husbands to great and knightly ideas on the subject of protecting the fair. True, never did a duel actually take place, since all the husbands were officials belonging to the Civil Service; but at least a given combatant would strive to heap contumely upon his rival, and, as we all know, that is a resource which may prove even more effectual than a duel. As regards morality, the ladies of N. were nothing if not censorious, and would at once be fired with virtuous indignation when they heard of a case of vice or seduction. Nay, even to mere frailty they would award the lash without mercy. On the other hand, should any instance of what they called " third personism " occur among *their own* circle, it was always kept dark—not a hint of what was going on being allowed to transpire, and even the wronged husband holding himself ready, should he meet with, or hear of, the " third person," to quote, in a mild and rational manner, the proverb, " Whom concerns it that a friend should consort with friend ? " In addition, I may say that, like most of the female world of St. Petersburg, the ladies of N. were pre-eminently careful and refined in their choice of words and phrases. Never did a lady say, " I blew my nose," or " I perspired," or " I spat." No, it had to be, " I relieved my nose through the expedient of wiping it with my handkerchief," and so forth. Again, to say, " This glass, or this plate, smells badly " was forbidden. No, not even a hint to such an effect was to be dropped. Rather, the proper phrase, in such a case, was " This glass, or this plate, is not behaving very well,"—or some such formula.

In fact, to refine the Russian tongue the more thoroughly, something like half the words in it were cut out: which circumstance necessitated very frequent recourse to the tongue of France, since the same words, if spoken in French, were another matter altogether, and one could use even blunter ones than the ones originally objected to.

So much for the ladies of N., provided that one confines one's observations to the surface; yet hardly need it be said that, should one penetrate deeper than that, a great deal more would come to light. At the same time, it is never a very safe proceeding to peer deeply into the hearts of ladies; wherefore, restricting ourselves to the foregoing superficialities, let us proceed further on our way.

Hitherto the ladies had paid Chichikov no particular attention, though giving him full credit for his gentlemanly and urbane demeanour; but from the moment that there arose rumours of his being a millionaire other qualities of his began to be canvassed. Nevertheless, not *all* the ladies were governed by interested motives, since it is due to the term " millionaire," rather than to the character of the person who bears it, that the mere sound of the word exercises upon rascals, upon decent folk,

and upon folk who are neither the one nor the other, an un-
definable influence. A millionaire suffers from the disadvantage
of everywhere having to behold meanness, including the sort of
meanness which, though not actually based upon calculations
of self-interest, yet runs after the wealthy man with smiles, and
doffs his hat, and begs for invitations to houses where the
millionaire is known to be going to dine. That a similar inclination to meanness seized upon the ladies of N. goes without
saying; with the result that many a drawing-room heard it
whispered that, if Chichikov was not exactly a beauty, at least
he was sufficiently good-looking to serve for a husband, though
he could have borne to have been a little more rotund and stout.
To that there would be added scornful references to lean husbands, and hints that they resembled tooth-brushes rather than
men—with many other feminine additions. Also, such crowds
of feminine shoppers began to repair to the Bazaar as almost to
constitute a crush, and something like a procession of carriages
ensued, so long grew the rank of vehicles. For their part, the
tradesmen had the joy of seeing highly priced dress materials
which they had bought at fairs, and then been unable to dispose
of, now suddenly become tradeable, and go off with a rush. For
instance, on one occasion a lady appeared at Mass in a bustle
which filled the church to an extent which led the verger on
duty to bid the commoner folk withdraw to the porch, lest the
lady's toilet should be soiled in the crush. Even Chichikov could
not help privately remarking the attention which he aroused.
On one occasion, when he returned to the inn, he found on his
table a note addressed to himself. Whence it had come, and who
had delivered it, he failed to discover, for the waiter declared
that the person who had brought it had omitted to leave the
name of the writer. Beginning abruptly with the words " I *must*
write to you," the letter went on to say that between a certain
pair of souls there existed a bond of sympathy; and this verity
the epistle further confirmed with rows of full stops to the
extent of nearly half a page. Next there followed a few reflections of a correctitude so remarkable that I have no choice but
to quote them. " What, I would ask, is this life of ours? "
inquired the writer. " 'Tis nought but a vale of woe. And what,
I would ask, is the world? 'Tis nought but a mob of unthinking
humanity." Thereafter, incidentally remarking that she had
just dropped a tear to the memory of her dear mother, who
had departed this life twenty-five years ago, the (presumably)
lady writer invited Chichikov to come forth into the wilds, and

to leave for ever the city where, penned in noisome haunts, folk could not even draw their breath. In conclusion, the writer gave way to unconcealed despair, and wound up with the following verses:

> " Two turtle doves to thee, one day,
> My dust will show, congealed in death;
> And, cooing wearily, they'll say:
> ' In grief and loneliness she drew her closing breath.' "

True, the last line did not scan, but that was a trifle, since the quatrain at least conformed to the mode then prevalent. Neither signature nor date were appended to the document, but only a postcript expressing a conjecture that Chichikov's own heart would tell him who the writer was, and stating, in addition, that the said writer would be present at the Governor's ball on the following night.

This greatly interested Chichikov. Indeed, there was so much that was alluring and provocative of curiosity in the anonymous missive that he read it through a second time, and then a third, and finally said to himself: " I *should* like to know who sent it! " In short, he took the thing seriously, and spent over an hour in considering the same. At length, muttering a comment upon the epistle's efflorescent style, he refolded the document, and committed it to his dispatch-box in company with a play-bill and an invitation to a wedding—the latter of which had for the last seven years reposed in the self-same receptacle and in the self-same position. Shortly afterwards there arrived a card of invitation to the Governor's ball already referred to. In passing, it may be said that such festivities are not infrequent phenomena in county towns, for the reason that where Governors exist there must take place balls if from the local gentry there is to be evoked that respectful affection which is every Governor's due.

Thenceforth all extraneous thoughts and considerations were laid aside in favour of preparing for the coming function. Indeed, this conjunction of exciting and provocative motives led to Chichikov devoting to his toilet an amount of time never witnessed since the creation of the world. Merely in the contemplation of his features in the mirror, as he tried to communicate to them a succession of varying expressions, was an hour spent. First of all he strove to make his features assume an air of dignity and importance, and then an air of humble, but faintly satirical, respect, and then an air of respect guiltless of any alloy whatsoever. Next, he practised performing a series of bows to his reflection, accompanied with certain murmurs intended

to bear a resemblance to a French phrase (though Chichikov
knew not a single word of the Gallic tongue). Lastly came the
performing of a series of what I might call " agreeable surprises,"
in the shape of twitchings of the brow and lips and certain
motions of the tongue. In short, he did all that a man is apt
to do when he is not only alone, but also certain that he is
handsome and that no one is regarding him through a chink.
Finally he tapped himself lightly on the chin, and said, " Ah,
good old face!" In the same way, when he started to dress
himself for the ceremony, the level of his high spirits remained
unimpaired throughout the process. That is to say, while
adjusting his braces and tying his tie, he shuffled his feet in
what was not exactly a dance, but might be called the *entr'acte*
of a dance: which performance had the not very serious result of
setting a wardrobe a-rattle, and causing a brush to slide from
the table to the floor.

Later, his entry into the ballroom produced an extraordinary
effect. Every one present came forward to meet him, some
with cards in their hands, and one man even breaking off a
conversation at the most interesting point—namely, the point
that " the Inferior Land Court must be made responsible for
everything." Yes, in spite of the responsibility of the Inferior
Land Court, the speaker cast all thoughts of it to the winds as
he hurried to greet our hero. From every side resounded acclama-
tions of welcome, and Chichikov felt himself engulfed in a sea
of embraces. Thus, scarcely had he extricated himself from the
arms of the President of the Local Council when he found himself
just as firmly clasped in the arms of the Chief of Police, who, in
turn, surrendered him to the Inspector of the Medical Department, who, in turn, handed him over to the Commissioner of
Taxes, who, again, committed him to the charge of the Town
Architect. Even the Governor, who hitherto had been standing
among his womenfolk with a box of sweets in one hand and a
lap-dog in the other, now threw down both sweets and lap-dog
(the lap-dog giving vent to a yelp as he did so) and added his
greeting to those of the rest of the company. Indeed, not a face
was there to be seen on which ecstatic delight—or, at all events,
the reflection of other people's ecstatic delight—was not painted.
The same expression may be discerned on the faces of subordinate officials when, the newly-arrived Director having made his
inspection, the said officials are beginning to get over their first
sense of awe on perceiving that he has found much to commend,
and that he can even go so far as to jest and utter a few words

of smiling approval. Thereupon every *tchinovnik* responds with a smile of double strength, and those who (it may be) have not heard a single word of the Director's speech smile out of sympathy with the rest, and even the gendarme who is posted at the distant door—a man, perhaps, who has never before compassed a smile, but is more accustomed to dealing out blows to the populace—summons up a kind of a grin, even though the grin resembles the grimace of a man who is about to sneeze after inadvertently taking an over-large pinch of snuff. To all and sundry Chichikov responded with a bow, and felt extraordinarily at his ease as he did so. To right and left did he incline his head in the sidelong, yet unconstrained, manner that was his wont and never failed to charm the beholder. As for the ladies, they clustered around him in a shining bevy that was redolent of every species of perfume—of roses, of spring violets, and of mignonette; so much so that instinctively Chichikov raised his nose to snuff the air. Likewise the ladies' dresses displayed an endless profusion of taste and variety; and though the majority of their wearers evinced a tendency to *embonpoint*, those wearers knew how to call upon art for the concealment of the fact. Confronting them, Chichikov thought to himself: " Which of these beauties is the writer of the letter?" Then again he snuffed the air. When the ladies had, to a certain extent, returned to their seats, he resumed his attempts to discern (from glances and expressions) which of them could possibly be the unknown authoress. Yet, though those glances and expressions were too subtle, too insufficiently open, the difficulty in no way diminished his high spirits. Easily and gracefully did he exchange agreeable badinage with one lady, and then approach another one with the short, mincing steps usually affected by young-old dandies who are fluttering around the fair. As he turned, not without dexterity, to right and left, he kept one leg slightly dragging behind the other, like a short tail or a comma. This trick the ladies particularly admired. In short, they not only discovered in him a host of recommendations and attractions, but also began to see in his face a sort of grand, Mars-like, military expression—a thing which, as we know, never fails to please the feminine eye. Certain of the ladies even took to bickering over him, and, on perceiving that he spent most of his time standing near the door, some of their number hastened to occupy chairs nearer to his post of vantage. In fact, when a certain dame chanced to have the good fortune to anticipate a hated rival in the race there very nearly ensued a most lamentable scene—which, to many of those who had been desirous of doing exactly the same thing, seemed a peculiarly horrible instance of brazen-faced audacity.

So deeply did Chichikov become plunged in conversation with his fair pursuers—or, rather, so deeply did those fair pursuers enmesh him in the toils of small talk (which they accomplished through the expedient of asking him endless subtle riddles which brought the sweat to his brow in his attempts to guess them) —that he forgot the claims of courtesy which required him first of all to greet his hostess. In fact, he remembered those claims only on hearing the Governor's wife herself addressing him. She had been standing before him for several minutes, and now greeted him with suave *empressement* and the words, " So *here* you are, Paul Ivanovitch! " But what she said next I am not in a position to report, for she spoke in the ultra-refined tone and vein wherein ladies and gentlemen customarily express themselves in high-class novels which have been written by experts more qualified than I am to describe *salons*, and able to boast of some acquaintance with good society. In effect, what the Governor's wife said was that she hoped—she greatly hoped—that Monsieur Chichikov's heart still contained a corner —even the smallest possible corner—for those whom he had so cruelly forgotten. Upon that Chichikov turned to her, and was on the point of returning a reply at least no worse than that which would have been returned, under similar circumstances, by the hero of a fashionable novelette, when he stopped short, as though thunderstruck.

For before him there was standing not only Madame, but also a young girl whom she was holding by the hand. The golden hair, the fine-drawn, delicate contours, the face with its bewitching oval—a face which might have served as a model for the countenance of the Madonna, since it was of a type rarely to be met with in Russia, where nearly everything, from plains to human feet, is, rather, on the gigantic scale; these features, I say, were those of the identical maiden whom Chichikov had encountered on the road when he had been fleeing from Nozdrev's. His emotion was such that he could not formulate a single intelligible syllable; he could merely murmur the devil only knows what, though certainly nothing of the kind which would have risen to the lips of the hero of a fashionable novel.

" I think that you have not met my daughter before? " said Madame. " She is just fresh from school."

He replied that he *had* had the happiness of meeting Mademoiselle before, and under rather unexpected circumstances; but on his trying to say something further his tongue completely failed him. The Governor's wife added a word or two, and then carried off her daughter to speak to some of the other guests.

Chichikov stood rooted to the spot, like a man who, after issuing into the street for a pleasant walk, has suddenly come to a halt on remembering that something has been left behind him. In a moment, as he struggles to recall what that something is, the mien of careless expectancy disappears from his face, and he no longer sees a single person or a single object in his vicinity. In the same way did Chichikov suddenly become oblivious to the scene around him. Yet all the while the melodious tongues of ladies were plying him with multitudinous hints and questions —hints and questions inspired with a desire to captivate. " Might we poor cumberers of the ground make so bold as to ask you what you are thinking of? " " Pray tell us where lie the happy regions in which your thoughts are wandering? " " Might we be informed of the name of her who has plunged you into this sweet abandonment of meditation? "—such were the phrases thrown at him. But to everything he turned a deaf ear, and the phrases in question might as well have been stones dropped into a pool. Indeed, his rudeness soon reached the pitch of his walking away altogether, in order that he might go and reconnoitre whither the Governor's wife and daughter had retreated. But the ladies were not going to let him off so easily. Every one of them had made up her mind to use upon him her every weapon, and to exhibit whatsoever might chance to constitute her best point. Yet the ladies' wiles proved useless, for Chichikov paid not the smallest attention to them, even when the dancing had begun, but kept raising himself on tiptoe to peer over people's heads and ascertain in which direction the bewitching maiden with the golden hair had gone. Also, when seated, he continued to peep between his neighbours' backs and shoulders, until at last he discovered her sitting beside her mother, who was wearing a sort of Oriental turban and feather. Upon that one would have thought that his purpose was to carry the position by storm; for, whether moved by the influence of spring, or whether moved by a push from behind, he pressed forward with such desperate resolution that his elbow caused the Commissioner of Taxes to stagger on his feet, and would have caused him to lose his balance altogether but for the supporting row of guests in the rear. Likewise the Postmaster was made to give ground; whereupon he turned and eyed

Chichikov with mingled astonishment and subtle irony. But
Chichikov never even noticed him; he saw in the distance only
the golden-haired beauty. At that moment she was drawing
on a long glove and, doubtless, pining to be flying over the
dancing-floor, where, with clicking heels, four couples had now
begun to thread the mazes of the mazurka. In particular was
a military staff-captain working body and soul and arms and
legs to compass such a series of steps as were never before
performed, even in a dream. However, Chichikov slipped past
the mazurka dancers, and, almost treading on their heels, made
his way towards the spot where Madame and her daughter were
seated. Yet he approached them with great diffidence and none
of his late mincing and prancing. Nay, he even faltered as he
walked; his every movement had about it an air of awkwardness.

It is difficult to say whether or not the feeling which had
awakened in our hero's breast was the feeling of love; for it is
problematical whether or not men who are neither stout nor
thin are capable of any such sentiment. Nevertheless, something
strange, something which he could not altogether explain, had
come upon him. It seemed as though the ball, with its talk and
its clatter, had suddenly become a thing remote—that the
orchestra had withdrawn behind a hill, and the scene grown
misty, like the carelessly painted-in background of a picture.
And from that misty void there could be seen glimmering only
the delicate outlines of the bewitching maiden. Somehow her
exquisite shape reminded him of an ivory toy, in such fair, white,
transparent relief did it stand out against the dull blur of the
surrounding throng.

Herein we see a phenomenon not infrequently observed—
the phenomenon of the Chichikovs of this world becoming
temporarily poets. At all events, for a moment or two our
Chichikov felt that he was a young man again, if not exactly
a military officer. On perceiving an empty chair beside the
mother and daughter, he hastened to occupy it, and though
conversation at first hung fire, things gradually improved, and
he acquired more confidence.

At this point I must reluctantly deviate to say that men of
weight and high office are always a trifle ponderous when
conversing with ladies. Young lieutenants—or, at all events,
officers not above the rank of captain—are far more successful
at the game. How they contrive to be so God only knows. Let
them but make the most inane of remarks, and at once the
maiden by their side will be rocking with laughter; whereas,

should a State Councillor enter into conversation with a damsel, and remark that the Russian Empire is one of vast extent, or utter a compliment which he has elaborated not without a certain measure of intelligence (however strongly the said compliment may smack of a book), of a surety the thing will fall flat. Even a witticism from him will be laughed at far more by him himself than it will by the lady who may happen to be listening to his remarks.

These comments I have interposed for the purpose of explaining to the reader why, as our hero conversed, the maiden began to yawn. Blind to this, however, he continued to relate to her sundry adventures which had befallen him in different parts of the world. Meanwhile (as need hardly be said) the rest of the ladies had taken umbrage at his behaviour. One of them purposely stalked past him to intimate to him the fact, as well as to jostle the Governor's daughter, and let the flying end of a scarf flick her in the face; while from a lady seated behind the pair came both a whiff of violets and a very venomous and sarcastic remark. Nevertheless, either he did not hear the remark or he *pretended* not to hear it. This was unwise of him, since it never does to disregard ladies' opinions. Later—but too late—he was destined to learn this to his cost.

In short, dissatisfaction began to display itself on every feminine face. No matter how high Chichikov might stand in society, and no matter how much he might be a millionaire and include in his expression of countenance an indefinable element of grandness and martial ardour, there are certain things which no lady will pardon, whosoever be the person concerned. We know that at Governors' balls it is customary for the onlookers to compose verses at the expense of the dancers; and in this case the verses were directed to Chichikov's address. Briefly, the prevailing dissatisfaction grew until a tacit edict of proscription had been issued against both him and the poor young maiden.

But an even more unpleasant surprise was in store for our hero; for whilst the young lady was still yawning as Chichikov recounted to her certain of his past adventures and also touched lightly upon the subject of Greek philosophy, there appeared from an adjoining room the figure of Nozdrev. Whether he had come from the buffet, or whether he had issued from a little green retreat where a game more strenuous than whist had been in progress, or whether he had left the latter resort unaided, or whether he had been expelled therefrom, is unknown; but at all events, when he entered the ballroom, he was in an elevated condition, and leading by the arm the Public Prosecutor, whom he seemed to have been dragging about for a long while past, seeing that the poor man was glancing from side to side as though seeking a means of putting an end to this personally conducted tour. Certainly he must have found the situation almost unbearable, in view of the fact that, after deriving inspiration from two glasses of tea not wholly undiluted with rum, Nozdrev was engaged in lying unmercifully. On sighting him in the distance, Chichikov at once decided to sacrifice himself. That is to say, he decided to vacate his present enviable position and make off with all possible speed, since he could see that an encounter with the newcomer would do him no good. Unfortunately at that moment the Governor buttonholed him with a request that he would come and act as arbiter between him (the Governor) and two ladies—the subject of dispute being the question as to whether or not woman's love is lasting. Simultaneously Nozdrev descried our hero and bore down upon him.

" Ah, my fine landowner of Kherson!" he cried with a smile which set his fresh, spring-rose-pink cheeks a-quiver. "Have you been doing much trade in departed souls lately?" With that he turned to the Governor. "I suppose your Excellency knows that this man traffics in dead peasants?" he bawled. "Look here, Chichikov. I tell you in the most friendly way possible that every one here likes you—yes, including even the Governor. Nevertheless, had I my way, I would hang you! Yes, by God I would!"

Chichikov's discomfiture was complete.

" And would you believe it, your Excellency," went on Nozdrev, " but this fellow actually said to me, ' Sell me your dead souls!' Why, I laughed till I nearly became as dead as the souls. And, behold, no sooner do I arrive here than I am told that he has bought three million roubles' worth of peasants for transferment! For transferment, indeed! And he wanted to bargain with me for my *dead* ones! Look here, Chichikov. You are a swine! Yes, by God, you are an utter swine! Is not that so, your Excellency? Is not that so, friend *Prokuror?* "[1]

But both his Excellency, the Public Prosecutor, and Chichikov were too taken aback to reply. The half-tipsy Nozdrev, without noticing them, continued his harangue as before.

" Ah, my fine sir!" he cried. " *This* time I don't mean to let you go. No, not until I have learnt what all this purchasing of dead peasants means. Look here. You ought to be ashamed of

[1] Public Prosecutor.

yourself. Yes, *I* say that—*I* who am one of your best friends."
Here he turned to the Governor again. " Your Excellency," he
continued, " you would never believe what inseparables this
man and I have been. Indeed, if you had stood there and said
to me, ' Nozdrev, tell me on your honour which of the two you
love best—your father or Chichikov? ' I should have replied,
' Chichikov, by God! " With that he tackled our hero again.
" Come, come, my friend! " he urged. " Let me imprint upon
your cheeks a *baiser* of two. You will excuse me if I kiss him,
will you not, your Excellency? No, do not resist me, Chichikov,
but allow me to imprint at least one *baiser* upon your lily-white
cheek." And in his efforts to force upon Chichikov what he
termed his " *baisers* " he came near to measuring his length
upon the floor.

Every one now edged away, and turned a deaf ear to his
further babblings; but his words on the subject of the purchase
of dead souls had none the less been uttered at the top of his
voice, and been accompanied with such uproarious laughter
that the curiosity even of those who had happened to be sitting
or standing in the remoter corners of the room had been aroused.
So strange and novel seemed the idea that the company stood
with faces expressive of nothing but a dumb, dull wonder.
Only some of the ladies (as Chichikov did not fail to remark)
exchanged meaning, ill-natured winks and a series of sarcastic
smiles: which circumstance still further increased his confusion.
That Nozdrev was a notorious liar every one, of course, knew,
and that he should have given vent to an idiotic outburst of this
sort had surprised no one; but a dead soul—well, what was one
to make of Nozdrev's reference to such a commodity?

Naturally this unseemly *contretemps* had greatly upset our
hero; for, however foolish be a madman's words, they may yet
prove sufficient to sow doubt in the minds of saner individuals.
He felt much as does a man who, shod with well-polished boots,
has just stepped into a dirty, stinking puddle. He tried to put
away from him the occurrence, and to expand, and to enjoy
himself once more. Nay, he even took a hand at whist. But all
was of no avail—matters kept going as awry as a badly-bent
hoop. Twice he blundered in his play, and the President of the
Council was at a loss to understand how his friend, Paul Ivanovitch, lately so good and so circumspect a player, could perpe-
trate such a *mauvais pas* as to throw away a particular king of
spades which the President has been " trusting " as (to quote
his own expression) " he would have trusted God." At supper,

too, matters felt uncomfortable, even though the society at
Chichikov's table was exceedingly agreeable and Nozdrev had
been removed, owing to the fact that the ladies had found his
conduct too scandalous to be borne, now that the delinquent
had taken to seating himself on the floor and plucking at the
skirts of passing lady dancers. As I say, therefore, Chichikov
found the situation not a little awkward, and eventually put an
end to it by leaving the supper room before the meal was over,
and long before the hour when usually he returned to the inn.

In his little room, with its door of communication blocked
with a wardrobe, and black-beetles occasionally peeping out of
corners, his frame of mind remained as uncomfortable as the
chair in which he was seated. His heart ached with a dull,
unpleasant sensation, with a sort of oppressive emptiness.

"The devil take those who first invented balls!" was his
reflection. "Who derives any real pleasure from them? In this
province there exist want and scarcity everywhere: yet folk
go in for balls! How absurd, too, were those overdressed women!
One of them must have had a thousand roubles on her back, and
all acquired at the expense of the overtaxed peasant, or, worse
still, at that of the conscience of her neighbour. Yes, we all know
why bribes are accepted, and why men become crooked in soul.
It is all done to provide wives—yes, may the pit swallow them
up!—with fal-lals. And for what purpose? That some woman
may not have to reproach her husband with the fact that, say,
the Postmaster's wife is wearing a better dress than she is—a
dress which has cost a thousand roubles! 'Balls and gaiety,
balls and gaiety' is the constant cry. Yet what folly balls are!
They do not consort with the Russian spirit and genius, and
the devil only knows why we have them. A grown, middle-aged
man—a man dressed in black, and looking as stiff as a poker—
suddenly takes the floor and begins shuffling his feet about,
while another man, even though conversing with a companion
on important business, will, the while, keep capering to right
and left like a billy-goat! Mimicry, sheer mimicry! The fact
that the Frenchman is at forty precisely what he was at fifteen
leads us to imagine that we too, forsooth, ought to be the same.
No; a ball leaves one feeling that one has done a wrong thing—so
much so that one does not care even to think of it. It also
leaves one's head perfectly empty, even as does the exertion of
talking to a man of the world. A man of that kind chatters away,
and touches lightly upon every conceivable subject, and talks in
smooth, fluent phrases which he has culled from books without

grazing their substance; whereas go and have a chat with a tradesman who knows at least *one* thing thoroughly, and through the medium of experience, and see whether his conversation will not be worth more than the prattle of a thousand chatterboxes. For what good does one get out of balls? Suppose that a competent writer were to describe such a scene exactly as it stands? Why, even in a book it would seem senseless, even as it certainly is in life. Are, therefore, such functions right or wrong? One would answer that the devil alone knows, and then spit and close the book."

Such were the unfavourable comments which Chichikov passed upon balls in general. With it all, however, there went a second source of dissatisfaction. That is to say, his principal grudge was not so much against balls as against the fact that at this particular one he had been exposed, he had been made to disclose the circumstance that he had been playing a strange, an ambiguous part. Of course, when he reviewed the *contretemps* in the light of pure reason, he could not but see that it mattered nothing, and that a few rude words were of no account now that the chief point had been attained; yet man is an odd creature, and Chichikov actually felt pained by the cold-shouldering administered to him by persons for whom he had not an atom of respect, and whose vanity and love of display he had only that moment been censuring. Still more, on viewing the matter clearly, he felt vexed to think that he himself had been so largely the cause of the catastrophe.

Yet he was not angry with *himself*—of that you may be sure, seeing that all of us have a slight weakness for sparing our own faults, and always do our best to find some fellow-creature upon whom to vent our displeasure—whether that fellow-creature be a servant, a subordinate official, or a wife. In the same way Chichikov sought a scapegoat upon whose shoulders he could lay the blame for all that had annoyed him. He found one in Nozdrev, and you may be sure that the scapegoat in question received a good drubbing from every side, even as an experienced captain or chief of police will give a knavish *starosta* or postboy a rating not only in the terms become classical, but also in such terms as the said captain or chief of police may invent for himself. In short, Nozdrev's whole lineage was passed in review; and many of its members in the ascending line fared badly in the process.

Meanwhile, at the other end of the town there was in progress an event which was destined to augment still further the un-

pleasantness of our hero's position.   That is to say, through the
outlying streets and alleys of the town there was clattering a
vehicle to which it would be difficult precisely to assign a name,
seeing that, though it was of a species peculiar to itself, it most
nearly resembled a large, rickety water melon on wheels.
Eventually this monstrosity drew up at the gates of a house
where the archpriest of one of the churches resided, and from
its doors there leapt a damsel clad in a jerkin and wearing a
scarf over her head.   For a while she thumped the gates so
vigorously as to set all the dogs barking; then the gates stiffly
opened, and admitted this unwieldy phenomenon of the road.
Lastly, the *barinia* herself alighted, and stood revealed as
Madame Korobotchka, widow of a Collegiate Secretary!   The
reason of her sudden arrival was that she had felt so uneasy
about the possible outcome of Chichikov's whim, that during
the three nights following his departure she had been unable to
sleep a wink; whereafter, in spite of the fact that her horses
were not shod, she had set out for the town, in order to learn
at first hand how the dead souls were faring, and whether
(which might God forefend!) she had not sold them at something like a third of their true value.   The consequences of her
venture the reader will learn from a conversation between two
ladies.   We will reserve it for the ensuing chapter.

IX

NEXT morning, before the usual hour for paying calls, there
tripped from the portals of an orange-coloured wooden house
with an attic storey and a row of blue pillars a lady in an
elegant plaid cloak.   With her came a footman in a many-caped
greatcoat and a polished top hat with a gold band.   Hastily,
but gracefully, the lady ascended the steps let down from a
koliaska which was standing before the entrance, and as soon
as she had done so the footman shut her in, put up the steps
again, and, catching hold of the strap behind the vehicle,
shouted to the coachman, " Right away! "   The reason of all
this was that the lady was the possessor of a piece of intelligence
which she was burning to communicate to a fellow-creature.
Every moment she kept looking out of the carriage window, and
perceiving, with almost speechless vexation, that, as yet, she
was but half-way on her journey.   The fronts of the houses

appeared to her longer than usual, and in particular did the front of the white stone hospital, with its rows of narrow windows, seen interminable to a degree which at length forced her to ejaculate: " Oh, the cursed building! Positively there is no end to it!" Also, she twice adjured the coachman with the words, " Go quicker, Andrusha! You are a horribly long time over the journey this morning." But at length the goal was reached, and the *koliaska* stopped before a one-storied wooden mansion, dark grey in colour, and having white carvings over the windows, a tall wooden fence and narrow garden in front of the latter, and a few meagre trees looming white with an incongruous coating of road dust. In the windows of the building were also a few flower pots and a parrot that kept alternately dancing on the floor of its cage and hanging on to the ring of the same with its beak. Also, in the sunshine before the door two pet dogs were sleeping. Here there lived the lady's bosom friend. As soon as the bosom friend in question learnt of the newcomer's arrival, she ran down into the hall, and the two ladies kissed and embraced one another. Then they adjourned to the drawing-room.

" How glad I am to see you!" said the bosom friend. " When I heard some one arriving I wondered who could possibly be calling so early. Parasha declared that it must be the Vice-Governor's wife, so, as I did not want to be bored with her, I gave orders that I was to be reported ' not at home.' "

For her part, the guest would have liked to have proceeded to business by communicating her tidings, but a sudden exclamation from the hostess imparted (temporarily) a new direction to the conversation.

" What a pretty chintz!" she cried, gazing at the other's gown.

" Yes, it *is* pretty," agreed the visitor. " On the other hand, Praskovia Thedorovna thinks that——"

In others words, the ladies proceeded to indulge in a conversation on the subject of dress; and only after this had lasted for a considerable while did the visitor let fall a remark which led her entertainer to inquire:

" And how is the universal charmer? "

" My God!" replied the other. " There has been *such* a business! In fact, do you know why I am here at all? " And the visitor's breathing became more hurried, and further words seemed to be hovering between her lips like hawks preparing to stoop upon their prey. Only a person of the inhumanity of a

" true friend " would have had the heart to interrupt her; but
the hostess was just such a friend, and at once interposed with:

" I wonder how any one can see anything in the man to
praise or to admire. For my own part, I think—and I would
say the same thing straight to his face—that he is a perfect
rascal."

" Yes, but do listen to what I have got to tell you."

" Oh, I know that some people think him handsome," continued the hostess, unmoved; " but *I* say that he is nothing of
the kind—that, in particular, his nose is perfectly odious."

" Yes, but let me finish what I was saying." The guest's
tone was almost piteous in its appeal.

" What is it, then? "

" You cannot imagine my state of mind! You see, this
morning I received a visit from Father Cyril's wife—the Archpriest's wife—you know her, don't you? Well, whom do you
suppose that fine gentleman visitor of ours has turned out
to be? "

" The man who has built the Archpriest a poultry-run? "

" Oh dear no! Had that been all, it would have been nothing.
No. Listen to what Father Cyril's wife had to tell me. She
said that, last night, a lady landowner named Madame Korobotchka arrived at the Archpriest's house—arrived all pale and
trembling—and told her, oh, such things! They sound like a
piece out of a book. That is to say, at dead of night, just when
every one had retired to rest, there came the most dreadful
knocking imaginable, and some one screamed out, ' Open the
gates, or we will break them down!' Just think! After this,
how any one can say that the man is charming I cannot imagine."

" Well, what of Madame Korobotchka? Is she a young
woman or good looking? "

" Oh dear no! Quite an old woman."

" Splendid indeed! So he is actually engaged to a person
like that? One may heartily commend the taste of our ladies
for having fallen in love with him! "

" Nevertheless, it is not as you suppose. Think, now!
Armed with weapons from head to foot, he called upon this old
woman, and said: ' Sell me any souls of yours which have
lately died.' Of course Madame Korobotchka answered,
reasonably enough: ' I cannot sell you those souls, seeing that
they have departed this world;' but he replied: ' No, no!
They are *not* dead. 'Tis I who tell you that—I who ought to
know the truth of the matter. I swear that they are still alive.'

In short, he made such a scene that the whole village came running to the house, and children screamed, and men shouted, and no one could tell what it was all about. The affair seemed to me so horrible, so utterly horrible, that I trembled beyond belief as I listened to the story. ' My dearest madam,' said my maid, Mashka, ' pray look at yourself in the mirror, and see how white you are.' ' But I have no time for that,' I replied, ' as I must be off to tell my friend, Anna Grigorievna, the news.' Nor did I lose a moment in ordering the *koliuska*. Yet when my coachman, Andrusha, asked me for directions I could not get a word out —I just stood staring at him like a fool, until I thought he must think me mad. Oh, Anna Grigorievna, if you but knew how upset I am!"

"What a strange affair!" commented the hostess. "What on earth can the man have meant by ' dead souls '? I confess that the words pass my understanding. Curiously enough, this is the second time I have heard speak of those souls. True, my husband avers that Nozdrev was lying; yet in his lies there seems to have been a grain of truth."

"Well, just think of my state when I heard all this! ' And now,' apparently said Korobotchka to the Archpriest's wife, ' I am altogether at a loss what to do, for, throwing me fifteen roubles, the man forced me to sign a worthless paper—yes, me, an inexperienced, defenceless widow who knows nothing of business.' That such things should happen! *Try* and imagine my feelings!"

" In my opinion, there is in this more than the dead souls which meet the eye."

" I think so too," agreed the other. As a matter of fact, her friend's remark had struck her with complete surprise, as well as filled her with curiosity to know what the word " more " might possibly signify. In fact, she felt driven to inquire: " What do *you* suppose to be hidden beneath it all? "

" No; tell me what *you* suppose? "

" What *I* suppose? I am at a loss to conjecture."

" Yes, but tell me what is in your mind? "

Upon this the visitor had to confess herself nonplussed; for, though capable of growing hysterical, she was incapable of propounding any rational theory. Consequently she felt the more that she needed tender comfort and advice.

" Then *this* is what I think about the dead souls," said the hostess. Instantly the guest pricked up her ears (or, rather, they pricked themselves up) and straightened herself and

became, somehow, more modish, and, despite her not inconsiderable weight, posed herself to look like a piece of thistledown
floating on the breeze.

"The dead souls," began the hostess.

"Are what, are what?" inquired the guest in great excitement.

"Are, are——"

"Tell me, tell me, for heaven's sake!"

"They are an invention to conceal something else. The man's
real object is, is—*to abduct the Governor's daughter*."

So startling and unexpected was this conclusion that the
guest sat reduced to a state of pale, petrified, genuine amazement.

"My God!" she cried, clapping her hands, "I should *never*
have guessed it!"

"Well, to tell you the truth, I guessed it as soon as ever you
opened your mouth."

"So much, then, for educating girls like the Governor's
daughter at school! Just see what comes of it!"

"Yes, indeed! And they tell me that she says things which
I hesitate even to repeat."

"Truly it wrings one's heart to see to what lengths immorality
has come."

"Some of the men have quite lost their heads about her, but
for my part I think her not worth noticing."

"Of course. And her manners are unbearable. But what
puzzles me most is how a travelled man like Chichikov could
come to let himself in for such an affair. Surely he must have
accomplices?"

"Yes; and I should say that one of those accomplices is
Nozdrev."

"Surely not?"

"*Certainly* I should say so. Why, I have known him even try
to sell his own father! At all events he staked him at cards."

"Indeed? You interest me. I should never have thought
him capable of such things."

"I always guessed him to be so."

The two ladies were still discussing the matter with acumen
and success when there walked into the room the Public Prosecutor—bushy eyebrows, motionless features, blinking eyes, and
all. At once the ladies hastened to inform him of the events
related, adducing therewith full details both as to the purchase
of dead souls and as to the scheme to abduct the Governor's
daughter; after which they departed in different directions,

for the purpose of raising the rest of the town. For the execution
of this undertaking not more than half an hour was required.
So thoroughly did they succeed in throwing dust in the public's
eyes that for a while every one—more especially the army of
public officials—was placed in the position of a schoolboy who,
while still asleep, has had a bag of pepper thrown in his face by
a party of more early-rising comrades. The questions now to
be debated resolved themselves into two—namely, the question
of the dead souls and the question of the Governor's daughter.
To this end two parties were formed—the men's party and the
feminine section. The men's party—the more absolutely senseless of the two—devoted its attention to the dead souls: the
women's party occupied itself exclusively with the alleged
abduction of the Governor's daughter. And here it may be said
(to the ladies' credit) that the women's party displayed far more
method and caution than did its rival faction, probably because
the function in life of its members had always been that of
managing and administering a household. With the ladies,
therefore, matters soon assumed vivid and definite shape; they
became clearly and irrefutably materialised; they stood stripped
of all doubt and other impedimenta. Said some of the ladies in
question, Chichikov had long been in love with the maiden, and
the pair had kept tryst by the light of the moon, while the
Governor would have given his consent (seeing that Chichikov
was as rich as a Jew) but for the obstacle that Chichikov had
deserted a wife already (how the worthy dames came to know
that he was married remains a mystery), and the said deserted
wife, pining with love for her faithless husband, had sent the
Governor a letter of the most touching kind, so that Chichikov,
on perceiving that the father and mother would never give their
consent, had decided to abduct the girl. In other circles the
matter was stated in a different way. That is to say, this section
averred that Chichikov did *not* possess a wife, but that, as a
man of subtlety and experience, he had bethought him of obtain-
ing the daughter's hand through the expedient of first tackling
the mother and carrying on with her an ardent *liaison*, and that,
thereafter, he had made an application for the desired hand,
but that the mother, fearing to commit a sin against religion,
and feeling in her heart certain gnawings of conscience, had
returned a blank refusal to Chichikov's request; whereupon
Chichikov had decided to carry out the abduction alleged. To
the foregoing, of course, there became appended various additional
proofs and items of evidence, in proportion as the sensation

spread to more remote corners of the town. At length, with these perfectings, the affair reached the ears of the Governor's wife herself. Naturally, as the mother of a family, and as the first lady in the town, and as a matron who had never before been suspected of things of the kind, she was highly offended when she heard the stories, and very justly so: with the result that her poor young daughter, though innocent, had to endure about as unpleasant a *tête-à-tête* as ever befell a maiden of sixteen, while, for his part, the Swiss footman received orders never at any time to admit Chichikov to the house.

Having done their business with the Governor's wife, the ladies' party descended upon the male section, with a view to influencing it to their own side by asserting that the dead souls were an invention used solely for the purpose of diverting suspicion and successfully effecting the abduction. And, indeed, more than one man was converted, and joined the feminine camp, in spite of the fact that thereby such seceders incurred strong names from their late comrades—names such as " old women," " petticoats," and others of a nature peculiarly offensive to the male sex.

Also, however much they might arm themselves and take the field, the men could not compass such orderliness within their ranks as could the women. With the former everything was of the antiquated and rough-hewn and ill-fitting and unsuitable and badly-adapted and inferior kind; their heads were full of nothing but discord and triviality and confusion and slovenliness of thought. In brief, they displayed everywhere the male bent, the rude, ponderous nature which is incapable either of managing a household or of jumping to a conclusion, as well as remains always distrustful and lazy and full of constant doubt and everlasting timidity. For instance, the men's party declared that the whole story was rubbish—that the alleged abduction of the Governor's daughter was the work rather of a military than of a civilian culprit; that the ladies were lying when they accused Chichikov of the deed; that a woman was like a money-bag—whatsoever you put into her she thenceforth retained; that the subject which really demanded attention was the dead souls, of which the devil only knew the meaning, but in which there certainly lurked something that was contrary to good order and discipline. One reason why the men's party was so certain that the dead souls connoted something contrary to good order and discipline, was that there had just been appointed to the province a new Governor-General—an event which, of course, had thrown the whole army of provincial *tchinovniks* into a state of great excitement, seeing that they knew that before long there would ensue transferments and sentences of censure, as well as the series of official dinners with which a Governor-General is accustomed to entertain his subordinates. "Alas," thought the army of *tchinovniks*, "it is probable that, should he learn of the gross reports at present afloat in our town, he will make such a fuss that we shall never hear the last of them." In particular did the Director of the Medical Department turn pale at the thought that possibly the new Governor-General would surmise the term "dead folk" to connote patients in the local hospitals who, for want of proper preventive measures, had died of sporadic fever. Indeed, might it not be that Chichikov was neither more nor less than an emissary of the said Governor-General, sent to conduct a secret inquiry? Accordingly he (the Director of the Medical Department) communicated this last supposition to the President of the Council, who, though at first inclined to ejaculate "Rubbish!" suddenly turned pale on propounding to himself the theory, "What if the souls purchased by Chichikov should *really* be dead ones?"—a terrible thought considering that he, the President, had permitted their transferment to be registered, and had himself acted as Plushkin's representative! What if these things should reach the Governor-General's ears? He mentioned the matter to one friend and another, and they, in their turn, went white to the lips, for panic spreads faster, and is even more destructive, than the dreaded black death. Also, to add to the *tchinovniks'* troubles, it so befell that just at this juncture there came into the local Governor's hands two documents of great importance. The first of them contained advices that, according to received evidence and reports, there was operating in the province a forger of rouble-notes who had been passing under various aliases and must therefore be sought for with the utmost diligence; while the second document was a letter from the Governor of a neighbouring province with regard to a malefactor who had there evaded apprehension—a letter conveying also a warning that, if in the province of the town of N. there should appear any suspicious individual who could produce neither references nor passports, he was to be arrested forthwith. These two documents left every one thunderstruck, for they knocked on the head all previous conceptions and theories. Not for a moment could it be supposed that the former document referred to Chichikov; yet, as each man pondered the position from his own point of view, he remembered that no one *really* knew who Chichikov was; as also that his vague references to himself had—yes!—included statements that his career in the service had suffered much in the cause of Truth, and that he possessed a number of enemies who were seeking his life. This gave the *tchinovniks* further food for thought. Perhaps his life really *did* stand in danger? Perhaps he really *was* being sought for by some one? Perhaps he really *had* done something of the kind above referred to? As a matter of fact, who was he? —not that it could actually be supposed that he was a forger of notes, still less a brigand, seeing that his exterior was respectable in the highest degree. Yet who was he? At length the *tchinov-niks* decided to make inquiries among those of whom he had purchased souls, in order that at least it might be learnt what the purchases had consisted of, and what exactly underlay them, and whether, in passing, he had explained to any one his real intentions, or revealed to any one his identity. In the first instance, therefore, resort was had to Korobotchka. Yet little was gleaned from that source—merely a statement that he had bought of her some souls for fifteen roubles apiece, and also a quantity of feathers, while promising also to buy some other commodities in the future, seeing that, in particular, he had entered into a contract with the Treasury for lard, a fact constituting fairly presumptive proof that the man was a rogue, seeing that just such another fellow had bought a quantity of feathers, yet had cheated folk all round, and, in particular, had done the Archpriest out of over a hundred roubles. Thus the net result of Madame's cross-examination was to convince the *tchinovniks* that she was a garrulous, silly old woman. With regard to Manilov, he replied that he would answer for Chichikov as he would for himself, and that he would gladly sacrifice his property *in toto* if thereby he could attain even a tithe of the qualities which Paul Ivanovitch possessed. Finally he delivered on Chichikov, with acutely-knitted brows, a eulogy couched in the most charming of terms, and coupled with sundry sentiments on the subject of friendship and affection in general. True, these remarks sufficed to indicate the tender impulses of the speaker's heart, but also they did nothing to enlighten his examiners concerning the business that was actually in hand. As for Sobakevitch, that landowner replied that he considered Chichikov an excellent fellow, as well as that the souls whom he had sold to his visitor had been in the truest sense of the word alive, but that he could not answer for anything which might occur in the future, seeing that any difficulties which might arise in the course of the actual transferment of the souls would not be *his* fault, in view of the fact that God was lord of all, and that fevers and other mortal complaints were so numerous in the world, and that instances of whole villages perishing through the same could be found on record.

Finally, our friends the *tchinovniks* found themselves compelled to resort to an expedient which, though not particularly savoury, is not infrequently employed—namely, the expedient of getting lacqueys quietly to approach the servants of the person concerning whom information is desired, and to ascertain from them (the servants) certain details with regard to their master's past life and antecedents. Yet even from this source very little was obtained, since Petrushka provided his interrogators merely with a taste of the smell of his living-room, and Selifan confined his replies to a statement that the *barin* had " been in the employment of the State, and also had served in the Customs."

In short, the sum total of the results gathered by the *tchinovniks* was that they still stood in ignorance of Chichikov's identity, but that he *must* be some one; wherefore it was decided to hold a final debate on the subject on what ought to be done, and who Chichikov could possibly be, and whether or not he was a man who ought to be apprehended and detained as not respectable, or whether he was a man who might himself be able to apprehend and detain *them* as persons lacking in respectability. The debate in question, it was proposed, should be held at the residence of the Chief of Police, who is known to our readers as the father and the general benefactor of the town.

X

On assembling at the residence indicated, the *tchinovniks* had occasion to remark that, owing to all these cares and excitements, every one of their number had grown thinner. Yes, the appointment of a new Governor-General, coupled with the rumours described and the reception of the two serious documents abovementioned, had left manifest traces upon the features of every one present. More than one frockcoat had come to look too large for its wearer, and more than one frame had fallen away, including the frames of the President of the Council, the Director of the Medical Department, and the Public Prosecutor. Even a certain Semen Ivanovitch, who, for some reason or another, was never alluded to by his family name, but who wore on his index-finger a ring with which he was accustomed to dazzle his lady friends, had diminished in bulk. Yet, as always happens at such junctures, there were also present a score of brazen individuals who had succeeded in *not* losing their presence of mind, even though they constituted a mere sprinkling. Of them the Postmaster formed one, since he was a man of equable temperament who could always say: "*We* know you, you Governor-Generals! We have seen three or four of you come and go, whereas *we* have been sitting on the same stools these thirty years." Nevertheless a prominent feature of the gathering was the total absence of what is vulgarly known as "common sense." In general, we Russians do not make a good show at representative assemblies, for the reason that, unless there be in authority a leading spirit to control the rest, the affair always develops into confusion. Why this should be so one could hardly say, but at all events a success is scored only by such gatherings as have for their object dining and festivity—to wit, gatherings at clubs or in German-run restaurants. However, on the present occasion, the meeting was *not* one of this kind; it was a meeting convoked of necessity, and likely in view of the threatened calamity to affect every *tchinovnik* in the place. Also, in addition to the great divergency of views expressed thereat, there was visible in all the speakers an invincible tendency to indecision which led them at one moment to make assertions, and at the next to contradict the same. But on at least one point all seemed to agree—namely, that Chichikov's appearance and conversation were too respectable for him to be a forger or a disguised brigand. That is to say, all *seemed* to agree on the point; until a sudden shout arose from the direction of the Postmaster, who for some time past had been sitting plunged in thought.

"*I* can tell you," he cried, "who Chichikov is!"

"Who, then?" replied the crowd in great excitement.

"He is none other than Captain Kopeikin."

"And who may Captain Kopeikin be?"

Taking a pinch of snuff (which he did with the lid of his snuff-box half-open, lest some extraneous person should contrive to insert a not over-clean finger into the stuff), the Postmaster related the following story.[1]

---

[1] To reproduce this story with a raciness worthy of the Russian original is practically impossible. The translator has not attempted the task.

" After fighting in the campaign of 1812, there was sent home, wounded, a certain Captain Kopeikin—a headstrong, lively blade who, whether on duty or under arrest, made things lively for everybody. Now, since at Krasni or at Leipzig (it matters not which) he had lost an arm and a leg, and in those days no provision was made for wounded soldiers, and he could not work with his left arm alone, he set out to see his father. Unfortunately his father could only just support himself, and was forced to tell his son so; wherefore the Captain decided to go and apply for help in St. Petersburg, seeing that he had risked his life for his country, and had lost much blood in its service. You can imagine him arriving in the capital on a baggage waggon—in the capital which is like no other city in the world! Before him there lay spread out the whole field of life, like a sort of Arabian Nights—a picture made up of the Nevski Prospect, Gorokhovaia Street, countless tapering spires, and a number of bridges apparently supported on nothing—in fact, a regular second Nineveh. Well, he made shift to hire a lodging, but found everything so wonderfully furnished with blinds and Persian carpets and so forth that he saw it would mean throwing away a lot of money. True, as one walks the streets of St. Petersburg one seems to smell money by the thousand roubles, but our friend Kopeikin's bank was limited to a few score coppers and a little silver—not quite enough to buy a village with! At length, at the price of a rouble a day, he obtained a lodging in the sort of tavern where the daily ration is a bowl of cabbage soup and a crust of bread; and as he felt that he could not manage to live very long on fare of that kind he asked folk what he had better do. ' What you had better do? ' they said. ' Well the Government is not here—it is in Paris, and the troops have not yet returned from the war; but there is a *temporary* Commission sitting, and you had better go and see what *it* can do for you.' ' All right! ' he said. ' I will go and tell the Commission that I have shed my blood, and sacrificed my life, for my country.' And he got up early one morning, and shaved himself with his left hand (since the expense of a barber was not worth while), and set out, wooden leg and all, to see the President of the Commission. But first he asked where the President lived, and was told that his house was in Naberezhnaia Street. And you may be sure that it was no peasant's hut, with its glazed windows and great mirrors and statues and lacqueys and brass door-handles! Rather, it was the sort of place which you would enter only after you had bought a cheap cake of soap and indulged in a two hours' wash. Also, at the entrance there was posted a grand Swiss footman with a *bâton* and an embroidered collar—a fellow looking like a fat, over-fed pug dog. However, friend Kopeikin managed to get himself and his wooden leg into the reception room, and there squeezed himself away into a corner, for fear lest he should knock down the gilded china with his elbow. And he stood waiting in great satisfaction at having arrived before the President had so much as left his bed and been served with his silver wash-basin. Nevertheless, it was only when Kopeikin had been waiting four hours that a breakfast waiter entered to say, ' The President will soon be here.' By now the room was as full of people as a plate is of beans, and when the President left the breakfast-room he brought with him, oh, such dignity and refinement, and such an air of the metropolis! First he walked up to one person, and then up to another, saying: ' What do *you* want? And what do *you* want? What can I do for *you*? What is *your* business?' And at length he halted before Kopeikin, and Kopeikin said to him: ' I have shed my blood, and lost both an arm and a leg, for my country, and am unable to work. Might I therefore dare to ask for a little help, if the regulations should permit of it, or for a gratuity, or for a pension, or something of the kind?' Then the President looked at him, and saw that one of his legs was indeed a wooden one, and that an empty right sleeve was pinned to his uniform. ' Very well,' he said. ' Come to me again in a few days' time.' Upon this friend Kopeikin felt delighted. ' *Now* I have done my job! ' he thought to himself; and you may imagine how gaily he trotted along the pavement, and how he dropped into a tavern for a glass of *vodka*, and how he ordered a cutlet and some caper sauce and other things for luncheon, and how he called for a bottle of wine, and how he went to the theatre in the evening! In short, he did himself thoroughly well. Next, he saw in the street a young English lady, as graceful as a swan, and set off after her on his wooden leg. ' But no,' he thought to himself. ' To the devil with that sort of thing just now! I will wait until I have drawn my pension. For the present I have spent enough.' (And I may tell you that by now he had got through fully half his money.) Two or three days later he went to see the President of the Commission again. ' I should be glad to know,' he said, ' whether by now you can do anything for me in return for my having shed my blood and suffered sickness and wounds on military service.' ' First of all,' said the President, ' I must tell you that nothing can be decided in your case with-

out the authority of the Supreme Government. Without that
sanction we cannot move in the matter. Surely you see how
things stand until the army shall have returned from the war?
All that I can advise you to do is to wait for the Minister to
return, and, in the meanwhile, to have patience. Rest assured
that then you will not be overlooked. And if for the moment
you have nothing to live upon, this is the best that I can do for
you.' With that he handed Kopeikin a trifle until his case should
have been decided. However, that was not what Kopeikin
wanted. He had supposed that he would be given a gratuity
of a thousand roubles straight away; whereas, instead of
'Drink and be merry,' it was 'Wait, for the time is not yet.'
Thus, though his head had been full of soup plates and cutlets
and English girls, he now descended the steps with his ears and
his tail down—looking, in fact, like a poodle over which the cook
has poured a bucketful of water. You see, St. Petersburg life
had changed him not a little since first he had got a taste of it,
and, now that the devil only knew how he was going to live, it
came all the harder to him that he should have no more sweets
to look forward to. Remember that a man in the prime of years
has an appetite like a wolf; and as he passed a restaurant he
could see a round-faced, holland-shirted, snow-white aproned
fellow of a French *chef* preparing a dish delicious enough to make
it turn to and eat itself; while, again, as he passed a fruit shop
he could see delicacies looking out of a window for fools to come
and buy them at a hundred roubles apiece. Imagine, therefore,
his position! On the one hand, so to speak, were salmon and
water-melons, while on the other hand was the bitter fare which
passes at a tavern for luncheon. 'Well,' he thought to himself,
'let them do what they like with me at the Commission, but I
intend to go and raise the whole place, and to tell every blessed
functionary there that I have a mind to do as I choose.' And
in truth this bold impertinence of a man did have the hardihood
to return to the Commission. 'What do you want?' said the
President. 'Why are you here for the third time? You have
had your orders given you.' 'I daresay I have,' he retorted,
'but I am not going to be put off with *them*. I want some cutlets
to eat, and a bottle of French wine, and a chance to go and
amuse myself at the theatre.' 'Pardon me,' said the President.
'What you really need (if I may venture to mention it) is a little
patience. You have been given something for food until the
Military Committee shall have met, and then, doubtless, you
will receive your proper reward, seeing that it would not be

seemly that a man who has served his country should be left
destitute. On the other hand, if, in the meanwhile, you desire
to indulge in cutlets and theatre-going, please understand that
we cannot help you, but that you must make your own resources,
and try as best you can to help yourself.' You can imagine that
this went in at one of Kopeikin's ears, and out at the other; that
it was like shooting peas at a stone wall. Accordingly he raised
a turmoil which sent the staff flying. One by one, he gave the
mob of secretaries and clerks a real good hammering. 'You,
and you, and you,' he said, ' do not even know your duties. You
are law-breakers.' Yes, he trod every man of them under foot.
At length the General himself arrived from another office, and
sounded the alarm. What was to be done with a fellow like
Kopeikin? The President saw that strong measures were
imperative. 'Very well,' he said. 'Since you decline to rest
satisfied with what has been given you, and quietly to await the
decision of your case in St. Petersburg, I must find you a lodging.
Here, constable, remove the man to gaol.' Then a constable who
had been called to the door—a constable three ells in height, and
armed with a carbine—a man well fitted to guard a bank—
placed our friend in a police waggon. 'Well,' reflected Kopeikin,
' at least I shan't have to pay my fare for *this* ride. That's one
comfort.' Again, after he had ridden a little way, he said to
himself: 'They told me at the Commission to go and make my
own means of enjoying myself. Very good. I'll do so.' However,
what became of Kopeikin, and whither he went, is known to
no one. He sank, to use the poets' expression, into the waters
of Lethe, and his doings now lie buried in oblivion. But allow
me, gentlemen, to piece together the further threads of the story.
Not two months later there appeared in the forests of Riazan a
band of robbers: and of that band the chieftain was none other
than——"

"Allow me," put in the Head of the Police Department.
"You have said that Captain Kopeikin had lost an arm and a
leg; whereas Chichikov——"

To say anything more was unnecessary. The Postmaster
clapped his hand to his forehead, and publicly called himself a
fool, though, later, he tried to excuse his mistake by saying
that in England the science of mechanics had reached such a
pitch that wooden legs were manufactured which would enable
the wearer, on touching a spring, to vanish instantaneously
from sight.

Various other theories were then propounded, among them

a theory that Chichikov was Napoleon, escaped from St. Helena and travelling about the world in disguise. And if it should be supposed that no such notion could possibly have been broached, let the reader remember that these events took place not many years after the French had been driven out of Russia, and that various prophets had since declared that Napoleon was Antichrist, and would one day escape from his island prison to exercise universal sway on earth. Nay, some good folk had even declared the letters of Napoleon's name to constitute the Apocalyptic cipher!

As a last resort, the *tchinovniks* decided to question Nozdrev, since not only had the latter been the first to mention the dead souls, but also he was supposed to stand on terms of intimacy with Chichikov. Accordingly the Chief of Police dispatched a note by the hand of a commissionaire. At the time Nozdrev was engaged on some very important business—so much so that he had not left his room for four days, and was receiving his meals through the window, and no visitors at all. The business referred to consisted of the marking of several dozen selected cards in such a way as to permit of his relying upon them as upon his bosom friend. Naturally he did not like having his retirement invaded, and at first consigned the commissionaire to the devil; but as soon as he learnt from the note that, since a novice at cards was to be the guest of the Chief of Police that evening, a call at the latter's house might prove not wholly unprofitable he relented, unlocked the door of his room, threw on the first garments which came to hand, and set forth. To every question put to him by the *tchinovniks* he answered firmly and with assurance. Chichikov, he averred, had indeed purchased dead souls, and to the tune of several thousand roubles. In fact, he (Nozdrev) had himself sold him some, and still saw no reason why he should not have done so. Next, to the question of whether or not he considered Chichikov to be a spy, he replied in the affirmative, and added that, as long ago as his and Chichikov's joint schooldays, the said Chichikov had been known as " The Informer," and repeatedly been thrashed by his companions on that account. Again, to the question of whether or not Chichikov was a forger of currency notes the deponent, as before, responded in the affirmative, and appended thereto an anecdote illustrative of Chichikov's extraordinary dexterity of hand—namely, an anecdote to the effect that, once upon a time, on learning that two million roubles' worth of counterfeit notes were lying in Chichikov's house, the authorities had placed seals upon the building, and had surrounded it on every side with an armed guard; whereupon Chichikov had, during the night, changed each of these seals for a new one, and also so arranged matters that, when the house was searched, the forged notes were found to be genuine ones!

Again, to the question of whether or not Chichikov had schemed to abduct the Governor's daughter, and also whether it was true that he, Nozdrev, had undertaken to aid and abet him in the act, the witness replied that, had he not undertaken to do so, the affair would never have come off. At this point the witness pulled himself up, on realising that he had told a lie which might get him into trouble; but his tongue was not to be denied—the details trembling on its tip were too alluring, and he even went on to cite the name of the village church where the pair had arranged to be married, that of the priest who had performed the ceremony, the amount of the fees paid for the same (seventy-five roubles), and statements (1) that the priest had refused to solemnise the wedding until Chichikov had frightened him by threatening to expose the fact that he (the priest) had married Mikhail, a local corn dealer, to his paramour, and (2) that Chichikov had ordered both a *koliaska* for the couple's conveyance and relays of horses from the post-houses on the road. Nay, the narrative, as detailed by Nozdrev, even reached the point of his mentioning certain of the postillions by name! Next, the *tchinovniks* sounded him on the question of Chichikov's possible identity with Napoleon; but before long they had reason to regret the step, for Nozdrev responded with a rambling rigmarole such as bore no resemblance to anything possibly conceivable. Finally, the majority of the audience left the room, and only the Chief of Police remained to listen (in the hope of gathering something more); but at last even he found himself forced to disclaim the speaker with a gesture which said: " The devil only knows what the fellow is talking about! " and so voiced the general opinion that it was no use trying to gather figs of thistles.

Meanwhile Chichikov knew nothing of these events; for, having contracted a slight chill, coupled with a sore throat, he had decided to keep his room for three days; during which time he gargled his throat with milk and fig juice, consumed the fruit from which the juice had been extracted, and wore around his neck a poultice of camomile and camphor. Also, to while away the hours, he made new and more detailed lists of the souls which he had bought, perused a work by the Duchesse de la Vallière,[1] rummaged in his portmanteau, looked through various articles and papers which he discovered in his dispatch-box, and found every one of these occupations tedious. Nor could he understand why none of his official friends had come to see him and inquire after his health, seeing that, not long since, there had been standing in front of the inn the *drozhkis* both of the Postmaster, the Public Prosecutor, and the President of the Council. He wondered and wondered, and then, with a shrug of his shoulders, fell to pacing the room. At length he felt better, and his spirits rose at the prospect of once more going out into the fresh air; wherefore, having shaved a plentiful growth of hair from his face, he dressed with such alacrity as almost to cause a split in his trousers, sprinkled himself with *eau-de-Cologne*, and wrapping himself in warm clothes, and turning up the collar of his coat, sallied forth into the street. His first destination was intended to be the Governor's mansion, and, as he walked along, certain thoughts concerning the Governor's daughter would keep whirling through his head, so that almost he forgot where he was, and took to smiling and cracking jokes to himself.

Arrived at the Governor's entrance, he was about to divest himself of his scarf when a Swiss footman greeted him with the words, " I am forbidden to admit you."

" What? " he exclaimed. " You do not know me? Look at me again, and see if you do not recognise me."

" Of course I recognise you," the footman replied. " I have seen you before, but have been ordered to admit any one else rather than Monsieur Chichikov."

" Indeed? And why so? "

" Those are my orders, and they must be obeyed," said the footman, confronting Chichikov with none of that politeness with which, on former occasions, he had hastened to divest our hero of his wrappings. Evidently he was of opinion that, since the gentry declined to receive the visitor, the latter must certainly be a rogue.

" I cannot understand it," said Chichikov to himself. Then he departed, and made his way to the house of the President of the Council. But so put about was that official by Chichikov's entry that he could not utter two consecutive words—he could only murmur some rubbish which left both his visitor and himself out of countenance. Chichikov wondered, as he left the

---

[1] One of the mistresses of Louis XIV. of France. In 1680 she wrote a book called *Réflexions sur la Miséricorde de Dieu, par une Dame Pénitente.*

house, what the President's muttered words could have meant, but failed to make head or tail of them. Next, he visited, in turn, the Chief of Police, the Vice-Governor, the Postmaster, and others; but in each case he either failed to be accorded admittance or was received so strangely, and with such a measure of constraint and conversational awkwardness and absence of mind and embarrassment, that he began to fear for the sanity of his hosts. Again and again did he strive to divine the cause, but could not do so; so he went wandering aimlessly about the town, without succeeding in making up his mind whether he or the officials had gone crazy. At length, in a state bordering upon bewilderment, he returned to the inn—to the establishment whence, that very afternoon, he had set forth in such exuberance of spirits. Feeling the need of something to do, he ordered tea, and, still marvelling at the strangeness of his position, was about to pour out the beverage when the door opened and Nozdrev made his appearance.

"What says the proverb?" he began. "'To see a friend, seven versts is not too long a round to make.' I happened to be passing the house, saw a light in your window, and thought to myself: 'Now, suppose I were to run up and pay him a visit? It is unlikely that he will be asleep.' Ah, ha! I see tea on your table! Good! Then I will drink a cup with you, for I had wretched stuff for dinner, and it is beginning to lie heavy on my stomach. Also, tell your man to fill me a pipe. Where is your own pipe?"

"I never smoke," rejoined Chichikov drily.

"Rubbish! As if I did not know what a chimney-pot you are! What is your man's name? Hi, Vakhramei! Come here!"

"Petrushka is his name, not Vakhramei."

"Indeed? But you *used* to have a man called Vakhramei, didn't you?"

"No, never."

"Oh, well. Then it must be Derebin's man I am thinking of. What a lucky fellow that Derebin is! An aunt of his has gone and quarrelled with her son for marrying a serf woman, and has left all her property to *him*, to Derebin. Would that *I* had an aunt of that kind to provide against future contingencies! But why have you been hiding yourself away? I suppose the reason has been that you go in for abstruse subjects and are fond of reading" (why Nozdrev should have drawn these conclusions no one could possibly have said—least of all Chichikov himself). "By the way, I can tell you of something that would have found you scope for your satirical vein" (the conclusion as to Chichikov's "satirical vein" was, as before, altogether unwarranted on Nozdrev's part). "That is to say, you would have seen merchant Likhachev losing a pile of money at play. My word, you would have laughed! A fellow with me named Perependev said: 'Would that Chichikov had been here! It would have been the very thing for him!' (As a matter of fact, never since the day of his birth had Nozdrev met any one of the name of Perependev.) "However, my friend, you must admit that you treated me rather badly the day that we played that game of chess; but, as I won the game, I bear you no malice. *A propos,* I am just from the President's, and ought to tell you that the feeling against you in the town is very strong, for every one believes you to be a forger of currency notes. I myself was sent for and questioned about you, but I stuck up for you through thick and thin, and told the *tchinovniks* that I had been at school with you, and had known your father. In fact, I gave the fellows a knock or two for themselves."

"You say that I am believed to be a forger?" said Chichikov, starting from his seat.

"Yes," said Nozdrev. "Why have you gone and frightened everybody as you have done? Some of our folk are almost out of their minds about it, and declare you to be either a brigand in disguise or a spy. Yesterday the Public Prosecutor even died of it, and is to be buried to-morrow" (this was true in so far as that, on the previous day, the official in question had had a fatal stroke—probably induced by the excitement of the public meeting). "Of course *I* don't suppose you to be anything of the kind, but, you see, these fellows are in a blue funk about the new Governor-General, for they think he will make trouble for them over your affair. *A propos,* he is believed to be a man who puts on airs, and turns up his nose at everything; and if so, he will get on badly with the *dvoriané,* seeing that fellows of that sort need to be humoured a bit. Yes, my word! Should the new Governor-General shut himself up in his study, and give no balls, there will be the very devil to pay! By the way, Chichikov, that is a risky scheme of yours."

"What scheme do you mean?" Chichikov asked uneasily.

"Why, that scheme of carrying off the Governor's daughter. However, to tell the truth, I was expecting something of the kind. No sooner did I see you and her together at the ball than I said to myself: 'Ah, ha! Chichikov is not here for nothing!' For my own part, I think you have made a poor choice, for I can see nothing in her at all. On the other hand, the niece of a friend of mine named Bikusov—she *is* a girl, and no mistake! A regular what you might call ' miracle in muslin! ' "

" What on earth are you talking about? " asked Chichikov with his eyes distended. " *How* could I carry off the Governor's daughter? What on earth do you mean? "

" Come, come! What a secretive fellow you are! My only object in having come to see you is to lend you a helping hand in the matter. Look here. On condition that you will lend me three thousand roubles, I will stand you the cost of the wedding, the *koliaska*, and the relays of horses. I must have the money even if I die for it."

Throughout Nozdrev's maunderings Chichikov had been rubbing his eyes to ascertain whether or not he was dreaming. What with the charge of being a forger, the accusation of having schemed an abduction, the death of the Public Prosecutor (whatever might have been its cause), and the advent of a new Governor-General, he felt utterly dismayed.

" Things having come to their present pass," he reflected, " I had better not linger here—I had better be off at once."

Getting rid of Nozdrev as soon as he could, he sent for Selifan, and ordered him to be up at daybreak, in order to clean the *britchka* and to have everything ready for a start at six o'clock. Yet, though Selifan replied, " Very well, Paul Ivanovitch," he hesitated awhile by the door. Next, Chichikov bid Petrushka get out the dusty portmanteau from under the bed, and then set to work to cram into it, pell-mell, socks, shirts, collars (both clean and dirty), boot trees, a calendar, and a variety of other articles. Everything went into the receptacle just as it came to hand, since his one object was to obviate any possible delay in the morning's departure. Meanwhile the reluctant Selifan slowly, very slowly, left the room, as slowly descended the stair-case (on each separate step of which he left a muddy foot-print), and, finally, halted to scratch his head. What that scratching may have meant no one could say; for, with the Russian populace, such a scratching may mean any one of a hundred things.

XI

NEVERTHELESS events did not turn out as Chichikov had intended they should. In the first place, he overslept himself. That was check number one. In the second place, on his rising and inquiring whether the *britchka* had been harnessed and everything got ready, he was informed that neither of those two things had been done. That was check number two. Beside himself with rage, he prepared to give friend Selifan the wigging of his life, and, meanwhile, waited impatiently to hear what the delinquent had got to say in his defence. It goes without saying that when Selifan made his appearance in the doorway he had only the usual excuses to offer—the sort of excuses usually offered by servants when a hasty departure has become imperatively necessary.

"Paul Ivanovitch," he said, " the horses require shoeing."

" Blockhead! " exclaimed Chichikov. " Why did you not tell me of that before, you damned fool? Was there not time enough for them to be shod? "

" Yes, I suppose there was," agreed Selifan. " Also one of the wheels is in want of a new tyre, for the roads are so rough that the old tyre is worn through. Also, the body of the *britchka* is so rickety that probably it will not last more than a couple of stages."

"Rascal! " shouted Chichikov, clenching his fists and approaching Selifan in such a manner that, fearing to receive a blow, the man backed and dodged aside. " Do you mean to ruin me, and to break all our bones on the road, you cursed idiot? For these three weeks past you have been doing nothing at all; yet now, at the very last moment, you come here stammering and playing the fool! Do you think I keep you just to eat and to drive yourself about? You must have known this before? Did you, or did you not, know it? Answer me at once."

" Yes, I did know it," replied Selifan, hanging his head.

" Then why didn't you tell me about it? "

Selifan had no reply immediately ready, so continued to hang his head while quietly saying to himself: " See how well I have managed things! I knew what was the matter, yet I did not say."

" And now," continued Chichikov, " go you at once and fetch a blacksmith. Tell him that everything must be put right within two hours at the most. Do you hear? If that should not be done, I, I—I will give you the best flogging that ever you had in your life." Truly Chichikov was almost beside himself with fury.

Turning towards the door, as though for the purpose of going and carrying out his orders, Selifan halted and added:

"That skewbald, *barin*—you might think it well to sell him, seeing that he is nothing but a rascal? A horse like that is more of a hindrance than a help."

"What? Do you expect me to go *now* to the market-place and sell him?"

"Well, Paul Ivanovitch, he is good for nothing but show, since by nature he is a most cunning beast. Never in my life have I seen such a horse."

"Fool! Whenever I may wish to sell him I *shall* sell him. Meanwhile, don't you trouble your head about what doesn't concern you, but go and fetch a blacksmith, and see that everything is put right within two hours. Otherwise I will take the very hair off your head, and beat you till you haven't a face left. Be off! Hurry!"

Selifan departed, and Chichikov, his ill-humour vented, threw down upon the floor the poignard which he always took with him as a means of instilling respect into whomsoever it might concern, and spent the next quarter of an hour in disputing with a couple of blacksmiths—men who, as usual, were rascals of the type which, on perceiving that something is wanted in a hurry, at once multiplies its terms for providing the same. Indeed, for all Chichikov's storming and raging as he dubbed the fellows robbers and extortioners and thieves, he could make no impression upon the pair, since, true to their character, they declined to abate their prices, and, even when they had begun their work, spent upon it, not two hours, but five and a half. Meanwhile he had the satisfaction of experiencing that delightful time with which all travellers are familiar—namely, the time during which one sits in a room where, except for a litter of string, waste paper, and so forth, everything else has been packed. But to all things there comes an end, and there arrived also the longed-for moment when the *britchka* had received the luggage, the faulty wheel had been fitted with a new tyre, the horses had been re-shod, and the predatory blacksmiths had departed with their gains. "Thank God!" thought Chichikov as the *britchka* rolled out of the gates of the inn, and the vehicle began to jolt over the cobblestones. Yet a feeling which he could not altogether have defined filled his breast as he gazed upon the houses and the streets and the garden walls which he might never see again. Presently, on turning a corner, the *britchka* was brought to a halt through the fact that along the street there was filing a seemingly endless funeral procession. Leaning forward in his *britchka*, Chichikov asked Petrushka whose obsequies the procession represented, and was told that they represented those of the Public Prosecutor. Disagreeably shocked, our hero hastened to raise the hood of the vehicle, to draw the curtains across the windows, and to lean back into a corner. While the *britchka* remained thus halted Selifan and Petrushka, their caps doffed, sat watching the progress of the *cortège*, after they had received strict instructions not to greet any fellow-servant whom they might recognise. Behind the hearse walked the whole body of *tchinovniks*, bare-headed; and though, for a moment or two, Chichikov feared that some of their number might discern him in his *britchka*, he need not have disturbed himself, since their attention was otherwise engaged. In fact, they were not even exchanging the small talk customary among members of such processions, but thinking exclusively of their own affairs, of the advent of the new Governor-General, and of the probable manner in which he would take up the reins of administration. Next came a number of carriages, from the windows of which peered the faces of ladies in mourning toilets. Yet the movements of their hands and lips made it evident that they were indulging in animated conversation—probably about the Governor-General, the balls which he might be expected to give, and their own eternal fripperies and gewgaws. Lastly came a few empty *drozhkis*. As soon as the latter had passed, our hero was able to continue on his way. Throwing back the hood of the *britchka*, he said to himself:

"Ah, good friend, you have lived your life, and now it is over! In the newspapers they will say of you that you died regretted not only by your subordinates, but also by humanity at large, as well as that, a respected citizen, a kind father, and a husband beyond reproach, you went to your grave amid the tears of your widow and orphans. Yet, should those journals be put to it to name any particular circumstance which justified this eulogy of you, they would be forced to fall back upon the fact that you grew a pair of exceptionally thick eyebrows!"

With that Chichikov bid Selifan quicken his pace, and concluded: "After all, it is as well that I encountered the procession, for they say that to meet a funeral is lucky."

Presently the *britchka* turned into some less frequented streets, lines of wooden fencing of the kind which mark the outskirts of a town began to file by, the cobblestones came to an end, the macadam of the highroad succeeded to them, and once more there began on either side of the turnpike a procession of *verst* stones, road menders, and grey villages; inns with *samovars* and peasant women and landlords who came running out of yards with sievefuls of oats; pedestrians in worn shoes which, it might be, had covered eight hundred *versts ;* little towns, bright with booths for the sale of flour in barrels, boots, small loaves, and other trifles; heaps of slag; much repaired bridges; expanses of field to right and to left; stout landowners; a mounted soldier bearing a green, iron-clamped box inscribed: " The —th Battery of Artillery "; long strips of freshly-tilled earth which gleamed green, yellow, and black on the face of the countryside. With it mingled long-drawn singing, glimpses of elm-tops amid mist, the far-off notes of bells, endless clouds of rooks, and the illimitable line of the horizon.

Ah, Russia, Russia, from my beautiful home in a strange land I still can see you! In you everything is poor and disordered and unhomely; in you the eye is neither cheered nor dismayed by temerities of nature which a yet more temerarious art has conquered; in you one beholds no cities with lofty, many-windowed mansions, lofty as crags, no picturesque trees, no ivy-clad ruins, no waterfalls with their everlasting spray and roar, no beetling precipices which confuse the brain with their stony immensity, no vistas of vines and ivy and millions of wild roses and ageless lines of blue hills which look almost unreal against the clear, silvery background of the sky. In you everything is flat and open; your towns project like points or signals from smooth levels of plain, and nothing whatsoever enchants or deludes the eye. Yet what secret, what invincible force draws me to you? Why does there ceaselessly echo and re-echo in my ears the sad song which hovers throughout the length and the breadth of your borders? What is the burden of that song? Why does it wail and sob and catch at my heart? What say the notes which thus painfully caress and embrace my soul, and flit, uttering their lamentations, around me? What is it you seek of me, O Russia? What is the hidden bond which subsists between us? Why do you regard me as you do? Why does everything within you turn upon me eyes full of yearning? Even at this moment, as I stand dumbly, fixedly, perplexedly contemplating your vastness, a menacing cloud, charged with gathering rain, seems to overshadow my head. What is it that your boundless expanses presage? Do they not presage that one day there will arise in you ideas as boundless as yourself? Do they not presage that one day you too will know no limits? Do they not presage that one day, when again you shall have room for their exploits, there will spring to life the heroes of old? How the power of your immensity enfolds me, and reverberates through all my being with a wild, strange spell, and flashes in my eyes with an almost supernatural radiance! Yes, a strange, brilliant, unearthly vista indeed do you disclose, O Russia, country of mine!

"Stop, stop, you fool!" shouted Chichikov to Selifan; and even as he spoke a *troika*, bound on Government business, came clattering by, and disappeared in a cloud of dust. To Chichikov's curses at Selifan for not having drawn out of the way with more alacrity a rural constable with moustaches of the length of an *arshin* added his quota.

What a curious and attractive, yet also what an unreal, fascination the term "highway" connotes! And how interesting for its own sake is a highway! Should the day be a fine one (though chilly) in mellowing autumn, press closer your travelling cloak, and draw down your cap over your ears, and snuggle cosily, comfortably into a corner of the *britchka* before a last shiver shall course through your limbs, and the ensuing warmth shall put to flight the autumnal cold and damp. As the horses gallop on their way, how delightfully will drowsiness come stealing upon you, and make your eyelids droop! For a while, through your somnolence, you will continue to hear the hard breathing of the team and the rumbling of the wheels; but at length, sinking back into your corner, you will relapse into the stage of snoring. And when you awake—behold! you will find that five stages have slipped away, and that the moon is shining, and that you have reached a strange town of churches and old wooden cupolas and blackened spires and white, half-timbered houses! And as the moonlight glints hither and thither, almost you will believe that the walls and the streets and the pavements of the place are spread with sheets—sheets shot with coal-black shadows which make the wooden roofs look all the brighter under the slanting beams of the pale luminary. Nowhere is a soul to be seen, for every one is plunged in slumber. Yet no. In a solitary window a light is flickering where some good burgher is mending his boots, or a baker drawing a batch of dough. O night and powers of heaven, how perfect is the blackness of your infinite vault—how lofty, how remote its inaccessible depths where it lies spread in an intangible, yet audible, silence!

Freshly does the lulling breath of night blow in your face, until once more you relapse into snoring oblivion, and your poor neighbour turns angrily in his corner as he begins to be conscious of your weight. Then again you awake, but this time to find yourself confronted only with fields and steppes. Everywhere in the ascendant is the desolation of space. But suddenly the ciphers on a *verst* stone leap to the eye! Morning is rising, and on the chill, gradually paling line of the horizon you can see gleaming a faint gold streak. The wind freshens and grows keener, and you snuggle closer into your cloak; yet how glorious is that freshness, and how marvellous the sleep in which once again you become enfolded! A jolt!—and for the last time you return to consciousness. By now the sun is high in the heavens, and you hear a voice cry " gently, gently!" as a farm waggon issues from a by-road. Below, enclosed within an ample dike, stretches a sheet of water which glistens like copper in the sunlight. Beyond, on the side of a slope, lie some scattered peasants' huts, a manor house, and, flanking the latter, a village church with its cross flashing like a star. There also comes wafted to your ear the sound of peasants' laughter, while in your inner man you are becoming conscious of an appetite which is not to be withstood.

Oh long-drawn highway, how excellent you are! How often have I in weariness and despondency set forth upon your length, and found in you salvation and rest! How often, as I followed your leading, have I been visited with wonderful thoughts and poetic dreams and curious, wild impressions!

At this moment our friend Chichikov also was experiencing visions of a not wholly prosaic nature. Let us peep into his soul and share them. At first he remained unconscious of anything whatsoever, for he was too much engaged in making sure that he was really clear of the town; but as soon as he saw that it had completely disappeared, with its mills and factories and other urban appurtenances, and that even the steeples of the white stone churches had sunk below the horizon, he turned his attention to the road, and the town of N. vanished from his thoughts as completely as though he had not seen it since childhood. Again, in its turn, the road ceased to interest him, and he began to close his eyes and to loll his head against the cushions. Of this let the author take advantage, in order to speak at length concerning his hero; since hitherto he (the author) has been prevented from so doing by Nozdrev and balls and ladies and local intrigues—by those thousand trifles which seem trifles only when they are introduced into a book, but which, in real life, figure as affairs of importance. Let us lay them aside, and betake ourselves to business.

Whether the character whom I have selected for my hero has pleased my readers is, of course, exceedingly doubtful. At all events the ladies will have failed to approve him, for the fair sex demands in a hero perfection, and, should there be the least mental or physical stain on him—well, woe betide! Yes, no matter how profoundly the author may probe that hero's soul, no matter how clearly he may portray his figure as in a mirror, he will be given no credit for the achievement. Indeed, Chichikov's very stoutness and plenitude of years may have militated against him, for never is a hero pardoned for the former, and the majority of ladies will, in such case, turn away, and mutter to themselves: "Phew! What a beast!" Yes, the author is well aware of this. Yet, though he could not, to save his life, take a person of virtue for his principal character, it may be that this story contains themes never before selected, and that in it there projects the whole boundless wealth of Russian psychology; that it portrays, as well as Chichikov, the peasant who is gifted with the virtues which God has sent him, and the marvellous maiden of Russia who has not her like in all the world for her beautiful feminine spirituality, the roots of which lie buried in noble aspirations and boundless self-denial. In fact, compared with these types, the virtuous of other races seem lifeless, as does an inanimate volume when compared with the living word. Yes, each time that there arises in Russia a movement of thought, it becomes clear that that movement sinks deep into the Slavonic nature where it would but have skimmed the surface of other nations.—But why am I talking like this? Whither am I tending? It is indeed shameful that an author who long ago reached man's estate, and was brought up to a course of severe introspection and sober, solitary self-enlightenment, should give way to such jejune wandering from the point. To everything its proper time and place and turn. As I was saying, it does not lie in me to take a virtuous character for my hero: and I will tell you why. It is because it is high time that a rest were given to the "poor, but virtuous" individual; it is because the phrase "a man of worth" has grown into a by-word; it is because the "man of worth" has become converted into a horse, and there is not a writer but rides him and flogs him, in and out of season; it is because the "man of worth" has been starved until he has not a shred of his virtue left, and all that remains of his body is but the ribs and the hide; it is because the " man of worth " is for ever being smuggled upon the scene; it is because the "man of worth" has at length forfeited every one's respect. For these reasons do I reaffirm that it is high time to yoke a rascal to the shafts. Let us yoke that rascal.

Our hero's beginnings were both modest and obscure. True, his parents were *dvoriané*, but he in no way resembled them. At all events, a short, squab female relative who was present at his birth exclaimed as she lifted up the baby: " He is altogether different from what I had expected him to be. He ought to have taken after his maternal grandmother, whereas he has been born, as the proverb has it, ' like nor father nor mother, but like a chance passer-by.' " Thus from the first life regarded the little Chichikov with sour distaste, and as through a dim, frost-encrusted window. A tiny room with diminutive casements which were never opened, summer or winter; an invalid father in a dressing-gown lined with lambskin, and with an ailing foot swathed in bandages—a man who was continually drawing deep breaths, and walking up and down the room, and spitting into a sandbox; a period of perpetually sitting on a bench with pen in hand and ink on lips and fingers; a period of being eternally confronted with the copy-book maxim, " Never tell a lie, but obey your superiors, and cherish virtue in your heart; " an everlasting scraping and shuffling of slippers up and down the room; a period of continually hearing a well-known, strident voice exclaim: " So you have been playing the fool again! " at times when the child, weary of the mortal monotony of his task, had added a superfluous embellishment to his copy; a period of experiencing the ever-familiar, but ever-unpleasant, sensation which ensued upon those words as the boy's ear was painfully twisted between two long fingers bent backwards at the tips—such is the miserable picture of that youth of which, in later life, Chichikov preserved but the faintest of memories! But in this world everything is liable to swift and sudden change; and, one day in early spring, when the rivers had melted, the father set forth with his little son in a *teliezhka*[1] drawn by a sorrel steed of the kind known to horsy folk as a *soroka*, and having as coachman the diminutive hunchback who, father of the only serf family belonging to the elder Chichikov, served as general factotum in the Chichikov establishment. For a day and a half the *soroka* conveyed them

[1] Four-wheeled open waggon.

on their way; during which time they spent the night at a roadside inn, crossed a river, dined off cold pie and roast mutton, and eventually arrived at the county town. To the lad the streets presented a spectacle of unwonted brilliancy, and he gaped with amazement. Turning into a side alley wherein the mire necessitated both the most strenuous exertions on the *soroka's* part and the most vigorous castigation on the part of the driver and the *barin*, the conveyance eventually reached the gates of a courtyard which, combined with a small fruit garden containing various bushes, a couple of apple-trees in blossom, and a mean, dirty little shed, constituted the premises attached to an antiquated-looking villa. Here there lived a relative of the Chichikovs, a wizened old lady who went to market in person and dried her stockings at the *samovar*. On seeing the boy, she patted his cheek and expressed satisfaction at his physique; whereupon the fact became disclosed that here he was to abide for a while, for the purpose of attending a local school. After a night's rest his father prepared to betake himself homeward again; but no tears marked the parting between him and his son, he merely gave the lad a copper or two and (a far more important thing) the following injunctions. " See here, my boy. Do your lessons well, do not idle or play the fool, and, above all things, see that you please your teachers. So long as you observe these rules you will make progress, and surpass your fellows, even if God shall have denied you brains, and you should fail in your studies. Also, do not consort over-much with your comrades, for they will do you no good; but, should you do so, then make friends with the richer of them, since one day they may be useful to you. Also, never entertain or treat any one, but see that every one entertains and treats *you*. Lastly, and above all else, keep and save your every kopeck. To save money is the most important thing in life. Always a friend or a comrade may fail you, and be the first to desert you in a time of adversity; but never will a *kopeck* fail you, whatever may be your plight. Nothing in the world cannot be done, cannot be attained, with the aid of money." These injunctions given, the father embraced his son, and set forth on his return; and though the son never again beheld his parent, the latter's words and precepts sank deep into the little Chichikov's soul.

The next day young Pavlusha made his first attendance at school. But no special aptitude in any branch of learning did he display. Rather, his distinguishing characteristics were diligence and neatness. On the other hand, he developed great intelligence as regards the *practical* aspect of life. In a trice he divined and comprehended how things ought to be worked, and, from that time forth, bore himself towards his school-fellows in such a way that, though they frequently gave him presents, he not only never returned the compliment, but even on occasions pocketed the gifts for the mere purpose of selling them again. Also, boy though he was, he acquired the art of self-denial. Of the trifle which his father had given him on parting he spent not a kopeck, but, the same year, actually added to his little store by fashioning a bullfinch of wax, painting it, and selling the same at a handsome profit. Next, as time went on, he engaged in other speculations—in particular, in the scheme of buying up eatables, taking his seat in class beside boys who had plenty of pocket-money, and, as soon as such opulent individuals showed signs of failing attention (and, therefore, of growing appetite), tendering them, from beneath the desk, a roll of pudding or a piece of gingerbread, and charging according to degree of appetite and size of portion. He also spent a couple of months in training a mouse, which he kept confined in a little wooden cage in his bedroom. At length, when the training had reached the point that, at the several words of command, the mouse would stand upon its hind legs, lie down, and get up again, he sold the creature for a respectable sum. Thus, in time, his gains attained the amount of five roubles; whereupon he made himself a purse and then started to fill a second receptacle of the kind. Still more studied was his attitude towards the authorities. No one could sit more quietly in his place on the bench than he. In the same connection it may be remarked that his teacher was a man who, above all things, loved peace and good behaviour, and simply could not abide clever, witty boys, since he suspected them of laughing at him. Consequently any lad who had once attracted the master's attention with a manifestation of intelligence needed but to shuffle in his place, or unintentionally to twitch an eyebrow, for the said master at once to burst into a rage, to turn the supposed offender out of the room, and to visit him with unmerciful punishment. "Ah, my fine fellow," he would say, "*I'll* cure you of your impudence and want of respect! I know you through and through far better than you know yourself, and will take good care that you have to go down upon your knees and curb your appetite." Whereupon the wretched lad would, for no cause of which he was aware, be forced to wear out his breeches on the floor and go hungry for days. "Talents and gifts," the schoolmaster would declare, "are so much rubbish. I respect only good behaviour, and shall award full marks to those who conduct themselves properly, even if they fail to learn a single letter of their alphabet: whereas to those in whom I may perceive a tendency to jocularity I shall award nothing, even though they should outdo Solon himself." For the same reason he had no great love for the author Krylov, in that the latter says in one of his Fables: "In my opinion, the more one sings, the better one works;" and often the pedagogue would relate how, in a former school of his, the silence had been such that a fly could be heard buzzing on the wing, and for the space of a whole year not a single pupil sneezed or coughed in class, and so complete was the absence of all sound that no one could have told that there was a soul in the place. Of this mentor young Chichikov speedily appraised the mentality; wherefore he fashioned his behaviour to correspond with it. Not an eyelid, not an eyebrow, would he stir during school hours, howsoever many pinches he might receive from behind; and only when the bell rang would he run to anticipate his fellows in handing the master the three-cornered cap which that dignitary customarily sported, and then to be the first to leave the class-room, and contrive to meet the master not less than two or three times as the latter walked homeward, in order that, on each occasion, he might doff his cap. And the scheme proved entirely successful. Throughout the period of his attendance at school he was held in high favour, and, on leaving the establishment, received full marks for every subject, as well as a diploma and a book inscribed (in gilt letters) "For Exemplary Diligence and the Perfection of Good Conduct." By this time he had grown into a fairly good-looking youth of the age when the chin first calls for a razor; and at about the same period his father died, leaving behind him, as his estate, four waistcoats completely worn out, two ancient frockcoats, and a small sum of money. Apparently he had been skilled only in *recommending* the saving of kopecks—not in *actually practising* the art. Upon that Chichikov sold the old house and its little parcel of land for a thousand roubles, and removed, with his one serf and the serf's family, to the capital, where he set about organising a new establishment and entering the Civil Service. Simultaneously with his doing so, his old schoolmaster lost (through stupidity or otherwise) the establishment over which he had hitherto presided, and in which he had set so much store by silence and good behaviour. Grief drove him to drink, and when nothing was left, even for that purpose, he retired—ill, helpless, and starving—into a broken-down, cheerless hovel. But certain of his former pupils—the same clever, witty lads whom he had once been wont to accuse of impertinence and evil conduct generally—heard of his pitiable plight, and collected for him what money they could, even to the point of selling their own necessaries. Only Chichikov, when appealed to, pleaded inability, and compromised with a contribution of a single *piatak*:[1] which his old schoolfellows straightway returned him—full in the face, and accompanied with a shout of " Oh, you skinflint! " As for the poor schoolmaster, when he heard what his former pupils had done, he buried his face in his hands, and the tears gushed from his failing eyes as from those of a helpless infant. " God has brought you but to weep over my death-bed," he murmured feebly; and added with a profound sigh, on hearing of Chichikov's conduct: " Ah, Pavlushka, how a human being may become changed! Once you were a good lad, and gave me no trouble; but now you are become proud indeed! "

Yet let it not be inferred from this that our hero's character had grown so *blasé* and hard, or his conscience so blunted, as to preclude his experiencing a particle of sympathy or compassion. As a matter of fact, he was capable both of the one and the other, and would have been glad to assist his old teacher had no great sum been required, or had he not been called upon to touch the fund which he had decided should remain intact. In other words, the father's injunction, " Guard and save every kopeck," had become a hard and fast rule of the son's. Yet the youth had no particular attachment to money for money's sake; he was not possessed with the true instinct for hoarding and niggardliness. Rather, before his eyes there floated ever a vision of life and its amenities and advantages—a vision of carriages and an elegantly furnished house and *récherché* dinners; and it was in the hope that some day he might attain these things that he saved every kopeck and, meanwhile, stinted both himself and others. Whenever a rich man passed him by in a splendid *drozhki* drawn by swift and handsomely-caparisoned horses, he would halt as though deep in thought, and then say to himself, like a man awakening from a long sleep: " That gentleman must have been a financier, he has so little hair on his brow." In short, everything connected with wealth and plenty produced upon him an ineffaceable impression. Even when he left school he took no holiday, so strong in him was the desire to get to work and enter the Civil Service. Yet, for all the encomiums

[1] Silver five kopeck piece.

contained in his diploma, he had much ado to procure a nomination to a Government Department; and only after a long time was a minor post found for him, at a salary of thirty or forty roubles a year. Nevertheless, wretched though this appointment was, he determined, by strict attention to business, to overcome all obstacles, and to win success. And, indeed, the self-denial, the patience, and the economy which he displayed were remarkable. From early morn until late at night he would, with indefatigable zeal of body and mind, remain immersed in his sordid task of copying official documents—never going home, snatching what sleep he could on tables in the building, and dining with the watchman on duty. Yet all the while he contrived to remain clean and neat, to preserve a cheerful expression of countenance, and even to cultivate a certain elegance of movement. In passing, it may be remarked that his fellow *tchinovniks* were a peculiarly plain, unsightly lot, some of them having faces like badly baked bread, swollen cheeks, receding chins, and cracked and blistered upper lips. Indeed, not a man of them was handsome. Also, their tone of voice always contained a note of sullenness, as though they had a mind to knock some one on the head; and by their frequent sacrifices to Bacchus they showed that even yet there remains in the Slavonic nature a certain element of paganism. Nay, the Director's room itself they would invade while still licking their lips, and since their breath was not over-aromatic, the atmosphere of the room grew not over-pleasant. Naturally, among such an official staff a man like Chichikov could not fail to attract attention and remark, since in everything—in cheerfulness of demeanour, in suavity of voice, and in complete neglect of the use of strong potions—he was the absolute antithesis of his companions. Yet his path was not an easy one to tread, for over him he had the misfortune to have placed in authority a Chief Clerk who was a graven image of elderly insensibility and inertia. Always the same, always unapproachable, this functionary could never in his life have smiled or asked civilly after an acquaintance's health. Nor had any one ever seen him a whit different in the street or at his own home from what he was in the office, or showing the least interest in anything whatever, or getting drunk and relapsing into jollity in his cups, or indulging in that species of wild gaiety which, when intoxicated, even a burglar affects. No, not a particle of this was there in him. Nor, for that matter, was there in him a particle of anything at all, whether good or bad: which complete negativeness of character produced rather a strange effect. In the same way, his wizened, marble-like features reminded one of nothing in particular, so primly proportioned were they. Only the numerous pockmarks and dimples with which they were pitted placed him among the number of those over whose faces, to quote the popular saying, "The Devil has walked by night to grind peas." In short, it would seem that no human agency could have approached such a man and gained his goodwill. Yet Chichikov made the effort. As a first step, he took to consulting the other's convenience in all manner of insignificant trifles —to cleaning his pens carefully, and, when they had been prepared exactly to the Chief Clerk's liking, laying them ready at his elbow; to dusting and sweeping from his table all super-fluous sand and tobacco ash; to procuring a new mat for his inkstand; to looking for his hat—the meanest-looking hat that ever the world beheld—and having it ready for him at the exact moment when business came to an end; to brushing his back if it happened to become smeared with whitewash from a wall. Yet all this passed as unnoticed as though it had never been done. Finally, Chichikov sniffed into his superior's family and domestic life, and learnt that he possessed a grown-up daughter on whose face also there had taken place a nocturnal, dia-bolical grinding of peas. *Here* was a quarter whence a fresh attack might be delivered! After ascertaining what church the daughter attended on Sundays, our hero took to contriving to meet her in a neat suit and a well-starched dickey: and soon the scheme began to work. The surly Chief Clerk wavered for a while; then ended by inviting Chichikov to tea. Nor could any man in the office have told you how it came about that before long Chichikov had removed to the Chief Clerk's house, and become a person necessary — indeed, indispensable — to the household, seeing that he bought the flour and the sugar, treated the daughter as his betrothed, called the Chief Clerk " *Papenka*," and occasionally kissed " *Papenka's* " hand. In fact, every one at the office supposed that, at the end of February (*i.e.* before the beginning of Lent) there would take place a wedding. Nay, the surly father even began to agitate with the authorities on Chichikov's behalf, and so enabled our hero, on a vacancy occurring, to attain the stool of a Chief Clerk. Apparently this marked the consummation of Chichikov's relations with his host, for he hastened stealthily to pack his trunk, and, the next day, figured in a fresh lodging. Also, he ceased to call the Chief Clerk " *Papenka*," or to kiss his hand; and the matter of the wedding came to as abrupt a termination as though it had never been mooted. Yet also he never failed to press his late host's hand, whenever he met him, and to invite him to tea; while, on the other hand, for all his immobility and dry indifference, the Chief Clerk never failed to shake his head with a muttered, " Ah, my fine fellow, you have grown too proud, you have grown too proud."

The foregoing constituted the most difficult step that our hero had to negotiate. Thereafter things came with greater ease and swifter success. Everywhere he attracted notice, for he developed within himself everything necessary for this world—namely, charm of manner and bearing, and great diligence in business matters. Armed with these resources, he next obtained promotion to what is known as " a fat post," and used it to the best advantage; and even though, at that period, strict inquiry had begun to be made into the whole subject of bribes, such inquiry failed to alarm him—nay, he actually turned it to account and thereby manifested the Russian resourcefulness which never fails to attain its zenith where extortion is concerned. His method of working was the following. As soon as a petitioner or a suitor put his hand into his pocket, to extract thence the necessary letters of recommendation for signature, Chichikov would smilingly exclaim as he detained his interlocutor's hand: " No, no! Surely you do not think that I——? But no, no! It is our duty, it is our obligation, and we do not require rewards for doing our work properly. So far as *your* matter is concerned, you may rest easy. Everything shall be carried through to-morrow. But may I have your address? There is no need for you to trouble yourself, seeing that the documents can easily be brought to you at your residence." Upon which the delighted suitor would return home in raptures, thinking: " Here, at long last, is the sort of man so badly needed. A man of that kind is a jewel beyond price." Yet for a day, for two days—nay, even for three—the suitor would wait in vain so far as any messengers with documents were concerned. Then he would repair to the office—to find that his business had not so much as been entered upon! Lastly, he would confront the " jewel beyond price." " Oh, pardon me, pardon me! " Chichikov would exclaim in the politest of tones as he seized and grasped the visitor's hands. " The truth is that we have *such* a quantity of business on hand! But the matter shall be put through to-morrow, and in the meanwhile I am most sorry about it." And with this would go the most fascinating of gestures.

Yet neither on the morrow, nor on the day following, nor on the third would documents arrive at the suitor's abode. Upon that he would take thought as to whether something more ought not to have been done; and, sure enough, on his making inquiry, he would be informed that "something will have to be given to the copyists." "Well, there can be no harm in that," he would reply. "As a matter of fact, I have ready a *tchetvertak*[1] or two." "Oh, no, no," the answer would come. "Not a *tchetvertak* per copyist, but a rouble, is the fee." "What? A rouble per copyist?" "Certainly. What is there to grumble at in that? Of the money the copyists will receive a *tchetvertak* apiece, and the rest will go to the Government." Upon that the disillusioned suitor would fly out upon the new order of things brought about by the inquiry into illicit fees, and curse both the *tchinovniks* and their uppish, insolent behaviour. "Once upon a time," would the suitor lament, "one *did* know what to do. Once one had tipped the Director a bank-note, one's affair was, so to speak, in the hat. But now one has to pay a rouble per copyist after waiting a week because otherwise it was impossible to guess how the wind might set! The devil fly away with all 'disinterested' and 'trustworthy' *tchinovniks!*" And certainly the aggrieved suitor had reason to grumble, seeing that, now that bribe-takers had ceased to exist, and Directors had uniformly become men of honour and integrity, secretaries and clerks ought not with impunity to have continued their thievish ways. In time there opened out to Chichikov a still wider field, for a Commission was appointed to supervise the erection of a Government building, and, on his being nominated to that body, he proved himself one of its most active members. The Commission got to work without delay, but for a space of six years had some trouble with the building in question. Either the climate hindered operations or the materials used were of the kind which prevents official edifices from ever rising higher than the basement. But, meanwhile, *other* quarters of the town saw arise, for each member of the Commission, a handsome house of the *non*-official style of architecture. Clearly the foundation afforded by the soil of those parts was better than that where the Government building was still engaged in hanging fire! Likewise the members of the Commission began to look exceedingly prosperous, and to blossom out into family life; and, for the first time in his existence, even Chichikov also departed from the iron laws of his self-imposed restraint and inexorable self-denial,

---

[1] A silver quarter rouble.

and so far mitigated his heretofore asceticism as to show himself a man not averse to those amenities which, during his youth, he had been capable of renouncing. That is to say, certain superfluities began to make their appearance in his establishment. He engaged a good cook, took to wearing linen shirts, bought for himself cloth of a pattern worn by no one else in the province, figured in checks shot with the brightest of reds and browns, fitted himself out with two splendid horses (which he drove with a single pair of reins, added to a ring attachment for the trace horse), developed a habit of washing with a sponge dipped in *eau-de-Cologne*, and invested in soaps of the most expensive quality, in order to communicate to his skin a more elegant polish.

But suddenly there appeared upon the scene a new Director —a military man, and a martinet as regarded his hostility to bribe-takers and anything which might be called irregular. On the very day after his arrival he struck fear into every breast by calling for accounts, discovering hosts of deficits and missing sums, and directing his attention to the aforesaid fine houses of civilian architecture. Upon that there ensued a complete reshuffling. *Tchinovniks* were retired wholesale, and the houses were sequestrated to the Government, or else converted into various pious institutions and schools for soldiers' children. Thus the whole fabric, and especially Chichikov, came crashing to the ground. Particularly did our hero's agreeable face displease the new Director. Why that was so it is impossible to say, but frequently, in cases of the kind, no reason exists. However, the Director conceived a mortal dislike to him, and also extended that enmity to the whole of Chichikov's colleagues. But inasmuch as the said Director was a military man, he was not fully acquainted with the myriad subtleties of the civilian mind; wherefore it was not long before, by dint of maintaining a discreet exterior, added to a faculty for humouring all and sundry, a fresh gang of *tchinovniks* succeeded in restoring him to mildness, and the General found himself in the hands of greater thieves than before, but thieves whom he did not even suspect, seeing that he believed himself to have selected men fit and proper, and even ventured to boast of possessing a keen eye for talent. In a trice the *tchinovniks* concerned appraised his spirit and character; with the result that the entire sphere over which he ruled became an agency for the detection of irregularities. Everywhere, and in every case, were those irregularities pursued as a fisherman pursues a fat sturgeon

with a gaff; and to such an extent did the sport prove successful
that almost in no time each participator in the hunt was seen
to be in possession of several thousand roubles of capital. Upon
that a large number of the former band of *tchinovniks* also
became converted to paths of rectitude, and were allowed to
re-enter the Service; but not by hook or by crook could Chichikov worm his way back, even though, incited thereto by sundry
items of paper currency, the General's first secretary and
principal bear leader did all he could on our hero's behalf. It
seemed that the General was the kind of man who, though
easily led by the nose (provided it was done without his knowledge) no sooner got an idea into his head than it stuck there like
a nail, and could not possibly be extracted; and all that the
wily secretary succeeded in procuring was the tearing up of a
certain dirty fragment of paper—even that being effected only
by an appeal to the General's compassion, on the score of the
unhappy fate which, otherwise, would befall Chichikov's wife
and children (who, luckily, had no existence in fact).

" Well," said Chichikov to himself, " I have done my best,
and now everything has failed. Lamenting my misfortune won't
help me, but only action." And with that he decided to begin
his career anew, and once more to arm himself with the weapons
of patience and self-denial. The better to effect this, he had, of
course, to remove to another town. Yet somehow, for a while,
things miscarried. More than once he found himself forced to
exchange one post for another, and at the briefest of notice;
and all of them were posts of the meanest, the most wretched,
order. Yet, being a man of the utmost nicety of feeling, the fact
that he found himself rubbing shoulders with anything but nice
companions did not prevent him from preserving intact his
innate love of what was decent and seemly, or from cherishing
the instinct which led him to hanker after office fittings of
lacquered wood, with neatness and orderliness everywhere.
Nor did he at any time permit a foul word to creep into his
speech, and would feel hurt even if in the speech of others there
occurred a scornful reference to anything which pertained to
rank and dignity. Also, the reader will be pleased to know that
our hero changed his linen every other day, and in summer,
when the weather was hot, *every* day, seeing that the very
faintest suspicion of an unpleasant odour offended his fastidious-
ness. For the same reason it was his custom, before being valeted
by Petrushka, always to plug his nostrils with a couple of cloves.
In short, there were many occasions when his nerves suffered

rackings as cruel as a young girl's, and so helped to increase his disgust at having once more to associate with men who set no store by the decencies of life. Yet, though he braced himself to the task, this period of adversity told upon his health, and he even grew a trifle shabby. More than once, on happening to catch sight of himself in the mirror, he could not forbear exclaiming: " Holy Mother of God, but what a nasty-looking brute I have become ! " and for a long while afterwards could not with anything like *sang froid* contemplate his reflection. Yet throughout he bore up stoutly and patiently—and ended by being transferred to the Customs Department. It may be said that the department had long constituted the secret goal of his ambition, for he had noted the foreign elegancies with which its officials always contrived to provide themselves, and had also observed that invariably they were able to send presents of china and cambric to their sisters and aunts—well, to their lady friends generally. Yes, more than once he had said to himself with a sigh: " *That* is the department to which I ought to belong, for, given a town near the frontier, and a sensible set of colleagues, I might be able to fit myself out with excellent linen shirts." Also, it may be said that most frequently of all had his thoughts turned to a certain quality of French soap which imparted a peculiar whiteness to the skin and a peerless freshness to the cheeks. Its name is known to God alone, but at least it was to be procured only in the immediate neighbourhood of the frontier. So, as I say, Chichikov had long felt a leaning towards the Customs, but for a time had been restrained from applying for the same by the various current advantages of the Building Commission; since rightly he had adjudged the latter to constitute a bird in the hand, and the former to constitute only a bird in the bush. But now he decided that, come what might, into the Customs he must make his way. And that way he made, and then applied himself to his new duties with a zeal born of the fact that he realised that fortune had specially marked him out for a Customs officer. Indeed, such activity, perspicuity, and ubiquity as his had never been seen or thought of. Within four weeks at the most he had so thoroughly got his hand in that he was conversant with Customs procedure in every detail. Not only could he weigh and measure, but also he could divine from an invoice how many *arshins* of cloth or other material a given piece contained, and then, taking a roll of the latter in his hand, could specify at once the number of pounds at which it would tip the scale. As for searchings, well, even his colleagues had to admit that he possessed the nose of a veritable bloodhound, and that it was impossible not to marvel at the patience wherewith he would try every button of the suspected person, yet preserve, throughout, a deadly politeness and an icy *sang-froid* which surpass belief. And while the searched were raging, and foaming at the mouth, and feeling that they would give worlds to alter his smiling exterior with a good, resounding slap, he would move not a muscle of his face, nor abate by a jot the urbanity of his demeanour, as he murmured, " Do you mind so far incommoding yourself as to stand up? " or " Pray step into the next room, madam, where the wife of one of our staff will attend you," or " Pray allow me to slip this penknife of mine into the lining of your coat " (after which he would extract thence shawls and towels with as much nonchalance as he would have done from his own travelling-trunk). Even his superiors acknowledged him to be a devil at the job, rather than a human being, so perfect was his instinct for looking into cart-wheels, carriage-poles, horses' ears, and places whither an author ought not to penetrate even in thought —places whither only a Customs official is permitted to go. The result was that the wretched traveller who had just crossed the frontier would, within a few minutes, become wholly at sea, and, wiping away the perspiration, and breaking out into body flushes, would be reduced to crossing himself and muttering, " Well, well, well! " In fact, such a traveller would feel in the position of a schoolboy who, having been summoned to the presence of the headmaster for the ostensible purpose of being given an order, has found that he receives, instead, a sound flogging. In short, for some time Chichikov made it impossible for smugglers to earn a living. In particular, he reduced Polish Jewry almost to despair, so invincible, so almost unnatural, was the rectitude, the incorruptibility which led him to refrain from converting himself into a small capitalist with the aid of confiscated goods and articles which, " to save excessive clerical labour," had failed to be handed over to the Government. Also, without saying it goes that such phenomenally zealous and disinterested service attracted general astonishment, and, eventually, the notice of the authorities; whereupon he received promotion, and followed that up by mooting a scheme for the infallible detection of contrabandists, provided that he could be furnished with the necessary authority for carrying out the same. At once such authority was accorded him, as also unlimited power to conduct every species of search and investigation. And that was all he wanted. It happened that previously there had been formed a well-found association for smuggling on regular, carefully prepared lines, and that this daring scheme seemed to promise profit to the extent of some millions of money: yet, though he had long had knowledge of it, Chichikov had said to the association's emissaries, when sent to buy him over, "The time is not yet." But now that he had got all the reins into his hands, he sent word of the fact to the gang, and with it the remark, "The time is *now*." Nor was he wrong in his calculations, for, within the space of a year, he had acquired what he could not have made during twenty years of non-fraudulent service. With similar sagacity he had, during his early days in the department, declined altogether to enter into relations with the association, for the reason that he had then been a mere cipher, and would have come in for nothing large in the way of takings; but now—well, now it was another matter altogether, and he could dictate what terms he liked. Moreover, that the affair might progress the more smoothly, he suborned a fellow *tchinovnik* of the type which, in spite of grey hairs, stands powerless against temptation; and, the contract concluded, the association duly proceeded to business. Certainly business began brilliantly. But probably most of my readers are familiar with the oft-repeated story of the passage of Spanish sheep across the frontier in double fleeces which carried between their outer layers and their inner enough lace of Brabant to sell to the tune of millions of roubles; wherefore I will not recount the story again beyond saying that those journeys took place just when Chichikov had become head of the Customs, and that, had he not a hand in the enterprise, not all the Jews in the world could have brought it to success. By the time that three or four of these ovine invasions had taken place, Chichikov and his accomplice had come to be the possessors of four hundred thousand roubles apiece; while some even aver that the former's gains totalled half a million, owing to the greater industry which he had displayed in the matter. Nor can any one but God say to what a figure the fortunes of the pair might not eventually have attained, had not an awkward *contretemps* cut right across their arrangements. That is to say, for some reason or another the devil so far deprived these *tchinovnik*-conspirators of sense as to make them come to words with one another, and then to engage in a quarrel. Beginning with a heated argument, this quarrel reached the point of Chichikov—who was, possibly, a trifle tipsy—calling his colleague a priest's son; and though

that description of the person so addressed was perfectly
accurate, he chose to take offence, and to answer Chichikov with
the words (loudly and incisively uttered), " It is *you* who have
a priest for your father," and to add to that (the more to incense
his companion), " Yes, mark you! *That* is how it is." Yet,
though he had thus turned the tables upon Chichikov with a
tu quoque, and then capped that exploit with the words last
quoted, the offended *tchinovnik* could not remain satisfied, but
went on to send in an anonymous document to the authorities.
On the other hand, some aver that it was over a woman that the
pair fell out—over a woman who, to quote the phrase then
current among the staff of the Customs Department, was " as
fresh and as strong as the pulp of a turnip," and that night-birds
were hired to assault our hero in a dark alley, and that the
scheme miscarried, and that in any case both Chichikov and his
friend had been deceived, seeing that the person to whom the
lady had really accorded her favours was a certain staff-captain
named Shamsharev. However, only God knows the truth of
the matter. Let the inquisitive reader ferret it out for himself.
The fact remains that a complete exposure of the dealings with
the contrabandists followed, and that the two *tchinovniks* were
put to the question, deprived of their property, and made to
formulate in writing all that they had done. Against this
thunderbolt of fortune the State Councillor could make no head-
way, and in some retired spot or another sank into oblivion;
but Chichikov put a brave face upon the matter, for, in spite of
the authorities' best efforts to smell out his gains, he contrived
to conceal a portion of them, and also resorted to every subtle
trick of intellect which could possibly be employed by an
experienced man of the world who has a wide knowledge of his
fellows. Nothing which could be effected by pleasantness of
demeanour, by moving oratory, by clouds of flattery, and by
the occasional insertion of a coin into a palm did he leave undone;
with the result that he was retired with less ignominy than was
his companion, and escaped actual trial on a criminal charge.
Yet he issued stripped of all his capital, stripped of his imported
effects, stripped of everything. That is to say, all that remained
to him consisted of ten thousand roubles which he had stored
against a rainy day, two dozen linen shirts, a small *britchka* of
the type used by bachelors, and two serving-men named Selifan
and Petrushka. Yes, and an impulse of kindness moved the
tchinovniks of the Customs also to set aside for him a few cakes
of the soap which he had found so excellent for the freshness of

the cheeks. Thus once more our hero found himself stranded. And what an accumulation of misfortunes had descended upon his head!—though, true, he termed them "suffering in the Service in the cause of Truth." Certainly one would have thought that, after these buffetings and trials and changes of fortune— after this taste of the sorrows of life—he and his precious ten thousand roubles would have withdrawn to some peaceful corner in a provincial town, where, clad in a stuff dressing-gown, he could have sat and listened to the peasants quarrelling on festival days, or (for the sake of a breath of fresh air) have gone in person to the poulterer's to finger chickens for soup, and so have spent a quiet, but not wholly useless, existence; but nothing of the kind took place, and therein we must do justice to the strength of his character. In other words, although he had undergone what, to the majority of men, would have meant ruin and discouragement and a shattering of ideals, he still preserved his energy. True, downcast and angry, and full of resentment against the world in general, he felt furious with the injustice of fate, and dissatisfied with the dealings of men; yet he could not forbear courting additional experiences. In short, the patience which he displayed was such as to make the wooden persistency of the German—a persistency merely due to the slow, lethargic circulation of the Teuton's blood—seem nothing at all, seeing that by nature Chichikov's blood flowed strongly, and that he had to employ much force of will to curb within himself those elements which longed to burst forth and revel in freedom. He thought things over, and, as he did so, a certain spice of reason appeared in his reflections.

"How have I come to be what I am?" he said to himself. "Why has misfortune overtaken me in this way? Never have I wronged a poor person, or robbed a widow, or turned any one out of doors: I have always been careful only to take advantage of those who possess more than their share. Moreover, I have never gleaned anywhere but where every one else was gleaning; and, had I not done so, others would have gleaned in my place. Why, then, should those others be prospering, and I be sunk as low as a worm? What am I? What am I good for? How can I, in future, hope to look any honest father of a family in the face? How shall I escape being tortured with the thought that I am cumbering the ground? What, in the years to come, will my children say, save that 'our father was a brute, for he left us nothing to live upon?'"

Here I may remark that we have seen how much thought

Chichikov devoted to his future descendants. Indeed, had not there been constantly recurring to his mind the insistent question, " What will my children say? " he might not have plunged into the affair so deeply. Nevertheless, like a wary cat which glances hither and thither to see whether its mistress be not coming before it can make off with whatsoever first falls to its paw (butter, fat, lard, a duck, or anything else), so our future founder of a family continued, though weeping and bewailing his lot, to let not a single detail escape his eye. That is to say, he retained his wits ever in a state of activity, and kept his brain constantly working. All that he required was a plan. Once more he pulled himself together, once more he embarked upon a life of toil, once more he stinted himself in everything, once more he left clean and decent surroundings for a dirty, mean existence. In other words, until something better should turn up, he embraced the calling of an ordinary attorney—a calling which, not then possessed of a civic status, was jostled on every side, enjoyed little respect at the hands of the minor legal fry (or, indeed, at its own), and perforce met with universal slights and rudeness. But sheer necessity compelled Chichikov to face these things. Among commissions entrusted to him was that of placing in the hands of the Public Trustee several hundred peasants who belonged to a ruined estate. The estate had reached its parlous condition through cattle disease, through rascally bailiffs, through failures of the harvest, through such epidemic diseases that had killed off the best workmen, and, last, but not least, through the senseless conduct of the owner himself, who had furnished a house in Moscow in the latest style, and then squandered his every kopeck, so that nothing was left for his further maintenance, and it became necessary to mortgage the remains—including the peasants—of the estate. In those days mortgage to the Treasury was an innovation looked upon with reserve, and, as attorney in the matter, Chichikov had first of all to " entertain " every official concerned (we know that, unless that be previously done, unless a whole bottle of madeira first be emptied down each clerical throat, not the smallest legal affair can be carried through), and to explain, for the barring of future attachments, that half the peasants were dead.

" And are they entered on the revision lists? " asked the secretary. " Yes," replied Chichikov. " Then what are you boggling at? " continued the Secretary. " Should one soul die, another will be born, and in time grow up to take the first one's place." Upon that there dawned on our hero one of the most inspired ideas which ever entered the human brain. " What a simpleton I am! " he thought to himself. " Here am I looking about for my mittens when all the time I have got them tucked into my belt. Why, were I myself to buy up a few souls which are dead—to buy them before a new revision list shall have been made, the Council of Public Trust might pay me two hundred roubles apiece for them, and I might find myself with, say, a capital of two hundred thousand roubles! The present moment is particularly propitious, since in various parts of the country there has been an epidemic, and, glory be to God, a large number of souls have died of it. Nowadays landowners have taken to card-playing and junketting and wasting their money, or to joining the Civil Service in St. Petersburg; consequently their estates are going to rack and ruin, and being managed in any sort of fashion, and succeeding in paying their dues with greater difficulty each year. That being so, not a man of the lot but would glady surrender to me his dead souls rather than continue paying the poll-tax; and in this fashion I might make— well, not a few kopecks. Of course there are difficulties, and, to avoid creating a scandal, I should need to employ plenty of *finesse ;* but man was given his brain to *use,* not to neglect. One good point about the scheme is that it will seem so improbable that in case of an accident, no one in the world will believe in it. True, it is illegal to buy or mortgage peasants without land, but I can easily pretend to be buying them only for transferment elsewhere. Land is to be acquired in the provinces of Taurida and Kherson almost for nothing, provided that one undertakes subsequently to colonise it; so to Kherson I will ' transfer ' them, and long may they live there! And the removal of my dead souls shall be carried out in the strictest legal form; and if the authorities should want confirmation by testimony, I shall produce a letter signed by my own superintendent of the Khersonian rural police—that is to say, by myself. Lastly, the supposed village in Kherson shall be called Chichikovöe—better still Pavlovsköe, according to my Christian name."

In this fashion there germinated in our hero's brain that strange scheme for which the reader may or may not be grateful, but for which the author certainly is so, seeing that, had it never occurred to Chichikov, this story would never have seen the light.

After crossing himself, according to the Russian custom, Chichikov set about carrying out his enterprise. On pretence of selecting a place wherein to settle, he started forth to inspect various corners of the Russian Empire, but more especially those which had suffered from such unfortunate accidents as failures of the harvest, a high rate of mortality, or whatsoever else might enable him to purchase souls at the lowest possible rate. But he did not tackle his landowners haphazard: he rather selected such of them as seemed more particularly suited to his taste, or with whom he might with the least possible trouble conclude identical agreements; though, in the first instance, he always tried, by getting on terms of acquaintanceship—better still, of friendship—with them, to acquire the souls for nothing, and so to avoid purchase at all. In passing, my readers must not blame me if the characters whom they have encountered in these pages have not been altogether to their liking. The fault is Chichikov's rather than mine, for he is the master, and where he leads we must follow. Also, should my readers gird at me for a certain dimness and want of clarity in my principal characters and actors, that will be tantamount to saying that never do the broad tendency and the general scope of a work become immediately apparent. Similarly does the entry to every town— the entry even to the Capital itself—convey to the traveller such an impression of vagueness that at first everything looks grey and monotonous, and the lines of smoky factories and workshops seem never to be coming to an end; but in time there will begin also to stand out the outlines of six-storied mansions, and of shops and balconies, and wide perspectives of streets, and a medley of steeples, columns, statues, and turrets—the whole framed in rattle and roar and the infinite wonders which the hand and the brain of men have conceived. Of the manner in which Chichikov's first purchases were made the reader is aware. Subsequently he will see also how the affair progressed, and with what success or failure our hero met, and how Chichikov was called upon to decide and to overcome even more difficult problems than the foregoing, and by what colossal forces the levers of this far-flung tale are moved, and how eventually the horizon will become extended until everything assumes a grandiose and a lyrical tendency. Yes, many a *verst* of road remains to be travelled by a party made up of an elderly gentleman, a *britchka* of the kind affected by bachelors, a valet named Petrushka, a coachman named Selifan, and three horses which, from the Assessor to the skewbald, are known to us individually by name. Again, although I have given a full description of our hero's exterior (such as it is), I may yet be asked for an inclusive definition also of his moral personality. That he is no hero compounded of virtues and perfections must be already clear. Then *what* is he? A villain? Why should we call him a villain? Why should we be so hard upon a fellow man? In these days our villains have ceased to exist. Rather it would be fairer to call him an *acquirer*. The love of acquisition, the love of gain, is a fault common to many, and gives rise to many and many a transaction of the kind generally known as "not strictly honourable." True, such a character contains an element of ugliness, and the same reader who, during his journey through life, would sit at the board of a character of this kind, and spend a most agreeable time with him, would be the first to look at him askance if he should appear in the guise of the hero of a novel or a play. But wise is the reader who, on meeting such a character, scans him carefully, and, instead of shrinking from him with distaste, probes him to the springs of his being. The human personality contains nothing which may not, in the twinkling of an eye, become altogether changed—nothing in which, before you can look round, there may not spring to birth some canker-worm which is destined to suck thence the essential juice. Yes, it is a common thing to see not only an overmastering passion, but also a passion of the most petty order, arise in a man who was born to better things, and lead him both to forget his greatest and most sacred obligations, and to see only in the veriest trifles the Great and the Holy. For human passions are as numberless as is the sand of the seashore, and infinitely more various: and all of them, whether elevated or debased, may begin by acting as man's servants, and go on to become his most insistent of masters. Happy, therefore, the man who may choose from among the gamut of human passions one which is noble! Hour by hour will that instinct grow and multiply in its measureless beneficence; hour by hour will it sink deeper and deeper into the infinite paradise of his soul. But there are passions of which a man cannot rid himself, seeing that they are born with him at his birth, and he has no power to abjure them. Higher powers govern those passions, and in them is something which will call to him, and refuse to be silenced, to the end of his life. Yes, whether in a guise of darkness, or whether in a guise which will become converted into a light to lighten the world, they will and must attain their consummation on life's field: and in either case they have been evoked for man's good. In the same way may the passion which drew our Chichikov onwards have been one that was independent of himself; in the same way may there have lurked even in his cold essence something which will one day cause men to humble themselves in the dust before the infinite wisdom of God.

Yet that folk should be dissatisfied with my hero matters nothing. What matters is the fact that, under different circumstances, their approval could have been taken as a foregone conclusion. That is to say, had not the author pried over-deeply into Chichikov's soul, nor stirred up in its depths what shunned and lay hidden from the light, nor disclosed those of his hero's thoughts which that hero would not have disclosed even to his most intimate friend; had the author, indeed, exhibited Chichikov just as he exhibited himself to the townsmen of N. and Manilov and the rest; well, then we may rest assured that every reader would have been delighted with him, and have voted him a most interesting person. For it is not nearly so necessary that Chichikov should figure before the reader as though his form and person were actually present to the eye as that, on concluding a perusal of this work, the reader should be able to return, unharrowed in soul, to that cult of the card-table which is the solace and delight of all good Russians. Yes, readers of this book, none of you really care to see humanity revealed in its nakedness. " Why should we do so? " you say. " What would be the use of it? Do we not know for ourselves that human life contains much that is gross and contemptible? Do we not with our own eyes have to look upon much that is anything but comforting? Far better would it be if you would put before us what is comely and attractive, so that we might forget ourselves a little." In the same fashion does a landowner say to his bailiff: " Why do you come and tell me that the affairs of my estate are in a bad way? I know that without *your* help. Have you nothing else to tell me? Kindly allow me to forget the fact, or else to remain in ignorance of it, and I shall be much obliged to you." Whereafter the said landowner probably proceeds to spend on his diversion the money which ought to have gone towards the rehabilitation of his affairs.

Possibly the author may also incur censure at the hands of those so-called " patriots " who sit quietly in corners, and become capitalists through making fortunes at the expense of others. Yes, let but something which they conceive to be derogatory to their country occur—for instance, let there be published some book which voices the bitter truth—and out they will come from their hiding-places like a spider which perceives a fly to be caught in its web. " Is it well to proclaim this to the world, and to set folk talking about it? " they will cry. " What you have described touches *us*, is *our* affair. Is conduct of that kind right? What will foreigners say? Does any one care calmly to sit by and hear himself traduced? Why should you lead foreigners to suppose that all is not well with us, and that we are not patriotic? " Well, to these sage remarks no answer can really be returned, especially to such of the above as refer to foreign opinion. But see here. There once lived in a remote corner of Russia two natives of the region indicated. One of those natives was a good man named Kifa Mokievitch, and a man of kindly disposition; a man who went through life in a dressing-gown, and paid no heed to his household, for the reason that his whole being was centred upon the province of speculation, and that, in particular, he was preoccupied with a philosophical problem usually stated by him thus: " A beast," he would say, " is born naked. Now, why should that be? Why should not a beast be born as a bird is born—that is to say, through the process of being hatched from an egg? Nature is beyond the understanding, however much one may probe her." This was the substance of Kifa Mokievitch's reflections. But herein is not the chief point. The other of the pair was a fellow named Moki Kifovitch, and son to the first named. He was what we Russians call a " hero," and whilst his father was pondering the parturition of beasts, his, the son's, lusty, twenty-year-old temperament was violently struggling for development. Yet that son could tackle nothing without some accident occurring. At one moment would he crack some one's fingers in half, and at another would he raise a bump on somebody's nose; so that both at home and abroad every one and everything—from the serving-maid to the yard-dog—fled on his approach, and even the bed in his bedroom became shattered to splinters. Such was Moki Kifovitch; and with it all he had a kindly soul. But herein is not the chief point. " Good sir, good Kifa Mokievitch," servants and neighbours would come and say to the father, " what are you going to do about your Moki Kifovitch? We get no rest from him, he is so above himself." " That is only his play, that is only his play," the father would reply. " What else can you expect? It is too late now to start a quarrel with him, and, moreover, every one would accuse me of harshness. True, he is a little conceited; but, were I to reprove him in public, the whole thing would become common talk, and folk would begin giving him a dog's name. And if they did that, would not their opinion touch me also, seeing that I am his father? Also, I am busy with philosophy, and have no time for such things. Lastly, Moki Kifovitch is my son, and very dear to my heart." And, beating his breast, Kifa Mokievitch again asserted that, even though his son should elect to continue his pranks, it would not be for *him*, for the father, to proclaim the fact, or to fall out with his offspring. And, this expression of paternal feeling uttered, Kifa Mokievitch left Moki Kifovitch to his heroic exploits, and himself returned to his beloved subject of speculation, which now included also the problem, " Suppose elephants were to take to being hatched from eggs, would not the shell of such eggs be of a thickness proof against cannon-balls, and necessitate the invention of some new type of fire-arm ? " Thus at the end of this little story we have these two denizens of a peaceful corner of Russia looking thence, as from a window, in less terror of doing what was scandalous than of having it *said* of them that they were acting scandalously. Yes, the feeling animating our so-called " patriots " is not true patriotism at all. Something else lies beneath it. Who, if not an author, is to speak aloud the truth? Men like you, my pseudo-patriots, stand in dread of the eye which is able to discern, yet shrink from using your own, and prefer, rather, to glance at everything unheedingly. Yes, after laughing heartily over Chichikov's misadventures, and perhaps even commending the author for his dexterity of observation and pretty turn of wit, you will look at yourselves with redoubled pride and a self-satisfied smile, and add: " Well, we agree that in certain parts of the provinces there exists strange and ridiculous individuals, as well as unconscionable rascals."

Yet which of you, when quiet, and alone, and engaged in solitary self-communion, would not do well to probe *your own* souls, and to put to *yourselves* the solemn question, " Is there not in *me* an element of Chichikov? " For how should there not be? Which of you is not liable at any moment to be passed in the street by an acquaintance who, nudging his neighbour, may say of you, with a barely suppressed sneer: " Look! there goes Chichikov! That is Chichikov who has just gone by! "

But here are we talking at the top of our voices whilst all the time our hero lies slumbering in his *britchka !* Indeed, his name has been repeated so often during the recital of his life's history that he must almost have heard us! And at any time he is an irritable, irascible fellow when spoken of with disrespect. True, to the reader Chichikov's displeasure cannot matter a jot; but for the author it would mean ruin to quarrel with his hero, seeing that, arm in arm, Chichikov and he have yet far to go.

" Tut, tut, tut! " came in a shout from Chichikov. " Hi, Selifan! "

" What is it? " came the reply, uttered with a drawl.

" What is it? Why, how dare you drive like that? Come! Bestir yourself a little! "

And, indeed, Selifan had long been sitting with half-closed eyes, and hands which bestowed no encouragement upon his somnolent steeds save an occasional flicking of the reins against their flanks; whilst Petrushka had lost his cap, and was leaning backwards until his head had come to rest against Chichikov's knees—a position which necessitated his being awakened with a cuff. Selifan also roused himself, and apportioned to the skew-bald a few cuts across the back of a kind which at least had the effect of inciting that animal to trot; and when, presently, the other two horses followed their companion's example, the light *britchka* moved forward like a piece of thistledown. Selifan flourished his whip and shouted, " Hi, hi! " as the inequalities of the road jerked him vertically on his seat; and meanwhile, reclining against the leather cushions of the vehicle's interior, Chichikov smiled with gratification at the sensation of driving fast. For what Russian does not love to drive fast? Which of us does not at times yearn to give his horses their head, and to let them go, and to cry, " To the devil with the world! "? At such moments a great force seems to uplift one as on wings; and one flies, and everything else flies, but contrariwise—both the *verst* stones, and traders riding on the shafts of their waggons, and the forest with dark lines of spruce and fir amid which may be heard the axe of the woodcutter and the croaking of the raven. Yes, out of a dim, remote distance the road comes towards one, and while nothing save the sky and the light clouds through which the moon is cleaving her way seem halted, the brief glimpses wherein one can discern nothing clearly have in them a pervading touch of mystery. Ah *troika, troika,* swift as a bird, who was it first invented you? Only among a hardy race of folk can you have come to birth—only in a land which, though poor and rough, lies spread over half the world, and spans *versts* the counting whereof would leave one with aching eyes. Nor are you a modishly-fashioned vehicle of the road—a thing of clamps and iron. Rather, you are a vehicle but shapen and fitted with the axe or chisel of some handy peasant of Yaroslav. Nor are you driven by a coachman clothed in German livery, but by a man bearded and mittened. See him as he mounts, and flourishes his whip, and breaks into a long-drawn song! Away like the wind go the horses, and the wheels, with their spokes, become transparent circles, and the road seems to quiver beneath them, and a pedestrian, with a cry of astonishment, halts to watch the vehicle as it flies, flies, flies on its way until it becomes lost on the ultimate horizon—a speck amid a cloud of dust!

And you, Russia of mine—are not you also speeding like a *troika* which nought can overtake? Is not the road smoking beneath your wheels, and the bridges thundering as you cross them, and everything being left in the rear, and the spectators, struck with the portent, halting to wonder whether you be not a thunderbolt launched from heaven? What does that awe-inspiring progress of yours foretell? What is the unknown force which lies within your mysterious steeds? Surely the winds themselves must abide in their manes, and every vein in their bodies be an ear stretched to catch the celestial message which bids them, with iron-girded breasts, and hooves which barely touch the earth as they gallop, fly forward on a mission of God? Whither, then, are you speeding, O Russia of mine? Whither? Answer me! But no answer comes—only the weird sound of your collar-bells. Rent into a thousand shreds, the air roars past you, for you are overtaking the whole world, and shall one day force all nations, all empires to stand aside, to give you way!

1841.

PART II

I

WHY do I so persistently paint the poverty, the imperfections of Russian life, and delve in the remotest depths, the most retired holes and corners, of our Empire for my subjects? The answer is that there is nothing else to be done when an author's idiosyncrasy happens to incline him that way. So again we find ourselves in a retired spot. But what a spot!

Imagine, if you can, a mountain range like a gigantic fortress, with embrasures and bastions which appear to soar a thousand *versts* towards the heights of heaven, and, towering grandly over a boundless expanse of plain, are broken up into precipitous, overhanging limestone cliffs. Here and there those cliffs are seamed with water-courses and gullies, while at other points they are rounded off into spurs of green—spurs now coated with fleece-like tufts of young undergrowth, now studded with the stumps of felled trees, now covered with timber which has, by some miracle, escaped the woodman's axe. Also, a river winds awhile between its banks, then leaves the meadow land, divides into runlets (all flashing in the sun like fire), plunges, re-united, into the midst of a thicket of elder, birch, and pine, and, lastly, speeds triumphantly past bridges and mills and weirs which seem to be lying in wait for it at every turn.

At one particular spot the steep flank of the mountain range is covered with billowy verdure of denser growth than the rest; and here the aid of skilful planting, added to the shelter afforded by a rugged ravine, has enabled the flora of north and south so to be brought together that, twined about with sinuous hop-tendrils, the oak, the spruce fir, the wild pear, the maple, the cherry, the thorn, and the mountain ash either assist or check one another's growth, and everywhere cover the declivity with their straggling profusion. Also, at the edge of the summit there can be seen mingling with the green of the trees the red roofs of a manorial homestead, while behind the upper stories of the mansion proper and its carved balcony and a great semi-circular window there gleam the tiles and gables of some peasants' huts.

Lastly, over this combination of trees and roofs there rises—overtopping everything with its gilded, sparkling steeple—an old village church. On each of its pinnacles a cross of carved gilt is stayed with supports of similar gilding and design; with the result that from a distance the gilded portions have the effect of hanging without visible agency in the air. And the whole—the three successive tiers of woodland, roofs, and crosses —lies exquisitely mirrored in the river below, where hollow willows, grotesquely shaped (some of them rooted on the river's banks, and some in the water itself, and all drooping their branches until their leaves have formed a tangle with the water lilies which float on the surface), seem to be gazing at the marvellous reflection at their feet.

Thus the view from below is beautiful indeed. But the view from above is even better. No guest, no visitor, could stand on the balcony of the mansion and remain indifferent. So boundless is the panorama revealed that surprise would cause him to catch at his breath, and exclaim: "Lord of Heaven, but what a prospect!" Beyond meadows studded with spinneys and water-mills lie forests belted with green; while beyond, again, there can be seen showing through the slightly misty air strips of yellow heath, and, again, wide-rolling forests (as blue as the sea or a cloud), and more heath, paler than the first, but still yellow. Finally, on the far horizon a range of chalk-topped hills gleams white, even in dull weather, as though it were lightened with perpetual sunshine; and here and there on the dazzling whiteness of its lower slopes some plaster-like, nebulous patches represent far-off villages which lie too remote for the eye to discern their details. Indeed, only when the sunlight touches a steeple to gold does one realise that each such patch is a human settlement. Finally, all is wrapped in an immensity of silence which even the far, faint echoes of persons singing in the void of the plain cannot shatter.

Even after gazing at the spectacle for a couple of hours or so, the visitor would still find nothing to say, save: "Lord of Heaven, but what a prospect!" Then who is the dweller in, the proprietor of, this manor—a manor to which, as to an impregnable fortress, entrance cannot be gained from the side where we have been standing, but only from the other approach, where a few scattered oaks offer hospitable welcome to the visitor, and then, spreading above him their spacious branches (as in friendly embrace), accompany him to the façade of the mansion whose top we have been regarding from the reverse aspect, but which now stands frontwise on to us, and has, on one side of it, a row of peasants' huts with red tiles and carved gables, and, on the other, the village church, with those glittering golden crosses and gilded open-work charms which seem to hang suspended in the air? Yes, indeed!—to what fortunate individual does this corner of the world belong? It belongs to Andrei Ivanovitch Tientietnikov, landowner of the canton of Tremalakhan, and, withal, a bachelor of about thirty.

Should my lady readers ask of me what manner of man is Tientietnikov, and what are his attributes and peculiarities, I should refer them to his neighbours. Of these, a member of the almost extinct tribe of intelligent staff officers on the retired list once summed up Tientietnikov in the phrase, " He is an absolute blockhead; " while a General who resided ten *versts* away was heard to remark that " he is a young man who, though not exactly a fool, has at least too much crowded into his head. I myself might have been of use to him, for not only do I maintain certain connections with St. Petersburg, but also——" And the General left his sentence unfinished. Thirdly, a captain-superintendent of rural police happened to remark in the course of conversation: " To-morrow I must go and see Tientietnikov about his arrears." Lastly, a peasant of Tientietnikov's own village, when asked what his *barin* was like, returned no answer at all. All of which would appear to show that Tientietnikov was not exactly looked upon with favour.

To speak dispassionately, however, he was not a bad sort of fellow—merely a star-gazer; and since the world contains many watchers of the skies, why should Tientietnikov not have been one of them? However, let me describe in detail a specimen day of his existence—one that will closely resemble the rest, and then the reader will be enabled to judge of Tientietnikov's character, and how far his life corresponded to the beauties of nature with which he lived surrounded.

On the morning of the specimen day in question he awoke very late, and, raising himself to a sitting posture, rubbed his eyes. And since those eyes were small, the process of rubbing them occupied a very long time, and throughout its continuance there stood waiting by the door his valet, Mikhailo, armed with a towel and basin. For one hour, for two hours, did poor Mikhailo stand there: then he departed to the kitchen, and returned to find his master still rubbing his eyes as he sat on the bed. At length, however, Tientietnikov rose, washed himself, donned a dressing-gown, and moved into the drawing-room for morning tea, coffee, cocoa, and warm milk; of all of which he partook but sparingly, while munching a piece of bread, and scattering tobacco ash with complete *insouciance*. Two hours did he sit over this meal, then poured himself out another cup of the rapidly cooling tea, and walked to the window. This faced the courtyard, and outside it, as usual, there took place the following daily altercation between a serf named Grigory (who purported to act as butler) and the housekeeper, Perfilievna.

Grigory. Ah, you nuisance, you good-for-nothing, you had far better hold your stupid tongue.

Perfilievna. Yes; and don't you wish that I would?

Grigory. What? You so thick with that bailiff of yours, you housekeeping jade!

Perfilievna. Nay, he is as big a thief as you are. Do you think the *barin* doesn't know you? And there he is! He must have heard everything!

Grigory. Where?

Perfilievna. There—sitting by the window, and looking at us!

Next, to complete the hubbub, a serf child which had been clouted by its mother broke out into a bawl, while a *borzoi* puppy which had happened to get splashed with boiling water by the cook fell to yelping vociferously. In short, the place soon became a babel of shouts and squeals, and, after watching and listening for a time, the *barin* found it so impossible to concentrate his mind upon anything that he sent out word that the noise would have to be abated.

The next item was that, a couple of hours before luncheon time, he withdrew to his study, to set about employing himself upon a weighty work which was to consider Russia from every point of view: from the political, from the philosophical, and from the religious, as well as to resolve various problems which had arisen to confront the Empire, and to define clearly the great future to which the country stood ordained. In short, it was to be the species of compilation in which the man of the day so much delights. Yet the colossal undertaking had progressed but little beyond the sphere of projection, since, after a pen had been gnawed awhile, and a few strokes had been committed to paper, the whole would be laid aside in favour of the reading of some book; and that reading would continue also during luncheon and be followed by the lighting of a pipe, the playing of a solitary game of chess, and the doing of more or less nothing for the rest of the day.

The foregoing will give the reader a pretty clear idea of the manner in which it was possible for this man of thirty-three to waste his time. Clad constantly in slippers and a dressing-gown, Tientietnikov never went out, never indulged in any form of dissipation, and never walked upstairs. Nothing did he care for fresh air, and would bestow not a passing glance upon all those beauties of the countryside which moved visitors to such ecstatic admiration. From this the reader will see that Andrei Ivanovitch Tientietnikov belonged to that band of sluggards whom we always have with us, and who, whatever be their present appellation, used to be known by the nicknames of "lollopers," "bed pressers," and "marmots." Whether the type is a type originating at birth, or a type resulting from untoward circumstances in later life, it is impossible to say. A better course than to attempt an answer to that question would be to recount the story of Tientietnikov's boyhood and upbringing.

Everything connected with the latter seemed to promise success, for at twelve years of age the boy—keen-witted, but dreamy of temperament, and inclined to delicacy—was sent to an educational establishment presided over by an exceptional type of master. The idol of his pupils, and the admiration of his assistants, Alexander Petrovitch was gifted with an extraordinary measure of good sense. How thoroughly he knew the peculiarities of the Russian of his day! How well he understood boys! How capable he was of drawing them out! Not a practical joker in the school but, after perpetrating a prank, would voluntarily approach his preceptor and make to him free confession. True, the preceptor would put a stern face upon the matter, yet the culprit would depart with head held higher, not lower, than before, since in Alexander Petrovitch there was something which heartened—something which seemed to say to a delinquent: "Forward, you! Rise to your feet again, even though you have fallen!" Not lectures on good behaviour was it, therefore, that fell from his lips, but rather the injunction, "I want to see intelligence, and nothing else. The boy who devotes his attention to becoming clever will never play the fool, for under such circumstances, folly disappears of itself." And so folly did, for the boy who failed to strive in the desired direction incurred the contempt of all his comrades, and even dunces and fools of senior standing did not dare to raise a finger when saluted by their juniors with opprobrious epithets. Yet "This is too much" certain folk would say to Alexander. "The result will be that your pupils will turn out prigs." "But no," he would reply. "Not at all. You see, I make it my principle to

keep the incapables for a single term only, since that is enough
for them; but to the clever ones I allot a double course of
instruction." And, true enough, any lad of brains was retained
for this finishing course. Yet he did not repress all boyish
playfulness, since he declared it to be as necessary to him as a
rash to a doctor, inasmuch as it enabled him to diagnose what
lay hidden within.

Consequently, how the boys loved him! Never was there such
an attachment between master and pupils. And even later,
during the foolish years, when foolish things attract, the measure
of affection which Alexander Petrovitch retained was extraordinary. In fact, to the day of his death, every former pupil
would celebrate the birthday of his late master by raising his
glass in gratitude to the mentor dead and buried—then close
his eyelids upon the tears which would come trickling through
them. Even the slightest word of encouragement from Alexander Petrovitch could throw a lad into a transport of tremulous
joy, and arouse in him an honourable emulation of his fellows.
Boys of small capacity he did not long retain in his establishment; whereas those who possessed exceptional talent he put
through an extra course of schooling. This senior class—a class
composed of specially-selected pupils—was a very different
affair from that which usually obtains in other colleges. Only
when a boy had attained its ranks did Alexander demand of him
what other masters indiscreetly demand of mere infants—namely
the superior frame of mind which, while never indulging in
mockery, can itself bear ridicule, and disregard the fool, and
keep its temper, and repress itself, and eschew revenge, and
calmly, proudly retain its tranquillity of soul. In short, whatever avails to form a boy into a man of assured character,
that did Alexander Petrovitch employ during the pupil's
youth, as well as constantly put him to the test. How well
he understood the art of life!

Of assistant tutors he kept but a few, since most of the necessary instruction he imparted in person, and, without pedantic
terminology and inflated diction and views, could so transmit
to his listeners the inmost spirit of a lesson that even the youngest
present absorbed its essential elements. Also, of studies he
selected none but those which may help a boy to become a good
citizen; and therefore most of the lectures which he delivered
consisted of discourses on what may be awaiting a youth, as
well as of such demarcations of life's field that the pupil, though
seated, as yet, only at the desk, could beforehand bear his part

in that field both in thought and spirit. Nor did the master
conceal anything. That is to say, without mincing words, he
invariably set before his hearers the sorrows and the difficulties
which may confront a man, the trials and the temptations which
may beset him. And this he did in terms as though, in every
possible calling and capacity, he himself had experienced the
same. Consequently, either the vigorous development of self-
respect or the constant stimulus of the master's eye (which
seemed to say to the pupil, " Forward! "—that word which
has become so familiar to the contemporary Russian, that word
which has worked such wonders upon his sensitive temperament); one or the other, I repeat, would from the first cause
the pupil to tackle difficulties, and only difficulties, and to
hunger for prowess only where the path was arduous, and
obstacles were many, and it was necessary to display the utmost
strength of mind. Indeed, few completed the course of which
I have spoken without issuing therefrom reliable, seasoned
fighters who could keep their heads in the most embarrassing
of official positions, and at times when older and wiser men,
distracted with the annoyances of life, had either abandoned
everything or, grown slack and indifferent, had surrendered to
the bribe-takers and the rascals. In short, no ex-pupil of Alexander Petrovitch ever wavered from the right road, but, familiar
with life and with men, armed with the weapons of prudence,
exerted a powerful influence upon wrongdoers.

For a long time past the ardent young Tientietnikov's excitable heart also had beat at the thought that one day he might
attain the senior class described. And, indeed, what better
teacher could he have had befall him than its preceptor? Yet
just at the moment when he had been transferred thereto, just
at the moment when he had reached the coveted position, did
his instructor come suddenly by his death! This was indeed a
blow for the boy—indeed a terrible initial loss! In his eyes
everything connected with the school seemed to undergo a
change—the chief reason being the fact that to the place of
the deceased headmaster there succeeded a certain Thedor
Ivanovitch, who at once began to insist upon certain external
rules, and to demand of the boys what ought rightly to have
been demanded only of adults. That is to say, since the lads'
frank and open demeanour savoured to him only of lack of
discipline, he announced (as though in deliberate spite of his
predecessor) that he cared nothing for progress and intellect, but
that heed was to be paid only to good behaviour. Yet, curiously

enough, good behaviour was just what he never obtained, for
every kind of secret prank became the rule; and while, by day,
there reigned restraint and conspiracy, by night there began to
take place chambering and wantonness.

Also, certain changes in the curriculum of studies came about,
for there were engaged new teachers who held new views and
opinions, and confused their hearers with a multitude of new
terms and phrases, and displayed in their exposition of things
both logical sequence and a zest for modern discovery and
much warmth of individual bias. Yet their instruction, alas!
contained no *life*——in the mouths of those teachers a dead
language savoured merely of carrion. Thus everything connected
with the school underwent a radical alteration, and respect for
authority and the authorities waned, and tutors and ushers
alike began to be treated with ridicule, and even the headmaster
came to be dubbed " Old Thedor," " Crusty," and the like.
And sundry other things began to take place—things which
necessitated many a penalty and expulsion; until, within a
couple of years, no one who had known the school in former
days would now have recognised it.

Nevertheless Tientietnikov, a youth of retiring disposition,
experienced no leanings towards the nocturnal orgies of his
companions—orgies during which the latter used to flirt with
damsels before the very windows of the headmaster's rooms,
nor yet towards their mockery of all that was sacred, simply
because fate had cast in their way an injudicious priest. No,
despite its dreaminess, his soul ever remembered its celestial
origin, and could not be diverted from the path of virtue. Yet
still he hung his head, for, while his ambition had come to life,
it could find no sort of outlet. Truly 'twere well if it had *not*
come to life, for throughout the time that he was listening to
professors who gesticulated on their chairs he could not help
remembering the old preceptor who, invariably cool and calm,
had yet known how to make himself understood. To what
subjects, to what lectures, did the boy not have to listen!—to
lectures on medicine, and on philosophy, and on law, and on a
version of general history so enlarged that even three years
failed to enable the professor to do more than finish the introduction thereto, and also the account of the development of
some self-governing towns in Germany. None of the stuff
remained fixed in Tientietnikov's brain save as shapeless clots;
for though his native intellect could not tell him how instruction
ought to be imparted, it at least told him that *this* was not the

way. And frequently, at such moments he would recall Alexander Petrovitch, and give way to such grief that scarcely did he know what he was doing.

But youth is fortunate in the fact that always before it there lies a future; and in proportion as the time for his leaving school drew nigh, Tientietnikov's heart began to beat higher and higher, and he said to himself: "This is not life, but only a preparation for life. True life is to be found in the Public Service. There at least will there be scope for activity." So, bestowing not a glance upon that beautiful corner of the world which never failed to strike the guest or chance visitor with amazement, and reverencing not a whit the dust of his ancestors, he followed the example of most ambitious men of his class by repairing to St. Petersburg (whither, as we know, the more spirited youth of Russia from every quarter gravitates—there to enter the Public Service, to shine, to obtain promotion, and, in a word, to scale the topmost peaks of that pale, cold, deceptive elevation which is known as society). But the real starting-point of Tientietnikov's ambition was the moment when his uncle (one State Councillor Onifri Ivanovitch) instilled into him the maxim that the only means to success in the Service lay in good handwriting, and that, without that accomplishment, no one could ever hope to become a Minister or Statesman. Thus, with great difficulty, and also with the help of his uncle's influence, young Tientietnikov at length succeeded in being posted to a Department. On the day that he was conducted into a splendid, shining hall—a hall fitted with inlaid floors and laquered desks as fine as though this were actually the place where the great ones of the Empire met for discussion of the fortunes of the State; on the day that he saw legions of handsome gentlemen of the quill-driving profession making loud scratchings with pens, and cocking their heads on one side; lastly on the day that he saw himself also allotted a desk, and requested to copy a document which appeared purposely to be one of the pettiest possible order (as a matter of fact it related to a sum of three roubles, and had taken half a year to produce)—well, at that moment a curious, an unwonted sensation seized upon the inexperienced youth, for the gentlemen around him appeared so exactly like a lot of college students. And, the further to complete the resemblance, some of them were engaged in reading trashy translated novels, which they kept hurriedly thrusting between the sheets of their apportioned work whenever the Director appeared, as though to convey the impression that it was to that work alone that they were applying themselves. In short, the scene seemed to Tientietnikov strange, and his former pursuits more important than his present, and his preparation for the Service preferable to the Service itself. Yes, suddenly he felt a longing for his old school; and as suddenly, and with all the vividness of life, there appeared before his vision the figure of Alexander Petrovitch. He almost burst into tears as he beheld his old master, and the room seemed to swim before his eyes, and the *tchinovniks* and the desks to become a blur, and his sight to grow dim. Then he thought to himself with an effort: " No, no! I *will* apply myself to my work, however petty it be at first." And, hardening his heart and recovering his spirit, he determined then and there to perform his duties in such a manner as should be an example to the rest.

But where are compensations not to be found? Even in St. Petersburg, despite its grim and murky exterior, they exist. Yes, even though thirty degrees of keen, cracking frost may have bound the streets, and the family of the North Wind be wailing there, and the Snowstorm Witch have heaped high the pavements, and be blinding the eyes, and powdering beards and fur collars and the shaggy manes of horses—even *then* there will be shining hospitably through the swirling snowflakes a fourth-floor window where, in a cosy room, and by the light of modest candles, and to the hiss of the *samovar*, there will be in progress a discussion which warms the heart and soul, or else a reading aloud of a brilliant page of one of those inspired Russian poets with whom God has dowered us, while the breast of each member of the company is heaving with a rapture unknown under a noontide sky.

Gradually, therefore, Tientietnikov grew more at home in the Service. Yet never did it become, for him, the main pursuit, the main object in life, which he had expected. No, it remained but one of a secondary kind. That is to say, it served merely to divide up his time, and enable him the more to value his hours of leisure. Nevertheless, just when his uncle was beginning to flatter himself that his nephew was destined to succeed in the profession, the said nephew elected to ruin his every hope. Thus it befell. Tientietnikov's friends (he had many) included among their number a couple of young fellows of the species known as " embittered." That is to say, though good-natured souls of that curiously restless type which cannot endure injustice, nor anything which it conceives to be such, they were thoroughly unbalanced of conduct themselves, and, while demanding general agreement with their views, treated those of others with the scantiest of ceremony. Nevertheless these two associates exercised upon Tientietnikov—both by the fire of their eloquence and by the form of their noble dissatisfaction with society—a very strong influence; with the result that, through arousing in him an innate tendency to nervous resentment, they led him also to notice trifles which before had escaped his attention. An instance of this is seen in the fact that he conceived against Theodor Thedorovitch Lienitsin, Director of one of the Departments which was quartered in the splendid range of offices before mentioned, a dislike which proved the cause of his discerning in the man a host of hitherto unmarked imperfections. Above all things did Tientietnikov take it into his head that, when conversing with his superiors, Lienitsin became, for the moment, a stick of luscious sweetmeat, but that, when conversing with his inferiors, he approximated more to a vinegar cruet. Certain it is that, like all petty-minded individuals, Lienitsin made a note of any one who failed to offer him a greeting on festival days, and that he revenged himself upon any one whose visiting-card had not been handed to his butler. Eventually the youth's aversion almost attained the point of hysteria; until he felt that, come what might, he *must* insult the fellow in some fashion. To that task he applied himself *con amore;* and so thoroughly that he met with complete success. That is to say, he seized an occasion to address Lienitsin in such fashion that the delinquent received notice either to apologise or to leave the Service; and when of these two alternatives he chose the latter his uncle came to him, and made a terrified appeal. "For God's sake remember what you are doing!" he cried. "To think that, after beginning your career so well, you should abandon it merely for the reason that you have not fallen in with the sort of Director whom you prefer! What do you mean by it, what do you mean by it? Were others to regard things in the same way, the Service would find itself left without a single individual. Reconsider your conduct—forego your pride and conceit, and make Lienitsin amends."

"But, dear Uncle," the nephew replied, "that is not the point. The point is, not that I should find an apology difficult to offer, seeing that, since Lienitsin is my superior, and I ought not to have addressed him as I did, I am clearly in the wrong. Rather, the point is the following. To my charge there has been committed the performance of another kind of service. That is to say, I am the owner of three hundred peasant souls, a badly administered estate, and a fool of a bailiff. That being so, whereas the State will lose little by having to fill my stool with another copyist, it will lose very much by causing three hundred peasant souls to fail in the payment of their taxes. As I say (how am I to put it?), I am a landowner who has preferred to enter the Public Service. Now, should I employ myself henceforth in conserving, restoring, and improving the fortunes of the souls whom God has entrusted to my care, and thereby provide the State with three hundred law-abiding, sober, hardworking taxpayers, how will that service of mine rank as inferior to the service of a department-directing fool like Lienitsin?"

On hearing this speech, the State Councillor could only gape, for he had not expected Tientietnikov's torrent of words. He reflected a few moments, and then murmured:

" Yes, but, but—but how can a man like you retire to rustication in the country? What society will you get there? Here one meets at least a general or a prince sometimes; indeed, no matter whom you pass in the street, that person represents gas lamps and European civilisation; but in the country, no matter what part of it you be in, not a soul is to be encountered save *muzhiks* and their women. Why should you go and condemn yourself to a state of vegetation like that?"

Nevertheless the uncle's expostulations fell upon deaf ears, for already the nephew was beginning to think of his estate as a retreat of a type likely to nourish the intellectual faculties and afford the only profitable field of activity. After unearthing one or two modern works on agriculture, therefore, he, two weeks later, found himself in the neighbourhood of the home where his boyhood had been spent, and approaching the spot which never failed to enthral the chance visitor or guest. And in the young man's breast there was beginning to palpitate a new feeling —in the young man's soul there were reawakening old, long-concealed impressions; with the result that many a spot which had long been faded from his memory now filled him with interest, and the beautiful views on the estate found him gazing at them like a newcomer, and with a beating heart. Yes, as the road wound through a narrow ravine, and became engulfed in a forest where, both above and below, he saw three-centuries-old oaks which three men could not have spanned, and where Siberian firs and elms overtopped even the poplars, and as he asked the peasants to tell him to whom the forest belonged, and they replied " To Tientietnikov," and he issued from the forest, and proceeded on his way through meadows, and past spinneys of elder, and of old and young willows, and arrived in sight of the distant range of hills, and, crossing by two different bridges the winding river (which he left successively to right and to left of him as he did so), he again questioned some peasants concerning the ownership of the meadows and the flooded lands, and was again informed that they all belonged to Tientietnikov, and then, ascending a rise, reached a tableland where, on one side, lay ungarnered fields of wheat and rye and barley, and, on the other, the country already traversed (but which now showed in shortened perspective), and then plunged into the shade of some forked, umbrageous trees which stood scattered over turf and extended to the manor-house itself, and caught glimpses of the carved huts of the peasants, and of the red roofs of the stone manorial outbuildings, and of the glittering pinnacles of the church, and felt his heart beating, and knew, without being told by any one, whither he had at length arrived—well, then the feeling which had been growing within his soul burst forth, and he cried in ecstasy:

" Why have I been a fool so long? Why, seeing that fate has appointed me to be ruler of an earthly paradise, did I prefer to bind myself in servitude as a scribe of lifeless documents? To think that, after I had been nurtured and schooled and stored with all the knowledge necessary for the diffusion of good among those under me, and for the improvement of my domain, and for the fulfilment of the manifold duties of a landowner who is at once judge, administrator, and constable of his people, I should have entrusted my estate to an ignorant bailiff, and sought to maintain an absentee guardianship over the affairs of serfs whom I have never met, and of whose capabilities and characters I am yet ignorant! To think that I should have deemed true estate-management inferior to a documentary, fantastic management of provinces which lie a thousand *versts* away, and which my foot has never trod, and where I could never have effected aught but blunders and irregularities ! "

Meanwhile another spectacle was being prepared for him. On learning that the *barin* was approaching the mansion, the *muzhiks* collected on the verandah in every variety of picturesque dress and tonsure; and when these good folk surrounded him, and there arose a resounding shout of " Here is our Foster Father ! He has remembered us ! " and, in spite of themselves, some of the older men and women began weeping as they recalled his grandfather and great-grandfather, he himself could not restrain his tears, but reflected: " How much affec-

tion! And in return for what? In return for my never having
come to see them—in return for my never having taken the
least interest in their affairs!" And then and there he registered
a mental vow to share their every task and occupation.

So he applied himself to supervising and administering. He
reduced the amount of the *barstchina*,[1] he decreased the number
of working-days for the owner, and he augmented the sum of
the peasants' leisure time. He also dismissed the fool of a bailiff,
and took to bearing a personal hand in everything—to being
present in the fields, at the threshing-floor, at the kilns, at the
wharf, at the freighting of barges and rafts, and at their conveyance down the river: wherefore even the lazy hands began to
look to themselves. But this did not last long. The peasant
is an observant individual, and Tientietnikov's *muzhiks* soon
scented the fact that, though energetic and desirous of doing
much, the *barin* had no notion how to do it, nor even how to set
about it—that, in short, he spoke by the book rather than out
of his personal knowledge. Consequently things resulted, not
in master and men failing to understand one another, but in
their not singing together, in their not producing the very same
note.

That is to say, it was not long before Tientietnikov noticed
that on the manorial lands, nothing prospered to the extent
that it did on the peasants'. The manorial crops were sown in
good time, and came up well, and every one appeared to work
his best, so much so that Tientietnikov, who supervised the
whole, frequently ordered mugs of *vodka* to be served out as a
reward for the excellence of the labour performed. Yet the rye
on the peasants' lands had formed into ear, and the oats had
begun to shoot their grain, and the millet had filled before, on
the manorial lands, the corn had so much as grown to stalk, or
the ears had sprouted in embryo. In short, gradually the *barin*
realised that, in spite of favours conferred, the peasants were
playing the rogue with him. Next, he resorted to remonstrance,
but was met with the reply, " How could we not do our best
for our *barin* ? You yourself saw how well we laboured at the
ploughing and the sowing, for you gave us mugs of *vodka* for
our pains."

" Then why have things turned out so badly? " the *barin*
persisted.

" Who can say? It must be that a grub has eaten the crop

[1] In the days of serfdom, the rate of forced labour—so many hours or
so many days per week—which the serf had to perform for his proprietor.

from below. Besides, what a summer it has been—never a drop of rain!"

Nevertheless the *barin* noted that no grub had eaten *the peasants'* crops, as well as that the rain had fallen in the most curious fashion—namely, in patches. It had obliged the *muzhiks*, but had shed a mere sprinkling for the *barin*.

Still more difficult did he find it to deal with the peasant women. Ever and anon they would beg to be excused from work, or start making complaints of the severity of the *barstchina*. Indeed, they were terrible folk! However, Tientietnikov abolished the majority of the tithes of linen, hedge fruit, mushrooms, and nuts, and also reduced by one-half other tasks proper to the women, in the hope that they would devote their spare time to their own domestic concerns—namely, to sewing and mending, and to making clothes for their husbands, and to increasing the area of their kitchen gardens. Yet no such result came about. On the contrary, such a pitch did the idleness, the quarrelsomeness, and the intriguing and caballing of the fair sex attain that their helpmeets were for ever coming to the *barin* with a request that he would rid one or another of his wife, since she had become a nuisance, and to live with her was impossible.

Next, hardening his heart, the *barin* attempted severity. But of what avail was severity? The peasant woman remained always the peasant woman, and would come and whine that she was sick and ailing, and keep pitifully hugging to herself the mean and filthy rags which she had donned for the occasion. And when poor Tientietnikov found himself unable to say more to her than just, "Get out of my sight, and may the Lord go with you!" the next item in the comedy would be that he would see her, even as she was leaving his gates, fall to contending with a neighbour for, say, the possession of a turnip, and dealing out slaps in the face such as even a strong, healthy man could scarcely have compassed!

Again, amongst other things, Tientietnikov conceived the idea of establishing a school for his people; but the scheme resulted in a farce which left him in sackcloth and ashes. In the same way he found that, when it came to a question of dispensing justice and of adjusting disputes, the host of juridical subtleties with which the professors had provided him proved absolutely useless. That is to say, the one party lied, and the other party lied, and only the devil could have decided between them. Consequently he himself perceived that a knowledge of mankind would have availed him more than all the legal refinements and philosophical maxims in the world could do. He lacked something; and though he could not divine what it was, the situation brought about was the common one of the *barin* failing to understand the peasant, and the peasant failing to understand the *barin*, and both becoming disaffected. In the end, these difficulties so chilled Tientietnikov's enthusiasm that he took to supervising the labours of the field with greatly diminished attention. That is to say, no matter whether the scythes were softly swishing through the grass, or ricks were being built, or rafts were being loaded, he would allow his eyes to wander from his men, and to fall to gazing at, say, a red-billed, reg-legged heron which, after strutting along the bank of a stream, would have caught a fish in its beak, and be holding it awhile, as though in doubt whether to swallow it. Next he would glance towards the spot where a similar bird, but one not yet in possession of a fish, was engaged in watching the doings of its mate. Lastly, with eyebrows knitted, and face turned to scan the zenith, he would drink in the smell of the fields, and fall to listening to the winged population of the air as from earth and sky alike the manifold music of winged creatures combined in a single harmonious chorus. In the rye the quail would be calling, and, in the grass, the corncrake, and over them would be wheeling flocks of twittering linnets. Also, the jacksnipe would be uttering its croak, and the lark executing its roulades where it had become lost in the sunshine, and cranes sending forth their trumpet-like challenge as they deployed towards the zenith in triangle-shaped flocks. In fact, the neighbourhood would seem to have become converted into one great concert of melody. O Creator, how fair is Thy world where, in remote, rural seclusion, it lies apart from cities and from highways!

But soon even this began to pall upon Tientietnikov, and he ceased altogether to visit his fields, or to do aught but shut himself up in his rooms, where he refused to receive even the bailiff when that functionary called with his reports. Again, although, until now, he had to a certain extent associated with a retired colonel of hussars—a man saturated with tobacco smoke—and also with a student of pronounced, but immature, opinions who culled the bulk of his wisdom from contemporary newspapers and pamphlets, he found, as time went on, that these companions proved as tedious as the rest, and came to think their conversation superficial, and their European method of comporting themselves—that is to say, the method of conversing with much slapping of knees and a great deal of bowing and gesticulation—too direct and unadorned. So these and every one else he decided to " drop," and carried this resolution into effect with a certain amount of rudeness. On the next occasion that Varvar Nikolaievitch Vishnepokromov called to indulge in a free-and-easy symposium on politics, philosophy, literature, morals, and the state of financial affairs in England (he was, in all matters which admit of superficial discussion, the pleasantest fellow alive, seeing that he was a typical representative both of the retired fire-eater and of the school of thought which is now becoming the rage)—when, I say, this next happened, Tientietnikov merely sent out to say that he was not at home, and then carefully showed himself at the window. Host and guest exchanged glances, and, while the one muttered through his teeth " The cur! " the other relieved his feelings with a remark or two on swine. Thus the acquaintance came to an abrupt end, and from that time forth no visitor called at the mansion.

Tientietnikov in no way regretted this, for he could now devote himself wholly to the projection of a great work on Russia. Of the scale on which this composition was conceived the reader is already aware. The reader also knows how strange, how unsystematic, was the system employed in it. Yet to say that Tientietnikov never awoke from his lethargy would not be altogether true. On the contrary, when the post brought him newspapers and reviews, and he saw in their printed pages, perhaps, the well-known name of some former comrade who had succeeded in the great field of Public Service, or had conferred upon science and the world's work some notable contribution, he would succumb to secret and suppressed grief, and involuntarily there would burst from his soul an expression of aching, voiceless regret that he himself had done so little. And at these times his existence would seem to him odious and repellent; at these times there would uprise before him the memory of his school days, and the figure of Alexander Petrovitch, as vivid as in life. And, slowly welling, the tears would course over Tientietnikov's cheeks.

What meant these repinings? Was there not disclosed in them the secret of his galling spiritual pain—the fact that he had failed to order his life aright, to confirm the lofty aims with which he had started his course; the fact that, always poorly equipped with experience, he had failed to attain the better and the higher state, and there to strengthen himself for the overcoming of hindrances and obstacles; the fact that, dissolving like overheated metal, his bounteous store of superior instincts had failed to take the final tempering; the fact that the tutor of his boyhood, a man in a thousand, had prematurely died, and left to Tientietnikov no one who could restore to him the moral strength shattered by vacillation and the will power weakened by want of virility—no one, in short, who could cry hearteningly to his soul "Forward!"—the word for which the Russian of every degree, of every class, of every occupation, of every school of thought, is for ever hungering.

Indeed, *where* is the man who can cry aloud for any of us, in the Russian tongue dear to our soul, the all-compelling command "Forward!"? Who is there who, knowing the strength and the nature and the inmost depths of the Russian genius, can by a single magic incantation divert our ideals to the higher life? Were there such a man, with what tears, with what affection, would not the grateful sons of Russia repay him! Yet age succeeds to age, and our callow youth still lies wrapped in shameful sloth, or strives and struggles to no purpose. God has not yet given us the man able to sound the call.

One circumstance which almost aroused Tientietnikov, which almost brought about a revolution in his character, was the fact that he came very near to falling in love. Yet even this resulted in nothing. Ten *versts* away there lived the General whom we have heard expressing himself in highly uncomplimentary terms concerning Tientietnikov. He maintained a General-like establishment, dispensed hospitality (that is to say, was glad when his neighbours came to pay him their respects, though he himself never went out), spoke always in a hoarse voice, read a certain number of books, and had a daughter—a curious, unfamiliar type, but full of life as life itself. This maiden's name was Ulinka, and she had been strangely brought up, for, losing her mother in early childhood, she had subsequently received instruction at the hands of an English governess who knew not a single word of Russian. Moreover her father, though excessively fond of her, treated her always as a toy; with the result that, as she grew to years of discretion, she became wholly wayward and spoilt. Indeed, had any one seen the sudden rage which would gather on her beautiful young forehead when she was engaged in a heated dispute with her father, he would have thought her one of the most capricious beings in the world. Yet that rage gathered only when she had heard of injustice or harsh treatment, and never because she desired to argue on her own behalf, or to attempt to justify her own conduct. Also, that anger would disppear as soon as ever she saw any one whom she had formerly disliked fall upon evil times, and, at his first request for alms would, without consideration or subsequent regret, hand him her purse and its whole contents. Yes, her every act was strenuous, and when she spoke her whole personality seemed to be following hot-foot upon her thought—both her expression of face and her diction and the movements of her hands. Nay, the very folds of her frock had a similar appearance of striving; until one would have thought that all her self were flying in pursuit of her words. Nor did she know reticence: before any one she would disclose her mind, and no force could compel her to maintain silence when she desired to speak. Also, her enchanting, peculiar gait—a gait which belonged to her alone —was so absolutely free and unfettered that every one involuntarily gave her way. Lastly, in her presence churls seemed to become confused and fall to silence, and even the roughest and most outspoken would lose their heads, and have not a word to say; whereas the shy man would find himself able to converse as never in his life before, and would feel, from the first, as though he had seen her and known her at some previous period—during the days of some unremembered childhood, when he was at home, and spending a merry evening among a crowd of romping children. And for long afterwards he would feel as though his man's intellect and estate were a burden.

This was what now befell Tientietnikov; and as it did so a new feeling entered into his soul, and his dreamy life lightened for a moment.

At first the General used to receive him with hospitable civility, but permanent concord between them proved impossible; their conversation always merged into dissension and soreness, seeing that, while the General could not bear to be contradicted or worsted in argument, Tientietnikov was a man of extreme sensitiveness. True, for the daughter's sake, the father was for a while deferred to, and thus peace was maintained; but this lasted only until the time when there arrived, on a visit to the General, two kinswomen of his—the Countess Bordirev and the Princess Uziakin, retired Court dames, but ladies who still kept up a certain connection with Court circles, and therefore were much fawned upon by their host. No sooner had they appeared on the scene than (so it seemed to Tientietnikov) the General's attitude towards the young man became colder—either he ceased to notice him at all or he spoke to him familiarly, and as to a person having no standing in society.

H

This offended Tientietnikov deeply, and though, when at length he spoke out on the subject, he retained sufficient presence of mind to compress his lips, and to preserve a gentle and courteous tone, his face flushed, and his inner man was boiling.

"General," he said, "I thank you for your condescension. By addressing me in the second person singular, you have admitted me to the circle of your most intimate friends. Indeed, were it not that a difference of years forbids any familiarity on my part, I should answer you in similar fashion."

The General sat aghast. At length, rallying his tongue and his faculties, he replied that, though he had spoken with a lack of ceremony, he had used the term "thou" merely as an elderly man naturally employs it towards a junior (he made no reference to difference of rank).

Nevertheless, the acquaintance broke off here, and with it any possibility of love-making. The light which had shed a momentary gleam before Tientietnikov's eyes had become extinguished for ever, and upon it there followed a darkness denser than before. Henceforth everything conduced to evolve the *régime* which the reader has noted—that *régime* of sloth and inaction which converted Tientietnikov's residence into a place of dirt and neglect. For days at a time would a broom and a heap of dust be left lying in the middle of a room, and trousers tossing about the *salon*, and pairs of worn-out braces adorning the whatnot near the sofa. In short, so mean and untidy did Tientietnikov's mode of life become, that not only his servants, but even his very poultry ceased to treat him with respect. Taking up a pen, he would spend hours in idly sketching houses, huts, waggons, *troikas*, and flourishes on a piece of paper; while at other times, when he had sunk into a reverie, the pen would, all unknowingly, sketch a small head which had delicate features, a pair of quick, penetrating eyes, and a raised *coiffure*. Then suddenly the dreamer would perceive, to his surprise, that the pen had executed the portrait of a maiden whose picture no artist could adequately have painted; and therewith his despondency would become greater than ever, and, believing that happiness did not exist on earth, he would relapse into increased *ennui*, increased neglect of his responsibilities.

But one morning he noticed, on moving to the window after breakfast, that not a word was proceeding either from the butler or the housekeeper, but that, on the contrary, the courtyard seemed to smack of a certain bustle and excitement. This was because through the entrance gates (which the kitchen maid and the scullion had run to open) there were appearing the noses of three horses—one to the right, one in the middle, and one to the left, after the fashion of triumphal groups of statuary. Above them, on the box seat, were seated a coachman and a valet, while behind, again, there could be discerned a gentleman in a scarf and a fur cap. Only when the equipage had entered the courtyard did it stand revealed as a light spring *britchka*. And as it came to a halt, there leapt on to the verandah of the mansion an individual of respectable exterior, and possessed of the art of moving with the neatness and alertness of a military man.

Upon this Tientietnikov's heart stood still. He was unused to receiving visitors, and for the moment conceived the new arrival to be a Government official, sent to question him concerning an abortive society to which he had formerly belonged. (Here the author may interpolate the fact that, in Tientietnikov's early days, the young man had become mixed up in a very absurd affair. That is to say, a couple of philosophers belonging to a regiment of hussars had, together with an æsthete who had not yet completed his student's course and a gambler who had squandered his all, formed a secret society of philanthropic aims under the presidency of a certain old rascal of a freemason and the ruined gambler aforesaid. The scope of the society's work was to be extensive: it was to bring lasting happiness to humanity at large, from the banks of the Thames to the shores of Kamtchatka. But for this much money was needed: wherefore from the noble-minded members of the society generous contributions were demanded, and then forwarded to a destination known only to the supreme authorities of the concern. As for Tientietnikov's adhesion, it was brought about by the two friends already alluded to as " embittered " —good-hearted souls whom the wear and tear of their efforts on behalf of science, civilisation, and the future emancipation of mankind had ended by converting into confirmed drunkards. Perhaps it need hardly be said also that Tientietnikov soon discovered how things stood, and withdrew from the association; but, meanwhile, the latter had had the misfortune so to have engaged in dealings not wholly creditable to gentlemen of noble origin as likewise to have become entangled in dealings with the police. Consequently, it is not to be wondered at that, though Tientietnikov had long severed his connection with the society and its policy, he still remained uneasy in his mind as to what might even yet be the result.)

However, his fears vanished the instant that the guest saluted him with marked politeness and explained, with many deferential poises of the head, and in terms at once civil and concise, that for some time past he (the newcomer) had been touring the Russian Empire on business and in the pursuit of knowledge, that that Empire abounded in objects of interest—not to mention a plenitude of manufactures and a great diversity of soil, and that, in spite of the fact that he was greatly struck with the amenities of his host's domain, he would certainly not have presumed to intrude at such an inconvenient hour but for the circumstance that the inclement spring weather, added to the state of the roads, had necessitated sundry repairs to his carriage at the hands of wheelwrights and blacksmiths. Finally he declared that, even if this last had *not* happened, he would still have felt unable to deny himself the pleasure of offering to his host that meed of homage which was the latter's due.

This speech—a speech of fascinating *bonhomie*—delivered, the guest executed a sort of shuffle with a half-boot of patent leather studded with buttons of mother-of-pearl, and followed that up by (in spite of his pronounced rotundity of figure) stepping backwards with all the *élan* of an india-rubber ball.

From this the somewhat reassured Tientietnikov concluded that his visitor must be a literary, knowledge-seeking professor who was engaged in roaming the country in search of botanical specimens and fossils; wherefore he hastened to express both his readiness to further the visitor's objects (whatever they might be) and his personal willingness to provide him with the requisite wheelwrights and blacksmiths. Meanwhile he begged his guest to consider himself at home, and, after seating him in an armchair, made preparations to listen to the newcomer's discourse on natural history.

But the newcomer applied himself, rather, to phenomena of the internal world, saying that his life might be likened to a barque tossed on the crests of perfidious billows, that in his time he had been fated to play many parts, and that on more than one occasion his life had stood in danger at the hands of foes. At the same time, these tidings were communicated in a manner calculated to show that the speaker was also a man of *practical* capabilities. In conclusion, the visitor took out a cambric pocket-handkerchief, and sneezed into it with a vehemence wholly new to Tientietnikov's experience. In fact, the sneeze rather resembled the note which, at times, the trombone of an orchestra appears to utter not so much from its proper place on the platform as from the immediate neighbourhood of the listener's ear. And as the echoes of the drowsy mansion re-sounded to the report of the explosion there followed upon the same a wave of perfume, skilfully wafted abroad with a flourish of the *eau-de-Cologne*-scented handkerchief.

By this time the reader will have guessed that the visitor was none other than our old and respected friend Paul Ivanovitch Chichikov. Naturally, time had not spared him his share of anxieties and alarms; wherefore his exterior had come to look a trifle more elderly, his frockcoat had taken on a suggestion of shabbiness, and *britchka*, coachman, valet, horses, and harness alike had about them a sort of second-hand, worse-for-wear effect. Evidently the Chichikovian finances were not in the most flourishing of conditions. Nevertheless, the old expression of face, the old air of breeding and refinement, remained unimpaired, and our hero had even improved in the art of walking and turning with grace, and of dexterously crossing one leg over the other when taking a seat. Also, his mildness of diction, his discreet moderation of word and phrase, survived in, if anything, increased measure, and he bore himself with a skill which caused his tactfulness to surpass itself in sureness of *aplomb*. And all these accomplishments had their effect further heightened by a snowy immaculateness of collar and dickey, and an absence of dust from his frockcoat, as complete as though he had just arrived to attend a nameday festival. Lastly, his cheeks and chin were of such neat clean-shavenness that no one but a blind man could have failed to admire their rounded contours.

From that moment onwards great changes took place in Tientietnikov's establishment, and certain of its rooms assumed an unwonted air of cleanliness and order. The rooms in question were those assigned to Chichikov, while one other apartment—a little front chamber opening into the hall—became permeated with Petrushka's own peculiar smell. But this lasted only for a little while, for presently Petrushka was transferred to the servants' quarters, a course which ought to have been adopted in the first instance.

During the initial days of Chichikov's sojourn, Tientietnikov feared rather to lose his independence, inasmuch as he thought that his guest might hamper his movements, and bring about alterations in the established routine of the place. But these fears proved groundless, for Paul Ivanovitch displayed an extraordinary aptitude for accommodating himself to his new position.

To begin with, he encouraged his host in his philosophical inertia by saying that the latter would help Tientietnikov to become a centenarian. Next, in the matter of a life of isolation, he hit things off exactly by remarking that such a life bred in a man a capacity for high thinking. Lastly, as he inspected the library and dilated on books in general, he contrived an opportunity to observe that literature safeguarded a man from a tendency to waste his time. In short, the few words of which he delivered himself were brief, but invariably to the point. And this discretion of speech was outdone by his discretion of conduct. That is to say, whether entering or leaving the room, he never wearied his host with a question if Tientietnikov had the air of being disinclined to talk; and with equal satisfaction the guest could either play chess or hold his tongue. Consequently Tientietnikov said to himself:

"For the first time in my life I have met with a man with whom it is possible to live. In general, not many of the type exist in Russia, and, though clever, good-humoured, well-educated men abound, one would be hard put to it to find an individual of equable temperament with whom one could share a roof for centuries without a quarrel arising. Anyway, Chichikov is the first of his sort that I have met."

For his part, Chichikov was only too delighted to reside with a person so quiet and agreeable as his host. Of a wandering life he was temporarily weary, and to rest, even for a month, in such a beautiful spot, and in sight of green fields and the slow flowering of spring, was likely to benefit him also from the hygienic point of view. And, indeed, a more delightful retreat in which to recuperate could not possibly have been found. The spring, long retarded by previous cold, had now begun in all its comeliness, and life was rampant. Already, over the first emerald of the grass, the dandelion was showing yellow, and the red-pink anemone was hanging its tender head; while the surface of every pond was a swarm of dancing gnats and midges, and the water-spider was being joined in their pursuit by birds which gathered from every quarter to the vantage-ground of the dry reeds. Every species of creature also seemed to be assembling in concourse, and taking stock of one another. Suddenly the earth had become populous, the forest had opened its eyes, and the meadows were lifting up their voice in song. In the same way had choral dances begun to be weaved in the village, and everywhere that the eye turned there was merriment. What brightness in the green of nature, what freshness in the air, what singing of birds in the gardens of the mansion, what general joy and rapture and exultation! Particularly in the village might the shouting and singing have been in honour of a wedding!

Chichikov walked hither, thither, and everywhere—a pursuit for which there was ample choice and facility. At one time he would direct his steps along the edge of the flat tableland, and contemplate the depths below, where still there lay sheets of water left by the floods of winter, and where the island-like patches of forest showed leafless boughs; while at another time he would plunge into the thicket and ravine country, where nests of birds weighted branches almost to the ground, and the sky was darkened with the criss-cross flight of cawing rooks. Again, the drier portions of the meadows could be crossed to the river wharves, whence the first barges were just beginning to set forth with pea-meal and barley and wheat, while at the same time one's ear would be caught with the sound of some mill resuming its functions as once more the water turned the wheel. Chichikov would also walk afield to watch the early tillage operations of the season, and observe how the blackness of a new furrow would make its way across the expanse of green, and how the sower, rhythmically striking his hand against the pannier slung across his breast, would scatter his fistfuls of seed with equal distribution, apportioning not a grain too much to one side or to the other.

In fact, Chichikov went everywhere. He chatted and talked, now with the bailiff, now with a peasant, now with a miller, and inquired into the manner and the nature of everything, and sought information as to how an estate was managed, and at what price corn was selling, and what species of grain was best for spring and autumn grinding, and what was the name of each peasant, and who were his kinsfolk, and where he had bought his cow, and what he fed his pigs on. Chichikov also made inquiry concerning the number of peasants who had lately died: but of these there appeared to be few. And suddenly his quick eye discerned the fact that Tientietnikov's estate was not being worked as it might have been—that much neglect and listlessness and pilfering and drunkenness was abroad; and on perceiving this, he thought to himself: "What a fool is that Tientietnikov! To think of letting a property like this decay when he might be drawing from it an income of fifty thousand roubles a year!"

Also, more than once, while taking these walks, our hero

pondered the idea of himself becoming a landowner—not now, of course, but later, when his chief aim should have been achieved, and he had got into his hands the necessary means for living the quiet life of the proprietor of an estate. Yes, and at these times there would include itself in his castle-building the figure of a young, fresh, fair-faced maiden of the mercantile or other rich grade of society, a woman who could both play and sing. He also dreamed of little descendants who should perpetuate the name of Chichikov; perhaps a frolicsome little boy and a fair young daughter, or, possibly, two boys and quite two or three daughters; so that all should know that he had really lived and had his being, that he had not merely roamed the world like a spectre or a shadow; so that for him and his the country should never be put to shame. And from that he would go on to fancy that a title appended to his rank would not be a bad thing—the title of State Councillor, for instance, which was deserving of all honour and respect. Ah, it is a common thing for a man who is taking a solitary walk so to detach himself from the irksome realities of the present that he is able to stir and to excite and to provoke his imagine to the conception of things he knows can never really come to pass!

Chichikov's servants also found the mansion to their taste, and, like their master, speedily made themselves at home in it. In particular did Petrushka make friends with Grigory the butler, although at first the pair showed a tendency to outbrag one another—Petrushka beginning by throwing dust in Grigory's eyes on the score of his (Petrushka's) travels, and Grigory taking him down a peg or two by referring to St. Petersburg (a city which Petrushka had never visited), and Petrushka seeking to recover lost ground by dilating on towns which he *had* visited, and Grigory capping this by naming some town which is not to be found on any map in existence, and then estimating the journey thither as at least thirty thousand versts—a statement which would so completely flabbergast the henchman of Chichikov's suite that he would be left staring open-mouthed, amid the general laughter of the domestic staff. However, as I say, the pair ended by swearing eternal friendship with one another, and making a practice of resorting to the village tavern in company.

For Selifan, however, the place had a charm of a different kind. That is to say, each evening there would take place in the village a singing of songs and a weaving of country dances; and so shapely and buxom were the maidens—maidens of a

type hard to find in our present-day villages on large estates—
that he would stand for hours wondering which of them was the
best. White-necked and white-bosomed, all had great roving
eyes, the gait of peacocks, and hair reaching to the waist. And
as, with his hands clasping theirs, he glided hither and thither
in the dance, or retired backwards towards a wall with a row of
other young fellows, and then, with them, returned to meet the
damsels—all singing in chorus (and laughing as they sang it),
" *Boyars*, show me my bridegroom! " and dusk was falling
gently, and from the other side of the river there kept coming
far, faint, plaintive echoes of the melody — well, then our
Selifan scarcely knew whether he were standing upon his head
or his heels. Later, when sleeping and when waking, both at
noon and at twilight, he would seem still to be holding a pair of
white hands, and moving in the dance.

Chichikov's horses also found nothing of which to disapprove.
Yes, both the bay, the Assessor, and the skewbald accounted
residence at Tientietnikov's a most comfortable affair, and
voted the oats excellent, and the arrangements of the stables
beyond all cavil. True, on this occasion each horse had a stall
to himself; yet, by looking over the intervening partition,
it was possible always to see one's fellows, and, should a
neighbour take it into his head to utter a neigh, to answer it
at once.

As for the errand which had hitherto led Chichikov to travel
about Russia, he had now decided to move very cautiously and
secretly in the matter. In fact, on noticing that Tientietnikov
went in absorbedly for reading and for talking philosophy, the
visitor said to himself, " No—I had better begin at the other
end," and proceeded first to feel his way among the servants of
the establishment. From them he learnt several things, and, in
particular, that the *barin* had been wont to go and call upon a
certain General in the neighbourhood, and that the General
possessed a daughter, and that she and Tientietnikov had had
an affair of some sort, but that the pair had subsequently parted,
and gone their several ways. For that matter, Chichikov himself had noticed that Tientietnikov was in the habit of drawing
heads of which each representation exactly resembled the rest.

Once, as he sat tapping his silver snuff-box after luncheon,
Chichikov remarked:

" One thing you lack, and only one, Andrei Ivanovitch."

" What is that? " asked his host.

" A female friend or two," replied Chichikov.

Tientietnikov made no rejoinder, and the conversation came temporarily to an end.

But Chichikov was not to be discouraged; wherefore, while waiting for supper and talking on different subjects, he seized an opportunity to interject:

" Do you know, it would do you no harm to marry."

As before, Tientietnikov did not reply, and the renewed mention of the subject seemed to have annoyed him.

For the third time—it was after supper—Chichikov returned to the charge by remarking:

" To-day, as I was walking round your property, I could not help thinking that marriage would do you a great deal of good. Otherwise you will develop into a hypochondriac."

Whether Chichikov's words now voiced sufficiently the note of persuasion, or whether Tientietnikov happened, at the moment, to be unusually disposed to frankness, at all events the young landowner sighed, and then responded as he expelled a puff of tobacco smoke:

" To attain anything, Paul Ivanovitch, one needs to have been born under a lucky star."

And he related to his guest the whole history of his acquaintanceship and subsequent rupture with the General.

As Chichikov listened to the recital, and gradually realised that the affair had arisen merely out of a chance word on the General's part, he was astounded beyond measure, and gazed at Tientietnikov without knowing what to make of him.

" Andrei Ivanovitch," he said at length, " what was there to take offence at? "

" Nothing, as regards the actual words spoken," replied the other. " The offence lay, rather, in the insult conveyed in the General's tone." Tientietnikov was a kindly and peaceable man, yet his eyes flashed as he said this, and his voice vibrated with wounded feeling.

" Yet, even then, need you have taken it so much amiss? "

" What? Could I have gone on visiting him as before? "

" Certainly. No great harm had been done? "

" I disagree with you. Had he been an old man in a humble station of life, instead of a proud and swaggering officer, I should not have minded so much. But, as it was, I could not, and would not, brook his words."

" A curious fellow, this Tientietnikov! " thought Chichikov to himself.

"A curious fellow, this Chichikov!" was Tientietnikov's inward reflection.

"I tell you what," resumed Chichikov. "To-morrow I myself will go and see the General."

"For what purpose?" asked Tientietnikov, with astonishment and distrust in his eyes.

"To offer him an assurance of my personal respect."

"A strange fellow, this Chichikov!" reflected Tientietnikov.

"A strange fellow, this Tientietnikov!" thought Chichikov, and then added aloud: "Yes, I will go and see him at ten o'clock to-morrow; but since my *britchka* is not yet altogether in travelling order, would you be so good as to lend me your *koliaska* for the purpose?"

II

TIENTIETNIKOV'S good horses covered the ten versts to the General's house in a little over half an hour. Descending from the *koliaska* with features attuned to deference, Chichikov inquired for the master of the house, and was at once ushered into his presence. Bowing with head held respectfully on one side and hands extended like those of a waiter carrying a trayful of teacups, the visitor inclined his whole body forward, and said:

"I have deemed it my duty to present myself to your Excellency. I have deemed it my duty because in my heart I cherish a most profound respect for the valiant men who, on the field of battle, have proved the saviours of their country."

That this preliminary attack did not wholly displease the General was proved by the fact that, responding with a gracious inclination of the head, he replied:

"I am glad to make your acquaintance. Pray be so good as to take a seat. In what capacity or capacities have your yourself seen service?"

"Of my service," said Chichikov, depositing his form, not exactly on the centre of a chair, but rather on one side of it, and resting a hand upon one of its arms, "—of my service the scene was laid, in the first instance, in the Treasury; while its further course bore me successively into the employ of the Public Buildings Commission, of the Customs Board, and of other Government Offices. But, throughout, my life has resembled a barque tossed on the crests of perfidious billows. In suffering I have been swathed and wrapped until I have come to be, as it were, suffering personified; while of the extent to which my life has been sought by foes, no words, no colouring, no (if I may so express it?) painter's brush could ever convey to you an adequate idea. And now, at length, in my declining years, I am seeking a corner in which to eke out the remainder of my miserable existence, while at the present moment I am enjoying the hospitality of a neighbour of your acquaintance."

" And who is that? "

" Your neighbour Tientietnikov, your Excellency."

Upon that the General frowned.

" Let me add," put in Chichikov hastily, " that he greatly regrets that on a former occasion he should have failed to show a proper respect for—for——"

" For what? " asked the General.

" For the services to the public which your Excellency has rendered. Indeed, he cannot find words to express his sorrow, but keeps repeating to himself: ' Would that I had valued at their true worth the men who have saved our fatherland ! ' "

" And why should he say that? " asked the mollified General. " I bear him no grudge. In fact, I have never cherished aught but a sincere liking for him, a sincere esteem, and do not doubt but that, in time, he may become a useful member of society."

" In the words which you have been good enough to utter," said Chichikov with a bow, " there is embodied much justice. Yes, Tientietnikov is in very truth a man of worth. Not only does he possess the gift of eloquence, but also he is a master of the pen."

" Ah, yes; he *does* write rubbish of some sort, doesn't he? Verses, or something of the kind? "

" Not rubbish, your Excellency, but practical stuff. In short, he is inditing a history."

" A *history* ? But a history of what? "

" A history of, of—" For a moment or two Chichikov hesitated. Then, whether because it was a General that was seated in front of him, or because he desired to impart greater importance to the subject which he was about to invent, he concluded: " A history of Generals, your Excellency."

" Of Generals? Of *what* Generals? "

" Of Generals generally — of Generals at large. That is to say, and to be more precise, a history of the Generals of our fatherland."

By this time Chichikov was floundering badly. Mentally he

spat upon himself and reflected: "Gracious heavens! What rubbish I am talking!"

"Pardon me," went on his interlocutor, "but I do not quite understand you. Is Tientietnikov producing a history of a given period, or only a history made up of a series of biographies? Also, is he including *all* our Generals, or only those who took part in the campaign of 1812?"

"The latter, your Excellency—only the Generals of 1812," replied Chichikov. Then he added beneath his breath: "Were I to be killed for it, I could not say what that may be supposed to mean."

"Then why should he not come and see me in person?" went on his host. "Possibly I might be able to furnish him with much interesting material?"

"He is afraid to come, your Excellency."

"Nonsense! Just because of a hasty word or two! I am not that sort of man at all. In fact, I should be very happy to call upon *him*."

"Never would he permit that, your Excellency. He would greatly prefer to be the first to make advances." And Chichikov added to himself: "What a stroke of luck those Generals were! Otherwise, the Lord knows where my tongue might have landed me!"

At this moment the door into the adjoining room opened, and there appeared in the doorway a girl as fair as a ray of the sun—so fair, indeed, that Chichikov stared at her in amazement. Apparently she had come to speak to her father for a moment, but had stopped short on perceiving that there was some one with him. The only fault to be found in her appearance was the fact that she was too thin and fragile-looking.

"May I introduce my little pet?" said the General to Chichikov. "To tell you the truth, I do not know your name."

"That you should be unacquainted with the name of one who has never distinguished himself in the manner of which you yourself can boast is scarcely to be wondered at." And Chichikov executed one of his sidelong, deferential bows.

"Well, I should be delighted to know it."

"It is Paul Ivanovitch Chichikov, your Excellency." With that went the easy bow of a military man and the agile backward movement of an india-rubber ball.

"Ulinka, this is Paul Ivanovitch," said the General, turning to his daughter. "He has just told me some interesting news—

namely, that our neighbour Tientietnikov is not altogether the
fool we had at first thought him. On the contrary, he is engaged
upon a very important work—upon a history of the Russian
Generals of 1812."

"But who ever supposed him to be a fool?" asked the girl
quickly. "What happened was that you took Vishnepokromov's
word—the word of a man who is himself both a fool and a good-
for-nothing.

"Well, well," said the father after further good-natured dispute on the subject of Vishnepokromov. "Do you now run
away, for I wish to dress for luncheon. And you, sir," he added
to Chichikov, "will you not join us at table?"

Chichikov bowed so low and so long that, by the time that
his eyes had ceased to see nothing but his own boots, the
General's daughter had disappeared, and in her place was standing a bewhiskered butler, armed with a silver soap-dish and a
hand-basin.

"Do you mind if I wash in your presence?" asked the host.

"By no means," replied Chichikov. "Pray do whatsoever
you please in that respect."

Upon that the General fell to scrubbing himself—incidentally,
to sending soapsuds flying in every direction. Meanwhile he
seemed so favourably disposed that Chichikov decided to sound
him then and there, more especially since the butler had left
the room.

"May I put to you a problem?" he asked.

"Certainly," replied the General. "What is it?"

"It is this, your Excellency. I have a decrepit old uncle who
owns three hundred souls and two thousand roubles-worth of
other property. Also, except for myself, he possesses not a
single heir. Now, although his infirm state of health will not
permit of his managing his property in person, he will not allow
me either to manage it. And the reason for his conduct—his
very strange conduct—he states as follows: ' I do not know my
nephew, and very likely he is a spendthrift. If he wishes to show
me that he is good for anything, let him go and acquire as many
souls as *I* have acquired; and when he has done that I will
transfer to him my three hundred souls as well."

"The man must be an absolute fool," commented the General.

"Possibly. And were that all, things would not be as bad
as they are. But, unfortunately, my uncle has gone and taken
up with his housekeeper, and has had children by her. Consequently everything will now pass to *them*."

" The old man must have taken leave of his senses," remarked the General. " Yet how *I* can help you I fail to see."

" Well, I have thought of a plan. If you will hand me over all the dead souls on your estate—hand them over to me exactly as though they were still alive, and were purchasable property —I will offer them to the old man, and then he will leave me his fortune."

At this point the General burst into a roar of laughter such as few can ever have heard. Half-dressed, he subsided into a chair, threw back his head, and guffawed until he came near to choking. In fact, the house shook with his merriment, so much so that the butler and his daughter came running into the room in alarm.

It was long before he could produce a single articulate word; and even when he did so (to reassure his daughter and the butler) he kept momentarily relapsing into spluttering chuckles which made the house ring and ring again.

Chichikov was greatly taken aback.

" Oh, that uncle! " bellowed the General in paroxysms of mirth. " Oh, that blessed uncle! *What* a fool he'll look! Ha, ha, ha! Dead souls offered him instead of live ones! Oh, my goodness! "

" I suppose I've put my foot in it again," ruefully reflected Chichikov. " But, good Lord, what a man the fellow is to laugh! Heaven send that he doesn't burst of it! "

" Ha, ha, ha! " broke out the General afresh. " *What* a donkey the old man must be! To think of his saying to you: ' You go and fit yourself out with three hundred souls, and I'll cap them with my own lot '! My word! What a jackass! "

" A jackass, your Excellency? "

" Yes, indeed! And to think of the jest of putting him off with dead souls! Ha, ha, ha! *What* wouldn't I give to see you handing him the title deeds? Who is he? What is he like? Is he very old? "

" He is eighty, your Excellency."

" But still brisk and able to move about, eh? Surely he must be pretty strong to go on living with his housekeeper like that? "

" Yes. But what does such strength mean? Sand runs away, your Excellency."

" The old fool! But is he really such a fool? "

" Yes, your Excellency."

" And does he go out at all? Does he see company? Can he still hold himself upright? "

" Yes, but with great difficulty."

" And has he any teeth left? "

" No more than two at the most."

" The old jackass! Don't be angry with me, but I must say that, though your uncle, he is also a jackass."

" Quite so, your Excellency. And though it grieves *me* to have to confess that he is my uncle, what am I to do with him? "

Yet this was not altogether the truth. What would have been a far harder thing for Chichikov to have confessed was the fact that he possessed no uncles at all.

" I beg of you, your Excellency," he went on, " to hand me over those, those——"

" Those dead souls, eh? Why, in return for the jest I will give you some land as well. Yes, you can take the whole grave-yard if you like. Ha, ha, ha! The old man! Ha, ha, ha! *What* a fool he'll look! Ha, ha, ha! "

And once more the General's guffaws went ringing through the house.

[At this point there occurs a long hiatus in the original.]

III

" IF Colonel Koshkarev should turn out to be as mad as the last one it is a bad look-out," said Chichikov to himself on opening his eyes amid fields and open country—everything else having disappeared save the vault of heaven and a couple of low-lying clouds.

" Selifan," he went on, " did you ask how to get to Colonel Koshkarev's? "

" Yes, Paul Ivanovitch. At least, there was such a clatter around the *koliaska* that I could not; but Petrushka asked the coachman."

" You fool! How often have I told you not to rely upon Petrushka? Petrushka is a blockhead, an idiot. Besides, at the present moment I believe him to be drunk."

" No, you are wrong, *barin*," put in the person referred to, turning his head with a sidelong glance. " After we get down the next hill we shall need but to keep bending round it. That is all."

" Yes, and I suppose you'll tell me that *sivnkha* is the only thing that has passed your lips? Well, the view at least is beauti-ful. In fact, when one has seen this place one may say that one has seen one of the beauty spots of Europe." This said, Chichikov added to himself, smoothing his chin: "What a difference between the features of a civilised man of the world and those of a common lacquey!"

Meanwhile the *koliaska* quickened its pace, and Chichikov once more caught sight of Tientietnikov's aspen-studded meadows. Undulating gently on elastic springs, the vehicle cautiously descended the steep incline, and then proceeded past water-mills, rumbled over a bridge or two, and jolted easily along the rough-set road which traversed the flats. Not a molehill, not a mound jarred the spine. The vehicle was comfort itself.

Swiftly there flew by clumps of osiers, slender elder trees, and silver-leaved poplars, their branches brushing against Selifan and Petrushka, and at intervals depriving the valet of his cap. Each time that this happened, the sullen-faced servitor fell to cursing both the tree responsible for the occurrence and the landowner responsible for the tree being in existence; yet nothing would induce him thereafter either to tie on the cap or to steady it with his hand, so complete was his assurance that the accident would never be repeated. Soon to the foregoing trees there became added an occasional birch or spruce fir, while in the dense undergrowth around their roots could be seen the blue iris and the yellow wood-tulip. Gradually the forest grew darker, as though eventually the obscurity would become complete. Then through the trunks and the boughs there began to gleam points of light like glittering mirrors, and as the number of trees lessened, these points grew larger, until the travellers debouched upon the shore of a lake four *versts* or so in circumference, and having on its further margin the grey, scattered log huts of a peasant village. In the water a great commotion was in progress. In the first place, some twenty men, immersed to the knee, to the breast, or to the neck, were dragging a large fishing-net inshore, while, in the second place, there was entangled in the same, in addition to some fish, a stout man shaped precisely like a melon or a hogshead. Greatly excited, he was shouting at the top of his voice: "Let Kosma manage it, you lout of a Denis! Kosma, take the end of the rope from Denis! Don't bear so hard on it, Thoma Bolshoy![1] Go where Thoma Menshov[2] is! Damn it, bring the net to land, will you!" From this it became clear that it was not on his own account that the stout man was worrying. Indeed, he had no need to do so, since his fat would in any case have prevented him from

[1] The Elder.   [2] The Younger.

sinking. Yes, even if he had turned head over heels in an effort
to dive, the water would persistently have borne him up; and
the same if, say, a couple of men had jumped on his back—the
only result would have been that he would have become a trifle
deeper submerged, and forced to draw breath by spouting
bubbles through his nose. No, the cause of his agitation was
lest the net should break, and the fish escape: wherefore he
was urging some additional peasants who were standing on the
bank to lay hold of and to pull at, an extra rope or two.

"That must be the *barin*—Colonel Koshkarev," said Selifan.

"Why?" asked Chichikov.

"Because, if you please, his skin is whiter than the rest, and
he has the respectable paunch of a gentleman."

Meanwhile good progress was being made with the hauling in
of the *barin;* until, feeling the ground with his feet, he rose to
an upright position, and at the same moment caught sight of
the *koliaska*, with Chichikov seated therein, descending the
declivity.

"Have you dined yet?" shouted the *barin* as, still entangled
in the net, he approached the shore with a huge fish on his back.
With one hand shading his eyes from the sun, and the other
thrown backwards, he looked, in point of pose, like the Medici
Venus emerging from her bath.

"No," replied Chichikov, raising his cap, and executing a
series of bows.

"Then thank God for that," rejoined the gentleman.

"Why?" asked Chichikov with no little curiosity, and still
holding his cap over his head.

"Because of *this*. Cast off the net, Thoma Menshov, and
pick up that sturgeon for the gentleman to see. Go and help
him, Telepen Kuzma."

With that the peasants indicated picked up by the head what
was a veritable monster of a fish.

"Isn't it a beauty—a sturgeon fresh run from the river?"
exclaimed the stout *barin*. "And now let us be off home. Coachman, you can take the lower road through the kitchen garden.
Run, you lout of a Thoma Bolshoy, and open the gate for him.
He will guide you to the house, and I myself shall be along
presently."

Thereupon the barelegged Thoma Bolshoy, clad in nothing
but a shirt, ran ahead of the *koliaska* through the village, every
hut of which had hanging in front of it a variety of nets, for
the reason that every inhabitant of the place was a fisherman.

Next, he opened a gate into a large vegetable enclosure, and thence the *koliaska* emerged into a square near a wooden church, with, showing beyond the latter, the roofs of the manorial homestead.

" A queer fellow, that Koshkarev!" said Chichikov to himself.

" Well, whatever I may be, at least I'm here," said a voice by his side. Chichikov looked round, and perceived that, in the meanwhile, the *barin* had dressed himself and overtaken the carriage. With a pair of yellow trousers he was wearing a grass-green jacket, and his neck was as guiltless of a collar as Cupid's. Also, as he sat sideways in his *drozhki*, his bulk was such that he completely filled the vehicle. Chichikov was about to make some remark or another when the stout gentleman disappeared; and presently his *drozhki* re-emerged into view at the spot where the fish had been drawn to land, and his voice could be heard reiterating exhortations to his serfs. Yet when Chichikov reached the verandah of the house he found, to his intense surprise, the stout gentleman waiting to welcome the visitor. How he had contrived to convey himself thither passed Chichikov's comprehension. Host and guest embraced three times, according to a bygone custom of Russia. Evidently the *barin* was one of the old school.

" I bring you," said Chichikov, " a greeting from his Excellency."

" From whom? "

" From your relative, General Alexander Dmitrievitch."

" Who is Alexander Dmitrievitch? "

" What? You do not know General Alexander Dmitrievitch Betrishev? " exclaimed Chichikov with a touch of surprise.

" No, I do not," replied the gentleman.

Chichikov's suprise grew to absolute astonishment.

" How comes that about? " he ejaculated. " I hope that I have the honour of addressing Colonel Koshkarev? "

" Your hopes are vain. It is to my house, not to his, that you have come; and I am Peter Petrovitch Pietukh—yes, Peter Petrovitch Pietukh."

Chichikov, dumbfounded, turned to Selifan and Petrushka.

" What do you mean? " he exclaimed. " I told you to drive to the house of Colonel Koshkarev, whereas you have brought me to that of Peter Petrovitch Pietukh."

" All the same, your fellows have done quite right," put in the gentleman referred to. " Do you " (this to Selifan and Petrushka) " go to the kitchen, where they will give you a glassful of *vodka* apiece. Then put up the horses, and be off to the servants' quarters."

"I regret the mistake extremely," said Chichikov.

"But it is not a mistake. When you have tried the dinner which I have in store for you, just see whether you think *it* a mistake. Enter, I beg of you." And, taking Chichikov by the arm, the host conducted him within, where they were met by a couple of youths.

"Let me introduce my two sons, home for their holidays from the Gymnasium," [1] said Pietukh. "Nikolasha, come and entertain our good visitor, while you, Aleksasha, follow me." And with that the host disappeared.

Chichikov turned to Nikolasha, whom he found to be a budding man about town, since at once he opened a conversation by stating that, as no good was to be derived from studying at a provincial institution, he and his brother desired to remove, rather, to St. Petersburg the provinces not being worth living in.

"I quite understand," Chichikov thought to himself. "The end of the chapter will be confectioners' assistants and the boulevards."

"Tell me," he added aloud, "how does your father's property at present stand?"

"It is all mortgaged," put in the father himself as he re-entered the room. "Yes, it is all mortgaged, every bit of it."

"What a pity!" thought Chichikov. "At this rate it will not be long before the man has no property at all left. I must hurry my departure." Aloud he said with an air of sympathy: "That you have mortgaged the estate seems to me a matter for regret."

"No, not at all," replied Pietukh. "In fact, they tell me that it is a good thing to do, and that every one else is doing it. Why should I act differently from my neighbours? Moreover, I have had enough of living here, and should like to try Moscow —more especially since my sons are always begging me to give them a metropolitan education."

"Oh, the fool, the fool!" reflected Chichikov. "He is for throwing up everything and making spendthrifts of his sons. Yet this is a nice property, and it is clear that the local peasants are doing well, and that the family, too, is comfortably off. On the other hand, as soon as ever these lads begin their education in restaurants and theatres, the devil will away with every

[1] Secondary School.

stick of their substance. For my own part, I could desire nothing better than this quiet life in the country."

"Let me guess what is in your mind," said Pietukh.

"What, then?" asked Chichikov, rather taken aback.

"You are thinking to yourself: 'That fool of a Pietukh has asked me to dinner, yet not a bite of dinner do I see.' But wait a little. It will be ready presently, for it is being cooked as fast as a maiden who has had her hair cut off plaits herself a new set of tresses."

"Here comes Platon Mikhalitch, father!" exclaimed Aleksasha, who had been peeping out of the window.

"Yes, and on a grey horse," added his brother.

"Who is Platon Mikhalitch?" inquired Chichikov.

"A neighbour of ours, and an excellent fellow."

The next moment Platon Mikhalitch himself entered the room, accompanied by a sporting dog named Yarb. He was a tall, handsome man, with extremely red hair. As for his companion, it was of the keen-muzzled species used for shooting.

"Have you dined yet?" asked the host.

"Yes," replied Platon.

"Indeed? What do you mean by coming here to laugh at us all? Do I ever go to *your* place after dinner?"

The newcomer smiled. "Well, if it can bring you any comfort," he said, "let me tell you that I ate nothing at the meal, for I had no appetite."

"But you should see what I have caught—what sort of a sturgeon fate has brought my way! Yes, and what crucians and carp!"

"Really it tires one to hear you. How come you always to be so cheerful?"

"And how come *you* always to be so gloomy?" retorted the host.

"How, you ask? Simply because I am so."

"The truth is you don't eat enough. Try the plan of making a good dinner. Weariness of everything is a modern invention. Once upon a time one never heard of it."

"Well, boast away, but have you yourself never been tired of things?"

"Never in my life. I do not so much as know whether I should find time to be tired. In the morning, when one awakes, the cook is waiting, and the dinner has to be ordered. Then one drinks one's morning tea, and then the bailiff arrives for *his* orders, and then there is fishing to be done, and then one's dinner has to be eaten. Next, before one has even had a chance to utter a snore, there enters once again the cook, and one has to order supper; and when she has departed, behold, back she comes with a request for directions for the following day's dinner! What time does *that* leave one to be weary of things?"

Throughout this conversation, Chichikov had been taking stock of the newcomer, who astonished him with his good looks, his upright, picturesque figure, his appearance of fresh, unwasted youthfulness, and the boyish purity, innocence, and clarity of his features. Neither passion nor care nor aught of the nature of agitation or anxiety of mind had ventured to touch his unsullied face, or to lay a single wrinkle thereon. Yet the touch of life which those emotions might have imparted was wanting. The face was, as it were, dreaming, even though from time to time an ironical smile disturbed it.

"I, too, cannot understand," remarked Chichikov, "how a man of your appearance can find things wearisome. Of course, if a man is hard pressed for money, or if he has enemies who are lying in wait for his life (as have certain folk of whom I know), well, then——"

"Believe me when I say," interrupted the handsome guest, "that, for the sake of a diversion, I should be glad of *any* sort of an anxiety. Would that some enemy would conceive a grudge against me! But no one does so. Everything remains eternally dull."

"But perhaps you lack a sufficiency of land or souls?"

"Not at all. I and my brother own ten thousand *desiatins* [1] of land, and over a thousand souls."

"Curious! I do not understand it. But perhaps the harvest has failed, or you have sickness about, and many of your male peasants have died of it?"

"On the contrary, everything is in splendid order, for my brother is the best of managers."

"Then to find things wearisome!" exclaimed Chichikov. "It passes my comprehension." And he shrugged his shoulders.

"Well, we will soon put weariness to flight," interrupted the host. "Aleksasha, do you run helter-skelter to the kitchen, and there tell the cook to serve the fish pasties. Yes, and where have that gawk of an Emelian and that thief of an Antoshka got to? Why have they not handed round the *zakuski* ?"

At this moment the door opened, and the " gawk " and the " thief " in question made their appearance with napkins and

---

[1] The desiatin = 2.86 English acres.

a tray—the latter bearing six decanters of variously-coloured beverages. These they placed upon the table, and then ringed them about with glasses and platefuls of every conceivable kind of appetiser. That done, the servants applied themselves to bringing in various comestibles under covers, through which could be heard the hissing of hot roast viands. In particular did the " gawk " and the " thief " work hard at their tasks. As a matter of fact, their appellations had been given them merely to spur them to greater activity, for, in general, the *barin* was no lover of abuse, but, rather, a kind-hearted man who, like most Russians, could not get on without a sharp word or two. That is to say, he needed them for his tongue as he needed a glass of *vodka* for his digestion. What else could you expect? It was his nature to care for nothing mild.

To the *zakuski* succeeded the meal itself, and the host became a perfect glutton on his guests' behalf. Should he notice that a guest had taken but a single piece of a comestible, he added thereto another one, saying: " Without a mate, neither man nor bird can live in this world." Should any one take two pieces, he added thereto a third, saying: " What is the good of the number 2? God loves a trinity." Should any one take three pieces, he would say: " Where do you see a waggon with three wheels? Who builds a three-cornered hut? " Lastly, should any one take four pieces, he would cap them with a fifth, and add thereto the punning quip, " *Na piat opiat.*" [1] After devouring at least twelve steaks of sturgeon, Chichikov ventured to think to himself, " My host cannot possibly add to *them*," but found that he was mistaken, for, without a word, Pietukh heaped upon his plate an enormous portion of spit-roasted veal, and also some kidneys. But what veal it was!

" That calf was fed two years on milk," he explained. " I cared for it like my own son."

" Nevertheless I can eat no more," said Chichikov.

" Do you try the veal before you say that you can eat no more."

" But I could not get it down my throat. There is no room left."

" If there be no room in a church for a newcomer, the beadle is sent for, and room is very soon made—yes, even though before there was such a crush that an apple couldn't have been dropped between the people. Do you try the veal, I say. That piece is the titbit of all."

[1] " One more makes five."

So Chichikov made the attempt; and in very truth the veal was beyond all praise, and room was found for it, even though one would have supposed the feat impossible.

"Fancy this good fellow removing to St. Petersburg or Moscow!" said the guest to himself. "Why, with a scale of living like this, he would be ruined in three years." For that matter, Pietukh might well have been ruined already, for hospitality can dissipate a fortune in three months as easily as it can in three years.

The host also dispensed the wine with a lavish hand, and what the guests did not drink he gave to his sons, who thus swallowed glass after glass. Indeed, even before coming to table, it was possible to discern to what department of human accomplishment their bent was turned. When the meal was over, however, the guests had no mind for further drinking. Indeed, it was all that they could do to drag themselves on to the balcony, and there to relapse into easy chairs. Indeed, the moment that the host subsided into his seat—it was large enough for four—he fell asleep, and his portly presence, converting itself into a sort of blacksmith's bellows, started to vent, through open mouth and distended nostrils, such sounds as can have greeted the reader's ear but seldom—sounds as of a drum being beaten in combination with the whistling of a flute and the strident howling of a dog.

"Listen to him!" said Platon.

Chichikov smiled.

"Naturally, on such dinners as that," continued the other, "our host does *not* find the time dull. And as soon as dinner is ended there can ensue sleep."

"Yes, but, pardon me, I still fail to understand why you find life wearisome. There are so many resources against *ennui!*"

"As for instance?"

"For a young man, dancing, the playing of one or another musical instrument, and—well, yes, marriage."

"Marriage to whom?"

"To some maiden who is both charming and rich. Are there none in these parts?"

"No."

"Then, were I you, I should travel, and seek a maiden elsewhere." And a brilliant idea therewith entered Chichikov's head. "This last resource," he added, "is the best of all resources against *ennui.*"

" What resource are you speaking of? "

" Of travel."

" But whither? "

" Well, should it so please you, you might join me as my companion." This said, the speaker added to himself as he eyed Platon: " Yes, that would suit me exactly, for then I should have half my expenses paid, and could charge him also with the cost of mending the *koliaska*."

" And whither should we go? "

" In that respect I am not wholly my own master, as I have business to do for others as well as for myself. For instance General Betristchev—an intimate friend and, I might add, a generous benefactor of mine—has charged me with commissions to certain of his relatives. However, though relatives are relatives, I am travelling likewise on my own account, since I wish to see the world and the whirligig of humanity—which, in spite of what people may say, is as good as a living book or a second education." As a matter of fact, Chichikov was reflecting: " Yes, the plan is an excellent one. I might even contrive that he should have to bear the whole of our expenses, and that his horses should be used while my own should be put out to graze on his farm."

" Well, why should I not adopt the suggestion? " was Platon's thought. " There is nothing for me to do at home, since the management of the estate is in my brother's hands, and my going would cause him no inconvenience. Yes, why should I not do as Chichikov has suggested? "

Then he added aloud:

" Would you come and stay with my brother for a couple of days? Otherwise he might refuse me his consent."

" With great pleasure," said Chichikov. " Or even for three days."

" Then here is my hand on it. Let us be off at once." Platon seemed suddenly to have come to life again.

" Where are you off to? " put in their host unexpectedly as he roused himself and stared in astonishment at the pair. " No, no, my good sirs. I have had the wheels removed from your *koliaska*, Monsieur Chichikov, and have sent your horse, Platon Mikhalitch, to a grazing ground fifteen *versts* away. Consequently you must spend the night here, and depart to-morrow morning after breakfast."

What could be done with a man like Pietukh? There was no help for it but to remain. In return, the guests were rewarded with a beautiful spring evening, for, to spend the time, the host organised a boating expedition on the river, and a dozen rowers, with a dozen pairs of oars, conveyed the party (to the accompaniment of song) across the smooth surface of the lake and up a great river with towering banks. From time to time the boat would pass under ropes, stretched across for purposes of fishing, and at each turn of the rippling current new vistas unfolded themselves as tier upon tier of woodland delighted the eye with a diversity of timber and foliage. In unison did the rowers ply their sculls, yet it was as though of itself that the skiff shot forward, bird-like, over the glassy surface of the water; while at intervals the broad-shouldered young oarsmen who was seated third from the bow would raise, as from a nightingale's throat, the opening staves of a boat song, and then be joined by five or six more, until the melody had come to pour forth in a volume as free and boundless as Russia herself. And Pietukh, too, would give himself a shake, and help lustily to support the chorus; and even Chichikov felt acutely conscious of the fact that he was a Russian. Only Platon reflected: "What is there so splendid in these melancholy songs? They do but increase one's depression of spirits."

The journey homeward was made in the gathering dusk. Rhythmically the oars smote a surface which no longer reflected the sky, and darkness had fallen when they reached the shore, along which lights were twinkling where the fisherfolk were boiling live eels for soup. Everything had now wended its way homeward for the night; the cattle and poultry had been housed, and the herdsmen, standing at the gates of the village cattle-pens, amid the trailing dust lately raised by their charges, were awaiting the milk-pails and a summons to partake of the eel-broth. Through the dusk came the hum of humankind, and the barking of dogs in other and more distant villages; while, over all, the moon was rising, and the darkened countryside was beginning to glimmer to light again under her beams. What a glorious picture! Yet no one thought of admiring it. Instead of galloping over the countryside on frisky cobs, Nikolasha and Aleksasha were engaged in dreaming of Moscow, with its confectioners' shops and the theatres of which a cadet, newly arrived on a visit from the capital, had just been telling them; while their father had his mind full of how best to stuff his guests with yet more food, and Platon was given up to yawning. Only in Chichikov was a spice of animation visible. "Yes," he reflected, "some day I, too, will become lord of such a country place."

And before his mind's eye there arose also a helpmeet and some little Chichikovs.

By the time that supper was finished the party had again over-eaten themselves, and when Chichikov entered the room allotted him for the night, he lay down upon the bed, and prodded his stomach. " It is as tight as a drum," he said to himself. " Not another titbit of veal could now get into it." Also, circumstances had so brought it about that next door to him there was situated his host's apartment; and since the intervening wall was thin, Chichikov could hear every word that was said there. At the present moment the master of the house was engaged in giving the cook orders for what, under the guise of an early breakfast, promised to constitute a veritable dinner. You should have heard Pietukh's behests! They would have excited the appetite of a corpse.

" Yes," he said, sucking his lips, and drawing a deep breath, " in the first place, make a pasty in four divisions. Into one of the divisions put the sturgeon's cheeks and some *viaziga*,[1] and into another division some buckwheat porridge, young mushrooms and onions, sweet milk, calves' brains, and anything else that you may find suitable—anything else that you may have got handy. Also, bake the pasty to a nice brown on one side, and but lightly on the other. Yes, and, as to the under side, bake it so that it will be all juicy and flaky, so that it shall not crumble into bits, but melt in the mouth like the softest snow that ever you heard of." And as he said this Pietukh fairly smacked his lips.

" The devil take him!" muttered Chichikov, thrusting his head beneath the bedclothes to avoid hearing more. " The fellow won't give one a chance to sleep."

Nevertheless he heard through the blankets:

" And garnish the sturgeon with beetroot, smelts, peppered mushrooms, young radishes, carrots, beans, and anything else you like, so as to have plenty of trimmings. Yes, and put a lump of ice into the pig's bladder, so as to swell it up."

Many other dishes did Pietukh order, and nothing was to be heard but his talk of boiling, roasting, and stewing. Finally, just as mention was being made of a turkey cock, Chichikov fell asleep.

Next morning the guests' state of repletion had reached the point of Platon being unable to mount his horse; wherefore the latter was dispatched homeward with one of Pietukh's

---

[1] Dried spinal marrow of the sturgeon.

grooms, and the two guests entered Chichikov's *koliaska*. Even the dog trotted lazily in the rear; for he, too, had over-eaten himself.

" It has been rather too much of a good thing," remarked Chichikov as the vehicle issued from the courtyard.

" Yes, and it vexes me to see the fellow never tire of it," replied Platon.

" Ah," thought Chichikov to himself, " if *I* had an income of seventy thousand roubles, as you have, I'd very soon give tiredness one in the eye ! Take Murazov, the tax-farmer—he, again, must be worth ten millions. What a fortune ! "

" Do you mind where we drive ? " asked Platon. " I should like first to go and take leave of my sister and my brother-in-law."

" With pleasure," said Chichikov.

" My brother-in-law is the leading landowner hereabouts. At the present moment he is drawing an income of two hundred thousand roubles from a property which, eight years ago, was producing a bare twenty thousand."

" Truly a man worthy of the utmost respect ! I shall be most interested to make his acquaintance. To think of it ! And what may his family name be ? "

" Kostanzhoglo."

" And his Christian name and patronymic ? "

" Constantine Thedorovitch."

" Constantine Thedorovitch Kostanzhoglo. Yes, it will be a most interesting event to make his acquaintance. To know such a man must be a whole education."

Here Platon set himself to give Selifan some directions as to the way, a necessary proceeding in view of the fact that Selifan could scarcely maintain his seat on the box. Twice Petrushka, too, had fallen headlong, and thus necessitated his being tied to his perch with a piece of rope. " What a clown ! " had been Chichikov's only comment.

" This is where my brother-in-law's lands begin," said Platon. " They give one a change of view."

And, indeed, from this point the countryside became planted with timber; the rows of trees running as straight as pistol-shots, and having beyond them, and on higher ground, a second expanse of forest, newly planted like the first; while beyond it, again, loomed a third plantation of older trees. Next there succeeded a flat piece of the same nature.

" All this timber," said Platon, " has grown up within eight or ten years at the most; whereas on another man's land it would have taken twenty to attain the same growth."

"And how has your brother-in-law effected this?"

"You must ask him himself. He is so excellent a husbandman that nothing ever fails with him. You see, he knows the soil, and also knows what ought to be planted beside what, and what kinds of timber are the best neighbours for grain. Again, everything on his estate is made to perform at least three or four different functions. For instance, he makes his timber not only serve as timber, but also serve as a provider of moisture and shade to a given stretch of land, and then as a fertiliser with its fallen leaves. Consequently, when everywhere else there is drought, he still has water, and when everywhere else there has been a failure of the harvest, on his lands it will have proved a success. But it is a pity that I know so little about it all as to be unable to explain to you his many expedients. Folk call him a wizard, for he produces so much. Nevertheless, personally I find what he does uninteresting."

"Truly an astonishing fellow!" reflected Chichikov with a glance at his companion. "It is sad indeed to see a man so superficial as to be unable to explain matters of this kind."

At length the manor appeared in sight—an establishment looking almost like a town, so numerous were the huts where they stood arranged in three tiers, crowned with three churches, and surrounded with huge ricks and barns. "Yes," thought Chichikov to himself, "one can see that a jewel of a landowner lives here." The huts in question were stoutly built and the intervening alleys well laid-out; while, wherever a waggon was visible, it looked serviceable and more or less new. Also, the local peasants bore an intelligent look on their faces, the cattle were of the best possible breed, and even the peasant's pig belonged to the porcine aristocracy. Clearly there dwelt here peasants who, to quote the song, were accustomed to "pick up silver by the shovelful." Nor were Englishified gardens and *parterres* and other conceits in evidence, but, on the contrary, there ran an open view from the manor house to the farm buildings and the workmen's cots, so that, after the old Russian fashion, the *barin* should be able to keep an eye upon all that was going on around him. For the same purpose, the mansion was topped with a tall lantern and a superstructure—a device designed, not for ornament, nor for a vantage-spot for the contemplation of the view, but for supervision of the labourers engaged in distant fields. Lastly, the brisk, active servants who received the visitors on the verandah were very different menials from the drunken Petrushka, even though they did not wear swallow-tailed coats, but only Cossack *tchekmeni* [1] of blue homespun cloth.

The lady of the house also issued on to the verandah. With her face of the freshness of " blood and milk " and the brightness of God's daylight, she as nearly resembled Platon as one pea resembles another, save that, whereas he was languid, she was cheerful and full of talk.

" Good day, brother! " she cried. " How glad I am to see you! Constantine is not at home, but will be back presently."

" Where is he? "

" Doing business in the village with a party of factors," replied the lady as she conducted her guests to the drawing-room.

With no little curiosity did Chichikov gaze at the interior of the mansion inhabited by the man who received an annual income of two hundred thousand roubles; for he thought to discern therefrom the nature of its proprietor, even as from a shell one may deduce the species of oyster or snail which has been its tenant, and has left therein its impression. But no such conclusions were to be drawn. The rooms were simple, and even bare. Not a fresco nor a picture nor a bronze nor a flower nor a china what-not nor a book was there to be seen. In short, everything appeared to show that the proprietor of this abode spent the greater part of his time, not between four walls, but in the field, and that he thought out his plans, not in sybaritic fashion by the fireside, nor in an easy chair beside the stove, but on the spot where work was actually in progress—that, in a word, where those plans were conceived, there they were put into execution. Nor in these rooms could Chichikov detect the least trace of a feminine hand, beyond the fact that certain tables and chairs bore drying-boards whereon were arranged some sprinklings of flower petals.

" What is all this rubbish for? " asked Platon.

" It is not rubbish," replied the lady of the house. " On the contrary, it is the best possible remedy for fever. Last year we cured every one of our sick peasants with it. Some of the petals I am going to make into an ointment, and some into an infusion. You may laugh as much as you like at my potting and preserving, yet you yourself will be glad of things of the kind when you set out on your travels."

Platon moved to the piano, and began to pick out a note or two.

[1] Long, belted Tartar blouses.

" Good Lord, what an ancient instrument!" he exclaimed.
" Are you not ashamed of it, sister?"

" Well, the truth is that I get no time to practise my music.
You see," she added to Chichikov, " I have an eight-year-old
daughter to educate; and to hand her over to a foreign governess
in order that I may have leisure for my own piano-playing—well
that is a thing which I could never bring myself to do."

" You have become a wearisome sort of person," commented
Platon, and walked away to the window. " Ah, here comes
Constantine," presently he added.

Chichikov also glanced out of the window, and saw approaching the verandah a brisk, swarthy-complexioned man of about
forty, a man clad in a rough cloth jacket and a velveteen cap.
Evidently he was one of those who care little for the niceties of
dress. With him, bareheaded, there came a couple of men of a
somewhat lower station in life, and all three were engaged in an
animated discussion. One of the *barin's* two companions was a
plain peasant, and the other (clad in a blue Siberian smock) a
travelling factor. The fact that the party halted awhile by the
entrance steps made it possible to overhear a portion of their
conversation from within.

" This is what you peasants had better do," the *barin* was
saying. " Purchase your release from your present master. I
will lend you the necessary money, and afterwards you can
work for me."

" No, Constantine Thedorovitch," replied the peasant.
" Why should we do that? Remove us just as we are. You will
know how to arrange it, for a cleverer gentleman than you is
nowhere to be found. The misfortune of us *muzhiks* is that we
cannot protect ourselves properly. The tavern-keepers sell us
such liquor that, before a man knows where he is, a glassful of it
has eaten a hole in his stomach, and made him feel as though he
could drink a pail of water. Yes, it knocks a man over before he
can look round. Everywhere temptation lies in wait for the
peasant, and he needs to be cunning if he is to get through the
world at all. In fact, things seem to be contrived for nothing
but to make us peasants lose our wits, even to the tobacco which
they sell us. What are folk like ourselves to do, Constantine
Thedorovitch? I tell you it is terribly difficult for a *muzhik* to
look after himself."

" Listen to me. This is how things are done here. When I
take on a serf, I fit him out with a cow and a horse. On the other
hand, I demand of him thereafter more than is demanded of a

peasant anywhere else. That is to say, first and foremost I make him work. Whether a peasant be working for himself or for me, never do I let him waste time. I myself toil like a bullock, and I force my peasants to do the same, for experience has taught me that that is the only way to get through life. All the mischief in the world comes through lack of employment. Now, do you go and consider the matter, and talk it over with your *mir*.[1]

" We have done that already, Constantine Thedorovitch, and our elders' opinion is: ' There is no need for further talk. Every peasant belonging to Constantine Thedorovitch is well off, and hasn't to work for nothing. The priests of his village, too, are men of good heart, whereas ours have been taken away, and there is no one to bury us.' "

" Nevertheless, do you go and talk the matter over again."

" We will, *barin*."

Here the factor who had been walking on the *barin's* other side put in a word.

" Constantine Thedorovitch," he said, " I beg of you to do as I have requested."

" I have told you before," replied the *barin*, " that I do not care to play the huckster. I am not one of those landowners whom fellows of your sort visit on the very day that the interest on a mortgage is due. Ah, I know your fraternity thoroughly, and know that you keep lists of all who have mortgages to repay. But what is there so clever about that? Any man, if you pinch him sufficiently, will surrender you a mortgage at half-price,— any man, that is to say, except myself, who care nothing for your money. Were a loan of mine to remain out three years, I should never demand a kopeck of interest on it."

" Quite so, Constantine Thedorovitch," replied the factor. " But I am asking this of you more for the purpose of establishing us on a business footing than because I desire to win your favour. Pray, therefore, accept this earnest money of three thousand roubles." And the man drew from his breast pocket a dirty roll of bank-notes, which, carelessly receiving, Kostanzhoglo thrust, uncounted, into the back pocket of his overcoat.

" Hm!" thought Chichikov. " For all he cares, the notes might have been a handkerchief."

When Kostanzhoglo appeared at closer quarters—that is to say, in the doorway of the drawing-room—he struck Chichikov more than ever with the swarthiness of his complexion, the dishevelment of his black, slightly grizzled locks, the alertness

[1] Village commune.

of his eye, and the impression of fiery southern origin which his whole personality diffused. For he was not wholly a Russian, nor could he himself say precisely who his forefathers had been. Yet, inasmuch as he accounted genealogical research no part of the science of estate-management, but a mere superfluity, he looked upon himself as, to all intents and purposes, a native of Russia, and the more so since the Russian language was the only tongue he knew.

Platon presented Chichikov, and the pair exchanged greetings.

"To get rid of my depression, Constantine," continued Platon, "I am thinking of accompanying our guest on a tour through a few of the provinces."

"An excellent idea," said Kostanzhoglo. "But precisely whither?" he added, turning hospitably to Chichikov.

"To tell you the truth," replied that personage with an affable inclination of the head as he smoothed the arm of his chair with his hand, "I am travelling less on my own affairs than on the affairs of others. That is to say, General Betristchev, an intimate friend, and, I might add, a generous benefactor, of mine, has charged me with commissions to some of his relatives. Nevertheless, though relatives are relatives, I may say that I am travelling on my own account as well, in that, in addition to possible benefit to my health, I desire to see the world and the whirligig of humanity, which constitute, so to speak, a living book, a second course of education."

"Yes, there is no harm in looking at other corners of the world besides one's own."

"You speak truly. There *is* no harm in such a proceeding. Thereby one may see things which one has not before encountered, one may meet men with whom one has not before come in contact. And with some men of that kind a conversation is as precious a benefit as has been conferred upon me by the present occasion. I come to you, most worthy Constantine Thedorovitch, for instruction, and again for instruction, and beg of you to assuage my thirst with an exposition of the truth as it is. I hunger for the favour of your words as for manna."

"But how so? What can *I* teach you?" exclaimed Kostanzhoglo in confusion. "I myself was given but the plainest of educations."

"Nay, most worthy sir, you possess wisdom, and again wisdom. Wisdom only can direct the management of a great estate, that can derive a sound income from the same, that can acquire wealth of a real, not a fictitious, order while also ful-

I

filling the duties of a citizen and thereby earning the respect of
the Russian public. All this I pray you to teach me."

"I tell you what," said Kostanzhoglo, looking meditatively
at his guest. "You had better stay with me for a few days,
and during that time I can show you how things are managed
here, and explain to you everything. Then you will see for
yourself that no great wisdom is required for the purpose."

"Yes, certainly you must stay here," put in the lady of the
house. Then, turning to her brother, she added: "And you
too must stay. Why should you be in such a hurry?"

"Very well," he replied. "But what say *you*, Paul Ivanovitch?"

"I say the same as you, and with much pleasure," replied
Chichikov. "But also I ought to tell you this: that there is a
relative of General Betristchev's, a certain Colonel Koshkarev——"

"Yes, we know him; but he is quite mad."

"As you say, he is mad, and I should not have been intending to visit him, were it not that General Betristchev is an
intimate friend of mine, as well as, I might add, my most
generous benefactor."

"Then," said Kostanzhoglo, "do you go and see Colonel
Koshkarev *now*. He lives less than ten *versts* from here, and I
have a gig ready harnessed. Go to him at once, and return
here for tea."

"An excellent idea!" cried Chichikov, and with that he
seized his cap.

Half an hour's drive sufficed to bring him to the Colonel's
establishment. The village attached to the manor was in a state
of utter confusion, since in every direction building and repairing operations were in progress, and the alleys were choked
with heaps of lime, bricks, and beams of wood. Also, some of
the huts were arranged to resemble offices, and superscribed in
gilt letters "Depot for Agricultural Implements," "Chief
Office of Accounts," "Estate Works Committee," "Normal
School for the Education of Colonists," and so forth.

Chichikov found the Colonel posted behind a desk and holding a pen between his teeth. Without an instant's delay the
master of the establishment—who seemed a kindly, approachable man, and accorded his visitor a very civil welcome—
plunged into a recital of the labour which it had cost him to
bring the property to its present condition of affluence. Then
he went on to lament the fact that he could not make his

peasantry understand the incentives to labour which the riches of science and art provide; for instance, he had failed to induce his female serfs to wear corsets, whereas in Germany, where he had resided for fourteen years, every humble miller's daughter could play the piano. None the less, he said, he meant to peg away until every peasant on the estate should, as he walked behind the plough, indulge in a regular course of reading Franklin's *Notes on Electricity*, Virgil's *Georgics*, or some work on the chemical properties of soil.

" Good gracious! " mentally exclaimed Chichikov. " Why, I myself have not had time to finish that book by the Duchesse de la Vallière! "

Much else the Colonel said. In particular did he aver that, provided the Russian peasant could be induced to array himself in German costume, science would progress, trade increase, and the Golden Age dawn in Russia.

For a while Chichikov listened with distended eyes. Then he felt constrained to intimate that with all that he had nothing to do, seeing that his business was merely to acquire a few souls, and thereafter to have their purchase confirmed.

" If I understand you aright," said the Colonel, " you wish to present a Statement of Plea? "

" Yes, that is so."

" Then kindly put it into writing, and it shall be forwarded to the Office for the Reception of Reports and Returns. Thereafter that Office will consider it, and return it to me, who will, in turn, dispatch it to the Estate Works Committee, who will, in turn, revise it, and present it to the Administrator, who, jointly with the Secretary, will——"

" Pardon me," expostulated Chichikov, " but that procedure will take up a great deal of time. Why need I put the matter into writing at all? It is simply this. I want a few souls which are—well, which are, so to speak, dead."

" Very good," commented the Colonel. " Do you write down in your State of Plea that the souls which you desire are, ' so to speak, dead.' "

" But what would be the use of my doing so? Though the souls are dead, my purpose requires that they should be represented as alive."

" Very good," again commented the Colonel. " Do you write down in your Statement that ' it is necessary ' (or, should you prefer an alternative phrase, ' it is requested,' or ' it is desiderated,' or ' it is prayed ') ' that the souls be represented as alive.' At all events, *without* documentary process of that kind, the matter cannot possibly be carried through. Also, I will appoint a Commissioner to guide you round the various Offices."

And he sounded a bell; whereupon there presented himself a man whom, addressing as " Secretary," the Colonel instructed to summon the " Commissioner." The latter, on appearing, was seen to have the air, half of a peasant, half of an official.

" This man," the Colonel said to Chichikov, " will act as your escort."

What could be done with a lunatic like Koshkarev? In the end, curiosity moved Chichikov to accompany the Commissioner. The Committee for the Reception of Reports and Returns was discovered to have put up its shutters, and to have locked its doors, for the reason that the Director of the Committee had been transferred to the newly-formed Committee of Estate Management, and his successor had been annexed by the same Committee. Next, Chichikov and his escort rapped at the doors of the Department of Estate Affairs; but that Department's quarters happened to be in process of repair, and no one could be made to answer the summons save a drunken peasant from whom not a word of sense was to be extracted. At length the escort himself felt moved to remark:

" There is a deal of foolishness going on here. Fellows like that drunkard lead the *barin* by the nose, and everything is ruled by the Committee of Management, which takes men from their proper work, and sets them to do any other it likes. Indeed, only through the Committee does *anything* get done."

By this time Chichikov felt that he had seen enough; wherefore he returned to the Colonel, and informed him that the Office for the Reception of Reports and Returns had ceased to exist. At once the Colonel flamed to noble rage. Pressing Chichikov's hand in token of gratitude for the information which the guest had furnished, he took paper and pen, and noted eight searching questions for presentation under three separate headings: (1) " Why has the Committee of Management presumed to issue orders to officials not under its jurisdiction? " (2) " Why has the Chief Manager permitted his predecessor, though still in retention of his post, to follow him to another Department? " and (3) " Why has the Committee of Estate Affairs suffered the Office for the Reception of Reports and Returns to lapse? "

" Now for a row! " thought Chichikov to himself, and turned to depart; but his host stopped him, saying:

" I cannot let you go, for, in addition to my honour having become involved, it behoves me to show my people how the regular, the organised, administration of an estate may be conducted. Herewith I will hand over the conduct of your affair to a man who is worth all the rest of the staff put together, and has had a university education. Also, the better to lose no time, may I humbly beg you to step into my library, where you will find notebooks, paper, pens, and everything else that you may require. Of these articles pray make full use, for you are a gentleman of letters, and it is your and my joint duty to bring enlightenment to all."

So saying, he ushered his guest into a large room lined from floor to ceiling with books and stuffed specimens. The books in question were divided into sections—a section on forestry, a section on cattle-breeding, a section on the raising of swine, and a section on horticulture, together with special journals of the type circulated merely for purposes of reference, and not for general reading. Perceiving that these works were scarcely of a kind calculated to while away an idle hour, Chichikov turned to a second bookcase. But to do so was to fall out of the frying-pan into the fire, for the contents of the second bookcase proved to be works on philosophy, while, in particular, six huge volumes confronted him under a label inscribed " A Preparatory Course to the Province of Thought, with the Theory of Community of Effort, Co-operation, and Subsistence, in its Application to a Right Understanding of the Organic Principles of a Mutual Division of Social Productivity." Indeed, wheresoever Chichikov looked, every page presented to his vision some such words as " phenomenon," " development," " abstract," " contents," and " synopsis." " This is not the sort of thing for me," he murmured, and turned his attention to a third bookcase, which contained books on the Arts. Extracting a huge tome in which some by no means reticent mythological illustrations were contained, he set himself to examine these pictures. They were of the kind which pleases mostly middle-aged bachelors and old men who are accustomed to seek in the ballet and similar frivolities a further spur to their waning passions. Having concluded his examination, Chichikov had just extracted another volume of the same species when Colonel Koshkarev returned with a document of some sort and a radiant countenance.

" Everything has been carried through in due form ! " he cri[es?]
" The man whom I mentioned is a genius indeed, ar[nd I]
intend not only to promote him over the rest, but also to

for him a special Department. Herewith shall you hear what a splendid intellect is his, and how in a few minutes he has put the whole affair in order."

"May the Lord be thanked for that!" thought Chichikov. Then he settled himself to listen while the Colonel read aloud:

"'After giving full consideration to the Reference which your Excellency has entrusted to me, I have the honour to report as follows:

"'(1) In the Statement of Plea presented by one Paul Ivanovitch Chichikov, Gentleman, Chevalier, and Collegiate Councillor, there lurks an error, in that an oversight has led the Petitioner to apply to Revisional Souls the term "Dead." Now, from the context it would appear that by this term the Petitioner desires to signify Souls Approaching Death rather than Souls Actually Deceased: wherefore the term employed betrays such an empirical instruction in letters as must, beyond doubt, have been confined to the Village School, seeing that in truth the Soul is Deathless.'"

"The rascal!" Koshkarev broke off to exclaim delightedly. "He has got you there, Monsieur Chichikov. And you will admit that he has a sufficiently incisive pen?"

"'(2) On this Estate there exist no Unmortgaged Souls whatsoever, whether Approaching Death or Otherwise; for the reason that all Souls thereon have been pledged not only under a First Deed of Mortgage, but also (for the sum of One Hundred and Fifty Roubles per Soul) under a Second,—the village of Gurmailovka alone excepted, in that, in consequence of a Suit having been brought against Landowner Priadistchev, and of a *caveat* having been pronounced by the Land Court, and of such *caveat* having been published in No. 42 of the *Gazette of Moscow*, the said Village has come within the Jurisdiction of the Court Above-Mentioned.'"

"Why did you not tell me all this before?" cried Chichikov furiously. "Why have you kept me dancing about for nothing?"

"Because it was absolutely necessary that you should view the matter through forms of documentary process. This is no jest on my part. The inexperienced may see things subconsciously, yet it is imperative that he should also see them *consciously*."

But to Chichikov's patience an end had come. Seizing his cap, and casting all ceremony to the winds, he fled from the house, and rushed through the courtyard. As it happened, the man who had driven him thither had, warned by experience, not troubled even to take out the horses, since he knew that such a proceeding would have entailed not only the presentation of a Statement of Plea for fodder, but also a delay of twenty-four hours until the Resolution granting the same should have been passed. Nevertheless the Colonel pursued his guest to the gates, and pressed his hand warmly as he thanked him for having enabled him (the Colonel) thus to exhibit in operation the proper management of an estate. Also, he begged to state that, under the circumstances, it was absolutely necessary to keep things moving and circulating, since, otherwise, slackness was apt to supervene, and the working of the machine to grow rusty and feeble; but that, in spite of all, the present occasion had inspired him with a happy idea—namely, the idea of instituting a Committee which should be entitled "The Committee of Supervision of the Committee of Management," and which should have for its function the detection of backsliders among the body first mentioned.

It was late when, tired and dissatisfied, Chichikov regained Kostanzhoglo's mansion. Indeed, the candles had long been lit.

"What has delayed you?" asked the master of the house as Chichikov entered the drawing-room.

"Yes; what has kept you and the Colonel so long in conversation together?" added Platon.

"This—the fact that never in my life have I come across such an imbecile," was Chichikov's reply.

"Never mind," said Kostanzhoglo. "Koshkarev is a most reassuring phenomenon. He is necessary in that in him we see expressed in caricature all the more crying follies of our intellectuals—of the intellectuals who, without first troubling to make themselves acquainted with their own country, borrow sillinesses from abroad. Yet that is how certain of our landowners are now carrying on. They have set up 'offices' and factories and schools and 'commissions,' and the devil knows what else besides. A fine lot of wiseacres! After the French War of 1812 they had to reconstruct their affairs: and see how they have done it! Yet so much worse have they done it than a Frenchman would have done that any fool of a Peter Petrovitch Pietukh now ranks as a good landowner!"

"But he has mortgaged the whole of his estate?" remarked Chichikov.

"Yes, nowadays everything is being mortgaged, or is going to be." This said, Kostanzhoglo's temper rose still further. "Out upon your factories of hats and candles!" he cried. "Out upon procuring candle-makers from London, and then turning land-owners into hucksters! To think of a Russian *pomiestchik*,[1] a member of the noblest of callings, conducting workshops and cotton mills! Why, it is for the wenches of towns to handle looms for muslin and lace."

" But you yourself maintain workshops? " remarked Platon.

" I do; but who established them? They established them-selves. For instance, wool had accumulated, and since I had nowhere to store it, I began to weave it into cloth—but, mark you, only into good, plain cloth of which I can dispose at a cheap rate in the local markets, and which is needed by peasants, including my own. Again, for six years on end did the fish factories keep dumping their offal on my bank of the river; wherefore at last, as there was nothing to be done with it, I took to boiling it into glue, and cleared forty thousand roubles by the process.

" The devil! " thought Chichikov to himself as he stared at his host. " What a fist this man has for making money! "

" Another reason why I started those factories," continued Kostanzhoglo, " is that they might give employment to many peasants who would otherwise have starved. You see, the year happened to have been a lean one—thanks to those same industry-mongering landowners, in that they had neglected to sow their crops; and now my factories keep growing at the rate of a factory a year, owing to the circumstance that such quanti-ties of remnants and cuttings become so accumulated that, if a man looks carefully to his management, he will find every sort of rubbish to be capable of bringing in a return—yes, to the point of his having to reject money on the plea that he has no need of it. Yet I do not find that to do all this I require to build a mansion with façades and pillars! "

" Marvellous! " exclaimed Chichikov. " Beyond all things does it surprise me that refuse can be so utilised."

" Yes, and that is what can be done by *simple* methods. But nowadays every one is a mechanic, and wants to open the money chest with an instrument instead of simply. For that purpose he hies him to England. Yes, *that* is the thing to do. What folly! " Kostanzhoglo spat and added: " Yet when he returns from abroad he is a hundred times more ignorant than when he went.

" Ah, Constantine," put in his wife anxiously, " you know how bad for you it is to talk like this."

[1] Landowner.

"Yes, but how am I to help losing my temper? The thing touches me too closely, it vexes me too deeply to think that the Russian character should be degenerating. For in that character there has dawned a sort of Quixotism which never used to be there. Yes, no sooner does a man get a little education into his head than he becomes a Don Quixote, and establishes schools on his estate such as even a madman would never have dreamed of. And from that school there issues a workman who is good for nothing, whether in the country or in the town—a fellow who drinks and is for ever standing on his dignity. Yet still our landowners keep taking to philanthropy, to converting themselves into philanthropic knights-errant, and spending millions upon senseless hospitals and institutions, and so ruining themselves and turning their families adrift. Yes, that is all that comes of philanthropy."

Chichikov's business had nothing to do with the spread of enlightenment, he was but seeking an opportunity to inquire further concerning the putting of refuse to lucrative uses; but Kostanzhoglo would not let him get a word in edgeways, so irresistibly did the flow of sarcastic comment pour from the speaker's lips.

"Yes," went on Kostanzhoglo, "folk are always scheming to educate the peasant. But first make him well-off and a good farmer. *Then* he will educate himself fast enough. As things are now, the world has grown stupid to a degree that passes belief. Look at the stuff that our present-day scribblers write! Let any sort of a book be published, and at once you will see every one making a rush for it. Similarly will you find folk saying: 'The peasant leads an over-simple life. He ought to be familiarised with luxuries, and so led to yearn for things above his station.' And the result of such luxuries will be that the peasant will become a rag rather than a man, and suffer from the devil only knows what diseases, until there will remain in the land not a boy of eighteen who will not have experienced the whole gamut of them, and found himself left with not a tooth in his jaws or a hair on his pate. Yes, that is what will come of infecting the peasant with such rubbish. But, thank God, there is still one healthy class left to us—a class which has never taken up with the 'advantages' of which I speak. For that we ought to be grateful. And since, even yet, the Russian agriculturist remains the most respect-worthy man in the land, why should he be touched? Would to God every one were an agriculturist!"

"Then you believe agriculture to be the most profitable of occupations?" said Chichikov.

"The best, at all events—if not the most profitable. 'In the sweat of thy brow shalt thou till the land.' To quote that requires no great wisdom, for the experience of ages has shown us that, in the agricultural calling, man has ever remained more moral, more pure, more noble than in any other. Of course I do not mean to imply that no other calling ought to be practised: simply that the calling in question lies at the root of all the rest. However much factories may be established privately or by the law, there will still lie ready to man's hand all that he needs— he will still require none of those amenities which are sapping the vitality of our present-day folk, nor any of those industrial establishments which make their profit, and keep themselves going, by causing foolish measures to be adopted which, in the end, are bound to deprave and corrupt our unfortunate masses. I myself am determined never to establish any manufacture, however profitable, which will give rise to a demand for 'higher things,' such as sugar and tobacco—no not if I lose a million by my refusing to do so. If corruption *must* overtake the *mir*, it shall not be through my hands. And I think that God will justify me in my resolve. Twenty years have I lived among the common folk, and I know what will inevitably come of such things."

"But what surprises me most," persisted Chichikov, "is that from refuse it should be possible, with good management, to make such an immensity of profit."

"And as for political economy," continued Kostanzhoglo, without noticing him, and with his face charged with bilious sarcasm, "—as for political economy, it is a fine thing indeed. Just one fool sitting on another fool's back, and flogging him along, even though the rider can see no further than his own nose! Yet into the saddle will that fool climb—spectacles and all! Oh, the folly, the folly of such things!" And the speaker spat derisively.

"That may be true," said his wife. "Yet you must not get angry about it. Surely one can speak on such subjects without losing one's temper?"

"As I listen to you, most worthy Constantine Thedorovitch," Chichikov hastened to remark, "it becomes plain to me that you have penetrated to the meaning of life, and laid your finger upon the essential root of the matter. Yet supposing, for a moment, we leave the affairs of humanity in general, and turn our attention to a purely individual affair, might I ask you how, in the case of a man becoming a landowner, and having a mind to grow wealthy as quickly as possible (in order that he may fulfil his bounden obligations as a citizen), he can best set about it?"

"How he can best set about growing wealthy?" repeated Kostanzhoglo. "Why,——"

"Let us go to supper," interrupted the lady of the house, rising from her chair, and moving towards the centre of the room, where she wrapped her shivering young form in a shawl. Chichikov sprang up with the alacrity of a military man, offered her his arm, and escorted her, as on parade, to the dining-room, where awaiting them there was the soup-tureen. From it the lid had just been removed, and the room was redolent of the fragrant odour of early spring roots and herbs. The company took their seats, and at once the servants placed the remainder of the dishes (under covers) upon the table and withdrew, for Kostanzhoglo hated to have servants listening to their employers' conversation, and objected still more to their staring at him all the while that he was eating.

When the soup had been consumed, and glasses of an excellent vintage resembling Hungarian wine had been poured out, Chichikov said to his host:

"Most worthy sir, allow me once more to direct your attention to the subject of which we were speaking at the point when the conversation became interrupted. You will remember that I was asking you how best a man can set about, proceed in, the matter of growing . . ."

[Here from the original two pages are missing.]

. . ."A property for which, had he asked forty thousand, I should still have demanded a reduction."

"Hm!" thought Chichikov; then added aloud: "But why do you not purchase it yourself?"

"Because to everything there must be assigned a limit. Already my property keeps me sufficiently employed. Moreover, I should cause our local *dvoriané* to begin crying out in chorus that I am exploiting their extremities, their ruined position, for the purpose of acquiring land for under its value. Of that I am weary."

"How readily folk speak evil!" exclaimed Chichikov.

"Yes, and the amount of evil-speaking in our province surpasses belief. Never will you hear my name mentioned without my being called also a miser and a usurer of the worst possible sort; whereas my accusers justify themselves in everything, and say that, ‘though we have wasted our money, we have started a demand for the higher amenities of life, and therefore encouraged industry with our wastefulness, a far better way of doing things than that practised by Kostanzhoglo, who lives like a pig.’ ”

“ Would *I* could live in your ‘ piggish ’ fashion! ” ejaculated Chichikov.

“ And so forth, and so forth. Yet what are the ‘ higher amenities of life ’? What good can they do to any one? Even if a landowner of the day sets up a library, he never looks at a single book in it, but soon relapses into card-playing — the usual pursuit. Yet folk call me names simply because I do not waste my means upon the giving of dinners! One reason why I do not give such dinners is that they weary me; and another reason is that I am not used to them. But come you to my house for the purpose of taking pot luck, and I shall be delighted to see you. Also, folk foolishly say that I lend money on interest; whereas the truth is that if you should come to me when you are really in need, and should explain to me openly how you propose to employ my money, and I should perceive that you are purposing to use that money wisely, and that you are really likely to profit thereby—well, in that case you would find me ready to lend you all that you might ask without interest at all.”

“ That is a thing which it is as well to know,” reflected Chichikov.

“ Yes,” repeated Kostanzhoglo, “ under those circumstances I should never refuse you my assistance. But I do object to throwing my money to the winds. Pardon me for expressing myself so plainly. To think of lending money to a man who is merely devising a dinner to his mistress, or planning to furnish his house like a lunatic, or thinking of taking his paramour to a masked ball or a jubilee in honour of some one who had better never have been born! ”

And, spitting, he came near to venting some expression which would scarcely have been becoming in the presence of his wife. Over his face the dark shadow of hypochondria had cast a cloud, and furrows had formed on his brow and temples, and his every gesture bespoke the influence of a hot, nervous rancour.

“ But allow me once more to direct your attention to the subject of our recently interrupted conversation,” persisted Chichikov as he sipped a glass of excellent raspberry wine.

" That is to say, supposing I were to acquire the property which you have been good enough to bring to my notice, how long would it take me to grow rich? "

" That would depend upon yourself," replied Kostanzhoglo with grim abruptness and evident ill-humour. " You might either grow rich quickly or you might never grow rich at all. If you made up your mind to grow rich, sooner or later you would find yourself a wealthy man."

" Indeed? " ejaculated Chichikov.

" Yes," replied Kostanzhoglo, as sharply as though he were angry with Chichikov. " You would merely need to be fond of work: otherwise you would effect nothing. The main thing is to like looking after your property. Believe me, you would never grow weary of doing so. People would have it that life in the country is dull; whereas, if I were to spend a single day as it is spent by some folk, with their stupid clubs and their restaurants and their theatres, I should die of *ennui*. The fools, the idiots, the generation of blind dullards! But a landowner never finds the days wearisome—he has not the time. In his life not a moment remains unoccupied; it is full to the brim. And with it all goes an endless variety of occupations. And what occupations! Occupations which genuinely uplift the soul, seeing that the landowner walks with nature and the seasons of the year, and takes part in, and is intimate with, everything which is evolved by creation. For let us look at the round of the year's labours. Even before spring has arrived there will have begun a general watching and a waiting for it, and a preparing for sowing, and an apportioning of crops, and a measuring of seed grain by byres, and a drying of seed, and a dividing of the workers into teams. For everything needs to be examined beforehand, and calculations must be made at the very start. And as soon as ever the ice shall have melted, and the rivers be flowing, and the land have dried sufficiently to be workable, the spade will begin its task in kitchen and flower garden, and the plough and the harrow their tasks in the field; until everywhere there will be tilling and sowing and planting. And do you understand what the sum of that labour will mean? It will mean that the harvest is being sown, that the welfare of the world is being sown, that the food of millions is being put into the earth. And thereafter will come summer, the season of reaping, endless reaping; for suddenly the crops will have ripened, and rye-sheaf will be lying heaped upon rye-sheaf, with, elsewhere, shocks of barley, and of oats. and of wheat. And everything will be teeming with life, and not a moment will there be to be lost, seeing that, had you even twenty eyes, you would have need for them all. And after the harvest festivities there will be grain to be carted to byre or stacked in ricks, and stores to be prepared for the winter, and storehouses and kilns and cattle-sheds to be cleaned for the same purpose, and the women to be assigned their tasks, and the totals of everything to be calculated, so that one may see the value of what has been done. And lastly will come winter, when in every threshing-floor the flail will be working, and the grain, when threshed, will need to be carried from barn to binn, and the mills require to be seen to, and the estate factories to be inspected, and the workmen's huts to be visited for the purpose of ascertaining how the *muzhik* is faring (for, given a carpenter who is clever with his tools, I, for one, am only too glad to spend an hour or two in his company, so cheering to me is labour). And if, in addition, one discerns the end to which everything is moving, and the manner in which the things of earth are everywhere multiplying and multiplying, and bringing forth more and more fruit to one's profiting, I cannot adequately express what takes place in a man's soul. And that, not because of the growth in his wealth—money is money and no more—but because he will feel that everything is the work of his own hands, and that he has been the cause of everything, and its creator, and that from him, as from a magician, there has flowed bounty and goodness for all. In what other calling will you find such delights in prospect?" As he spoke, Kostanzhoglo raised his face, and it became clear that the wrinkles had fled from it, and that, like the Tsar on the solemn day of his crowning, Kostanzhoglo's whole form was diffusing light, and his features had in them a gentle radiance. "In all the world," he repeated, "you will find no joys like these, for herein man imitates the God who projected creation as the supreme happiness, and now demands of man that he, too, should act as the creator of prosperity. Yet there are folk who call such functions tedious!"

Kostanzhoglo's mellifluous periods fell upon Chichikov's ear like the notes of a bird of paradise. From time to time he gulped, and his softened eyes expressed the pleasure which it gave him to listen.

"Constantine, it is time to leave the table," said the lady of the house, rising from her seat. Every one followed her example, and Chichikov again acted as his hostess's escort—though with less dexterity of deportment than before, owing to the fact that this time his thoughts were occupied with more essential matters of procedure.

" In spite of what you say," remarked Platon as he walked behind the pair, " I, for my part, find these things wearisome."

But the master of the house paid no attention to his remark, for he was reflecting that his guest was no fool, but a man of serious thought and speech who did not take things lightly. And, with the thought, Kostanzhoglo grew lighter in soul, as though he had warmed himself with his own words, and were exulting in the fact that he had found some one capable of listening to good advice.

When they had settled themselves in the cosy, candle-lighted drawing-room, with its balcony and the glass door opening out into the garden—a door through which the stars could be seen glittering amid the slumbering tops of the trees—Chichikov felt more comfortable than he had done for many a day past. It was as though, after long journeying, his own roof-tree had received him once more—had received him when his quest had been accomplished, when all that he wished for had been gained, when his travelling-staff had been laid aside with the words " It is finished." And of this seductive frame of mind the true source had been the eloquent discourse of his hospitable host. Yes, for every man there exist certain things which, instantly that they are said, seem to touch him more closely, more intimately, than anything has done before. Nor is it an uncommon occurrence that in the most unexpected fashion, and in the most retired of retreats, one will suddenly come face to face with a man whose burning periods will lead one to forget oneself and the tracklessness of the route and the discomfort of one's nightly halting-places, and the futility of crazes and the falseness of the tricks by which one human being deceives another. And at once there will become engraven upon one's memory—vividly, and for all time—the evening thus spent. And of that evening one's remembrance will hold true, both as to who was present, and where each such person sat, and what he or she was wearing, and what the walls and the stove and other trifling features of the room looked like.

In the same way did Chichikov note each detail that evening —both the appointments of the agreeable, but not luxuriously furnished, room, and the good-humoured expression which reigned on the face of the thoughtful host, and the design of the curtains, and the amber-mounted pipe smoked by Platon, and the way in which he kept puffing smoke into the fat jowl of the

dog Yarb, and the sneeze which, on each such occasion, Yarb
vented, and the laughter of the pleasant-faced hostess (though
always followed by the words " Pray do not tease him any
more "), and the cheerful candle-light, and the cricket chirping
in a corner, and the glass door, and the spring night which,
laying its elbows upon the tree-tops, and spangled with stars,
and vocal with the nightingales which were pouring forth
warbled ditties from the recesses of the foliage, kept glancing
through the door, and regarding the company within.

" How it delights me to hear your words, good Constantine
Thedorovitch! " said Chichikov. " Indeed, nowhere in Russia
have I met with a man of equal intellect."

Kostanzhoglo smiled, while realising that the compliment was
scarcely deserved.

" If you want a man of *genuine* intellect," he said, " I can tell
you of one. He is a man whose boot soles are worth more than
my whole body."

" Who may he be? " asked Chichikov in astonishment.

" Murazov, our local Commissioner of Taxes."

" Ah! I have heard of him before," remarked Chichikov.

" He is a man who, were he not the director of an estate,
might well be a director of the Empire. And were the Empire
under my direction, I should at once appoint him my Minister
of Finance."

" I have heard tales beyond belief concerning him — for
instance, that he has acquired ten million roubles."

" Ten? More than forty. Soon half Russia will be in his
hands."

" You don't say so? " cried Chichikov in amazement.

" Yes, certainly. The man who has only a hundred thousand
roubles to work with grows rich but slowly, whereas he who has
millions at his disposal can operate over a greater radius, and
so back whatsoever he undertakes with twice or thrice the
money which can be brought against him. Consequently his
field becomes so spacious that he ends by having no rivals.
Yes, no one can compete with him, and, whatsoever price he
may fix for a given commodity, at that price it will have to
remain, nor will any man be able to outbid it."

" My God! " muttered Chichikov, crossing himself, and staring at Kostanzhoglo with his breath catching in his throat.
" The mind cannot grasp it—it petrifies one's thoughts with
awe. You see folk marvelling at what Science has achieved in
the matter of investigating the habits of cowbugs, but to me it

is a far more marvellous thing that in the hands of a single mortal there can become accumulated such gigantic sums of money. But may I ask whether the great fortune of which you speak has been acquired through honest means?"

"Yes; through means of the most irreproachable kind—through the most honourable of methods."

"Yet so improbable does it seem that I can scarcely believe it. Thousands I could understand; but millions——!"

"On the contrary, to make thousands honestly is a far more difficult matter than to make millions. Millions are easily come by, for a millionaire has no need to resort to crooked ways; the way lies straight before him, and he needs but to annex whatsoever he comes across. No rival will spring up to oppose him, for no rival will be sufficiently strong, and since the millionaire can operate over an extensive radius, he can bring (as I have said) two or three roubles to bear upon any one else's one. Consequently, what interest will he derive from a thousand roubles? Why, ten or twenty per cent. at the least."

"And it is beyond measure marvellous that the whole should have started from a single kopeck."

"Had it started otherwise, the thing could never have been done at all. Such is the normal course. He who is born with thousands, and is brought up to thousands, will never acquire a single kopeck more, for he will have been set up with the amenities of life in advance, and so never come to stand in need of anything. It is necessary to begin from the beginning rather than from the middle; from a kopeck rather than from a rouble; from the bottom rather than from the top. For only thus will a man get to know the men and conditions among which his career will have to be carved. That is to say, through encountering the rough and the tumble of life, and through learning that every kopeck has to be beaten out with a three-kopeck nail, and through worsting knave after knave, he will acquire such a degree of perspicuity and wariness that he will err in nothing which he may tackle, and never come to ruin. Believe me, it is so. The beginning, not the middle, is the right starting point. No one who comes to me and says, ' Give me a hundred thousand roubles, and I will grow rich in no time,' do I believe, for he is likely to meet with failure rather than with the success of which he is so assured. 'Tis with a kopeck, and with a kopeck only, that a man must begin."

"If that is so, *I* shall grow rich," said Chichikov, involuntarily remembering the dead souls. " For of a surety *I* began with nothing."

" Constantine, pray allow Paul Ivanovitch to retire to rest," put in the lady of the house. " It is high time, and I am sure you have talked enough."

" Yes, beyond a doubt you will grow rich," continued Kostanzhoglo, without heeding his wife. " For towards you there will run rivers and rivers of gold, until you will not know what to do with all your gains."

As though spellbound, Chichikov sat in an aureate world of ever-growing dreams and fantasies. All his thoughts were in a whirl, and on a carpet of future wealth his tumultuous imagination was weaving golden patterns, while ever in his ears were ringing the words " towards you there will run rivers and rivers of gold."

" Really, Constantine, *do* allow Paul Ivanovitch to go to bed."

" What on earth is the matter? " retorted the master of the house testily. " Pray go yourself if you wish to." Then he stopped short, for the snoring of Platon was filling the whole room, and also—outrivalling it—that of the dog Yarb. This caused Kostanzhoglo to realise that bedtime really had arrived; wherefore, after he had shaken Platon out of his slumbers, and bidden Chichikov good night, all dispersed to their several chambers, and became plunged in sleep.

All, that is to say, except Chichikov, whose thoughts remained wakeful, and who kept wondering and wondering how best he could become the owner, not of a fictitious, but of a real, estate. The conversation with his host had made everything clear, had made the possibility of his acquiring riches manifest, had made the difficult art of estate management at once easy and understandable; until it would seem as though particularly was his nature adapted for mastering the art in question. All that he would need to do would be to mortgage the dead souls, and then to set up a genuine establishment. Already he saw himself acting and administering as Kostanzhoglo had advised him —energetically, and through personal oversight, and undertaking nothing new until the old had been thoroughly learned, and viewing everything with his own eyes, and making himself familiar with each member of his peasantry, and abjuring all superfluities, and giving himself up to hard work and husbandry. Yes, already could he taste the pleasure which would be his when he had built up a complete industrial organisation, and the springs of the industrial machine were in vigorous working order, and each had become able to reinforce the other. Labour should be kept in active operation, and, even as, in a mill, flour comes flowing from grain, so should cash, and yet more cash, come flowing from every atom of refuse and remnant. And all the while he could see before him the landowner who was one of the leading men in Russia, and for whom he had conceived such an unbounded respect. Hitherto only for rank or for opulence had Chichikov respected a man—never for mere intellectual power; but now he made a first exception in favour of Kostanzhoglo, seeing that he felt that nothing undertaken by his host could possibly come to naught. And another project which was occupying Chichikov's mind was the project of purchasing the estate of a certain landowner named Khlobuev. Already Chichikov had at his disposal ten thousand roubles, and a further fifteen thousand he would try and borrow of Kostanzhoglo (seeing that the latter had himself said that he was prepared to help any one who really desired to grow rich); while, as for the remainder, he would either raise the sum by mortgaging the estate or force Khlobuev to wait for it—just tell him to resort to the courts if such might be his pleasure.

Long did our hero ponder the scheme; until at length the slumber which had, these four hours past, been holding the rest of the household in its embraces enfolded also Chichikov, and he sank into oblivion.

IV

NEXT day, with Platon and Constantine, Chichikov set forth to interview Khlobuev, the owner whose estate Constantine had consented to help Chichikov to purchase with a non-interest-bearing, uncovenanted loan of ten thousand roubles. Naturally, our hero was in the highest of spirits. For the first fifteen *versts* or so the road led through forest land and tillage belonging to Platon and his brother-in-law; but directly the limit of these domains was reached, forest land began to be replaced with swamp, and tillage with waste. Also, the village on Khlobuev's estate had about it a deserted air, and as for the proprietor himself, he was discovered in a state of drowsy dishevelment, having not long left his bed. A man of about forty, he had his cravat crooked, his frockcoat adorned with a large stain, and one of his boots worn through. Nevertheless he seemed delighted to see his visitors.

"What?" he exclaimed. "Constantine Thedorovitch and Platon Mikhailovitch? Really I must rub my eyes! Never again in this world did I look to see callers arriving. As a rule, folk avoid me like the devil, for they cannot disabuse their minds of the idea that I am going to ask them for a loan. Yes, it is my own fault, I know, but what would you? To the end will swine cheat swine. Pray excuse my costume. You will observe that my boots are in holes. But how can I afford to get them mended?"

"Never mind," said Constantine. "We have come on business only. May I present to you a possible purchaser of your estate, in the person of Paul Ivanovitch Chichikov?"

"I am indeed glad to meet you!" was Khlobuev's response. "Pray shake hands with me, Paul Ivanovitch."

Chichikov offered not one hand, but both.

"I can show you a property worth your attention," went on the master of the estate. "May I ask if you have yet dined?"

"Yes, we have," put in Constantine, desirous of escaping as soon as possible. "To save you further trouble, let us go and view the estate at once."

"Very well," replied Khlobuev. "Pray come and inspect my irregularities and futilities. You have done well to dine beforehand, for not so much as a fowl is left in the place, so dire are the extremities to which you see me reduced."

Sighing deeply, he took Platon by the arm (it was clear that he did not look for any sympathy from Constantine), and walked ahead, while Constantine and Chichikov followed.

"Things are going hard with me, Platon Mikhailovitch," continued Khlobuev. "How hard you cannot imagine. No money have I, no food, no boots. Were I still young and a bachelor, it would have come easy to me to live on bread and cheese; but when a man is growing old, and has got a wife and five children, such trials press heavily upon him, and, in spite of himself, his spirits sink."

"But, should you succeed in selling the estate, that would help to put you right, would it not?" said Platon.

"How could it do so?" replied Khlobuev with a despairing gesture. "What I might get for the property would have to go towards discharging my debts, and I should find myself left with less than a thousand roubles besides."

"Then what do you intend to do?"

" God knows! "

" But is there *nothing* to which you could set your hand in order to clear yourself of your difficulties? "

" How could there be? "

" Well, you might accept a Government post."

" Become a provincial secretary, you mean? How could I obtain such a post? They would not offer me one of the meanest possible kind. Even supposing that they did, how could I live on a salary of five hundred roubles—I who have a wife and five children? "

" Then try and obtain a bailiff's post."

" Who would entrust their property to a man who has squandered his own estate? "

" Nevertheless, when death and destitution threaten, a man must either do something or starve. Shall I ask my brother to use his influence to procure you a post? "

" No, no, Platon Mikhailovitch," sighed Khlobuev, gripping the other's hand. " I am no longer serviceable—I am grown old before my time, and find that liver and rheumatism are paying me for the sins of my youth. Why should the Government be put to a loss on my account?—not to speak of the fact that for every salaried post there are countless numbers of applicants. God forbid that, in order to provide me with a livelihood farther burdens should be imposed upon an impoverished public! "

" Such are the results of improvident management! " thought Platon to himself. " The disease is even worse than my sloth-fulness."

Meanwhile Kostanzhoglo, walking by Chichikov's side, was almost taking leave of his senses.

" Look at it! " he cried with a wave of his hand. " See to what wretchedness the peasant has become reduced! Should cattle disease come, Khlobuev will have nothing to fall back upon, but will be forced to sell his all—to leave the peasant without a horse, and therefore without the means to labour, even though the loss of a single day's work may take years of labour to rectify. Meanwhile it is plain that the local peasant has become a mere dissolute, lazy drunkard. Give a *muzhik* enough to live upon for twelve months without working, and you will corrupt him for ever, so inured to rags and vagrancy will he grow. And what is the good of that piece of pasture there—of that piece on the further side of those huts? It is a mere flooded tract. Were it mine, I should put it under flax, and clear five thousand roubles, or else sow it with turnips, and clear, perhaps, four thousand. And see how that rye is drooping, and nearly laid. As for wheat, I am pretty sure that he has not sown any. Look, too, at those ravines! Were they mine, they would be standing under timber which even a rook could not top. To think of wasting such quantities of land! Where land wouldn't bear corn, I should dig it up, and plant it with vegetables. What ought to be done is that Khlobuev ought to take a spade into his own hands, and to set his wife and children and servants to do the same; and even if they died of the exertion, they would at least die doing their duty, and not through guzzling at the dinner table."

This said, Kostanzhoglo spat, and his brow flushed with grim indignation.

Presently they reached an elevation whence the distant flashing of a river, with its flood waters and subsidiary streams, caught the eye, while, further off, a portion of General Betristchev's homestead could be discerned among the trees, and, over it, a blue, densely wooded hill which Chichikov guessed to be the spot where Tientietnikov's mansion was situated.

"This is where I should plant timber," said Chichikov. "And, regarded as a site for a manor house, the situation could scarcely be beaten for beauty of view."

"You seem to set great store upon views and beauty," remarked Kostanzhoglo with reproof in his tone. "Should you pay too much attention to those things, you might find yourself without crops or view. Utility should be placed first, not beauty. Beauty will come of itself. Take, for example, towns. The fairest and most beautiful towns are those which have built themselves—those in which each man has built to suit his own exclusive circumstances and needs; whereas towns which men have constructed on regular, string-taut lines are no better than collections of barracks. Put beauty aside, and look only to what is *necessary*."

"Yes, but to me it would always be irksome to have to wait. All the time that I was doing so I should be hungering to see in front of me the sort of prospect which I prefer."

"Come, come! Are you a man of twenty-five—you who have served as a *tchinovnik* in St. Petersburg? Have patience, have patience. For six years work, and work hard. Plant, sow, and dig the earth without taking a moment's rest. It will be difficult, I know—yes, difficult indeed; but at the end of that time, if you have thoroughly stirred the soil, the land will begin to help you as nothing else can do. That is to say, over and above your seventy or so pairs of hands, there will begin to assist in the work seven hundred pairs of hands which you cannot see. Thus everything will be multiplied tenfold. I myself have ceased even to have to lift a finger, for whatsoever needs to be done gets done of itself. Nature loves patience: always remember that. It is a law given her of God Himself, who has blessed all those who are strong to endure."

"To hear your words is to be both encouraged and strengthened," said Chichikov. To this Kostanzhoglo made no reply, but presently went on:

"And see how that piece of land has been ploughed! To stay here longer is more than I can do. For me, to have to look upon such want of orderliness and foresight is death. Finish your business with Khlobuev without me, and, whatsoever you do, get this treasure out of that fool's hands as quickly as possible, for he is dishonouring God's gifts."

And Kostanzhoglo, his face dark with the rage that was seething in his excitable soul, left Chichikov, and caught up the owner of the establishment.

"What, Constantine Thedorovitch?" cried Khlobuev in astonishment. "Just arrived, you are going already?"

"Yes; I cannot help it; urgent business requires me at home." And entering his gig, Kostanzhoglo drove rapidly away. Somehow Khlobuev seemed to divine the cause of his sudden departure.

"It was too much for him," he remarked. "An agriculturist of that kind does not like to have to look upon the results of such feckless management as mine. Would you believe it, Paul Ivanovitch, but this year I have been unable to sow any wheat! Am I not a fine husbandman? There was no seed for the purpose, nor yet anything with which to prepare the ground. No, I am not like Constantine Thedorovitch, who, I hear, is a perfect Napoleon in his particular line. Again and again the thought occurs to me, 'Why has so much intellect been put into that head, and only a drop or two into my own dull pate?' Take care of that puddle, gentlemen. I have told my peasants to lay down planks for the spring, but they have not done so. Nevertheless my heart aches for the poor fellows, for they need a good example, and what sort of an example am I? How am I to give them orders? Pray take them under your charge, Paul Ivanovitch, for I cannot teach them orderliness and method when I myself lack both. As a matter of fact, I should have given them their freedom long ago, had there been any use in my doing so:

for even I can see that peasants must first be afforded the means of earning a livelihood before they can live. What they need is a stern, yet just, master who shall live with them, day in, day out, and set them an example of tireless energy. The present-day Russian—I know it of myself—is helpless without a driver. Without one he falls asleep, and the mould grows over him."

"Yet I cannot understand *why* he should fall asleep and grow mouldy in that fashion," said Platon. "Why should he need continual surveillance to keep him from degenerating into a drunkard and a good-for-nothing?"

"The cause is lack of enlightenment," said Chichikov.

"Possibly — only God knows. Yet enlightenment has reached us right enough. Do we not attend university lectures and everything else that is befitting? Take my own education. I learnt not only the usual things, but also the art of spending money upon the latest refinement, the latest amenity—the art of familiarising oneself with whatsoever money can buy. How, then, can it be said that I was educated foolishly? And my comrades' education was the same. A few of them succeeded in annexing the cream of things, for the reason that they had the wit to do so, and the rest spent their time in doing their best to ruin their health and squander their money. Often I think there is no hope for the present-day Russian. While desiring to do everything, he accomplishes nothing. One day he will scheme to begin a new mode of existence, a new dietary; yet before evening he will have so over-eaten himself as to be unable to speak or do aught but sit staring like an owl. The same with every one."

"Quite so," agreed Chichikov with a smile. "'Tis everywhere the same story."

"To tell the truth, we are not born to common sense. I doubt whether Russia has ever produced a really sensible man. For my own part, if I see my neighbour living a regular life, and making money, and saving it, I begin to distrust him, and to feel certain that in old age, if not before, he too will be led astray by the devil—led astray in a moment. Yes, whether or not we be educated, there is something we lack. But what that something is passes my understanding."

On the return journey the prospect was the same as before. Everywhere the same slovenliness, the same disorder, was displaying itself unadorned: the only difference being that a fresh puddle had formed in the middle of the village street. This want and neglect was noticeable in the peasants' quarters equally with the quarters of the *barin*. In the village a furious woman in greasy sackcloth was beating a poor young wench within an ace of her life, and at the same time devoting some third person to the care of all the devils of hell; further away a couple of peasants were stoically contemplating the virago—one scratching his rump as he did so, and the other one yawning. The same yawn was discernible in the buildings, for not a roof was there but had a gaping hole in it. As he gazed at the scene Platon himself yawned. Patch was superimposed upon patch, and, in place of a roof, one hut had a piece of wooden fencing, while its crumbling window-frames were stayed with sticks purloined from the *barin's* barn. Evidently the system of upkeep in vogue was the system employed in the case of Trishkin's coat—the system of cutting up the cuffs and the collar into mendings for the elbows.

"No, I do not admire your way of doing things," was Chichikov's unspoken comment when the inspection had been concluded and the party had re-entered the house. Everywhere in the latter the visitors were struck with the way in which poverty went with glittering, fashionable profusion. On a writing-table lay a volume of Shakespeare, and, on an occasional table, a carved ivory back-scratcher. The hostess, too, was elegantly and fashionably attired, and devoted her whole conversation to the town and the local theatre. Lastly, the children—bright, merry little things—were well-dressed both as regards boys and girls. Yet far better would it have been for them if they had been clad in plain striped smocks, and running about the courtyard like peasant children. Presently a visitor arrived in the shape of a chattering, gossiping woman; whereupon the hostess carried her off to her own portion of the house, and, the children following them, the men found themselves alone.

"How much do you want for the property?" asked Chichikov of Khlobuev. "I am afraid I must request you to name the lowest possible sum, since I find the estate in a far worse condition than I had expected to do."

"Yes, it *is* in a terrible state, agreed Khlobuev. "Nor is that the whole of the story. That is to say, I will not conceal from you the fact that, out of a hundred souls registered at the last revision, only fifty survive, so terrible have been the ravages of cholera. And of these, again, some have absconded; wherefore they too must be reckoned as dead, seeing that, were one to enter process against them, the costs would end in the property having to pass *en bloc* to the legal authorities. For these reasons I am asking only thirty-five thousand roubles for the estate."

Chichikov (it need hardly be said) started to haggle.

" Thirty-five thousand? " he cried. " Come, come! Surely you will accept *twenty*-five thousand? "

This was too much for Platon's conscience.

" Now, now, Paul Ivanovitch! " he exclaimed. " Take the property at the price named, and have done with it. The estate is worth at least that amount—so much so that, should you not be willing to give it, my brother-in-law and I will club together to effect the purchase."

" That being so," said Chichikov, taken aback, " I beg to agree to the price in question. At the same time, I must ask you to allow me to defer payment of one-half the purchase money until a year from now."

" No, no, Paul Ivanovitch. Under no circumstances could I do that. Pay me half now, and the rest in . . .[1] You see, I need the money for the redemption of the mortgage."

" That places me in a difficulty," remarked Chichikov. " Ten thousand roubles is all that at the moment I have available." As a matter of fact, this was not true, seeing that, counting also the money which he had borrowed of Kostanzhoglo, he had at his disposal *twenty* thousand. His real reason for hesitating was that he disliked the idea of making so large a payment in a lump sum.

" I must repeat my request, Paul Ivanovitch," said Khlobuev, " —namely, that you pay me at least fifteen thousand immediately."

" The odd five thousand *I* will lend you," put in Platon to Chichikov.

" Indeed? " exclaimed Chichikov as he reflected: " So he also lends money! "

In the end Chichikov's dispatch-box was brought from the *koliaska*, and Khlobuev received thence ten thousand roubles, together with a promise that the remaining five thousand should be forthcoming on the morrow; though the promise was given only after Chichikov had first proposed that *three* thousand should be brought on the day named, and the rest be left over for two or three days longer, if not for a still more protracted period. The truth was that Paul Ivanovitch hated parting with money. No matter how urgent a situation might have been, he would still have preferred to pay a sum to-morrow rather than to-day. In other words, he acted as we all do, for we all like keeping a petitioner waiting. " Let him rub his back in the hall

---

[1] Here, in the original, a word is missing.

for a while," we say. " Surely he can bide his time a little? "
Yet of the fact that every hour may be precious to the poor
wretch, and that his business may suffer from the delay, we
take no account. " Good sir," we say, " pray come again to-
morrow. To-day I have no time to spare you."

" Where do you intend henceforth to live? " inquired Platon.
" Have you any other property to which you can retire? "

" No," replied Khlobuev. " I shall remove to the town,
where I possess a small villa. That would have been necessary
in any case, for the children's sake. You see, they must have
instruction in God's word, and also lessons in music and dancing;
and not for love or money can these things be procured in the
country.

" Nothing to eat, yet dancing lessons for his children! "
reflected Chichikov.

" An extraordinary man! " was Platon's unspoken comment.

" However, we must contrive to wet our bargain somehow,"
continued Khlobuev. " Hi, Kirushka! Bring that bottle of
champagne,"

" Nothing to eat, yet champagne to drink! " reflected Chichikov. As for Platon, he did not know *what* to think.

In Khlobuev's eyes it was *de rigueur* that he should provide
a guest with champagne; but, though he had sent to the town
for some, he had been met with a blank refusal to forward even
a bottle of *kvass* on credit. Only the discovery of a French dealer
who had recently transferred his business from St. Petersburg,
and opened a connection on a system of general credit, saved the
situation by placing Khlobuev under the obligation of patronis-
ing him.

The company drank three glassfuls apiece, and so grew more
cheerful. In particular did Khlobuev expand, and wax full of
civility and friendliness, and scatter witticisms and anecdotes to
right and left. What knowledge of men and the world did his
utterances display! How well and accurately could he divine
things! With what appositeness did he sketch the neighbouring
landowners! How clearly he exposed their faults and failings!
How thoroughly he knew the story of certain ruined gentry—
the story of how, why, and through what cause they had fallen
upon evil days! With what comic originality could he describe
their little habits and customs!

In short, his guests found themselves charmed with his
discourse, and felt inclined to vote him a man of first-rate
intellect.

"What most surprises me," said Chichikov, "is how, in view of your ability, you come to be so destitute of means or resources."

"But I have plenty of both," said Khlobuev, and with that went on to deliver himself of a perfect avalanche of projects. Yet those projects proved to be so uncouth, so clumsy, so little the outcome of a knowledge of men and things, that his hearers could only shrug their shoulders, and mentally exclaim: "Good Lord! What a difference between worldly wisdom and the capacity to use it!" In every case the projects in question were based upon the imperative necessity of at once procuring from somewhere two hundred—or at least one hundred—thousand roubles. That done (so Khlobuev averred), everything would fall into its proper place, the management of his affairs would begin to prosper, the holes in his pockets would become stopped, his income would be quadrupled, and he would find himself in a position to liquidate his debts in full. Nevertheless he ended by saying: "What would you advise me to do? I fear that the philanthropist who would lend me two hundred thousand roubles or even a hundred thousand, does not exist. It is not God's will that he should."

"Good gracious!" inwardly ejaculated Chichikov. "To suppose that God would send such a fool two hundred thousand roubles!"

"However," went on Khlobuev, "I possess an aunt worth three millions—a pious old woman who gives freely to churches and monasteries, but finds a difficulty in helping her neighbour. At the same time, she is a lady of the old school, and worth having a peep at. Her canaries alone number four hundred, and, in addition, there is an army of pug-dogs, hangers-on, and servants. Even the youngest of the servants is sixty, but she calls them all 'young fellows,' and if a guest happens to offend her during dinner, she orders them to leave him out when handing the dishes. *There's* a woman for you!"

Platon laughed.

"And what may her family name be?" asked Chichikov. "And where does she live?"

"She lives in the county town, and her name is Alexandra Ivanovna Khanasarov."

"Then why do you not apply to her?" asked Platon earnestly. "It seems to me that, once she realised the position of your family, she could not possibly refuse you."

"Alas! nothing is to be looked for from that quarter," replied Khlobuev. "My aunt is of a very stubborn disposition—

a perfect stone of a woman. Moreover, she has around her a sufficient band of favourites already. In particular is there a fellow who is aiming for a Governorship, and to that end has managed to insinuate himself into the circle of her kinsfolk. By the way," the speaker added, turning to Platon, "would you do me a favour? Next week I am giving a dinner to the associated guilds of the town."

Platon stared. He had been unaware that both in our capitals and in our provincial towns there exists a class of men whose lives are an enigma—men who, though they will seem to have exhausted their substance, and to have become enmeshed in debt, will suddenly be reported as in funds, and on the point of giving a dinner! And though, at this dinner, the guests will declare that the festival is bound to be their host's last fling, and that for a certainty he will be haled to prison on the morrow, ten years or more will elapse, and the rascal still be at liberty, even though, in the meanwhile, his debts will have increased!

In the same way did the conduct of Khlobuev's *ménage* afford a curious phenomenon, for one day the house would be the scene of a solemn Te Deum, performed by a priest in vestments, and the next of a stage play performed by a troupe of French actors in theatrical costume. Again, one day would see not a morsel of bread in the house, and the next day a banquet and generous *largesse* given to a party of artists and sculptors. During these seasons of scarcity (sufficiently severe to have led any one but Khlobuev to seek suicide by hanging or shooting), the master of the house would be preserved from rash action by his strongly religious disposition, which, contriving in some curious way to conform with his irregular mode of life, enabled him to fall back upon reading the lives of saints, ascetics, and others of the type which has risen superior to its misfortunes. And at such times his spirit would become softened, his thoughts full of gentleness, and his eyes wet with tears; he would fall to saying his prayers, and invariably some strange coincidence would bring an answer thereto in the shape of an unexpected measure of assistance. That is to say, some former friend of his would remember him, and send him a trifle in the way of money; or else some female visitor would be moved by his story to let her impulsive, generous heart proffer him a handsome gift; or else a suit whereof tidings had never even reached his ears would end by being decided in his favour. And when that happened he would reverently acknowledge the immensity of the mercy of Providence, gratefully tender thanksgiving for the same, and betake himself again to his irregular mode of existence.

"Somehow I feel sorry for the man," said Platon when he and Chichikov had taken leave of their host, and left the house.

"Perhaps so, but he is a hopeless prodigal," replied the other. "Personally I find it impossible to compassionate such fellows."

And with that the pair ceased to devote another thought to Khlobuev. In the case of Platon, this was because he contemplated the fortunes of his fellows with the lethargic, half-somnolent eye which he turned upon all the rest of the world; for though the sight of the distress of others would cause his heart to contract and feel full of sympathy, the impression thus produced never sank into the depths of his being. Accordingly, before many minutes were over he had ceased to bestow a single thought upon his late host. With Chichikov, however, things were different. Whereas Platon had ceased to think of Khlobuev no more than he had ceased to think of himself, Chichikov's mind had strayed elsewhere, for the reason that it had become taken up with grave meditation on the subject of the purchase just made. Suddenly finding himself no longer a fictitious proprietor, but the owner of a real, an actually existing, estate, he became contemplative, and his plans and ideas assumed such a serious vein as imparted to his features an unconsciously important air.

"Patience and hard work!" he muttered to himself. "The thing will not be difficult, for with those two requisites I have been familiar from the days of my swaddling clothes. Yes, no novelty will they be to me. Yet, in middle age, shall I be able to compass the patience whereof I was capable in my youth?"

However, no matter how he regarded the future, and no matter from what point of view he considered his recent acquisition, he could see nothing but advantage likely to accrue from the bargain. For one thing, he might be able to proceed so that, first the whole of the estate should be mortgaged, and then the better portions of land be sold outright. Or he might so contrive matters as to manage the property for a while (and thus become a landowner like Kostanzhoglo, whose advice, as his neighbour and his benefactor, he intended always to follow), and then to dispose of the property by private treaty (provided he did not wish to continue his ownership), and still to retain in his hands the dead and absconded souls. And another possible *coup* occurred to his mind. That is to say, he might contrive to withdraw from the district without having repaid

Kostanzhoglo at all! Truly a splendid idea! Yet it is only fair to say that the idea was not one of Chichikov's own conception. Rather, it had presented itself—mocking, laughing, and winking—unbidden. Yet the impudent, the wanton thing! Who is the procreator of suddenly born ideas of the kind? The thought that he was now a real, an actual, proprietor instead of a fictitious—that he was now a proprietor of real land, real rights of timber and pasture, and real serfs who existed not only in the imagination, but also in veritable actuality—greatly elated our hero. So he took to dancing up and down in his seat, to rubbing his hands together, to winking at himself, to holding his fist, trumpet-wise, to his mouth (while making believe to execute a march), and even to uttering aloud such self-encouraging nicknames and phrases as "bulldog" and "little fat capon." Then suddenly recollecting that he was not alone, he hastened to moderate his behaviour and endeavour to stifle the boundless flow of his good spirits; with the result that when Platon, mistaking certain sounds for utterances addressed to himself, inquired what his companion had said, the latter retained the presence of mind to reply "Nothing."

Presently, as Chichikov gazed about him, he saw that for some time past the *koliaska* had been skirting a beautiful wood, and that on either side the road was bordered with an edging of birch trees, the tenderly-green, recently-opened leaves of which caused their tall, slender trunks to show up with the whiteness of a snowdrift. Likewise nightingales were warbling from the recesses of the foliage, and some wood tulips were glowing yellow in the grass. Next (and almost before Chichikov had realised how he came to be in such a beautiful spot when, but a moment before, there had been visible only open fields) there glimmered among the trees the stony whiteness of a church, with, on the further side of it, the intermittent, foliage-buried line of a fence; while from the upper end of a village street there was advancing to meet the vehicle a gentleman with a cap on his head, a knotted cudgel in his hands, and a slender-limbed English dog by his side.

"This is my brother," said Platon. "Stop, coachman." And he descended from the *koliaska*, while Chichikov followed his example. Yarb and the strange dog saluted one another, and then the active, thin-legged, slender-tongued Azor relinquished his licking of Yarb's blunt jowl, licked Platon's hands instead, and, leaping upon Chichikov, slobbered right into his ear.

The two brothers embraced.

" Really, Platon," said the gentleman (whose name was Vassili), " what do you mean by treating me like this? "

" How so? " asked Platon indifferently.

" What? For three days past I have seen and heard nothing of you! A groom from Pietukh's brought your cob home, and told me you had departed on an expedition with some *barin*. At least you might have sent me word as to your destination and the probable length of your absence. What made you act so? God knows what I have not been wondering! "

" Does it matter? " rejoined Platon. " I forgot to send you word, and we have been no further than Constantine's (who, with our sister, sends you his greeting). By the way, may I introduce Paul Ivanovitch Chichikov? "

The pair shook hands with one another. Then, doffing their caps, they embraced.

" What sort of man is this Chichikov? " thought Vassili. " As a rule my brother Platon is not over-nice in his choice of acquaintances." And, eyeing our hero as narrowly as civility permitted, he saw that his appearance was that of a perfectly respectable individual.

Chichikov returned Vassili's scrutiny with a similar observance of the dictates of civility, and perceived that he was shorter than Platon, that his hair was of a darker shade, and that his features, though less handsome, contained far more life, animation, and kindliness than did his brother's. Clearly he indulged in less dreaming, though that was an aspect which Chichikov little regarded.

" I have made up my mind to go touring our Holy Russia with Paul Ivanovitch," said Platon. " Perhaps it will rid me of my melancholy."

" But what has made you come to such a sudden decision? " asked the perplexed Vassili (very nearly he added: " Fancy going travelling with a man whose acquaintance you have just made, and who may turn out to be a rascal or the devil knows what! " But, in spite of his distrust, he contented himself with another covert scrutiny of Chichikov, and this time came to the conclusion that there was no fault to be found with his exterior).

The party turned to the right, and entered the gates of an ancient courtyard attached to an old-fashioned house of a type no longer built—the type which has huge gables supporting a high-pitched roof. In the centre of the courtyard two great lime trees covered half the surrounding space with shade, while beneath them were ranged a number of wooden benches, and the whole was encircled with a ring of blossoming lilacs and cherry trees which, like a beaded necklace, reinforced the wooden fence, and almost buried it beneath their clusters of leaves and flowers. The house, too, stood almost concealed by this greenery, except that the front door and the windows peered pleasantly through the foliage, and that here and there between the stems of the trees there could be caught glimpses of the kitchen regions, the storehouses, and the cellar. Lastly, around the whole stood a grove, from the recesses of which came the echoing songs of nightingales.

Involuntarily the place communicated to the soul a sort of quiet, restful feeling, so eloquently did it speak of that care-free period when every one lived on good terms with his neighbour, and all was simple and unsophisticated. Vassili invited Chichikov to seat himself, and the party approached, for that purpose, the benches under the lime trees; after which a youth of about seventeen, and clad in a red shirt, brought decanters containing various kinds of *kvass* (some of them as thick as syrup, and others hissing like aerated lemonade), deposited the same upon the table, and, taking up a spade which he had left leaning against a tree, moved away towards the garden. The reason of this was that in the brothers' household, as in that of Kostanzhoglo, no servants were kept, since the whole staff were rated as gardeners, and performed that duty in rotation — Vassili holding that domestic service was not a specialised calling, but one to which any one might contribute a hand, and therefore one which did not require special menials to be kept for the purpose. Moreover, he held that the average Russian peasant remains active and willing (rather than lazy) only so long as he wears a shirt and a peasant's smock; but that as soon as ever he finds himself put into a German tailcoat, he becomes awkward, sluggish, indolent, disinclined to change his vest or take a bath, fond of sleeping in his clothes, and certain to breed fleas and bugs under the German apparel. And it may be that Vassili was right. At all events, the brothers' peasantry were exceedingly well clad—the women, in particular, having their head-dresses spangled with gold, and the sleeves of their blouses embroidered after the fashion of a Turkish shawl.

" You see here the species of *kvass* for which our house has long been famous," said Vassili to Chichikov. The latter poured himself out a glassful from the first decanter which he lighted upon, and found the contents to be linden honey of a kind never tasted by him even in Poland, seeing that it had a sparkle like

K

that of champagne, and also an effervescence which sent a pleasant spray from the mouth into the nose.

"Nectar!" he exclaimed. Then he took some from a second decanter. It proved to be even better than the first. "A beverage of beverages!" he exclaimed. "At your respected brother-in-law's I tasted the finest syrup which has ever come my way, but here I have tasted the very finest *kvass*."

"Yet the recipe for the syrup also came from here," said Vassili, "seeing that my sister took it with her. By the way, to what part of the country, and to what places, are you thinking of travelling?"

"To tell you the truth," replied Chichikov, rocking himself to and fro on the bench, and smoothing his knee with his hand, and gently inclining his head, "I am travelling less on my own affairs than on the affairs of others. That is to say, General Betristchev, an intimate friend, and, I might add, a generous benefactor of mine, has charged me with commissions to some of his relatives. Nevertheless, though relatives are relatives, I may say that I am travelling on my own account as well, in that, in addition to possible benefit to my health, I desire to see the world and the whirligig of humanity, which constitute, so to speak, a living book, a second course of education."

Vassili took thought. "The man speaks floridly," he reflected, "yet his words contain a certain element of truth." After a moment's silence he added to Platon: "I am beginning to think that the tour might help you to bestir yourself. At present you are in a condition of mental slumber. You have fallen asleep, not so much from weariness or satiety, as through a lack of vivid perceptions and impressions. For myself, I am your complete antithesis. I should be only too glad if I could feel less acutely, if I could take things less to heart."

"Emotion has become a disease with you," said Platon. "You seek your own troubles, and make your own anxieties."

"How can you say that when ready-made anxieties greet one at every step?" exclaimed Vassili. "For example, have you heard of the trick which Lienitsin has just played us—of his seizing the piece of vacant land whither our peasants resort for their sports? That piece I would not sell for all the money in the world. It has long been our peasants' play-ground, and all the traditions of our village are bound up with it. Moreover, for me, old custom is a sacred thing for which I would gladly sacrifice everything else."

"Lienitsin cannot have known of this, or he would not have

seized the land," said Platon. "He is a newcomer, just arrived from St. Petersburg. A few words of explanation ought to meet the case."

"But he *does* know of what I have stated; he *does* know of it. Purposely I sent him word to that effect, yet he has returned me the rudest of answers."

"Then go yourself and explain matters to him."

"No, I will not do that; he has tried to carry off things with too high a hand. But *you* can go if you like."

"I would certainly go were it not that I scarcely like to interfere. Also, I am a man whom he could easily hoodwink and outwit."

"Would it help you if *I* were to go?" put in Chichikov. "Pray enlighten me as to the matter."

Vassili glanced at the speaker, and thought to himself: "What a passion the man has for travelling!"

"Yes, pray give me an idea of the kind of fellow," repeated Chichikov, "and also outline to me the affair."

"I should be ashamed to trouble you with such an unpleasant commission," replied Vassili. "He is a man whom I take to be an utter rascal. Originally a member of a family of plain *dvoriané* in this province, he entered the Civil Service in St. Petersburg, then married some one's natural daughter in that city, and has returned to lord it with a high hand. I cannot bear the tone he adopts. Our folk are by no means fools. They do not look upon the current fashion as the Tsar's *ukaz* any more than they look upon St. Petersburg as the Church."

"Naturally," said Chichikov. "But tell me more of the particulars of the quarrel."

"They are these. He needs additional land and, had he not acted as he has done, I would have given him some land elsewhere for nothing; but, as it is, the pestilent fellow has taken it into his head to——"

"I think I had better go and have a talk with him. That might settle the affair. Several times have people charged me with similar commissions, and never have they repented of it. General Betristchev is an example."

"Nevertheless I am ashamed that you should be put to the annoyance of having to converse with such a fellow."

[At this point there occurs a long hiatus.]

"And above all things, such a transaction would need to be carried through in secret," said Chichikov. "True, the law does not forbid such things, but there is always the risk of a scandal."

"Quite so, quite so," said Lienitsin with head bent down.

"Then we agree!" exclaimed Chichikov. "How charming! As I say, my business is both legal and illegal. Though needing to effect a mortgage, I desire to put no one to the risk of having to pay the two roubles on each living soul; wherefore I have conceived the idea of relieving landowners of that distasteful obligation by acquiring dead and absconded souls who have failed to disappear from the revision list. This enables me at once to perform an act of Christian charity and to remove from the shoulders of our more impoverished proprietors the burden of tax-payment upon souls of the kinds specified. Should you yourself care to do business with me, we will draw up a formal purchase deed as though the souls in question were still alive."

"But it would be such a curious arrangement," muttered Lienitsin, moving his chair and himself a little further away. "It would be an arrangement which, er—er—"

"Would involve you in no scandal whatever, seeing that the affair would be carried through in secret. Moreover, between friends who are well-disposed towards one another——"

"Nevertheless——"

Chichikov adopted a firmer and more decided tone. "I repeat that there would be no scandal," he said. "The transaction would take place as between good friends, and as between friends of mature age, and as between friends of good status, and as between friends who know how to keep their own counsel." And, so saying, he looked his interlocutor frankly and generously in the eyes.

Nevertheless Lienitsin's resourcefulness and acumen in business matters failed to relieve his mind of a certain perplexity— and the less so since he had contrived to become caught in his own net. Yet, in general, he possessed neither a love for nor a talent for underhand dealings, and, had not fate and circumstances favoured Chichikov by causing Lienitsin's wife to enter the room at that moment, things might have turned out very differently from what they did. Madame was a pale, thin, insignificant-looking young lady, but none the less a lady who wore her clothes à la St. Petersburg, and cultivated the society of persons who were unimpeachably *comme il faut*. Behind her, borne in a nurse's arms, came the first fruits of the love of husband and wife. Adopting his most telling method of approach (the method accompanied with a sidelong inclination of the head and a sort of hop), Chichikov hastened to greet the lady from the metropolis, and then the baby. At first the latter started to bellow disapproval, but the words " Agoo, agoo, my pet! " added to a little cracking of the fingers and a sight of a beautiful seal on a watch chain, enabled Chichikov to wheedle the infant into his arms; after which he fell to swinging it up and down until he had contrived to raise a smile on its face—a circumstance which greatly delighted the parents, and finally inclined the father in his visitor's favour. Suddenly, however—whether from pleasure of from some other cause—the infant misbehaved itself!

" My God! " cried Madame. " He has gone and spoilt your frockcoat! "

True enough, on glancing downwards, Chichikov saw that the sleeve of his brand-new garment had indeed suffered a hurt. " If I could catch you alone, you little devil," he muttered to himself, " I'd shoot you! "

Host, hostess, and nurse all ran for *eau-de-Cologne*, and from three sides set themselves to rub the spot affected.

" Never mind, never mind; it is nothing," said Chichikov as he strove to communicate to his features as cheerful an expression as possible. " What does it matter what a child may spoil during the golden age of its infancy? "

To himself he remarked: " The little brute! Would it could be devoured by wolves! It has made only too good a shot, the cussed young ragamuffin! "

How, after this—after the guest had shown such innocent affection for the little one, and magnanimously paid for his so doing with a brand-new suit—could the father remain obdurate? Nevertheless, to avoid setting a bad example to the countryside, he and Chichikov agreed to carry through the transaction *privately*, lest, otherwise, a scandal should arise.

" In return," said Chichikov, " would you mind doing me the following favour? I desire to mediate in the matter of your difference with the Brothers Platonov. I believe that you wish to acquire some additional land? Is not that so? "

[*Here there occurs a hiatus in the original.*]

Everything in life fulfils its function, and Chichikov's tour in search of a fortune was carried out so successfully that not a little money passed into his pockets. The system employed was a good one: he did not steal, he merely used. And every one of us at times does the same: one man with regard to Government timber, and another with regard to a sum belonging to his

employer, while a third defrauds his children for the sake of an
actress, and a fourth robs his peasantry for the sake of smart
furniture or a carriage. What can one do when one is surrounded on every side with roguery, and everywhere there are
insanely expensive restaurants, masked balls, and dances to the
music of gipsy bands? To abstain when every one else is indulging in these things, and fashion commands, is difficult indeed!

Chichikov was for setting forth again, but the roads had now
got into a bad state, and, in addition, there was in preparation
a second fair—one for the *dvoriané* only. The former fair had
been held for the sale of horses, cattle, cheese, and other
peasant produce, and the buyers had been merely cattle-jobbers
and *kulaks;* but this time the function was to be one for the sale
of manorial produce which had been bought up by wholesale
dealers at Nizhni Novgorod, and then transferred hither. To
the fair, of course, came those ravishers of the Russian purse
who, in the shape of Frenchmen with pomades and French-
women with hats, make away with money earned by blood and
hard work, and, like the locusts of Egypt (to use Kostanzhoglo's
term), not only devour their prey, but also dig holes in the ground
and leave behind their eggs.

Although, unfortunately, the occurrence of a bad harvest
retained many landowners at their country houses, the local
tchinovniks (whom the failure of the harvest did *not* touch)
proceeded to let themselves go—as also, to their undoing, did
their wives. The reading of books of the type diffused, in these
modern days, for the inoculation of humanity with a craving for
new and superior amenities of life had caused every one to conceive a passion for experimenting with the latest luxury; and
to meet this want the French wine merchant opened a new
establishment in the shape of such a restaurant as had never
before been heard of in the province—a restaurant where supper
could be procured on credit as regarded one-half, and for an
unprecedentedly low sum as regarded the other. This exactly
suited both heads of boards and clerks who were living in hope
of being able some day to resume their bribes-taking from
suitors. There also developed a tendency to compete in the
matter of horses and liveried flunkeys; with the result that
despite the damp and snowy weather exceedingly elegant turn-
outs took to parading backwards and forwards. Whence these
equipages had come God only knows, but at least they would
not have disgraced St. Petersburg. From within them merchants
and attorneys doffed their caps to ladies, and inquired after

their health, and likewise it became a rare sight to see a bearded man in a rough fur cap, since every one now went about clean-shaven and with dirty teeth, after the European fashion.

"Sir, I beg of you to inspect my goods," said a tradesman as Chichikov was passing his establishment. "Within my doors you will find a large variety of clothing."

"Have you a cloth of a bilberry-coloured check?" inquired the person addressed.

"I have cloths of the finest kind," replied the tradesman, raising his cap with one hand, and pointing to his shop with the other. Chicikov entered, and in a trice the proprietor had dived beneath the counter, and appeared on the other side of it, with his back to his wares and his face towards the customer. Leaning forward on the tips of his fingers, and indicating his merchandise with just the suspicion of a nod, he requested the gentleman to specify exactly the species of cloth which he required.

"A cloth with an olive-coloured or a bottle-tinted spot in its pattern—anything in the nature of bilberry," explained Chichikov.

"That being so, sir, I may say that I am about to show you cloths of a quality which even our illustrious capitals could not surpass. Hi, boy! Reach down that roll up there—number 34. No, *not* that one, fool! Such fellows as you are always too good for your job. There—hand it to me. This is indeed a nice pattern!"

Unfolding the garment, the tradesman thrust it close to Chichikov's nose in order that he might not only handle, but also smell it.

"Excellent, but not what I want," pronounced Chichikov. "Formerly I was in the Customs Department, and therefore wear none but cloth of the latest make. What I want is of a ruddier pattern than this—not exactly a bottle-tinted pattern, but something approaching bilberry."

"I understand, sir. Of course you require only the very newest thing. A cloth of that kind I *do* possess, sir, and though expensive in price, it is of a quality to match."

Carrying the roll of stuff to the light—even stepping into the street for the purpose—the shopman unfolded his prize with the words, "A truly beautiful shade! A cloth of smoked grey, shot with flame colour!"

The material met with the customer's approval, a price was agreed upon, and with incredible celerity the vendor made up the purchase into a brown-paper parcel, and stowed it away in Chichikov's *koliaska*.

At this moment a voice asked to be shown a black frockcoat.

"The devil take me if that isn't Khlobuev!" muttered our hero, turning his back upon the newcomer. Unfortunately the other had seen him.

"Come, come, Paul Ivanovitch!" he expostulated. "Surely you do not intend to overlook me? I have been searching for you everywhere, for I have something important to say to you."

"My dear sir, my very dear sir," said Chichikov as he pressed Khlobuev's hand, "I can assure you that, had I the necessary leisure, I should at all times be charmed to converse with you." And mentally he added: "Would that the Evil One would fly away with you!"

Almost at the same moment Murazov, the great landowner, entered the shop. As he did so our hero hastened to exclaim: "Why, it is Athanasi Vassilievitch! How *are* you, my very dear sir?"

"Well enough," replied Murazov, removing his cap (Khlobuev and the shopman had already done the same). "How, may I ask, are *you?*"

"But poorly," replied Chichikov, "for of late I have been troubled with indigestion, and my sleep is bad. I do not get sufficient exercise."

However, instead of probing further into the subject of Chichikov's ailments, Murazov turned to Khlobuev.

"I saw you enter the shop," he said, "and therefore followed you, for I have something important for your ear. Could you spare me a minute or two?"

"Certainly, certainly," said Khlobuev, and the pair left the shop together.

"I wonder what is afoot between them," said Chichikov to himself.

"A wise and noble gentleman, Athanasi Vassilievitch!" remarked the tradesman. Chichikov made no reply save a gesture.

"Paul Ivanovitch, I have been looking for you everywhere," Lienitsin's voice said from behind him, while again the tradesman hastened to remove his cap. "Pray come home with me, for I have something to say to you."

Chichikov scanned the speaker's face, but could make nothing of it. Paying the tradesman for the cloth, he left the shop.

Meanwhile Murazov had conveyed Khlobuev to his rooms.

" Tell me," he said to his guest, " exactly how your affairs stand. I take it that, after all, your aunt left you something? "

" It would be difficult to say whether or not my affairs are improved," replied Khlobuev. " True, fifty souls and thirty thousand roubles came to me from Madame Khanasarova, but I had to pay them away to satisfy my debts. Consequently I am once more destitute. But the important point is that there was trickery connected with the legacy, and shameful trickery at that. Yes, though it may surprise you, it is a fact that that fellow Chichikov——"

" Yes, Semen Semenovitch, but, before you go on to speak of Chichikov, pray tell me something about yourself, and how much, in your opinion, would be sufficient to clear you of your difficulties? "

" My difficulties are grievous," replied Khlobuev. " To rid myself of them, and also to have enough to go on with, I should need to acquire at least a hundred thousand roubles, if not more. In short, things are becoming impossible for me."

" And, had you the money, what should you do with it? "

" I should rent a tenement, and devote myself to the education of my children. Not a thought should I give to myself, for my career is over, seeing that it is impossible for me to re-enter the Civil Service and I am good for nothing else."

" Nevertheless, when a man is leading an idle life he is apt to incur temptations which shun his better-employed brother."

" Yes, but beyond question I am good for nothing, so broken is my health, and such a martyr am I to dyspepsia."

" But how do you propose to live without working? How can a man like you exist without a post or a position of any kind? Look around you at the works of God. Everything has its proper function, and pursues its proper course. Even a stone can be used for one purpose or another. How, then, can it be right for a man who is a thinking being to remain a drone? "

" But I should not be a drone, for I should employ myself with the education of my children."

" No, Semen Semenovitch—no: *that* you would find the hardest task of all. For how can a man educate his children who has never even educated himself? Instruction can be imparted to children only through the medium of example; and would a life like yours furnish them with a profitable example —a life which has been spent in idleness and the playing of cards? No, Semen Semenovitch. You had far better hand your children over to me. Otherwise they will be ruined. Do not think that I am jesting. Idleness has wrecked your life, and you must flee from it. Can a man live with nothing to keep him in place? Even a journeyman labourer who earns the barest pittance may take an interest in his occupation."

"Athanasi Vassilievitch, I have tried to overcome myself, but what further resource lies open to me? Can I who am old and incapable re-enter the Civil Service and spend year after year at a desk with youths who are just starting their careers? Moreover, I have lost the trick of taking bribes; I should only hinder both myself and others; while, as you know, it is a department which has an established caste of its own. Therefore, though I have considered, and even attempted to obtain, every conceivable post, I find myself incompetent for them all. Only in a monastery should I——"

"Nay, nay. Monasteries, again, are only for those who have worked. To those who have spent their youth in dissipation such havens say what the ant said to the dragonfly—namely, 'Go you away, and return to your dancing.' Yes, even in a monastery do folk toil and toil—they do not sit playing whist." Murazov looked at Khlobuev, and added: "Semen Semenovitch, you are deceiving both yourself and me."

Poor Khlobuev could not utter a word in reply, and Murazov began to feel sorry for him.

"Listen, Semen Semenovitch," he went on. "I know that you say your prayers, and that you go to church, and that you observe both Matins and Vespers, and that, though averse to early rising, you leave your bed at four o'clock in the morning before the household fires have been lit."

"Ah, Athanasi Vassilievitch," said Khlobuev, "that is another matter altogether. That I do, not for man's sake, but for the sake of Him who has ordered all things here on earth. Yes, I believe that He at least can feel compassion for me, that He at least, though I be foul and lowly, will pardon me and receive me when all men have cast me out, and my best friend has betrayed me and boasted that he has done it for a good end."

Khlobuev's face was glowing with emotion, and from the older man's eyes also a tear had started.

"You will do well to hearken unto Him who is merciful," he said. "But remember also that, in the eyes of the All-Merciful, honest toil is of equal merit with a prayer. Therefore take unto yourself whatsoever task you may, and do it as though you were doing it, not unto man, but unto God. Even though to your lot there should fall but the cleaning of a floor, clean that floor as though it were being cleaned for Him alone. And thence at least this good you will reap: that there will remain to you no time for what is evil—for card playing, for feasting, for all the life of this gay world. Are you acquainted with Ivan Potapitch?"

"Yes, not only am I acquainted with him, but I also greatly respect him."

"Time was when Ivan Potapitch was a merchant worth half a million roubles. In everything did he look but for gain, and his affairs prospered exceedingly, so much so that he was able to send his son to be educated in France, and to marry his daughter to a General. And whether in his office or at the Exchange, he would stop any friend whom he encountered and carry him off to a tavern to drink, and spend whole days thus employed. But at last he became bankrupt, and God sent him other misfortunes also. His son! Ah, well! Ivan Potapitch is now my steward, for he had to begin life over again. Yet once more his affairs are in order, and, had it been his wish, he could have restarted in business with a capital of half a million roubles. 'But no,' he said. 'A steward am I, and a steward will I remain to the end; for, from being full-stomached and heavy with dropsy, I have become strong and well.' Not a drop of liquor passes his lips, but only cabbage soup and gruel. And he prays as none of the rest of us pray, and he helps the poor as none of the rest of us help them; and to this he would add yet further charity if his means permitted him so to do."

Poor Khlobuev remained silent, as before.

The elder man took his two hands in his.

"Semen Semenovitch," he said, "you cannot think how much I pity you, or how much I have had you in my thoughts. Listen to me. In the monastery there is a recluse who never looks upon a human face. Of all men whom I know he has the broadest mind, and he breaks not his silence save to give advice. To him I went and said that I had a friend (though I did not actually mention your name) who was in great trouble of soul. Suddenly the recluse interrupted me with the words: 'God's work first, and our own last. There is need for a church to be built, but no money wherewith to build it. Money must be collected to that end.' Then he shut to the wicket. I wondered to myself what this could mean, and concluded that the recluse had been unwilling to accord me his counsel. Next I repaired to the Archimandrite, and had scarce reached his door when he inquired of me whether I could commend to him a man meet to be entrusted with the collection of alms for a church—a man who should belong to the *dvoriané* or to the more lettered merchants, but who would guard the trust as he would guard the salvation of his soul. On the instant thought I to myself: 'Why should not the Holy Father appoint my friend Semen Semenovitch? For the way of suffering would benefit him greatly; and as he passed with his ledger from landowner to peasant, and from peasant to townsman, he would learn where folk dwell, and who stands in need of aught, and thus would become better acquainted with the countryside than folk who dwell in cities. And, thus become, he would find that his services were always in demand.' Only of late did the Governor-General say to me that, could be but be furnished with the name of a secretary who should know his work not only by the book but also by experience, he would give him a great sum, since nothing is to be learned by the former means, and, through it, much confusion arises."

"You confound me, you overwhelm me!" said Khlobuev, staring at his companion in open-eyed astonishment. "I can scarcely believe that your words are true, seeing that for such a trust an active, indefatigable man would be necessary. Moreover, how could I leave my wife and children unprovided for?"

"Have no fear," said Murazov, "I myself will take them under my care, as well as procure for the children a tutor. Far better and nobler were it for you to be travelling with a wallet, and asking alms on behalf of God, than to be remaining here and asking alms for yourself alone. Likewise, I will furnish you with a tilt-waggon, so that you may be saved some of the hardships of the journey, and thus be preserved in good health. Also, I will give you some money for the journey, in order that, as you pass on your way, you may give to those who stand in greater need than their fellows. Thus, if, before giving, you assure yourself that the recipient of the alms is worthy of the same, you will do much good; and as you travel you will become acquainted with all men and sundry, and they will treat you, not as a *tchinovink* to be feared, but as one to whom, as a petitioner on behalf of the Church, they may unloose their tongues without peril."

"I feel that the scheme is a splendid one, and would gladly bear my part in it were it not likely to exceed my strength."

"What is there that does *not* exceed our strength?" said Murazov. "Nothing is wholly proportionate to it—everything surpasses it. Help from above is necessary: otherwise we are all powerless. Strength comes of prayer, and of prayer alone. When a man crosses himself, and cries, ' Lord, have mercy upon me!' he soon stems the current and wins to the shore. Nor need you take any prolonged thought concerning this matter. All that you need do is to accept it as a commission sent of God. The tilt-waggon can be prepared for you immediately; and then, as soon as you have been to the Archimandrite for your book of accounts and his blessing, you will be free to start on your journey."

" I submit myself to you, and accept the commission as a divine trust."

And even as Khlobuev spoke he felt renewed vigour and confidence arise in his soul, and his mind begin to awake to a sense of hopefulness of eventually being able to put to flight his troubles. And even as it was, the world seemed to be growing dim to his eyes . . .

Meanwhile, plea after plea had been presented to the legal authorities, and daily were relatives whom no one had before heard of putting in an appearance. Yes, like vultures to a corpse did these good folk come flocking to the immense property which Madame Khanasarov had left behind her. Everywhere were heard rumours against Chichikov, rumours with regard to the validity of the second will, rumours with regard to will number one, and rumours of larceny and concealment of funds. Also, there came to hand information with regard both to Chichikov's purchases of dead souls and to his conniving at contraband goods during his service in the Customs Department. In short, every possible item of evidence was exhumed, and the whole of his previous history investigated. How the authorities had come to suspect and to ascertain all this God only knows, but the fact remains that there had fallen into the hands of those authorities information concerning matters of which Chichikov had believed only himself and four walls to be aware. True, for a time these matters remained within the cognisance of none but the functionaries concerned, and failed to reach Chichikov's ears; but at length a letter from a confidential friend gave him reason to think that the fat was about to fall into the fire. Said the letter briefly: " Dear sir, I beg to advise you that possibly legal trouble is pending, but that you have no cause for uneasiness, seeing that everything will be attended to by yours very truly." Yet, in spite of its tenor, the epistle reassured its recipient. " What a genius the fellow is!" thought Chichikov to himself. Next, to complete his satisfaction, his tailor arrived with the new suit which he had ordered. Not without a certain sense of pride did our hero inspect the frockcoat of smoked grey shot with flame colour, and look at it from every point of view, and then try on the breeches—the latter fitting him like a picture, and quite concealing any deficiencies in the matter of thighs and calves (though, when buckled behind, they left his stomach projecting like a drum). True, the customer remarked that there appeared to be a slight tightness under the right armpit, but the smiling tailor only rejoined that that would cause the waist to fit all the better. " Sir," he said triumphantly, " you may rest assured that the work has been executed exactly as it ought to have been executed. No one, except in St. Petersburg, could have done it better." As a matter of fact, the tailor himself hailed from St. Petersburg, but called himself on his signboard " Foreign Costumier from London and Paris "—the truth being that by the use of a double-barrelled flourish of cities superior to mere " Karlsruhe " and " Copenhagen " he designed to acquire business and cut out his local rivals.

Chichikov graciously settled the man's account, and, as soon as he had gone, paraded at leisure, and *con amore*, and after the manner of an artist of æsthetic taste, before the mirror. Somehow he seemed to look better than ever in the suit, for his cheeks had now taken on a still more interesting air, and his chin an added seductiveness, while his white collar lent tone to his neck, the blue satin tie heightened the effect of the collar, the fashionable dickey set off the tie, the rich satin waistcoat emphasised the dickey, and the smoked-grey-shot-with-flame-colour frockcoat, shining like silk, splendidly rounded off the whole. When he turned to the right he looked well: when he turned to the left he looked even better. In short, it was a costume worthy of a Lord Chamberlain or the species of dandy who shrinks from swearing in the Russian language, but amply relieves his feelings in the language of France. Next, inclining his head slightly to one side, our hero endeavoured to pose as though he were addressing a middle-aged lady of exquisite refinement; and the result of these efforts was a picture which any artist might have yearned to portray. Next, his delight led him gracefully to execute a hop in ballet fashion, so that the wardrobe trembled and a bottle of *eau-de-Cologne* came crashing to the floor. Yet even this *contretemps* did not upset him; he merely called the offending bottle a fool, and then debated whom first he should visit in his attractive guise.

Suddenly there resounded through the hall a clatter of spurred heels, and then the voice of a gendarme saying: "You are commanded to present yourself before the Governor-General!" Turning round, Chichikov stared in horror at the spectacle presented; for in the doorway there was standing an apparition wearing a huge moustache, a helmet surmounted with a horsehair plume, a pair of crossed shoulder-belts, and a gigantic sword! A whole army might have been combined into a single individual! And when Chichikov opened his mouth to speak the apparition repeated, "You are commanded to present yourself before the Governor-General," and at the same moment our hero caught sight both of a second apparition outside the door and of a coach waiting beneath the window. What was to be done? Nothing whatever was possible. Just as he stood—in his smoked-grey-shot-with-flame-colour suit—he had then and there to enter the vehicle, and, shaking in every limb, and with a gendarme seated by his side, to start for the residence of the Governor-General.

And even in the hall of that establishment no time was given him to pull himself together, for at once an aide-de-camp said: "Go inside immediately, for the Prince is awaiting you." And as in a dream did our hero see a vestibule where couriers were being handed dispatches, and then a *salon* which he crossed with the thought, "I suppose I am not to be allowed a trial, but shall be sent straight to Siberia!" And at the thought his heart started beating in a manner which the most jealous of lovers could not have rivalled. At length there opened a door, and before him he saw a study full of portfolios, ledgers, and dispatch-boxes, with, standing behind them, the gravely menacing figure of the Prince.

"There stands my executioner," thought Chichikov to himself. "He is about to tear me in pieces as a wolf tears a lamb."

Indeed, the Prince's lips were simply quivering with rage.

"Once before did I spare you," he said, "and allow you to remain in the town when you ought to have been in prison: yet your only return for my clemency has been to revert to a career of fraud—and of fraud as dishonourable as ever a man engaged in."

"To what dishonourable fraud do you refer, your Highness?" asked Chichikov, trembling from head to foot.

The Prince approached, and looked him straight in the eyes.

"Let me tell you," he said, "that the woman whom you induced to witness a certain will has been arrested, and that you will be confronted with her."

The world seemed suddenly to grow dim before Chichikov's sight.

" Your Highness," he gasped, " I will tell you the whole truth, and nothing but the truth. I am guilty—yes, I am guilty; but I am not so guilty as you think, for I was led away by rascals."

" That any one can have led you away is impossible," retorted the Prince. " Recorded against your name there stand more felonies than even the most hardened liar could have invented. I believe that never in your life have you done a deed not innately dishonourable—that not a kopeck have you ever obtained by aught but shameful methods of trickery and theft, the penalty for which is Siberia and the *knut*. But enough of this! From this room you will be conveyed to prison, where, with other rogues and thieves, you will be confined until your trial may come on. And this is lenient treatment on my part, for you are worse, far worse, than the felons who will be your companions. *They* are but poor men in smocks and sheepskins, whereas *you*——" Without concluding his words, the Prince cast a glance at Chichikov's smoked-grey-shot-with-flame-colour apparel.

Then he touched a bell.

" Your Highness," cried Chichikov, " have mercy upon me! You are the father of a family! Spare me for the sake of my aged mother!"

" Rubbish! " exclaimed the Prince. " Even as before you besought me for the sake of a wife and children whom you did not even possess, so now you would speak to me of an aged mother! "

" Your Highness," protested Chichikov, " though I am a wretch and the lowest of rascals, and though it is true that I lied when I told you that I possessed a wife and children, I swear that, as God is my witness, it has always been my *desire* to possess a wife, and to fulfil all the duties of a man and a citizen, and to earn the respect of my fellows and the authorities. But what could be done against the force of circumstances? By hook or by crook I have ever been forced to win a living, though confronted at every step by wiles and temptations and traitorous enemies and despoilers. So much has this been so that my life has, throughout, resembled a barque tossed by tempestuous waves, a barque driven at the mercy of the winds. Ah, I am only a man, your Highness! "

And in a moment the tears had gushed in torrents from his eyes, and he had fallen forward at the Prince's feet—fallen forward just as he was, in his smoked-grey-shot-with-flame-colour frockcoat, his velvet waistcoat, his satin tie, and his exquisitely fitting breeches, while from his neatly brushed pate, as again and again he struck his hand against his forehead, there came an odorous whiff of best-quality *eau-de-Cologne*.

" Away with him!" exclaimed the Prince to the gendarme who had just entered. " Summon the escort to remove him."

" Your Highness!" Chichikov cried again as he clasped the Prince's knees; but, shuddering all over, and struggling to free himself, the Prince repeated his order for the prisoner's removal.

" Your Highness, I say that I will not leave this room until you have accorded me mercy!" cried Chichikov as he clung to the Prince's leg with such tenacity that, frockcoat and all, he began to be dragged along the floor.

" Away with him, I say!" once more the Prince exclaimed with the sort of indefinable aversion which one feels at the sight of a repulsive insect which cannot summon up the courage to crush with his boot. So convulsively did the Prince shudder that Chichikov, clinging to his leg, received a kick on the nose. Yet still the prisoner retained his hold; until at length a couple of burly gendarmes tore him away and, grasping his arms, hurried him—pale, dishevelled, and in that strange, half-conscious condition into which a man sinks when he sees before him only the dark, terrible figure of death, the phantom which is so abhorrent to all our natures—from the building. But on the threshold the party came face to face with Murazov, and in Chichikov's heart the circumstance revived a ray of hope. Wresting himself with almost supernatural strength from the grasp of the escorting gendarmes, he threw himself at the feet of the horror-stricken old man.

" Paul Ivanovitch," Murazov exclaimed, " what has happened to you?"

" Save me!" gasped Chichikov. " They are taking me away to prison and death!"

Yet almost as he spoke the gendarmes seized him again, and hurried him away so swiftly that Murazov's reply escaped his ears.

A damp, mouldy cell which reeked of soldiers' boots and leggings, an unvarnished table, two sorry chairs, a window closed with a grating, a crazy stove which, while letting the smoke emerge through its cracks, gave out no heat—such was the den to which the man who had just begun to taste the sweets of life, and to attract the attention of his fellows with his new

suit of smoked-grey-shot-with-flame-colour, now found himself
consigned. Not even necessaries had he been allowed to bring
away with him, nor his dispatch-box which contained all his
booty. No, with the indenture deeds of the dead souls, it was
lodged in the hands of a *tchinovnik ;* and as he thought of these
things Chichikov rolled about the floor, and felt the canker-
worm of remorse seize upon and gnaw at his heart, and bite its
way ever further and further into that heart so defenceless
against its ravages, until he made up his mind that, should he
have to suffer another twenty-four hours of such misery, there
would no longer be a Chichikov in the world. Yet over him,
as over every one, there hung poised the All-Saving Hand; and,
an hour after his arrival at the prison, the doors of the gaol
opened to admit Murazov.

Compared with poor Chichikov's sense of relief when the old
man entered his cell, even the pleasure experienced by a thirsty,
dusty traveller when he is given a drink of clear spring water to
cool his dry, parched throat fades into insignificance.

" Ah, my deliverer ! " he cried as he rose from the floor, where
he had been grovelling in heartrending paroxysms of grief.
Seizing the old man's hand, he kissed it and pressed it to his
bosom. Then, bursting into tears, he added: " God Himself
will reward you for having come to visit an unfortunate wretch ! "

Murazov looked at him sorrowfully, and said no more than
" Ah, Paul Ivanovitch, Paul Ivanovitch ! What has happened ? "

" What has happened ? " cried Chichikov. " I have been
ruined by an accursed woman. That was because I could not
do things in moderation—I was powerless to stop myself in time.
Satan tempted me, and drove me from my senses, and bereft me
of human prudence. Yes, truly I have sinned, I have sinned !
Yet how came I so to sin ? To think that a *dvorianin*—yes, a
dvorianin—should be thrown into prison without process or
trial ! I repeat, a *dvorianin !* Why was I not given time to go
home and collect my effects ? whereas now they are left with
no one to look after them ! My dispatch-box, my dispatch-
box ! It contained my whole property, all that my heart's
blood and years of toil and want have been needed to acquire.
And now everything will be stolen, Athanasi Vassilievitch—
everything will be taken from me ! My God ! "

And, unable to stand against the torrent of grief which came
rushing over his heart once more, he sobbed aloud in tones which
penetrated even the thickness of the prison walls, and made dull
echoes awake behind them. Then, tearing off his satin tie, and

seizing by the collar the smoked-grey-shot-with-flame-colour frockcoat, he stripped the latter from his shoulders.

"Ah, Paul Ivanovitch," said the old man, "how even now the property which you have acquired is blinding your eyes, and causing you to fail to realise your terrible position!"

"Yes, my good friend and benefactor," wailed poor Chichikov despairingly, and clasping Murazov by the knees. "Yet save me if you can! The Prince is fond of you, and would do anything for your sake."

"No, Paul Ivanovitch; however much I might wish to save you, and however much I might try so to do, I could not help you as you desire; for it is to the power of an inexorable law, and not to the authority of any one man, that you have rendered yourself subject."

"Satan tempted me, and has ended by making of me an outcast from the human race!" Chichikov beat his head against the wall and struck the table with his fist until the blood spurted from his hand. Yet neither his head nor his hand seemed to be conscious of the least pain.

"Calm yourself, Paul Ivanovitch," said Murazov. "Calm yourself, and consider how best you can make your peace with God. Think of your miserable soul, and not of the judgment of man."

"I will, Athanasi Vassilievitch, I will. But what a fate is mine! Did ever such a fate befall a man? To think of all the patience with which I have gathered my kopecks, of all the toil and trouble which I have endured! Yet what I have done has not been done with the intention of robbing any one, nor of cheating the Treasury. Why, then, did I gather those kopecks? I gathered them to the end that one day I might be able to live in plenty, and also to have something to leave to the wife and children whom, for the benefit and the welfare of my country, I hoped eventually to win and to maintain. That was why I gathered those kopecks. True, I worked by devious methods —that I fully admit; but what else could I do? And even devious methods I employed only when I saw that the straight road would not serve my purpose so well as a crooked. Moreover, as I toiled, the appetite for those methods grew upon me. Yet what I took I took only from the rich; whereas villains exist who, while drawing thousands a year from the Treasury, despoil the poor, and take from the man with nothing even that which he has. Is it not the cruelty of fate, therefore, that, just when I was beginning to reap the harvest of my toil—to touch it, so to speak, with the tip of one finger—there should have arisen a sudden storm which has sent my barque to pieces on a rock? My capital had nearly reached the sum of three hundred thousand roubles, and a three-storied house was as good as mine, and twice over I could have bought a country estate. Why, then, should such a tempest have burst upon me? Why should I have sustained such a blow? Was not my life already like a barque tossed to and fro by the billows? Where is Heaven's justice—where is the reward for all my patience, for my boundless perseverance? Three times did I have to begin life afresh, and each time that I lost my all I began with a single kopeck at a moment when other men would have given themselves up to despair and drink. How much did I not have to overcome, how much did I not have to bear! Every kopeck which I gained I had to make with my whole strength; for though, to others, wealth may come easily, every coin of mine had to be ' forged with a nail worth three kopecks ' as the proverb has it. With such a nail—with the nail of an iron, unwearying perseverance—did *I* forge my kopecks."

Convulsively sobbing with a grief which he could not repress, Chichikov sank upon a chair, tore from his shoulders the last ragged, trailing remnants of his frockcoat, and hurled them from him. Then, thrusting his fingers into the hair which he had once been so careful to preserve, he pulled it out by handfuls at a time, as though he hoped through physical pain to deaden the mental agony which he was suffering.

Meanwhile Murazov sat gazing in silence at the unwonted spectacle of the man who had lately been mincing with the gait of a worldling or a military fop now writhing in dishevelment and despair as he poured out upon the hostile forces by which human ingenuity so often finds itself outwitted a flood of invective.

" Paul Ivanovitch, Paul Ivanovitch," at length said Murazov, " what could not each of us rise to be did we but devote to good ends the same measure of energy and of patience which we bestow upon unworthy objects! How much good would not you yourself have effected! Yet I do not grieve so much for the fact that you have sinned against your fellow as I grieve for the fact that you have sinned against yourself and the rich store of gifts and opportunities which has been committed to your care. Though originally destined to rise, you have wandered from the path and fallen."

" Ah, Athanasi Vassilievitch," cried poor Chichikov, clasping his friend's hands, " I swear to you that, if you would but restore me my freedom, and recover for me my lost property, I would lead a different life from this time forth. Save me, you who alone can work my deliverance! Save me! "

" How can I do that? So to do I should need to procure the setting aside of a law. Again, even if I were to make the attempt, the Prince is a strict administrator, and would refuse on any consideration to release you."

" Yes, but for you all things are possible. It is not the law that troubles me: with that I could find a means to deal. It is the fact that for no offence at all I have been cast into prison, and treated like a dog, and deprived of my papers and dispatch-box and all my property. Save me if you can."

Again clasping the old man's knees, he bedewed them with his tears.

" Paul Ivanovitch," said Murazov, shaking his head, " how that property of yours still seals your eyes and ears, so that you cannot so much as listen to the promptings of your own soul! "

" Ah, I will think of my soul, too, if only you will save me."

" Paul Ivanovitch," the old man began again, and then stopped. For a little while there was a pause.

" Paul Ivanovitch," at length he went on, " to save you does not lie within my power. Surely you yourself see that? But, so far as I can, I will endeavour to, at all events, lighten your lot and procure your eventual release. Whether or not I shall succeed I do not know; but I will make the attempt. And should I, contrary to my expectations, prove successful, I beg of you, in return for these my efforts, to renounce all thought of benefit from the property which you have acquired. Sincerely do I assure you that, were I myself to be deprived of my property (and my property greatly exceeds yours in magnitude), I should not shed a single tear. It is not the property of which men can deprive us that matters, but the property of which no one on earth can deprive or despoil us. You are a man who has seen something of life—to use your own words, you have been a barque tossed hither and thither by tempestuous waves: yet still will there be left to you a remnant of substance on which to live, and therefore I beseech you to settle down in some quiet nook where there is a church, and where none but plain, good-hearted folk abide. Or, should you feel a yearning to leave behind you posterity, take in marriage a good woman who shall bring you, not money, but an aptitude for simple, modest domestic life. But this life—the life of turmoil, with its long-ings and its temptations—forget, and let it forget *you;* for there is no peace in it. See for yourself how, at every step, it brings one but hatred and treachery and deceit."

"Indeed, yes!" agreed the repentant Chichikov. "Gladly will I do as you wish, since for many a day past have I been longing to amend my life, and to engage in husbandry, and to reorder my affairs. A demon, the tempter Satan himself, has beguiled me and led me from the right path."

Suddenly there had recurred to Chichikov long-unknown, long-unfamiliar feelings. Something seemed to be striving to come to life again in him—something dim and remote, some-thing which had been crushed out of his boyhood by the dreary, deadening education of his youthful days, by his desolate home, by his subsequent lack of family ties, by the poverty and niggardliness of his early impressions, by the grim eye of fate— an eye which had always seemed to be regarding him as through a misty, mournful, frost-encrusted window-pane, and to be mocking at his struggles for freedom. And as these feelings came back to the penitent a groan burst from his lips, and, covering his face with his hands, he moaned: "It is all true, it is all true!"

"Of little avail are knowledge of the world and experience of men unless based upon a secure foundation," observed Murazov. "Though you have fallen, Paul Ivanovitch, awake to better things, for as yet there is time."

"No, no!" groaned Chichikov in a voice which made Mura-zov's heart bleed. "It is too late, too late. More and more is the conviction gaining upon me that I am powerless, that I have strayed too far ever to be able to do as you bid me. The fact that I have become what I am is due to my early schooling; for, though my father taught me moral lessons, and beat me, and set me to copy maxims into a book, he himself stole land from his neighbours, and forced me to help him. I have even known him bring an unjust suit, and defraud the orphan whose guardian he was! Consequently I know and feel that, though my life has been different from his, I do not hate roguery as I ought to hate it, and that my nature is coarse, and that in me there is no real love for what is good, no real spark of that beautiful in-stinct for well-doing which becomes a second nature, a settled habit. Also, never do I yearn to strive for what is right as I yearn to acquire property. This is no more than the truth. What else could I do but confess it?"

The old man sighed.

"Paul Ivanovitch," he said, "I know that you possess will-power, and that you possess also perseverance. A medicine may be bitter, yet the patient will gladly take it when assured that only by its means can he recover. Therefore, if it really be that you have no genuine love for doing good, do good by *forcing* yourself so to do. Thus you will benefit yourself even more than you will benefit him for whose sake the act is performed. Only force yourself to do good just once and again, and, behold, you will suddenly conceive the *true* love for well-doing. That is so, believe me. 'A kingdom is to be won only by striving,' says the proverb. That is to say, things are to be attained only by putting forth one's whole strength, since nothing short of one's whole strength will bring one to the desired goal. Paul Ivanovitch, within you there is a source of strength denied to many another man. I refer to the strength of an iron perseverance. Cannot *that* help you to overcome? Most men are weak and lack will-power, whereas I believe that you possess the power to act a hero's part."

Sinking deep into Chichikov's heart, these words would seem to have aroused in it a faint stirring of ambition, so much so that, if it was not fortitude which shone in his eyes, at all events it was something virile, and of much the same nature.

"Athanasi Vassilievitch," he said firmly, "if you will but petition for my release, as well as for permission for me to leave here with a portion of my property, I swear to you on my word of honour that I will begin a new life, and buy a country estate, and become the head of a household, and save money, not for myself, but for others, and do good everywhere, and to the best of my ability, and forget alike myself and the feasting and debauchery of town life, and lead, instead, a plain, sober existence."

"In that resolve may God strengthen you!" cried the old man with unbounded joy. "And I, for my part, will do my utmost to procure your release. And though God alone knows whether my efforts will be successful, at all events I hope to bring about a mitigation of your sentence. Come, let me embrace you! How you have filled my heart with gladness! With God's help, I will now go to the Prince."

And the next moment Chichikov found himself alone. His whole nature felt shaken and softened, even as, when the bellows have fanned the furnace to a sufficient heat, a plate compounded even of the hardest and most fire-resisting metal dissolves, glows, and turns to the liquefied state.

" I myself can feel but little," he reflected, " but I intend to use my every faculty to help others to feel. I myself am but bad and worthless, but I intend to do my utmost to set others on the right road. I myself am but an indifferent Christian, but I intend to strive never to yield to temptation, but to work hard, and to till my land with the sweat of my brow, and to engage only in honourable pursuits, and to influence my fellows in the same direction. For, after all, am I so very useless? At least I could maintain a household, for I am frugal and active and intelligent and steadfast. The only thing is to make up my mind to it."

Thus Chichikov pondered; and as he did so his half-awakened energies of soul touched upon something. That is to say, dimly his instinct divined that every man has a duty to perform, and that that duty may be performed here, there, and everywhere, and no matter what the circumstances and the emotions and the difficulties which compass a man about. And with such clearness did Chichikov mentally picture to himself the life of grateful toil which lies removed from the bustle of towns and the temptations which man, forgetful of the obligation of labour, has invented to beguile an hour of idleness that almost our hero forgot his unpleasant position, and even felt ready to thank Providence for the calamity which had befallen him, provided that it should end in his being released, and in his receiving back a portion of his property.

Presently the massive door of the cell opened to admit a *tchinovnik* named Samosvitov, a robust, sensual individual who was reputed by his comrades to be something of a rake. Had he served in the army, he would have done wonders, for he would have stormed any point, however dangerous and inaccessible, and captured cannon under the very noses of the foe; but, as it was, the lack of a more warlike field for his energies caused him to devote the latter principally to dissipation. Nevertheless he enjoyed great popularity, for he was loyal to the point that, once his word had been given, nothing would ever make him break it. At the same time, some reason or another led him to regard his superiors in the light of a hostile battery which, come what might, he must breach at any weak or unguarded spot or gap which might be capable of being utilised for the purpose.

" We have all heard of your plight," he began as soon as the door had been safely closed behind him. " Yes, every one has heard of it. But never mind. Things will yet come right. We will do our very best for you, and act as your humble servants in everything. Thirty thousand roubles is our price—no more."

" Indeed? " said Chichikov. " And, for that, shall I be completely exonerated? "

" Yes, completely, and also given some compensation for your loss of time."

" And how much am I to pay in return, you say? "

" Thirty thousand roubles, to be divided among ourselves, the Governor-General's staff, and the Governor-General's secretary."

" But how is even that to be managed, for all my effects, including my dispatch-box, will have been sealed up and taken away for examination? "

" In an hour's time they will be in your hands again," said Samosvitov. " Shall we shake hands over the bargain? "

Chichikov did so with a beating heart, for he could scarcely believe his ears.

" For the present, then, farewell," concluded Samosvitov. " I have instructed a certain mutual friend that the important points are silence and presence of mind."

" Hm! " thought Chichikov. " It is to my lawyer he is referring."

Even when Samosvitov had departed the prisoner found it difficult to credit all that had been said. Yet not an hour had elapsed before a messenger arrived with his dispatch-box and the papers and money therein practically undisturbed and intact! Later it came out that Samosvitov had assumed complete authority in the matter. First, he had rebuked the gendarmes guarding Chichikov's effects for lack of vigilance, and then sent word to the Superintendent that additional men were required for the purpose; after which he had taken the dispatch-box into his own charge, removed from it every paper which could possibly compromise Chichikov, sealed up the rest in a packet, and ordered a gendarme to convey the whole to their owner on the pretence of forwarding him sundry garments necessary for the night. In the result Chichikov received not only his papers, but also some warm clothing for his hypersensitive limbs. Such a swift recovery of his treasures delighted him beyond expression, and, gathering new hope, he began once more to dream of such allurements as theatre-going and the ballet girl after whom he had for some time past been dangling. Gradually did the country estate and the simple life begin to recede into the distance: gradually did the town house and the life of gaiety begin to loom larger and larger in the foreground. Oh, life, life!

Meanwhile in Government offices and chancellories there had been set on foot a boundless volume of work. Clerical pens slaved, and brains skilled in legal *casus* toiled; for each official had the artist's liking for the curved line in preference to the straight. And all the while, like a hidden magician, Chichikov's lawyer imparted driving power to that machine which caught up a man into its mechanism before he could even look round. And the complexity of it increased and increased, for Samosvitov surpassed himself in importance and daring. On learning of the place of confinement of the woman who had been arrested, he presented himself at the doors, and passed so well for a smart young officer of gendarmery that the sentry saluted and sprang to attention.

" Have you been on duty long? " asked Samosvitov.

" Since this morning, your Excellency."

" And shall you soon be relieved? "

" In three hours from now, your Excellency."

" Presently I shall want you, so I will instruct your officer to have you relieved at once."

" Very good, your Excellency."

Hastening home, thereafter, at top speed, and donning the uniform of a gendarme, with a false moustache and a pair of false whiskers—an *ensemble* in which the devil himself would not have known him, Samosvitov then made for the gaol where Chichikov was confined, and, *en route*, impressed into the service the first street woman whom he encountered, and handed her over to the care of two young fellows of like sort with himself. The next step was to hurry back to the prison where the original woman had been interned, and there to intimate to the sentry that he, Samosvitov (with whiskers and rifle complete), had been sent to relieve the said sentry at his post—a proceeding which, of course, enabled the newly-arrived relief to ensure, while performing his self-assumed turn of duty, that for the woman lying under arrest there should be substituted the woman recently recruited to the plot, and that the former should then be conveyed to a place of concealment where she was highly unlikely to be discovered.

Meanwhile, Samosvitov's feats in the military sphere were being rivalled by the wonders worked by Chichikov's lawyer in the civilian field of action. As a first step, the lawyer caused it to be intimated to the local Governor that the Public Prosecutor was engaged in drawing up a report to his, the local Governor's, detriment; whereafter the lawyer caused it to be intimated also to the Chief of Gendarmery that a certain confidential official was engaged in doing the same by *him;* whereafter, again, the lawyer confided to the confidential official in question that, owing to the documentary exertions of an official of a still more confidential nature than the first, he (the confidential official first-mentioned) was in a fair way to find himself in the same boat as both the local Governor and the Chief of Gendarmery: with the result that the whole trio were reduced to a frame of mind in which they were only too glad to turn to him (Samosvitov) for advice. The ultimate and farcical upshot was that report came crowding upon report, and that such alleged doings were brought to light as the sun had never before beheld. In fact, the documents in question employed anything and everything as material, even to announcing that such and such an individual had an illegitimate son, that such and such another kept a paid mistress, and that such and such a third was troubled with a gadabout wife; whereby there became interwoven with and welded into Chichikov's past history and the story of the dead souls such a crop of scandals and innuendoes that by no manner of means could any mortal decide to which of these rubbishy romances to award the palm, since all of them presented an equal claim to that honour. Naturally, when, at length, the *dossier* reached the Governor-General himself it simply flabbergasted the poor man; and even the exceptionally clever and energetic secretary to whom he deputed the making of an abstract of the same very nearly lost his reason with the strain of attempting to lay hold of the tangled end of the skein. It happened that just at that time the Prince had several other important affairs on hand, and affairs of a very unpleasant nature. That is to say, famine had made its appearance in one portion of the province, and the *tchinovniks* sent to distribute food to the people had done their work badly; in another portion of the province certain *Raskolniki* [1] were in a state of ferment, owing to the spreading of a report that an Antichrist had arisen who would not even let the dead rest, but was purchasing them wholesale—wherefore the said *Raskolniki* were summoning folk to prayer and repentance, and, under cover of capturing the Antichrist in question, were bludgeoning non-Antichrists in batches; lastly, the peasants of a third portion of the province had risen against the local landowners and superintendents of

[1] Dissenters or Old Believers: *i.e.* members of the sect which refused to accept the revised version of the Church Service Books promulgated by the Patriarch Nikon in 1665.

police, for the reason that certain rascals had started a rumour that the time was come when the peasants themselves were to become landowners, and to wear frockcoats, while the land-owners in being were about to revert to the peasant state, and to take their own wares to market; wherefore one of the local *volosts*,[1] oblivious of the fact that an order of things of that kind would lead to a superfluity alike of landowners and of super-intendents of police, had refused to pay its taxes, and neces-sitated recourse to forcible measures. Hence it was in a mood of the greatest possible despondency that the poor Prince was sitting plunged when word was brought him that the old man who had gone bail for Chichikov was waiting to see him.

" Show him in," said the Prince; and the old man entered.

" A fine fellow your Chichikov! " began the Prince angrily. " You defended him, and went bail for him, even though he had been up to business which even the lowest thief would not have touched! "

" Pardon me, your Highness; I do not understand to what you are referring."

" I am referring to the matter of the fraudulent will. The fellow ought to have been given a public flogging for it."

" Although to exculpate Chichikov is not my intention, might I ask you whether you do not think that the case is non-proven? At all events, sufficient evidence against him is still lacking."

" What? We have as chief witness the woman who personated the deceased, and I will have her interrogated in your presence."

Touching a bell, the Prince ordered her to be sent for.

" It is a most disgraceful affair," he went on; " and, ashamed though I am to have to say it, some of our leading *tchinovniks*, including the local Governor himself, have become implicated in the matter. Yet you tell me that this Chichikov ought not to be confined among thieves and rascals! " Clearly the Governor-General's wrath was very great indeed.

" Your Highness," said Murazov, " the Governor of the town is one of the heirs under the will: wherefore he has a certain right to intervene. Also, the fact that extraneous persons have meddled in the matter is only what is to be expected from human nature. A rich woman dies, and no exact, regular dis-position of her property is made. Hence there comes flocking from every side a cloud of fortune hunters. What else could one expect? Such is human nature."

" Yes, but why should such persons go and commit fraud? "

[1] Fiscal districts.

asked the Prince irritably. " I feel as though not a single honest *tchinovnik* were available—as though every one of them were a rogue."

" Your Highness, which of us is altogether beyond reproach? The *tchinovniks* of our town are human beings, and no more. Some of them are men of worth, and nearly all of them men skilled in business—though also, unfortunately, largely inter-related."

" Now, tell me this, Athanasi Vassilievitch," said the Prince, " for you are about the only honest man of my acquaintance. What has inspired in you such a *penchant* for defending rascals? "

" This," replied Murazov. " Take any man you like of the persons whom you thus term rascals. That man none the less remains a human being. That being so, how can one refuse to defend him when all the time one knows that half his errors have been committed through ignorance and stupidity? Each of us commits faults with every step that we take; each of us entails unhappiness upon others with every breath that we draw—and that although we may have no evil intention what-ever in our minds. Your Highness himself has, before now, committed an injustice of the gravest nature."

" *I* have? " cried the Prince, taken aback by this unexpected turn given to the conversation.

Murazov remained silent for a moment, as though he were debating something in his thoughts. Then he said:

" Nevertheless it is as I say. You committed the injustice in the case of the lad Dierpiennikov."

" What, Athanasi Vassilievitch? The fellow had infringed one of the Fundamental Laws! He had been found guilty of treason! "

" I am not seeking to justify him; I am only asking you whether you think it right that an inexperienced youth who had been tempted and led away by others should have received the same sentence as the man who had taken the chief part in the affair. That is to say, although Dierpiennikov and the man Voron-Drianni received an equal measure of punishment, their *criminality* was not equal."

" If," exclaimed the Prince excitedly, " you know anything further concerning the case, for God's sake tell it me at once. Only the other day did I forward a recommendation that St. Petersburg should remit a portion of the sentence."

" Your Highness," replied Murazov, " I do not mean that I know of anything which does not lie also within your own cog-nisance, though one circumstance there was which might have told in the lad's favour had he not refused to admit it, lest another should suffer injury. All that I have in my mind is this. On that occasion were you not a little over-hasty in coming to a conclusion? You will understand, of course, that I am judging only according to my own poor lights, and for the reason that on more than one occasion you have urged me to be frank. In the days when I myself acted as a chief of gendarmery I came in contact with a great number of accused—some of them bad, some of them good; and in each case I found it well also to consider a man's past career, for the reason that, unless one views things calmly, instead of at once decrying a man, he is apt to take alarm, and to make it impossible thereafter to get any real confession from him. If, on the other hand, you question a man as friend might question friend, the result will be that straightway he will tell you everything, nor ask for mitigation of his penalty, nor bear you the least malice, in that he will understand that it is not you who have punished him, but the law."

The Prince relapsed into thought; until presently there entered a young *tchinovnik*. Portfolio in hand, this official stood waiting respectfully. Care and hard work had already imprinted their insignia upon his fresh young face; for evidently he had not been in the Service for nothing. As a matter of fact, his greatest joy was to labour at a tangled case, and successfully to unravel it.

[*At this point a long hiatus occurs in the original.*]

"I will send corn to the localities where famine is worst," said Murazov, "for I understand that sort of work better than do the *tchinovniks*, and will personally see to the needs of each person. Also, if you will allow me, your Highness, I will go and have a talk with the *Raskolniki*. They are more likely to listen to a plain man than to an official. God knows whether I shall succeed in calming them, but at least no *tchinovnik* could do so, for officials of the kind merely draw up reports and lose their way among their own documents—with the result that nothing comes of it. Nor will I accept from you any money for these purposes, since I am ashamed to devote so much as a thought to my own pocket at a time when men are dying of hunger. I have a large stock of grain lying in my granaries; in addition to which, I have sent orders to Siberia that a new consignment shall be forwarded me before the coming summer."

"Of a surety will God reward you for your services, Athanasi Vassilievitch! Not another word will I say to you on the subject, for you yourself must feel that any words from me would be inadequate. Yet tell me one thing: I refer to the case of which you know. Have I the right to pass over the case? Also, would it be just and honourable on my part to let the offending *tchinovniks* go unpunished?"

"Your Highness, it is impossible to return a definite answer to those two questions: and the more so because many rascals are at heart men of rectitude. Human problems are difficult things to solve. Sometimes a man may be drawn into a vicious circle, so that, having once entered it, he ceases to be himself."

"But what would the *tchinovniks* say if I allowed the case to be passed over? Would not some of them turn up their noses at me, and declare that they have effected my intimidation? Surely they would be the last persons in the world to respect me for my action?"

"Your Highness, I think this: that your best course would be to call them together, and to inform them that you know everything, and to explain to them your personal attitude (exactly as you have explained it to me), and to end by at once requesting their advice and asking them what each of them would have done had he been placed in similar circumstances."

"What? You think that those *tchinovniks* would be so accessible to lofty motives that they would cease thereafter to be venal and meticulous? I should be laughed at for my pains."

"I think not, your Highness. Even the baser section of humanity possesses a certain sense of equity. Your wisest plan, your Highness, would be to conceal nothing and to speak to them as you have just spoken to me. If, at present, they imagine you to be ambitious and proud and unapproachable and self-assured, your action would afford them an opportunity of seeing how the case really stands. Why should you hesitate? You would but be exercising your undoubted right. Speak to them as though delivering not a message of your own, but a message from God."

"I will think it over," the Prince said musingly, "and meanwhile I thank you from my heart for your good advice."

"Also, I should order Chichikov to leave the town," suggested Murazov.

"Yes, I will do so. Tell him from me that he is to depart hence as quickly as possible, and that the further he should remove himself, the better it will be for him. Also, tell him that it is only owing to your efforts that he has received a pardon at my hands."

Murazov bowed, and proceeded from the Prince's presence to

that of Chichikov. He found the prisoner cheerfully enjoying a hearty dinner which, under hot covers, had been brought him from an exceedingly excellent kitchen. But almost the first words which he uttered showed Murazov that the prisoner had been having dealings with the army of bribes-takers; as also that in those transactions his lawyer had played the principal part.

"Listen, Paul Ivanovitch," the old man said. "I bring you your freedom, but only on this condition—that you depart out of the town forthwith. Therefore gather together your effects, and waste not a moment, lest worse befall you. Also, of all that a certain person has contrived to devise on your behalf I am aware; wherefore let me tell you, as between ourselves, that should the conspiracy come to light, nothing on earth can save him, and in his fall he will involve others rather than be left unaccompanied in the lurch, and not see the guilt shared. How is it that when I left you but recently you were in a better frame of mind than you are now? I beg of you not to trifle with the matter. Ah me! what boots that wealth for which men dispute and cut one another's throats? Do they think that it is possible to prosper in this world without thinking of the world to come? Believe me when I say that, until a man shall have renounced all that leads humanity to contend without giving a thought to the ordering of spiritual wealth, he will never set his temporal goods either upon a satisfactory foundation. Yes, even as times of want and scarcity may come upon nations, so may they come upon individuals. No matter what may be said to the contrary, the body can never dispense with the soul. Why, then, will you not try to walk in the right way, and, by thinking no longer of dead souls, but only of your own living one, regain, with God's help, the better road? I too am leaving the town to-morrow. Hasten, therefore, lest, bereft of my assistance, you meet with some dire misfortune."

And the old man departed, leaving Chichikov plunged in thought. Once more had the gravity of life begun to loom large before him.

"Yes, Murazov was right," he said to himself. "It is time that I were moving."

Leaving the prison—a warder carrying his effects in his wake—he found Selifan and Petrushka overjoyed at seeing their master once more at liberty.

"Well, good fellows?" he said kindly. "And now we must pack and be off."

"True, true, Paul Ivanovitch," agreed Selifan. "And by

this time the roads will have become firmer, for much snow has fallen. Yes, high time is it that we were clear of the town. So weary of it am I that the sight of it hurts my eyes."

"Go to the coachbuilder's," commanded Chichikov, "and have sledge-runners fitted to the *koliaska*.

Chichikov then made his way into the town—though not with the object of paying farewell visits (in view of recent events, that might have given rise to some awkwardness), but for the purpose of paying an unobtrusive call at the shop where he had obtained the cloth for his latest suit. There he now purchased four more *arshins* of the same smoked-grey-shot-with-flame-colour material as he had had before, with the intention of having it made up by the tailor who had fashioned the previous costume; and by promising double renumeration he induced the tailor in question so to hasten the cutting out of the garments that, through sitting up all night over the work, the man might have the whole ready by break of day. True, the goods were delivered a trifle *after* the appointed hour, yet the following morning saw the coat and breeches completed; and while the horses were being put to, Chichikov tried on the clothes, and found them equal to the previous creation, even though during the process he caught sight of a bald patch on his head, and was led mournfully to reflect: "Alas! Why did I give way to such despair? Surely I need not have torn my hair out so freely?"

Then, when the tailor had been paid, our hero left the town. But no longer was he the old Chichikov—he was only a ruin of what he had been, and his frame of mind might have been compared to a building recently pulled down to make room for a new one, while the new one has not yet been erected owing to the non-receipt of the plans from the architect. Murazov, too, had departed, but at an earlier hour, and in a tilt-waggon with Ivan Potapitch.

An hour later the Governor-General issued to all and sundry officials a notice that, on the occasion of his departure for St. Petersburg, he would be glad to see the corps of *tchinovniks* at a private meeting. Accordingly all ranks and grades of officialdom repaired to his residence, and there awaited—not without a certain measure of trepidation and of searching of heart—the Governor-General's entry. When that took place he looked neither clear nor dull. Yet his bearing was proud, and his step assured. The *tchinovniks* bowed—some of them to the waist, and he answered their salutations with a slight inclination of the head. Then he spoke as follows:

" Since I am about to pay a visit to St. Petersburg, I have
thought it right to meet you, and to explain to you privately my
reasons for doing so. An affair of a most scandalous character
has taken place in our midst. To what affair I am referring I
think most of those present will guess. Now, an automatic
process has led to that affair bringing about the discovery also
of other matters. Those matters are no less dishonourable than
the primary one; and to that I regret to have to add that there
stand involved in them certain persons whom I had hitherto
believed to be honourable. Of the object aimed at by those who
have complicated matters to the point of making their resolution almost impossible by ordinary methods I am aware; as
also I am aware of the identity of the ringleader, despite the
skill with which he has sought to conceal his share in the
scandal. But the principal point is, that I propose to decide
these matters, not by formal documentary process, but by the
more summary process of court-martial, and that I hope, when
the circumstances have been laid before his Imperial Majesty, to
receive from him authority to adopt the course which I have
mentioned. For I conceive that when it has become impossible to
resolve a case by civil means, and some of the necessary documents have been burnt, and attempts have been made (both
through the adduction of an excess of false and extraneous
evidence and through the framing of fictitious reports) to cloud
an already sufficiently obscure investigation with an added
measure of complexity,—when all these circumstances have
arisen, I conceive that the only possible tribunal to deal with
them is a military tribunal. But on that point I should like
your opinion."

The Prince paused for a moment or two, as though awaiting
a reply; but none came, seeing that every man had his eyes
bent upon the floor, and many of the audience had turned white
in the face.

" Then," he went on, " I may say that I am aware also of a
matter which those who have carried it through believe to lie
only within the cognisance of themselves. The particulars of
that matter will not be set forth in documentary form, but only
through process of myself acting as plaintiff and petitioner, and
producing none but ocular evidence."

Among the throng of *tchinovniks* some one gave a start, and
thereby caused others of the more apprehensive to fall to
trembling in their shoes.

" Without saying does it go that the prime conspirators ought to undergo deprivation of rank and property, and that the remainder ought to be dismissed from their posts; for though that course would cause a certain proportion of the innocent to suffer with the guilty, there would seem to be no other course available, seeing that the affair is one of the most disgraceful nature, and calls aloud for justice. Therefore, although I know that to some my action will fail to serve as a lesson, since it will lead to their succeeding to the posts of dismissed officials, as well as that others hitherto considered honourable will lose their reputation, and others entrusted with new responsibilities will continue to cheat and betray their trust,—although all this is known to me, I still have no choice but to satisfy the claims of justice by proceeding to take stern measures. I am also aware that I shall be accused of undue severity; but, lastly, I am aware that it is my duty to put aside all personal feeling, and to act as the unconscious instrument of that retribution which justice demands.

Over every face there passed a shudder. Yet the Prince had spoken calmly, and not a trace of anger or any other kind of emotion had been visible on his features.

" Nevertheless," he went on, " the very man in whose hands the fate of so many now lies, the very man whom no prayer for mercy could ever have influenced, himself desires to make a request of you. Should you grant that request, all will be forgotten and blotted out and pardoned, for I myself will intercede with the Throne on your behalf. That request is this. I know that by no manner of means, by no preventive measures, and by no penalties will dishonesty ever be completely extirpated from our midst, for the reason that its roots have struck too deep, and that the dishonourable traffic in bribes has become a necessity to, even the mainstay of, some whose nature is not innately venal. Also, I know that, to many men, it is an impossibility to swim against the stream. Yet now, at this solemn and most critical juncture, when the country is calling aloud for saviours, and it is the duty of every citizen to contribute and to sacrifice his all, I feel that I cannot but issue an appeal to every man in whom a Russian heart and a spark of what we understand by the word ' nobility ' exist. For, after all, which of us is more guilty than his fellow? It may be that to *me* the greatest culpability should be assigned, in that at first I may have adopted towards you too reserved an attitude, that I may have been over-hasty in repelling those who desired but to serve me, even though of their services I did not actually stand in need. Yet, had they really loved justice and the good of their country, I think that they would have been less prone to take offence at the coldness of my attitude, but would have sacrificed their feelings and their personality to their superior convictions. For hardly can it be that I failed to note their overtures and the loftiness of their motives, or that I would not have accepted any wise and useful advice proffered. At the same time, it is for a subordinate to adapt himself to the tone of his superior, rather than for a superior to adapt himself to the tone of his subordinate. Such a course is at once more regular and more smooth of working, since a corps of subordinate has but one director, whereas a director may have a hundred subordinates. But let us put aside the question of comparative culpability. The important point is, that before us all lies the duty of rescuing our fatherland. Our fatherland is suffering, not from the incursion of a score of alien tongues, but from our own acts, in that, in addition to the lawful administration, there has grown up a second administration possessed of infinitely greater powers than the system established by law. And that second administration has established its conditions, fixed its tariff of prices, and published that tariff abroad; nor could any ruler, even though the wisest of legislators and administrators, do more to correct the evil than limit it in the conduct of his more venal *tchinovniks* by setting over them, as their supervisors, men of superior rectitude. No, until each of us shall come to feel that, just as arms were taken up during the period of the upheaval of the nations, so now each of us must make a stand against dishonesty, all remedies will end in failure. As a Russian, therefore—as one bound to you by consanguinity and identity of blood—I make to you my appeal. I make it to those of you who understand wherein lies nobility of thought. I invite those men to remember the duty which confronts us, whatsoever our respective stations; I invite them to observe more closely their duty, and to keep more constantly in mind their obligation of holding true to their country, in that before us the future looms dark, and that we can scarcely . . ."

[*Here the manuscript of the original comes abruptly to an end.*]

THE
TEMPLE PRESS   LETCHWORTH
ENGLAND

EVERYMAN,
I WILL GO WITH THEE,
& BE THY GVIDE
IN THY MOST NEED
TO GO BY THY SIDE